REBORN

Reborn

Seth Haddon

blindeyebooks.com

Reborn
By Seth Haddon
Published by Blind Eye Books
315 Prospect Street #5393, Bellingham WA 98227
www.blindeyebooks.com

Edited by Nicole Kimberling
Copyedit by Jennifer Ehrhardt
Page Proof by Jack Shapira
Cover Art by Julie Dillon
Book Design by Dawn Kimberling
Ebook design by Michael DeLuca

print ISBN: 978-1-956422-05-4
ebook ISBN: 978-1-956422-06-1
Library of Congress Control Number: 2023937553
Printed in the United States of America

CONTENTS

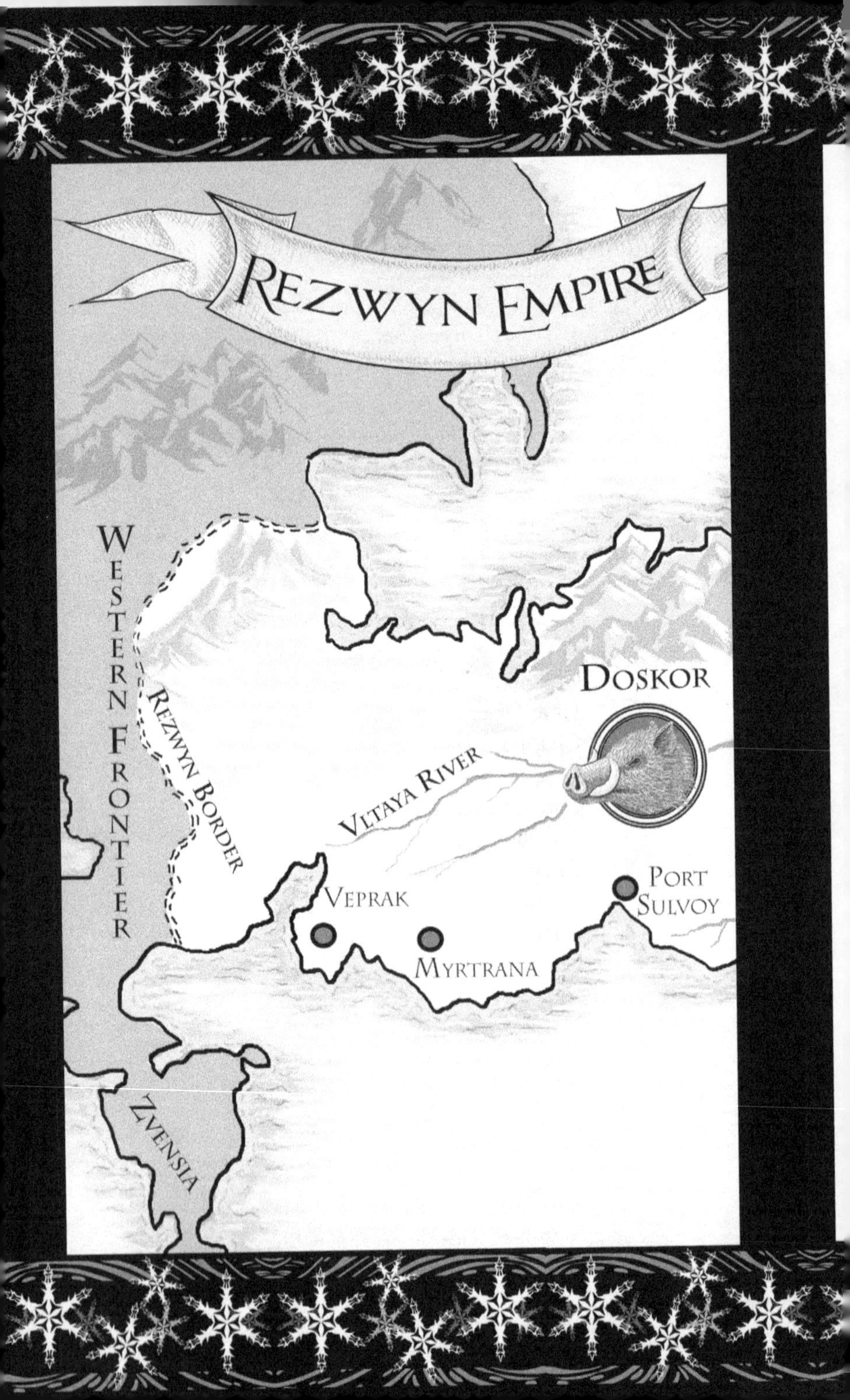
Rezwyn Empire
Western Frontier
Rezwyn Border
Doskor
Vitaya River
Veprak
Myrtrana
Port Sulvoy
Zvensia

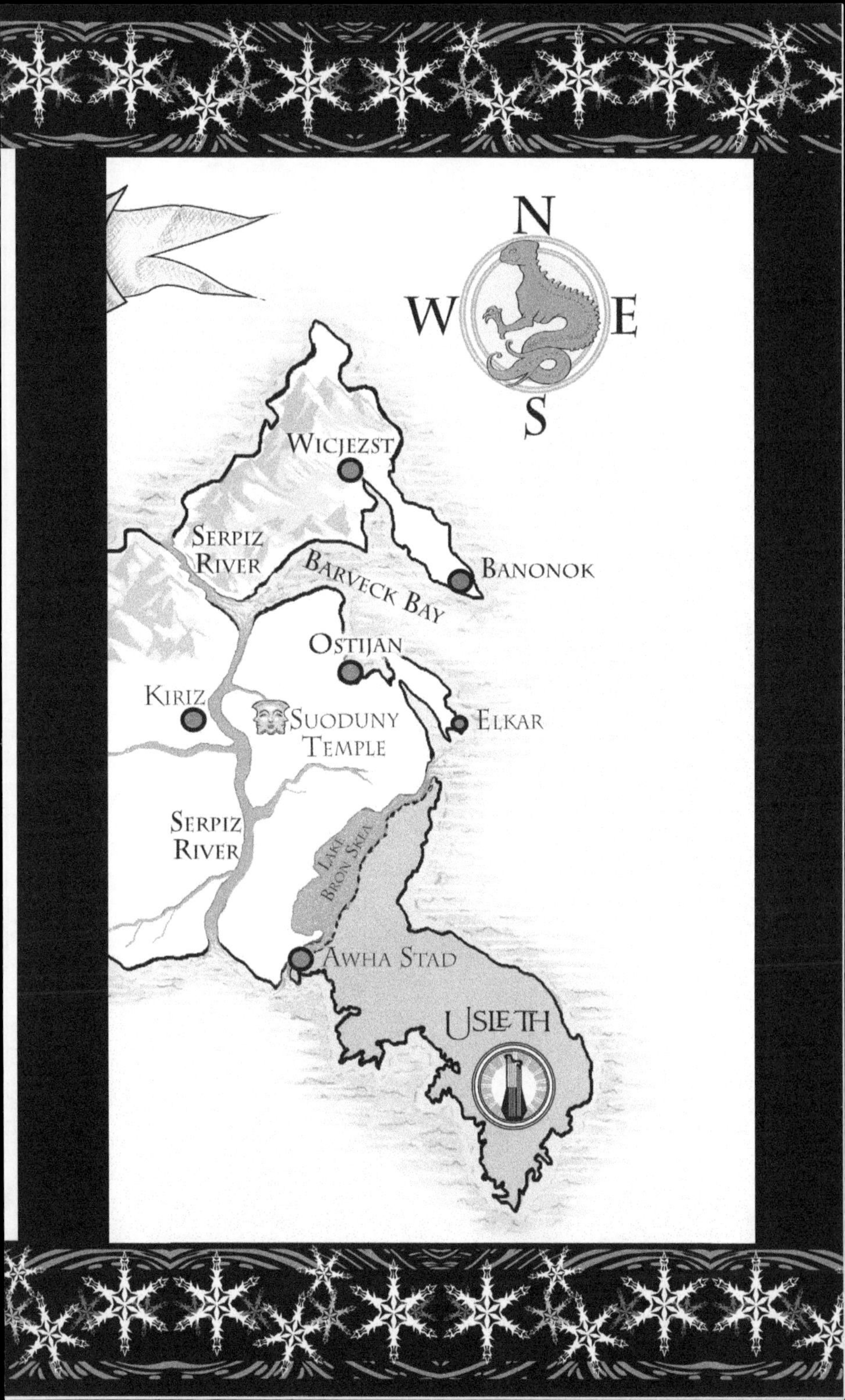
N
W
E
S
Wicjezst
Serpiz River
Barveck Bay
Banonok
Ostijan
Kiriz
Suoduny Temple
Elkar
Serpiz River
Lake Bron Skia
Awha Stad
Usleth

CHAPTER ONE

In the ninety-seventh year of Emperor Nio Beumeut's reign, Izra Dziove's visions ceased to be anything useful. From the cradle, Izra had been gifted dreams from his god, Suoduny, He Who Weaves Our Fates. Violent things, usually; portents of war, or threats against His Excellency, the True Commander's person—forewarnings useful to an emperor with a crumbling hold on his nation. But that year, for many months now, Izra had been dreaming of one thing only.

A man.

In the dream, Izra stood pressed against the cold glass of the window, watching his persistent visitor disappear into the sunset. As always, Izra was powerless to stop the man's retreat. Then, when at last the sun would dip below the horizon, the frigid landscape would be set ablaze. The departing man would be caught in the glare and seem to brighten from the inside, his russet-brown skin turning honey gold. He would look back at Izra once, but the brilliance of the sun concealed his face. It always happened this way. All his features were blotted out by the sunset's final flare.

Izra did not know the dream man's name, but he felt as familiar as Izra's own soul. He had had the dream for years, long before it became a fixture, and still had no explanation for that contradiction. He only knew it to be true. Each time Izra saw him—his nameless man—a feeling overcame him. A pull in his heart, in the very depths of his soul; this urge to step forward, to run after him.

Izra knew in some other life, the gods had made that man his.

Most often the dream would end there, just a brief and teasing image in the early hours before he woke. But tonight, in its final moments, the dream twisted into a new image. Two figures bubbling out of the sunlight, resolving into men. Both stood poring over something on a table, and from them burned something ancient and lingering, and a warmth in him that bordered on recognition.

Izra woke with a start. Sweat clung to his body, dripping in rivulets down his back. He wanted to spring up, shake the dream from his body, but he did not move. The shadows felt thick tonight, a veil hiding secrets. In the sharp, cold night, his awareness came back to him quickly. The sheets were damp, and the hearth burned low, but everything else in his chamber was as it should have been. He was alone.

Izra stared into the flames. He had never had that dream interrupted by the beginning of another. Apparently, the gods were toying with him tonight. But it did not make sense. His usual dream should not have been breached. He had slept through it a hundred times and never stirred. This time, thunderclap-quick he had awoken—in a sweat as if it had been a nightmare, in the heavy dark of night. So why now?

Izra walked to the mantle and peered at his dim reflection; a tired, pallid ghost. All the meat in his face seemed gaunt. He pulled his pure black hair back from his face, knotting half of it in a loose pile. Then he turned toward the window, pulled the curtain aside and stared out at the impenetrable night. A chill seeped through the glass and pricked his naked skin. Whatever he expected to see, he did not see it. Nothing outside but the dark.

He could have explained away the incident if he wanted to. But he was a strix, blessed with a god's power and consult to the emperor. He would not mistake a warning from the gods for his own human exhaustion.

Izra Dziove had learned long ago to never ignore the pull of fate.

Still naked, he knelt before the dying fire. If there was a threat somewhere in this castle, he would find it. The fingertips of his left hand glinted in the firelight. They were silver-tipped, conducive to magic and navigating the threads of fate.

Izra exhaled and plunged his hand into the ash that caked the embers. The heat stung his skin, but he ignored it, using his coated finger to mark his forehead. Every fireplace in this castle used wood from the same trees; stone and marble pulled from the same quarries. These threads linked each hearth to one another and were invisible to most, but not to Izra. They were veins of the same body. That was the power of a strix: his duty as Commander of the Uxbuh, his birthright as a member of the Dziove family. He exhaled, spoke his intention aloud, and blew the remaining ashes back into the fire.

In answer, the flame roared.

Izra raised his hand to shield his eyes from the sudden arc of flame. Somewhere in the tunneled corridors of the castle, another fire climbed high in its hearth. Izra's breath caught. His heart began to pound.

The mirrored flame marked the location of the intruder. He could feel the essence of it, the wrongness of their presence, but everything else seemed murky. He did not know who it was, but he knew whose chambers they had entered.

An assassin moved against the True Commander.

"As fate wills it, Suoduny." Izra shot to standing. Adrenaline dispelled the remains of sleep from his body. As he dressed, Izra watched that flame, monitoring the image of the True Commander's chambers shown through the bright link of the hearths.

He hefted his heavy wolf-pelt coat onto his back, grabbed his halberd, and slipped out into the corridor.

Izra sped through the curving space. Torches burned in sconces and cast a dim light. He slowed only once: to pound on the door of his second, a gaunt, lean man named

Kew. They had known each other for over a decade, now. Kew had come from a large family of artisans before he rejected the caste in favor of serving in the army. He was eager, a hard worker, and a good friend to Izra.

Izra was surprised when the door opened quickly.

"What the hell is it?" said Kew in a harried voice. He had not quite realized who had disturbed him. The man looked frazzled; his hair was a mess, his pale cheeks rosy and flushed. A pale leg disappeared as it slid hastily up the bed.

Kew somehow managed to flush further.

"Uh . . . Commander. I can explain—"

"I could not care less," Izra said, speaking truth. "Suoduny woke me. Someone is with the emperor. Someone who shouldn't be."

Kew froze. "What?"

But Izra had already turned away. He shouted, "Bring the guards with you!"

No one was awake, and no guards ever patrolled this wing of the castle. Seals blocked it on all sides, and those magic locks could only be opened by the most trusted of the Uxbuh, the god-filled—unless an emergency triggered them all to open. The locks were still intact. The hearth beckoned him down to the most protected part of the castle—and no alarm save his own god had alerted him. A pit as dark and dangerous as the Doskor night opened in his belly. He knew the truth. There had been no breach.

Someone inside the castle was about to do the unthinkable.

He sprinted down the stone spiral staircase that led deep into the castle's heart. The instant his feet touched the marble floor of the lower level, he readied his halberd. It had a beautifully elaborate head; an axe-blade shooting into a narrow spear. The multiple faces of Suoduny had been carved into the wooden shaft, and when the skin of his palm met the face of his god, he felt grounded and sturdy.

With this, he would drive out whichever treacherous soul threatened the True Commander.

This corridor shone with light. All shadows were banished: no one hid here. The seal at the end of the corridor curled in a complicated tapestry of metal. It would easily stump the uninitiated—only the True Commander's trusted few understood the magic that protected his doors. Izra leaned his halberd against a wall and raised both hands.

As a Dziove, the magic powering the seal felt familiar to him, a companion he had been raised with. With his right hand, he scooped his fingers beneath a taut magical thread. With the silver fingertips of his left hand, he urged the power to unwind.

The lock resisted.

Izra grunted. Intention was important; he reminded the lock of this truth.

"Suoduny commands it," he murmured.

At once, the lock unfurled. Iron whipped to the edges of the door, quick and efficient as if eager for Izra to enter.

His wrist throbbed; he shook it out, feeling the weight of the silver at the end of it. Then he retrieved the halberd and kicked open the doors.

Izra stepped inside the exquisite natural cavern of the emperor's chamber. The space was still. Unnaturally so. He heard the hearth fire-spitting, a distant drip of water. Nothing else.

Perhaps the traitor had fled. But Izra knew better than to be so optimistic. Suoduny had dragged him from sleep for this.

Stalactites hung from the ceiling in sharp points, and fire light shone through the limestone to make them glow. The hearth sat to the left, and the emperor's bed to the right. Izra stepped toward the bed silently.

Shrouded by curtains of near-sheer fabric, the emperor slept. Izra could see the silhouette of his recumbent form.

The emperor appeared to be alone. Carefully, halberd at the ready, he crept toward the curtain.

Izra still got a shock whenever he laid eyes on the True Commander. It was no different now, even with the informality of his approach, the intimacy of this moment.

He went to the emperor's side and pressed two fingers against the old man's throat. Izra had to close his eyes to feel the pulse; the faint, suppressed heartbeat fluttered inconsistently beneath the pad of his fingers. Izra exhaled. Alive, but still somewhere beyond the physical realm. The emperor's soul floated somewhere, lost in astrok-mer, the astral sea.

The sudden weight of grief filled him at the thought. Grief and guilt; a potent, cruel mix. He shuddered and closed his eyes.

"I am here, Emperor." Izra felt something within him shift as the stale air in the room chilled. With his senses pricked, he gripped the halberd. Silence stretched as he focused. He scanned for the silhouette of an attacker, or the movement of a blade. But no assault came.

Izra knew better than to relax. Suoduny had warned him, and the gods would never intervene for anything trivial. Holding his breath, he tried to connect with the god: to call upon the holy connection he shared as a strix to locate the source of the danger.

A body slammed into him from behind.

Izra rocked forward but didn't fall. He spun—just in time to catch the glint of a descending dagger. He brought the wooden shaft of his halberd to block, then threw his weight to the side, hurling the attacker off.

Afire with fury, Izra grounded himself. He scanned for movement. A shadow darted behind the curtains like dark vapor, stopping at Izra's left. Izra thrust without hesitation, satisfied as the spear point of his halberd slashed through the curtain and punctured solid flesh. The attacker yelped—a deep, outraged bark. Izra tried to twist the head, in a bid to end this terrible business, but the man dashed aside. Izra whipped the bloody halberd back through the half-torn curtain. All pretense of a cautious assassin fell away; the figure beneath the curtain twisted and slashed wildly, rushing against Izra with his dagger. With a burst of speed, Izra hauled the halberd to block. He kicked the soft pouch of the attacker's belly. A pained cry went up as they stumbled back. Before they could right themselves, Izra already had the halberd at their neck.

"Drop your dagger, filth."

No resistance. The dagger clattered to the stone immediately. Izra kicked it away and pressed forward with the spear point.

The attacker appeared short; their body concealed by a tunic several sizes too big. A plain, featureless mask obscured their face.

To Izra's great surprise, the wretch made no attempts to plead for their life. Instead, they murmured something that might have been a prayer. The fool. What were they expecting? That the gods would side with a traitor? That those great divinities would not only ignore, but endorse this sacrilege?

Izra sighed. "In this, fear will not serve you. Nor will regret."

With the head of the halberd, he hooked the mask and dragged it aside.

Horror rode over him.

Staring back at Izra were no bare eyes, but instead the beaded face covering of an initiated man—a priest of Borviet, He Who Rides on Chaos. His name was Semor.

"By the gods," Izra whispered, breath half-lost with his shock. "What are you doing?" Nausea swamped him. A fiery tempest of bile pushed into his throat. A priest. A priest here to murder the very heart of the empire. Not once in his life had Izra ever questioned the inherent goodness of the holy order. This was unthinkable.

He willed it to be a lie. The realization that a priest would plunge to such wicked depths infected his body like a disease he needed desperately to expel. Still, the priest stepped forward—either to attack or explain himself. It did not matter.

"Do not take another step, scum." Although the threat loomed, his voice faltered and undercut its strength. "What base things tempted you to betray both the gods and this empire?"

"His time has come to an end, strix," Semor said. Compared to Izra, his voice was calm, severe. "Both you and I know it." Semor was an old-guard, once a trusted advisor to the True Commander in matters of expansion. And now, with the emperor's condition, Semor had been ignored.

"Is this what you have come to, then? Betray the emperor—the very gods? This is wrong, Semor," Izra said, trying to sound calm. "You were a good man, once. You may still be. Something dark has swayed you, but you have done nothing you cannot come back from."

Semor seemed to consider this. Hope—that infernal and simple thing—swelled in Izra's heart like the rising tide. But by the time the priest had blinked, that optimism had died.

To confirm it, the final knife twist in Izra's heart, Semor shook his head. "I am not some misguided pup, Dziove. I have many years on you; many years serving the emperor in his prime. When we were conquerors. A true empire. Not some half-dead memory of glory." Semor paused to grit his teeth. "You have heard there are city-states to the east and south angling to break away. People renouncing the gods. And Beumeut languishes here in his stone tomb doing nothing. Bending the knee to Uslethian cizalecs. Praying to live forever."

Izra raised his chin. He heard the words, let them pass through his skin and into his soul and acknowledged the drop in his stomach without really feeling it.

"On your knees, Semor." To his credit, Semor accepted this. He sank slowly. Izra steadied himself. Outside, finally, he heard Kew bringing the guards.

Semor heard them too and looked Izra dead in the eye. "We are born to conquer. It is in our very nature; stitched into our souls by the gods. But Beumeut would stagnate us. Have us ignore the pull of our souls. Beumeut will—"

Incensed, Izra growled, "You will call him the True Commander!"

"I shall not give respect where it is not due!"

Izra slammed the butt of his halberd into Semor's nose without hesitation. The man howled and crumpled. A warm glow of satisfaction coursed through Izra at the sight. "This once, I will share in your sentiment, priest."

Guards swarmed in, encircling the traitor priest. General Neve followed—furious, frown pronounced, glinting cuirass thrown over her white nightgown. But when she saw the man at Izra's feet she skidded to a stop. Izra recognized her expression; the same tumultuous grief he had felt, flooded her. General Neve ran a hand over her shaved head and turned away.

"Seize him," Izra commanded. "Priest Semor has done the unthinkable. He has tried to murder the True Commander."

Gasps echoed in the stone chamber. Many of the guards bowed to the emperor, their swords unwavering against the priest's neck.

"Take him away," Izra said, "and prepare him for death."

CHAPTER TWO

Not far away from the frozen and unsettling Rezwyn capital at Doskor, on the single cobbled road that originated in Port Sulvoy on the Prauv Ocean, Oren Radek was experiencing perhaps the worst breath he'd ever smelled. It wafted out of a bandit who held a knife to Oren's jugular. He spoke in broken Uslethian, "What are you doing out here all alone, pretty boy?"

And Radek, who had just been weeks at sea without a single compliment, leaned into the blade and grinned. "Do you really think I'm pretty?"

This question prompted a shiver of revulsion from the bandit, which was rich coming from a man with two rows of blackened teeth.

"Don't make that face," Radek purred. "I know this tunic caught your eye." He was dressed deliciously, like a lord—in velvet, with ruching—which was exactly why he and his cart full of fine wares had been ambushed.

The bandit's lip curled. "Hand it over. And all your coin."

Beside him, the cart horse whinnied and stamped as the others rummaged in the cart she hauled. Somewhere in the distance, Radek thought he heard the answering whinny of his lovely steel-gray mare Deina—but he couldn't think about that now. He looked the bandit up and down and let himself scoff. "And why would I do that?"

The bandits totaled four, which in the grand scheme of things wasn't very many but still clearly enough.

They'd stationed themselves in a place where forested ridges on either side of the road prevented easy escape. This imperial road was meant to be protected; any foreigners getting waylaid this close to the capital would only embarrass both the Rezwyns and Emperor Nio Beumeut. Radek wondered if something very not good was happening in Doskor.

"Because I have a knife to your throat," the bandit spat, thick Doskorian accent rasping over his words. He cursed—Radek caught only part of it, which was "fucking idiot foreigner," and long enough a sentence Radek had to wonder what else had been said. With a gentle graze, the bandit urged him on. "Come now. The purse."

Radek moved slowly. As he did, he watched the other three pilfer all his lovely things. Jewelry, trinkets, a lavish armchair carved by the celebrated woodworker Szargrid of Teum Bett—gorgeous thing, inlaid with mother-of-pearl. Radek had sourced the finest fabrics, even sacrificed profit and pulled from other shipments to build the most breathtaking assortment of Uslethian gifts. Now he watched glumly as some idiot dragged an expensive red silk coverlet bordered with pearlescent gedrok through dirty snow.

Radek slipped one finger around the string looping the pouch to his belt and stopped. "Aren't you going to ask?"

A pause. A twitch. Then the bandit folded and took the bait. "Ask what?"

"Where all these pretty things have come from and to whom they're going?" Radek said, gesturing in the direction of Doskor. "Why some fancy foreign lord would be idiotic enough to wander into Doskor without an entourage?" The bandit blinked at him. Radek blinked back. "No?"

The bandit frowned. He wasn't spooked enough to turn around. He leaned forward and nicked Radek's neck with the blade. "Hand over the purse."

"Yes, yes," Radek said. He tried to maintain his composure. Skillfully, he untied the pouch and wrapped the string idly around the palm of his hand, feeling the hefty weight at its end. "Here it is then."

The bandit proffered his palm. Grip tight, Radek swung and launched the coin-filled pouch into the bandit's right eye.

An affronted scream. A wet crack. The bandit's head snapped around from the momentum. Radek danced back, assessing. The other three bandits dropped all his fine wares in the dirty snow and drew their weapons in an orchestra of steel along scabbard, and the whirring clink of a crossbow being drawn. But Radek couldn't split his attention. Blood trickled from the bandit's nose and turned his fair white skin a mottled pink.

"Oh, that's going to bruise," Radek hissed—absolutely the wrong thing to say.

"You'll regret that, cizalec."

The Doskorian came through hard on the last word. A bit of spittle landed squarely between Radek's eyes, making him flinch. Radek swallowed. Cizalec. Foreigner. Benign until said to you by any local of the Rezwyn empire. Then it was hissed at you, a guttural spit of some putrid collective feeling.

"Will I, now?" Radek whispered, swinging the pouch once more. "Are you sure about that?"

With an angry cry, the bandit launched forward. Even with one eye scrunched tight and a clear lack of finesse, he had the speed. Radek stepped back, first slowly then three steps at once. The bandit struck out low—and stabbed him.

Radek yelled out of habit. No pain blinded his senses. He felt nothing at all. Radek's scream cut off abruptly and he and the bandit considered one another before they both dropped their gazes. The dagger had gone through Radek's tunic, but instead of sinking into flesh, it was buried in the pack of cards for the strategy game called Gulek Des. It was a treasured possession. Radek's most favored toy. And now it had a hole in it.

"Those cards are hand-painted, you bastard!" Radek cried, ripping his leg away. And then, calling over his shoulder: "Mirakel, would you share your damned bodyguards?"

A crossbow bolt zipped past Radek's face and lodged itself in the bandit's neck. Radek squeaked at the suddenness. The bandit swayed for a second, scrabbling to hold onto breath, and then fell with a writhing finality that made Radek glance away. In his periphery, he saw the remaining three bandits lashing out, struggling and dying. It didn't take more than a minute, but that minute felt terribly long. Radek spent it staring out at the empire's landscape. When the cries gurgled out, he turned and exhaled sharply.

"Nasty business," he said when it was done.

The woman beside him scoffed. "Really," she said, gesturing to the militiamen in her employ to finish the job quickly. "And here I was thinking you were starting to enjoy yourself."

Radek didn't say anything to that, just gave her a warning glance to end the thought there. Mirakel was short and muscular, with the fair-taupe skin of Westgar, a province on the border between Usleth and the Rezwyn Empire. Dark, shaggy shoulder-length hair framed her face, with a choppy fringe cut haphazardly across her forehead. Her visible lack of enthusiasm left no doubt that she didn't want to be there—and she made no attempt to appear otherwise happy with her assignment.

As an officer of the Uslethian treasury, Mirakel had been sent along with Radek to pay their way, and also to ensure he burned no holes into Usleth's proverbial pockets. Which was a bit of a personal attack, Radek thought, but King Zavrius had decreed it.

Before Mirakel had further chance to berate him, a weaselly forty-something burst out from behind the ridge and made a beeline for Radek.

Radek braced himself for a lecture. The diplomat, Paqe, jabbed a finger toward his face. "You have a seal, you imbecile! From King Zavrius himself!" Panic wormed into his expression. "Instead, you—you're killing citizens of the empire. Putting us all in jeopardy!"

Radek felt the weight of King Zavrius's seal around his neck. Thick turquoise and crystal adorned the medallion, and its weight was accentuated by a heavy metal ring. The seal itself was not metal, but gedrokbone, harvested from the great and dead arcane beasts of Usleth and etched with a lute-harp—the king's mark.

"I could have whipped it out. Shoved it in the bandits' faces. But what would've been the point? This band had the audacity to rob me on the emperor's doorstep. Why would they quiver before a foreign king?" Radek asked.

Paqe scowled deeply. He had been named one of Usleth's diplomats after Zavrius took the throne and came recommended through Chancellor Petra, the king's paternal aunt. All of them were bound to listen to Paqe—but not necessarily obey him.

"Don't get above yourself," Paqe sniffed.

"Forgive me, Paqe. I'll do better when we're in the city."

Paqe stared, not fully believing him. Radek dipped his head a little. Men like Paqe liked to be consulted, but sometimes they were as prideful as anyone else. Paqe knew the minutiae of the law and would be invaluable once they began negotiating the international trade agreement. But out here on the road with the bandits—he was not so much the shining star.

"You'll do most of the talking, won't you? When we're before the emperor?" Radek knocked his shoulder against him. "I'll need you in there."

"Of course, you will," Paqe said hurriedly. "I'm not falling for your charming act, Radek," he claimed, though after he'd said it, he immediately stopped his lecture and wandered off.

Mirakel crossed her arms. "I wish the king had sent someone else."

Radek glanced at her. "You don't mean that."

She gave the kind of sigh of someone who had only just gotten comfortable sitting down and had since been asked to move. "Oh, what do you know? If those bandits had run off with all the gifts, I'm the poor sod who'd have to finance new ones."

Radek decided not to push her and began helping the militia reload the cart. He rescued that fine red brocade from the ground only to find someone had gone and bled on it.

"Shit," he muttered, rubbing uselessly at it. He hefted it high for Mirakel to see. "Do you think he'll notice?"

"The emperor?" She folded her arms. "He's a colonizer. Blood is practically decor for an empire; he'll love it. Now listen to me, Oren Radek. Look at me."

He looked. They'd done business for years. As a purser, Mirakel had loaned him the finances for Radek's early push into the empire's markets. Now they had spent four weeks traveling from Awha Stad. He liked her. Liked her enough he didn't want her to think little of him. Wasn't sure she liked him very much, though.

"Don't get ahead of the caravan anymore. And don't get smart with brigands. King Zavrius isn't here to be impressed by your wit."

Radek gave a deferential nod. He knew better than to argue. "Terribly sorry. It's a miracle I'm not dead yet."

"Good boy." Mirakel patted his back, her finger sliding under the necklace that held King Zavrius's mark. "Doing the king proud means keeping your head, Radek. Stop doing stupid shit."

He smiled at her and nodded, but he made no such promise aloud.

~~~
~~~

Within the hour, they were back on the road. In Deina's saddle—she really was a lovely horse—Radek had time to marinate on what such dangerous roads could mean. At Port Sulvoy, a party had meant to meet them to travel inland to Doskor. Instead, they were met with a cryptic and poorly translated letter conveying the emperor's apologies.

Radek paused at that, briefly considering.

It had been two years since King Zavrius had taken the throne. The months following the king's coronation had been rife with assassination attempts and betrayals. Much of the nobility had hated him—Zavrius's interest in peace and trade seemed more the mark of a lily-livered dandy than anyone fit to rule a country.

But for the most part, he'd proved them wrong. Usleth was prospering. With the discovery of a new gedrok, the ancient creatures whose bodies held arcane power, the Paladin order that protected the nation had been revitalized and expanded. Now, with a paladin in every major settlement ensuring the rule of law, Zavrius's rule had been secured.

Until, without rhyme or reason, Emperor Nio Beumeut had sent Usleth a missive declaring an end to their newly established trade partner status.

Though it would be nothing like the unrest that had clouded the early weeks of his rule, the king knew that a sudden end to trade would reignite the tensions between Usleth and the empire. For many in Usleth, engaging with the empire at all felt like a conversation between a sword and a neck. But trade had been good for Usleth and had disproved many fears.

Zavrius had said, "Radek, the fear is that any contact with the Rezwyns will eventuate in the annexing of Usleth. If you hear or see anything to suggest the emperor plans that, write me. But they haven't declared war in years. Not when my siblings died, not in the months when my throne was in flux. The emperor wanted trade as much as me. Find out what's going on."

And Radek believed an expansion of the current trade routes to be the way forward. Radek had a port at Awha Stad, in the south of Usleth, which was grand and all—only Uslethians weren't allowed up the Serpiz River and it took months to travel up the eastern empire coast to the warehouses he'd installed at Banonok, Elkar, and Ostijan. A port in the south of the empire lay much closer to both Awha Stad and Doskor, but any shipments to Port Sulvoy were heavily scrutinized and regulated. Merchants from Usleth made it no further than Doskor if they managed to circumvent buccaneers, and empire traders were contained to Westgar. The Ashmon settlements in the far west of Usleth had no tangible sense of the empire except the vision of them encroaching on Uslethian territory. Radek had proposed a set of protected trade routes between both nations.

So Zavrius had sent him to speak to the emperor personally.

Radek owed half of his success as a merchant to his decision to support King Zavrius's ascension to the throne. The decision had made him one of the richest merchants in Usleth, and if he could convince the emperor of these new routes, he could make his mark on the empire, too. More than that, the place fascinated him. The people too. Uslethian historians marked them all as vile killers. But Radek had lived through the war, too, and somehow he'd come out of it with a morbid curiosity for the people that had invaded his homeland and the sharp change in their demeanor the instant peace had been brokered. Never again had they invaded. He wanted to know every little thing about them, and if nothing came of that, at least he'd know his market well enough to provide the goods they wanted.

"It's my time," he'd told Mirakel upon their departure. "Reversing the emperor's decision and securing these trade routes is essential. If I'm the one to do it . . . king of the merchants, I'll be."

"King of the merchants," Mirakel repeated, not bothering to hide her disdain. "A step down from your usual fantasy."

The usual fantasy was no fantasy—it was a question of Radek's descent. His mother had always claimed that he descended from King Gedrok, that ancient ruler credited for the discovery of the eponymous Uslethian creatures.

"If the dynasty hadn't changed, you might be bowing to me right now," Radek murmured.

Mirakel smiled at him sweetly. "Then I'll count my blessings, Lord Radek."

Now they were here, within a day's travel of Doskor.

The closest Uslethian province, Westgar, boasted mountains and cool weather. However, the empire proved to be even colder, with a frigid wind assaulting them during their travels. On the way here they'd passed broad plains with low hills, a taiga crowded with pines and spruces, and a stretch of agricultural fields. But when the steep hilly ridges increased, the road had funneled them through a mountain pass. On either side of him, the forested ridges grew, looming above them and filling the sky.

Radek leaned back in Deina's saddle to stare up at them. Usleth was nothing like this. Moving through this pass, the lushness of the trees filled Radek with a sense of awe, even in the growing cold. Doskor felt like a protected bastion with these mountains, tucked away from the world.

Mirakel tilted her neck back and sighed at the gray sky. "How old are you, Radek?"

"Twenty-eight," he said. Then, self-consciously. "Why?"

"Well, if it weren't for the line on your forehead, I'd think you sixteen and desperate."

Radek's hand flew to his head like the right amount of pressure would smooth the divot etched in his skin. Mirakel continued her brutal attack with, "Flirting with a bandit. I swear you fall in love with any man who looks at you for more than a second."

Radek scoffed. "And I fall out of love even faster than that."

"At least you know it. . ." she grinned, tilting her head toward him. "Ah. Who knows. Perhaps you'll find someone to flirt with at court."

"I'm hopeful," Radek grinned. "Hopeful enough I've brought something in a bottle just for that potential," Radek said.

Mirakel rolled her eyes. "Of course, you did. And who are you planning to bed? The emperor himself?"

Radek shot her a look. "Can't say the elderly are my type."

"Eh, we'll see," she told him. "There might be no one else."

CHAPTER THREE

On the morning of Semor's public execution, the bells clanged incessantly. Even in the deep catacombs of Doskor's castle, the clamber resounded through Izra's skull.

Each dreary toll reminded him of the horror of what had happened. It made his heart ache to think too long about it. Izra stood in front of the emperor's chambers, in the basalt depths beneath the castle proper. These tunnels lacked the usual dampness of the underground, replaced instead by an unnatural yet comforting warmth. Gods-given, of course. He said a quick prayer to Suoduny—eyes closed, desperate reach into the ether to feel his god—ignored the sinking feeling and focused on his hands.

With both hands raised high, Izra felt the sparks of Suoduny's power in his blood and saw the intricate lock barring the way to the emperor. The convoluted spell brimmed with traps—something only adept fingers should have been able to unpick.

And yet that traitor priest had gotten in.

Every day since Semor had broken the lock, Izra had made it part of his duty to inspect its reliability. He was becoming obsessive—he had enough sense to recognize that—but it irked him to know that if Suoduny had not jolted him into consciousness, he might have slept through the emperor's murder. Anyone with enough magic in them could learn to unweave these locks, in theory. But such labyrinthine things should have been impossible to untangle without one of the high-ranking Uxbuh, the True Army, which he commanded by birthright. Those touched by the gods had enough magic for unpicking. Unless the emperor's daughters had leaked the secret of the emperor's private exit, someone had let Semor in.

Who had betrayed them?

"Stand down, Commander."

Izra pulled himself to attention at the sound of General Neve's voice. He turned and bowed to her, downcast eyes catching several pairs of feet trotting in beside her. He had not heard their approach, which made him flush with rage and shame. Some commander; some protector. He was losing his edge over grief for something he had managed to stop.

"Sir." He shook the self-pity out of himself and bowed to his general. As the emperor's first-born daughter, she would have been free to spend her days doing very little. But she had been called to greater things. Izra owed a great deal of his training and discipline to General Neve.

Standing tall, he surveyed the three attendants by her side. A short, wisp of a woman in her later years, a young man wearing his light hair in a long plait, and a genderless third, who gave Izra a withering stare. Each wore the bulky, high-necked vestments of the cuvari, which meant they were here to swarm the True Commander's chambers.

The cuvari were the empire's living library, consisting of scholars, philosophers, historians, and scribes, all dedicated to the preservation of the empire's history. And they were secular, or claimed to be; as perfectly neutral as humans could get. Rumors circulated that some of them had renounced the pantheon altogether, which made Izra nearly sick to think about since the Dzioves were descended from the gods.

One day they would be doing the same to him; committing a summary of his entire life to their dreary archives.

Izra grimaced, unsuccessfully keeping it from his face. The color in General Neve's eyes changed, brown-gray turning fathomlessly dark as her usual kindness blinked away to a warning glare. Izra took it like a blow, and stood straighter, made his face perfectly impassive, as if before a foreigner.

"The cuvari are here to record my father," General Neve said. "You will open the lock for them."

What else could he say except, "Of course."

Izra turned and raised his hands once more, letting his magic uncurl the lock. The cuvari stayed silent, but he could feel their hardened stares watching him. He considered whispering a prayer aloud just to make them squirm. In truth, their presence deeply unsettled him.

In the end, duty made him move. Izra bowed politely and stepped aside. He thought he had hidden his disdain quite well until General Neve's lips pursed, a quarter-inch of disapproval edging her eyebrow upward.

"That will be all, strix," she said.

The cuvari slipped past her, ugly little cretins come to feast on the True Commander's sub-potent, unnatural state. General Neve stopped as they disappeared into the chamber and put her shoulder to him, just enough warning for Izra to get his senses together. He readied himself to be scolded. He had been far too open with his thoughts without saying a single word.

She rocked her head toward him, eyes nearly amused. "You know what I am going to say."

"Yes, General Neve."

"You know why it is necessary."

"Yes, General Neve." And in truth, he did. An assassination attempt, of course, needed to be recorded.

"Izra," General Neve said. She folded into him, losing the harshness and smiling at him. "He would be proud. Not only for your conduct, but for the love with which you do it. The Dzioves have always served the head of the empire, and strixes are so rare that any emperor is blessed to have one. But to have a strix with such pride for his place?" Here she squeezed his shoulder, and the cadence of the speech reminded him of comforting a small, very sweet child. "Truly, you and your sister are wonderful protectors and advisors to my father. To the family. But also to the empire itself."

Ah. Izra tried to conceal it, but he cocked his head. She wanted something—which made sense. Without orders from the emperor, he only had General Neve to follow. She would put him on course.

The general bade him to walk. "My sister . . . she truly believes Borviet calls to purge the empire of foreign influence. And with the rumors coming from Ostijan and the territories at our borders . . ."—insurrection, defection, independence were just some of the rumors Izra had heard—"The rule of law is slipping. She believes she has the blessing of the gods to put things right."

Here the general gave him a pointed look, as if Izra could have forgotten this. Unspoken was the knowledge that Neala acted without orders.

Acted as if her father was dead.

When General Neve said, "If the True Commander cannot be awakened soon, Neala will act. Her supporters are already gathering." Izra felt a layer of his resolve slip, and guilt swam up into his stomach.

"You do not think. . ." he trailed off. It was not his place to openly question what he wanted to question. General Neve met his gaze, and there stretched a long moment of silence.

He wanted to ask: *You do not think she planned this?* And also: *You do not think the True Commander will ever wake?*

Both were awful things to think, let alone ask the general. But both were great fears of Izra's. And only four people knew of how the True Commander came to be in this state—both his daughters, Izra, and Kew. Which left very few people to speculate.

In a bid to keep the empire stable, the True Commander had sought the impossible. Immortality. This was not something to question; the emperor's will was absolute. Izra had prayed for guidance, for a vision, something that would lead the emperor in this journey; had done his duty as strix, and had failed in it. What kind of visionary advisor failed in his singular duty? He might never swallow that shame: he had only seen his fated man.

Neala had seen it, though. The thing in the northern mountains. The thing the gods had promised her would secure Emperor Nio Beumeut's eternal state.

Izra and Kew had gone solemnly to fulfill the order and retrieved the beast's blood. And Izra had returned, kneeling before his emperor, prideful and happy to be of service—only to condemn the True Commander to the astrok-mer. For when the blood had passed his lips, the emperor's spirit had been lifted out of him.

Izra glanced up at the general and felt ill. He knew he was overstepping but he felt compelled to ask. "Your sister believes she is favored. That all the visions she has received are. . . godly. What do you believe?"

General Neve glanced at him, furrow in her brow. "I think there is no use speculating on the wills of the gods, those unknowable forces. But what I do know is that you saved my father, and that I am grateful. Beyond measure."

Izra bowed his head. Not quite in support of her sister's infallible connection to the gods, then, which was a relief. As for Semor, Izra would always be loyal to the True Commander first. "It was my solemn duty. Though now I've earned the ire of nearly every priest in Doskor."

He said it loudly enough the priests scuttering through these halls would hear him. The general tried to contain her glare and failed. "Semor is well respected. And you would do well to at least acknowledge that."

"He is a traitor," Izra hissed, and this earned him outright disdain from several priests of Borviet.

Izra fought the urge to glare back. No honor in such revelry.

Doskor's castle echoed in its emptiness. Beyond the servants, soldiers, priests, and scattered cuvari in its walls, there were very few visitors. Most officials who had been appointed by the emperor himself had gone to govern the city-states and provinces that made up the empire's territory. They rarely returned to Doskor for a reason other than trouble. Though there had been a lot of that, recently. Izra had heard talk, and even seen the general drawing up plans to put down any insurrection, if a city-state decided it wanted independence once more.

Izra stared through the open door of the throne room.

The grand cavern seemed to stretch around its centerpiece, the great marble throne of the emperor.

Shrines lined the walls, facing the throne, so that the gods could look directly over the True Commander's well-being. Several priests lay prone, in ritual worship, desperately hoping to urge a holy vision from the gods. Each god required different worship; priests of Borviet self-flagellated for his blessing while Ognmoksh worshippers carved arrow shafts for her hunt as others skinned a deer to propitiate her.

In the center of the hall, stood the long marble tables where the Emperor's Guidance sat. These had only one occupant: High Priestess Neala

She ruled over the Emperor's Guidance, those priests who offered the True Commander counsel. She was partial to Borviet herself, but as the High Priestess, she worshipped at each of the main pantheon's altars regularly. But where the priests of Borviet favored her, they were now openly despising Izra. They saw Semor's death not as a slight, but as an act against Borviet.

The High Priestess gave him a wide smile as he entered and said, "Have you come to offer me guidance, Izra Dziove?"

Izra glanced at General Neve, who looked at him imploringly. Izra understood at once why she had brought him here.

"I'm here to make an offering for Semor," he said with great reluctance. "To ease his way in death."

"Come," Neala said. She reached for him. Izra hesitated but approached the table anyway. He had nothing to offer but his blood, a small cut in the way of Borviet's priests. Neala gently took his arm and pulled up the long sleeve, exposing the back of Izra's forearm.

"You have once again saved my father's life," Neala said as she reached for the ceremonial sickle at her side.

"But I have condemned one of your priests to do it," Izra whispered.

Neala smiled brightly. She laid the sharp edge of the blade against his skin but did not cut. "You must understand, Izra, that the priests of Borviet are filled with fervor and wanting. If you were to talk to them, commune with them, I am sure they would benefit from a man such as yourself."

The softness in her voice momentarily disarmed him, reminding Izra of their childhood. He had grown up here; he had known Neala his entire life. And as children it had been easier; the divide between their statuses had been blurred.

Izra had prophesized so much of the war with Usleth. He had received visions and helped the empire's army win—but the price had been, in part, his childhood. His sanity. When the blood got too much, when the gory visions overwhelmed him, Neala had helped him. She had mesmerized him by crafting puppets out of felt and string, making them dance for Izra, making him laugh. She had ensured he stayed a child as long as he could. And in this moment he yearned for that again; when Neala could recognize his pain and not exploit it.

But he braced himself to hear what kind of man Neala thought him now to be.

"A man who understands necessity. Who will do what needs to be done."

She looked at him for a long time, with such genuine sweetness that Izra's heart twisted. He had fallen for this before, lured by their shared history. Months ago, the High Priestess had come to him, held his hands, with a vision to preserve the emperor's life.

Please, Izra Dziove, you are strix and beloved of my father. Do this for me and I will be forever grateful.

Guilt swelled in him, and he forced the memory back down. He had believed her then and he found himself believing her now—which could not happen again.

He had done what needed to be done then, under her command. And now they shared something Izra did not want to share.

"My duty," he murmured, "is always to the True Commander."

"Of course," Neala said brightly. She gently opened his skin; blood for blood. "As mine is to the empire."

CHAPTER FOUR

They reached Doskor by mid-afternoon. Radek breathed deep, taking in the crisp, winter-cold air tinged with smoke.

The city stretched large in a basin ringed by high mountains and could only be approached by following the road that ran along the Vltaya River. With a natural fortification like that, the narrow pass at the bottom of the hill served as the city's only gate. From here, Radek could see that a river flowed west to east through the city, and two islets sat dotted with small structures Paqe informed him were shrines to the empire's many gods. To the west the castle sprawled, a fortress of gray stone and soaring spires—architecture to marvel at and be swallowed by.

The gates were massive, golden-gray wrought iron. Curling decorative hinges bloomed from either side, and spherical portraits filled each door. There were five in total, with the central portrait—a depiction of a multi-faceted Borviet, half-human and half-boar—split across the seam of both doors in an open-mouthed howl. Radek grimaced at the sight.

No one stopped or questioned them, but they were watched by soldiers in the turrets. Radek locked eyes with one of them and watched her face twist in disgust.

That stung. It always did. It would never matter how lordly he got, or how deep he dug his claws into this continent; he would always be a cizalec here—a foreigner. None of their party could blend in. The people here were ghost-white, not the light tawny of Westgar, like Mirakel, but a type of pale that made them near translucent. Blue veins split like roots beneath their skin and gave them all an unnerving, lifeless quality, as cold and near-dead as the continent they lived in. They stood in stark contrast to the people of Usleth, whom Radek mused were full of life; brown skin warmed in the sun.

"How many bloody gods do they have?" Mirakel hissed at him, shaking him from his thoughts. Radek was more than happy to show off his empire knowledge. The soldiers' cuirasses were decorated with the visages of their respective gods. Many wore the boar-human hybrid of Borviet, the war god. He pointed out the others.

"Ognmoksh," Radek told her, pointing to the depiction of a dying deer. "For the hunt. And there, the tree creature suckling the baby. Zimsmrt. Death, and winter. It's mostly farmers who worship her."

"What?" she said, wrinkling her nose. "That barely makes sense."

"Most of the gods are worshipped as propitiation—like appeasement," Radek explained. He'd learned that much from empire merchants he did business with, and from watching the way they prayed to the sea to spare their shipments.

Paqe gave him the kind of proud look one would reserve for a kindred spirit and added, "There are five in the main pantheon. Borviet, Ognmoksh, Zimsmrt, Suoduny, Zeljia. Then there're gods for anything you can think of."

Mirakel said nothing to this, but she frowned. For many years, Usleth and the empire had been at war. No wonder Mirakel felt uneasy here.

Radek turned his attention to the city. He had meant to make this trip too many times before. But the atmosphere was odd and the people sparse. It wasn't quite what he'd expected for the capital of the empire. Not many people considered him for long, and soon Radek became aware of a crowd gathering near the city center. He shot Paqe a look, expecting it to be some holiday or festival the diplomat had forgotten about, but he only got a sharp shake of the head. Paqe frowned, straining to listen to the chatter.

"Some event," Paqe translated with a shrug. "Something important."

A new group of people merged into the growing throng. They wore fringed head-coverings and stumbled through the crowd slowly, with a reverent pace the rest of the city dwellers did not share. They wove between the horses, dressed in pale beige and washed-out blue, their faces completely obscured. A few rung silver bells in front of their faces and carried incense, but they all had white tree branches curled around their headpieces.

Priests.

"Oh," Paqe said with a low whisper. "What an interesting thing to stumble upon."

"What is it?" Radek asked. Bodies packed tightly onto the road, squeezing close to Deina's flank. She stamped in agitation.

"Those are priests of Zimsmrt," Paqe told him, pointing to the branch-bearers holding incense in the air. He turned with a bright, unseemly grin. "There's going to be an important execution."

Radek raised a brow and turned to Mirakel, who only said, "What? King of the merchants can't stand a little blood?"

Radek would have hit her, if she hadn't been right. In any case, he hadn't much choice. The throng of bodies formed a current that swept them all forward. He had a chance to cast about at the buildings lining the streets. All of them were made of massive pine logs, stained dark, their roofs downward slopes for runoff snow. Carvings were etched into doorways or added as attachments at the ends of beams—symbols echoed on cuirasses or stamped into necklaces in the people around him. The gods were always watching here.

A persistent quiet settled; a stillness that felt unnatural, not reverential. Some people had their heads bowed, but others were eager, craning for the view. As they rounded the corner, people on foot were forced to step aside to give the horses room.

Radek saw it then. A set of wooden gallows loomed in the city center. Doskor's castle rose out of the riverbanks behind it. On the ground before the gallows, guards enforced a perimeter. They were twitchy. Several had their swords drawn. Radek gripped the reins tight.

"I don't like this," Mirakel murmured to him, tone vastly different to her earlier mockery. She made a quick gesture behind her for Conwa and Velki, her bodyguards, to stand to attention. The two moved their hands, ready to draw weapons.

Radek scanned for whatever threat had the soldiers on the defensive. As he did, movement rippled through the crowd, momentarily breaking the uneasy silence with hissing murmurs. They were quiet, too quiet to pick up what was being said, but Radek caught the tone. Anger. Grief. Whoever was about to die, the crowd seemed against it.

Two figures mounted the stairs to the raised platform. The first appeared to be a priest, hunched over and waddling. He wore a drab, sack-like garment covered in mud and grime. Compelled by something, he swung out toward the crowd and bowed. Even with his face covered, sadness occupied the movement; the crowd swayed, and a haunting, low wail sounded throughout many of the gathered priests. Radek jolted in the saddle. A wave of nausea went through him. The rattling, anguished sound ebbed and flowed, and seemed dragged from a deep and ancient place, as if being hauled through flesh itself.

Radek shot a horrified look to Mirakel. It was a terrible sound. Deeply unpleasant. It accompanied the first step of the other figure.

Radek lost his breath at the sight.

This one looked like a wolf wearing the skin of a man. Tall, broad, and austere in a way that demanded the crowd's attention. Radek stared, rapt. The man had that pale northern skin, but a mass of kohl surrounded his eyes, and ran like tears over his cheekbones and his chin. Shoulder-length black hair cascaded down like a mane. He had tied back half of it in a tail, while the remaining locks fell around his neck in slight curls. He wore livery; blue and silver, remnant of the glacial winter of the empire.

Paqe made a low noise of recognition beside Radek and leaned in to whisper.

"He's a Dziove," he murmured.

"A what?" Mirakel whispered.

"Prominent family. Very close to the emperor."

Radek swung away from Paqe and reconsidered the man. When the Dziove took his place near the drop lever, something in Radek squirmed.

This man would serve as executioner.

"Who is the condemned?" Radek murmured. "Ask someone."

Paqe lost all that earlier pride. He gave a flippant gesture to the stage, like it was obvious.

And it was. There were only two people on the platform, after all. Only one of them had been caked in mud.

"The priest?" Radek clarified, incredulous. Priests were sacred to the empire. Protected. At the pinnacle of society.

The droning lament continued, growing louder as the priest centered himself on the stage. Radek felt compelled to watch, drawn inexplicably to the scene. Sharp icy wind slashed across his cheeks.

Paqe murmured. "It is deeply sacred thing, the life of priest. Great honor to take it. All this tells you is this Dziove is of huge importance to the emperor. A strix, blessed with the arcane."

Radek held his breath. Talk of the arcane made him uncomfortable.

At least in Usleth, he knew where such power came from. There, drinking the ichor drawn from the bones of the fallen creatures known as gedroks gave the king's paladins access to arcane powers. But here? The idea of gods bestowing gifts of untold power to whomever they pleased?

The Dziove stood stock still as two soldiers in the blue-gray livery of the palace rushed to drag the priest into position. They draped a noose around his neck and pulled it tight.

From within his heavy wolf-skin cloak, the Dziove drew a long, wooden hornpipe, and blew. A full, deep note echoed on the stone, and, at last, the wailing stopped.

The man began to speak. Each word had a raspy, smoky quality to it. Radek could parse none of it. The Doskorian was thick and fluent. He looked to Paqe for help, and the man struggled through.

"Uh. . . he is Izra Dziove, Commander of the Uxbuh."

"Uxbuh," Radek repeated. "What is that?"

Paqe ground his jaw. "Would you—" he gestured to the platform, where the executioner continued to speak. "Look, it doesn't translate well. It's god-filled, I suppose. Soldiers with a calling, or somehow blessed. Just—he says this priest tried to assassinate the True Commander." A pause. "The emperor." Paqe's eyes went wide at that, perhaps anticipating the diplomatic struggles he would face with an emperor on the defensive.

Radek exhaled noisily. "What?" he said. "Did he manage it?"

"Well, we're not witnessing a bloody funeral, are we?" Mirakel murmured.

"I don't think you've quite grasped the gravity of the situation," Paqe said, but Radek's concern stemmed from his worry that now the emperor would be too paranoid for trade.

"He won't give me leave to travel north of Doskor now," he hissed. "Or at least I wouldn't, if I were him."

"Stop panicking," Mirakel muttered. "You haven't even spoken to him."

But what she did know? If the man couldn't trust his own people, why would he open the gates to foreigners?

The guttural sounds of Doskorian prayer stole Radek's attention. The accused priest swayed trance-like, deep in it and frantic, as if begging for intervention. None came. None but the Dziove, whose hand hesitated mid-air, poised to comfort him. Then he stood straighter. Radek felt drawn to the twitch of bulky muscle in his shoulders as he shucked off a thick, black coat made of pelts. It slumped to the floor like a slumbering wolf.

Izra Dziove rolled his shoulders back. His cuirass gleamed, and beneath it, the emperor's livery seemed to fold over his body. He did not move toward the lever. He threaded his fingers through a thick chain of office that hung low against his chest and brought the wide metal symbol at its end to his lips. The medallion depicted a three-headed boar, open mouthed, screaming.

The executioner kissed it.

"Ocinje!" he bellowed.

Without touching anything, the lever swung violently backward, and the platform dropped. The priest plunged.

Radek jumped and turned away.

No one had been near the lever—he hadn't been expecting it to move.

The moment seemed to drag. Even without the awful gurgling and choking he'd expected with a hanging, a heaviness sat over the crowd and bore down on their necks. No one spoke. A few people peeled away. Doors opened and closed. But a great number stood there, watching the creaking, swaying form. But whether it was reverential or not, a feeling of ceremony emanated from this that he couldn't ignore.

"Let's go," he murmured to Mirakel. She nodded and trotted her horse slowly through the thinning crowd. Her two militiamen tailed them, guiding the cart of gifts.

"Paqe." Radek touched the diplomat's forearm.

As if suddenly awakened from a dream, Paqe urged his horse to follow the slow-moving stream past the spectacle and continue to the palace. From the gallows, like an overbearing shadow, came the boring stare of the Dziove. Radek shifted his eyes away and tried to turn with a nonchalance he did not feel. The cart creaked forward, and the limping crowd led them out of the cramped square. Radek kept his focus on the bulk of the castle, looming behind the Dziove and the gallows, but paranoia swelled in him.

The Rezwyn soldiers stayed statuesque as they guarded the swinging corpse. He saw all this in his periphery. Radek told himself not to look. On horseback, Uslethian; he already stuck out like a sore thumb. But the massive form of Izra Dziove, like an oil blot on the sky, had made no move to stop them.

And then a deep bellow echoed in the square. It had the same rich quality of the horn, but it was a voice. His voice. The crowd froze and locked itself in an anticipatory stillness. In unison, the soldiers turned and yelled in time to the percussive beat of their sabatons upon the cobblestones. They fanned out from the gallows heading straight for them; Radek saw all this from the corner of his eye. As both lord and merchant, Radek had seen thugs and brutes and murderers, and built his life navigating their cruelty. He had made it this far with determination—and thus, with this same determination, he decided not to turn around.

"Paqe," Radek whispered, somewhat desperately. The diplomat did not reply. The Dziove was only getting closer to them; a great beast stalking prey. Radek clenched his jaw and hissed, "Paqe!"

"Off your horse," Paqe said through a gritted smile. "Now, now. Quickly."

Radek hesitated, then cursed, then did as he was told. Mirakel followed suit. Her militiamen were rigid, hands trained on their weapons.

"A great honor," Paqe said calmly over Radek's pathetic wheezing, "to be greeted by the True Commander's trusted Dziove."

When Izra Dziove stopped before him, everything in Radek's body shivered. He held himself as still as his body allowed. It didn't matter. It was involuntary. Up close, Radek was forced to take in the sheer size of him. The man stood tall, broad, severe. Radek hadn't seen it before, but a scar had split his left brow and curved down his face to his cheek. Another burst over his right lip. Jet black stubble filled his cheeks like shadow; unkempt, the mark of a man who hadn't shaved in days, not one trying to grow a beard. Gray streaked through his hair, though Radek wouldn't have put him over thirty.

Izra said nothing. Paqe had also stopped speaking—but the Dziove acted like the diplomat hadn't said a word in the first place. His severe gaze bored into Radek, who responded by pulling his best and biggest smile.

Shuffling, awkward movement; Radek reached toward his tunic and, inchworm-fashion, edged Zavrius's seal out from the warmth. The gedrokbone glinted. He held it toward the pale man's face and added helpfully, "King Zavrius's seal."

Izra breathed low and snorted. The frigid air steamed around his exhale. Radek felt so drawn to the faded hazel of his eyes and the remorseless shadow behind them that he practically tipped forward to be closer.

Izra looked at him. Deadpan, in Uslethian so articulated it almost sounded fake, he said, "You are the one I have been expecting."

Radek shuffled on the frosty cobbles. "Well, yes, I'd hope so. King Zavrius sent at least three letters in advance." Here Radek swallowed and nervously looked to Paqe. "Those were sent, weren't they?"

"He just said he's been expecting us," Mirakel mumbled.

Radek made a motion for her to stop with his hand and said in a frantic whisper, "And I think in this case an over-abundance of caution might serve us, Mirakel!"

She shut up. Paqe offered an unhelpful grin which Radek turned away from.

"As I was saying." He swallowed and once again proffered the seal. "We are the envoys sent by King Zavrius of Usleth for an audience with Emperor Nio Beumeut."

Izra considered this impassively. He was doing absolutely nothing with his face. Radek steeled himself anyway, waiting more for anger and murder than a simple acknowledgment.

Shit, why did he care this much? If such a lack of emotion could make Radek this jumpy, he could only imagine the visceral power a smile on Izra Dziove's face would hold.

"What is your name?" the commander asked coolly.

Radek blinked, surprised. "Oren Radek." And then, a little late, "Sir—General, I mean."

"You may put that away."

Oren Radek put the seal away. His palms were growing sweaty. The inside of Radek's velvet tunic had become its own muggy environment.

"May I touch your face, Oren Radek?"

Radek balked. He said nothing, which the Rezwyn took as acquiescence. In the achingly long moment before Izra touched his face, Radek tried to get help. He slid an eye to Paqe, hoping he'd get some encouraging gesture, something that would tell him this was all completely normal and fine. But Paqe wasn't looking at him. The bloody weasel was enchanted. His eyes were fixed on the careful, calculated motion of Izra's hand toward Radek's face; Paqe apparently lacked availability to assist him in any way. Radek didn't even bother with Mirakel. He flushed as two strong calloused hands enveloped his cheeks and urged them upward as if his head were a chalice.

The proximity put him in a stupor. Izra's intensity shocked him; beautiful, and big. He smelled earthy, faintly of woodsmoke. Radek dragged his gaze up to Izra's face, feeling inexplicably exhausted. The edge of his vision stormed. Izra's face blurred.

"What have you done?" he whispered.

But Izra Dziove said nothing. And though Radek tried to hold on to consciousness, it was slippery and frightening and fading. Before it all went dark, his body seemed to feel every bit of the cold in this continent. He started to shiver.

Then Oren Radek trembled so violently he fell into the other man's arms, unconscious.

Chapter Five

Izra felt alive.

He kicked open the nearest chamber door with a man named Oren Radek enveloped in his arms and rushed him to the bed. To his right, three servants shot up in surprise at his intrusion, but he completely disregarded them. Izra moved to the bed and lay the unconscious man down. Someone else behind him barked orders for the servants to leave. Time slowed down—in the way of dreaming. Izra heard his heartbeat in his ears and wondered if he had never woken up this morning.

Whoever had followed him in was causing a ruckus. A few swears were thrown about. Izra tuned them out and settled next to the body as if to pray. In truth, this motion had the same weight to it as worship, and Izra knew that. He had betrayed all common sense to do this, but his heart had been twisting with passion and fear. Izra had not expected this.

"What are you doing?" he heard called from behind him. He fought the urge to continue staring at the man on the bed. He felt foolish, like a boy half his age, but Oren Radek was gorgeous. The firelight burnished his brown skin and softened all the angles of his face. His hair curled darkly, and twin pearl earrings framed his jaw. Nestled in a black beard were his lips; crooked, a little chapped. Izra shifted to run a thumb over them.

"Izra!"

Izra jumped and rounded to find Kew, furious for no good reason.

Kew flinched at whatever dark look twisted on Izra's face and put his hands up to assuage the horror in him. "You have gone mad. Herding Uslethians into the castle as if we did not just prevent the emperor's death."

"Who are you to say so?" Izra repeated. Kew pressed his lips together until they disappeared into the rest of his face. Izra felt bad for it immediately and sighed. He turned back to the man on the bed.

Gods, it felt like one of his dreams. Oren Radek. He whispered the name aloud. Oren. Radek. Felt his tongue curve over it, until it felt familiar and intimate. This was his man. He knew it like Suoduny had told him himself. Rapidly, Izra got to his feet and pushed Kew outside. The other four Uslethians were standing there, in a kind of petrified wonder. The two mercenary types, and the other—who was she?—were fuming. But the other one, a tutor, or a scholar, perhaps—some caste that required very little physical movement—set his face to an impassive mask, free from all emotion, and knocked his head forward in a familiar custom.

Ah. So a diplomat, then. He knew the empire custom with all cizalecs was to maintain a sense of calm and inner unity. Emotion often betrayed this.

"We cannot keep a cizalec in an inner chamber. Not until the general is aware of it," Kew said.

Izra wanted to tell him he was wrong. In his soul, he knew Oren Radek to be trustworthy.

"He had King Zavrius's seal," Izra began.

Kew leaned forward with a frown and pressed his thumb against Izra's forehead. "Something is wrong with you."

Izra decided then and there that he could not continue this without telling Kew. It would kill any peace he had left. He tugged Kew forward and told him in a low whisper, "It's him."

Kew frowned. "What?"

"The one," Izra hissed impatiently. "The man. Whom Suoduny shows me."

A dubious expression clouded Kew's face. "Your fated man?"

"Yes. Yes!" Izra shook him.

Kew leaned to the side and stared at the two Uslethians his fated man had come with. After a long moment of consideration, he glanced back at Izra. That uncertain expression had decayed into complete disbelief. "Well." Kew gestured to the diplomat. "He looks . . . nothing like . . . I mean . . . I didn't think he would really be your type?"

Izra glared at him. Then at the Uslethians. The gaunt-faced diplomat stared back, wide-eyed, like a rabbit before a wolf.

Kew stepped in front of him, blocking off Izra's view. "The heart wants what it wants," he said.

Izra shoved Kew away. "You are as thick as they come. Obviously not the diplomat."

"The one you carried in?" Kew's expression lifted. He spoke easily, all that agitation apparently evaporated. "At least there's a decent reason for your breaching protocol. Now the whole of Doskor will have something to celebrate. The elusive soulmate of the infamous Dziove is, in fact, real. That scandal will certainly be forgotten."

"Scandal? Hardly. A miscommunication at best," Izra scoffed. It was too difficult not to take the bait on this one. He hated this memory, and all talk of it—but hated more to let it be spoken of without his input. The True Commander had wanted to make a pair of him and the Lord of Veprak, a large, warm city in the west of the empire. They had a strong army, and the lord had acquired several cities in the True Commander's name. A Dziove and a military lord—it would have been a secure and solid bond, and removed any chance for the Lord of Veprak to depose the True Commander, should his ambitions grow much further.

But if the gods showed you someone, a bond of marriage would not be enough to keep you from them. Besides Veprak was a little too dedicated to the mortification of the flesh required by the god Borviet for Izra's taste.

Izra pushed past his second with his jaw clenched. Kew's anxious nattering seemed only protocol, but it grated on Izra's nerves. At that moment, all Izra wanted to do was spin on his heel, march right back to lay prostrate before Oren Radek, and endlessly thank his god.

Izra gestured for the guards to peel away from the Uslethians, and gave them each a short bow. He turned first to the woman with a crop of brown hair, whose eyes were fire and rage—not because he in any way wanted the challenge, but because she had been the first to rush forward when Radek fell. It might have been delusional, but Izra felt a kinship by proxy.

But she did not speak—on the suggestion, Izra guessed, of the diplomat.

"I am Ambassador Paqe, and it is an honor to be within the walls of the great castle." The diplomat had stepped forward. He spoke in smooth Doskorian, flashing an anxious, wilting smile at Izra.

"Ambassador Paqe," Izra replied in Uslethian, for the courtesy of his companions. "You will forgive us for this, I hope."

"Oh, of course!" Paqe said, very happily.

The woman next to him balked and struggled. She tried to whisper to Paqe, but Izra still caught the words. "Are you fucking kidding me? If I have to negotiate for Radek's safe return, it'll be a hole in the treasury."

"Mirakel!" Paqe hissed, practically pleading now. The woman fell silent, albeit begrudgingly. "Oren Radek is here for a trade deal, you see. To reconfirm that which your True Commander, inexplicably, ceased. We. . . we wrote ahead.

Is Ambassador Odrica Dziove present in Doskor now? She can verify my identity."

"Ambassador, you speak so well!" Kew exclaimed when he had finished. "Almost native. Very impressive." Then he looped his arm through Izra's and dragged him flush against the opposite corridor, near Oren's door. "They have no idea what's happened here."

"No," Izra agreed.

"Why are you frowning?" Kew asked as his own brows came together. "Surely this is good. We can just send them back home."

Izra turned away to think. He'd been so stunned and excited to find the man from his dreams that he hadn't given a single thought to the man's origin. How could he be from Usleth? Why would Suoduny give him a . . . heathen?

Izra racked his brain. What did he even know about that tiny peninsula? Only that they recognized no gods save for the dead bodies of giant creatures from which they—rather disgustingly—harvested ichor to power arcane weapons. Izra's older sister had been an ambassador to the court at Cres Stros and had told him many strange tales of the bizarre necromancy practiced there.

He instructed Kew to show the rest of the party from Usleth to their rooms, but kept Oren Radek with him to watch him—to think.

He tucked Oren Radek into bed. Hours passed. The sun set.

Izra focused on the rise and fall of the other man's chest and allowed himself to be lulled by the ambient crackle of the hearth.

He had pushed Oren too hard; reached into the space between them with Suoduny's help and tried to pull a sense of recognition to the forefront of Oren's mind. It had been too much for him. Oren Radek had none of a strix's innate qualities. Even with divine guidance, Oren had not ventured so close to their realm the way Izra had his whole life.

"What are you doing, Dziove?"

It was not quite an accusation, but neither was it a wholly banal question.

General Neve stood at the door. Izra scrambled to his feet, only to dip into a bow once more.

The general's armor made her appear short and bulky. She kept her hair shorn close to her scalp, but she had not shaved it in weeks. A fine down of black hair had grown, a stark contrast against the white of her skin.

"You brought this Uslethian here without permission," she said. "You carried him up the stairs. You tucked him into bed like you were his nursemaid, or so the guards tell me."

Izra saw no point in lying when she already knew. He looked away. "I did, yes."

The general responded immediately with a sharp, disappointed exhale.

"Izra?" she said, more softly. She came and touched his arm; a touch to remind him of their closeness, of their family's closeness. "What is going on?"

"He's my fated man," he said. "I tried to reach into him to feel our soul connection and it was too much for him. That's why he's like this."

The general took this in without a single word. She seemed less interested in Oren's unconscious state than with his being here at all. Then she said, "I am happy for you. Truly." But then, slightly accusatory, she asked: "Did Suoduny show you his impending arrival? Or give any indication that he hailed from Usleth?"

Izra shook his head. General Neve did something strange with her mouth and glanced away. He knew enough about her to read it: she had not known either.

Boldly he asked, "And your sister? Did she know of the incoming diplomatic party?"

"You mean High Priestess Neala?" The general's hand slipped away from his arm.

Izra bit his tongue. He had overstepped. Forgotten the divide of their blood that made him servant and her the exalted daughter of the emperor. But the general told him. She shook her head unhappily. "I have since asked her. She said there have been letters from King Zavrius. She says she told them to turn back."

Neither of them spoke. A new emotion played out on the general's face, as if calculating something, trying to reason away what her sister had done. It did not matter to Izra. There could only be one reason the priestess would have kept this from them.

"General," Izra said softly. "What is she angry about? That the Uslethians made it here at all?"

He should not have said it. The general ignored most of his implication but spun back with barely contained fury. It lit her eyes, illuminated the weariness in the rest of her face. "This was stupid of you," she said, gesturing to Oren's form. "He cannot stay here. None of them should be here. It's not safe. For you or them. Tomorrow, send them back."

He stepped forward. Her stormy eyes widened at the move, shocked at the transgression, but he could not stop now. Izra said, "Have you ever questioned my loyalty?"

She looked at him, brows furrowed. Then she swallowed. "Not once."

"Do not start now. My loyalty is to the emperor. I am his servant. I know his wishes, and death to Uslethians was not among them. He wanted peace. Trade. I do not care if the Priestess shares his blood; my emperor is not yet dead." Izra finished and clamped his mouth shut. Cold sweat dripped down the back of his neck—which the general could order to be cut, if she liked. Or broken. He would be the next swaying body to line Doskor's walls. Izra braced himself. At the very least, Suoduny had let him and his fated man meet one time.

The general made no order. Strangely, her eyes softened. She turned away.

"You are right, Dziove. Neala will always prioritize Borviet over anything else. That is her devotion; it is overriding the True Commander's wishes. I do not wish to think she had anything to do with Semor . . ." Here she paused, refusing to give voice to the rest of the thought. But she looked at him, gaze full of meaning, before she continued. "She summoned several governors back here. Whilst you were with the cizalec, they have arrived. She has called a feast for tonight, you know. A gathering of the court, and like minds. Expansion to her and so many Rezwyns means gaining new territory. Not sharing ideas, or food, or clothes."

Izra froze. The empire's city-states were governed by military men and women appointed to the position by the emperor. They each held the fortresses, ensuring each city-state paid its dues. To have even a few here surprised him—or rather, concerned him. Who was overseeing the outer territories while they all gathered here? But more importantly, having them here whilst the True Commander lay unconscious implied something more sinister. Neala planned to build consensus among them. She wanted to gain their support.

General Neve left him after that; left him to marinate in the knowledge his blood and his caste did not make him safe from the will of her sister.

Izra sat with his legs crossed. He let his eyes drift. Fear and a godly love filled up Izra's chest, just by being close to the body of Oren Radek. But he had not been what Izra expected. And neither could Izra imagine Suoduny—the god of fate itself—had led a cizalec to Izra's arms, now, by anything short of design.

He must be meant to champion their cause. It felt wrong to stand up so boldly against the blood of the emperor, but he would have to. All the signs in the mortal world pointed him towards it.

Chapter Six

Radek woke with a headache that split his skull and, for one blissful minute, absolutely no memory of what had occurred.

The room was grand; carpet over the marble, four-poster bed, small round table for meals. A bow window showed the lush coniferous ridges in the distance. He was tucked into a warm, soft bed—which boded well—but when he got up and tried the door, he found it was locked—which did not. Then he realized the door didn't even have a bloody keyhole, which meant he couldn't even attempt lockpicking, and that silliness made him crack. Oren stumbled back to the bed, sat, and then shame walloped him with the mortifying memory of fainting into that executioner's arms.

He was in Doskor. He was King Zavrius's envoy. He had let a pretty man touch him and then swooned. And since he certainly hadn't walked into this castle chamber, he had been carried. When he realized the likelihood that either Mirakel or Paqe had held him in their arms was slim to none—and he knew the other militiamen wouldn't count hefting the unconscious body of their patron around as part of their duties—he nearly swooned again. Izra Dziove certainly had the broadness necessary to carry him. Then Radek imagined his twiggy neck lolling unattractively and shot upright in both embarrassment and anxiety. After that horrible image, he had an itch to move.

What the hell had happened to him? He fiddled with King Zavrius's seal and stumbled over to the frost-limned window, staring out over the city of Doskor to the far horizon. The sun was sinking, a dying firestorm smothered by snow-capped mountains. He saw a stand of trees bristling at the edge of a jagged precipice. Wind blew through them, forcing the trees to cascade into one another as the strength of the draught increased. Just as quickly the wind stopped, and the pines returned to their precarious place on the cold incline. Radek felt a strange brotherhood with those trees; the feeling of being on the edge, close to being uprooted and plummeting into a ravine.

The more he thought about it, the more nefarious all this seemed. What better way for the Rezwyns to gain the upper hand in a negotiation than this? Separation, isolation from his allies—Radek stopped that thought before it could get more of a footing but couldn't quite stop the swell of panic at being away from them. Were they alive? Was he alone?

But Radek had been the one to faint, so how could it be intentional? Still, his nerves were frayed, leaving him shaky. He would be easy to interrogate, if it came to that. Radek had to remember what kind of man Nio Beumeut's reputation purported him to be. More than a warmonger. A colonizer. Radek stood thinking about all the ways he could leave Doskor with nothing, and became so lulled by his own thoughts he almost missed the sound of the door opening.

Radek whipped around. He braced himself, expecting to see a hulking silhouette filling the doorway, backlit by the sconces in the hallway. But the figure standing was lithe and thin. She walked forward and the bloom behind her disrupted, revealing her face and complexion: alabaster pale and spotted with freckles. Much of her hair was hidden by a stiff headscarf. The girl saw him and startled, nearly dropping the bucket she carried. She bowed low and mumbled out a thickly accented, "Lord."

Radek felt his own head dipping with her. Before he could be discomfited by his body's reaction to the word 'lord'—which apparently was to bow self-consciously, rather than coolly acknowledge his own title—the servant stuttered out another sentence of half-formed Uslethian words. Put together with Radek's poor knowledge of Doskorian, they managed two full sentences.

She would alert the commander he'd awoken, and he would bathe and change for an audience. She offered him the water, bowed again, and left.

Radek followed her line of sight to the single heavy trunk he'd managed to cart over from Usleth. Someone must have brought it in whilst he slept (another thing to be embarrassed about).

The emperor was waiting for him, then.

Radek calmed himself, pressed his lips to Zavrius's seal for luck, and dropped to his knees and washed quickly with the tepid water and cloth provided.

After that, damp and shivering, he went to engage his luggage. The trunk was plain, not carved with anything, but of high quality and he liked it. It had been one of the first things he bought when he started to make coin; a symbol of becoming something greater than a boy confined to one small town. Something to travel with, to store precious things in. With the help of his militiamen, Radek had crammed seven heavy outfits in. The moment he opened the trunk, the compressed clothes sprung out like they were gasping for air. Before he dug through them, Radek stripped off the thick mustard velvet tunic he'd worn for days, shivering immediately as the warm layers were stripped away. Shuffling over to the fire, Radek caught his reflection in the etched mirror above the mantle and froze.

Traveling for so long had done something to him already. Radek had always boasted little more than an ounce of lean muscle, and if not covered by fat, it was masked by layers of clothing. But it wasn't his body that seemed different, but his face. He looked changed, like some flower that withered away from the sun. Sunken eyes, weathered warm flush beneath his skin. His beard itched, a scraggly mess long overdue for a shave. One patch on his chin had previously been shorn too close to the skin, and now grew at a substantially slower rate than the rest. He found his scissors and spent some time making himself presentable before turning to the main event—his clothes.

There was power in clothing, in fashion; it could make someone think highly of you before you opened your mouth. Radek had learned to dress the part from a young age. Nothing had changed here, in this foreign land; he would wear what he had to make the emperor listen. Flaunting some finely made thing was his specialty

He chose a layered kaftan tunic of red velvet and wool lined with a gold-beige silk, with paneled woolen pants he'd tried to make as tight as possible. His shoes were felted boots with leather soles. Heavy gold embroidery adorned the tunic's front to his waist, where the layers started to flare. From shoulder to elbow, gold lace windows were showing off his arms, but they disappeared when the lace connected to short velvet flounce sleeves. It was all a bit much, which made it perfect. Radek shook out his hands, trying to expel all the bothersome anxiety that had bubbled up in him. The bravado faltered. He remembered again that he was confined to this room—a prisoner, however well-kept—and that wouldn't do. Not if he intended to secure this deal for the king, and certainly not if he was to build himself an empire of trade routes. He needed to calm down.

To assist with this, Radek fished out his cards and shuffled them. He stared first at the wash of painted scenes, then let his eyes lose focus in the hopes he could be lulled by their blurring colors. When that didn't work, he thought about pulling one free, and managed to yank out a Rezwyn soldier card that depicted three screaming Rezwyns skewering an Uslethian on their halberds. Not ideal. He grimaced, replaced the card, and realized he'd started sweating profusely.

He was going to die. Was he going to die? Radek cast about for something else to focus on. A glinting decanter on the little table tempted him. Some bottled tension in him unfurled at the sight, and he moved to it at breakneck speed, yanking out the glass stopper before he'd ceased walking. Honey-gold liquid swirled inside, and when decanted into a small glass smelled strongly of plum and some other, bitter thing Radek didn't recognize. Haltingly, he brought the glass to his lips, and sipped.

A light, sweet taste coated his mouth until he swallowed. The taste distorted from sweet to a sour bite, increasingly more sour with every aching second it took the liquid to trickle down his throat. And then, all at once, fire.

Radek choked. He slammed the glass onto the table and staggered back, clawing at his throat. His stomach twisted with the vile liquid. Radek shivered and dropped to his knees, the carpet barely muffling the smack of his weight onto marble. Eyes watering, heart hammering, Radek had one clear thought: he was an idiot. He'd been poisoned.

The door burst open. Radek craned his neck, peering at the massive silhouetted form of Izra Dziove.

The commander blinked, unmoving. "What are you doing?"

"Dying," Radek wheezed. "I'm—" he managed to point to the poisoned wine on the table.

Izra stared. "Dramatic."

"What?"

"It is only snake wine," Izra said, gesturing to the ceiling like the gods were watching. He came and brushed his hand along Radek's back, the briefest of gentle touches, and then put his hands beneath Radek's arms and lifted him. "It has the burn of venom in it, but it is not poisoned. Are you comforted now?"

"Yes, alright, thank you." Radek decoupled from Izra and thought about running violently toward the window and crashing through the glass to a euphoric end. He stood facing it for a long moment feeling his cheeks burn with the kind of embarrassed rage he hoped would corrode his insides and kill him standing.

Izra stood ramrod straight and stared at him. Radek didn't know how to feel about that. He looked different than when Radek had encountered him on the road. Cleaner, actually. More put together. He had shaved and combed his hair back, put something like oil in it to keep the edges from frizzing. No longer in his uniform, Izra now donned a neat black tunic beneath his cuirass, which appeared to have been recently polished. His wolf cloak remained still wrapped around his shoulders. But when their eyes met, he flinched.

"You look very nice," Izra said. He seemed to belatedly register the awkwardness of this compliment, because he frowned immediately after he'd spoken.

A number of things flooded Radek's mind at that. But only an adolescent giggle emerged from his mouth.

When Radek didn't reply Izra advanced. There was an intimacy here that made Radek shiver. He found himself feeling very small. Izra kept looking at him like they were old friends. That warmth tempted Radek; he wanted to lean into it. To let his guard down. Though if the emperor had heard a single rumor about the merchant Lord Oren Radek, sending a tall, pretty man into a bedroom with him reeked of a ploy. Radek liked men; liked them often. Could this man be a kind of gift? Or was he a spy? Most likely both.

Radek stepped away—giant, startling man that Izra was—and put his hands up. The motion stopped Izra's advance, but probably only because Radek looked very silly cowering in his velvet robe. He was alone, without his allies, and this wouldn't do much longer.

"Am I your prisoner, then?" he asked.

Izra laughed. "What?"

"You locked me in," Radek said. "If I'm a prisoner in the empire, I would like to know."

Izra focused on him, eyes assessing. "You have a bed, a piss-pot, and a view. This is the best empire prison of them all."

"Yet here I am, locked in a room, alone. And speaking of that, where is the rest of my party?"

Izra slumped. "You are not a prisoner. Your diplomat has explained your reason for being here, and two of your party have already left. Your other companions are outside waiting for us."

"What kind of King of Merchants faints in the street?" Mirakel spat once he came into view.

Both she and Paqe were waiting in the corridor outside his room. Two soldiers flanked them, holding highly decorated halberds. There was little distinction between them and the soldiers in the city. They wore the same garb, the same stamped cuirasses, but he had no time to think on it. Once Radek realized Mirakel looked frightened, he couldn't think of anything else.

Arms wrapped around herself, body tense—Radek could almost hear her sweating. He had never seen her like this.

He sidled close and whispered, "What's wrong with you? You look ready to shit your pants."

"Eat me."

"No," Radek said. This exchange did not relieve Mirakel in the slightest. "Look. I apologize for my little fainting spell—"

"—a tall man looked at you and you literally passed out."

"—but I've had a decent nap, now, and I'm fine. You can stop mourning me."

Mirakel made a nasty expression. "Wasn't mourning you. But do you have any idea how expensive a funeral would be? Just extraditing your body would burn a hole." She stared at him. "Don't die here, okay?"

Radek glanced about. "Would be easier to stay alive if your bodyguards were here. Why did you let them go? You're paying them to protect you."

"Apparently not enough," she muttered.

"You didn't go with them," he said.

"No, I didn't," Mirakel agreed, without elaborating further.

Paqe looked haggard. After Mirakel had quieted, the diplomat looked Radek's way, and gave a subtle nod of his head. "Glad you're still with us."

Radek frowned. Why were they both acting like he'd come so close to death?

"Do you know something I don't?" Radek whispered, to no reply.

He wanted to pick the diplomat's brains, but Izra Dziove lurked like a waiting shadow. Radek's urge to speak calcified.

"This way," Izra said.

Radek shored up his confidence and followed him down the wide corridor. The walls were made of a gray stone and shot into an arched ceiling; the floor consisted of an eerie white marble struck through with blue veins. Dozens of torches burned along the wall, but a darkness still sat in the castle, a vignette at the edge of Radek's vision.

Radek glanced back. The soldiers at the rear had dropped back to a polite distance, clearly unconcerned about the three of them overpowering Izra.

There was a great tension here. Not knowing why that priest had been executed meant they were likely to wander into some great political blunder.

"Tell me your thoughts," Radek whispered, when he thought they were comfortably out of earshot.

Paqe spoke urgently. "The Rezwyns are a cautious, if somewhat unknowable, people. But this treatment is . . . quite unheard of. Mirakel and I were interrogated."

"They didn't know we were coming," Radek said.

Paqe said tensely, "I am aware."

Izra ushered them along until they reached a door. Radek had very little sense of what the castle should look like, given his unconsciousness upon arrival, but after a few of these thin vestibules ended in a doorway, his spatial understanding had all but evaporated. Much of his attention stayed on Izra, anyway. The firelight bled into Izra's hair, streaking it the way the setting sun splits along the horizon.

"We are not being ferried to the throne room," Paqe whispered suddenly. It broke Radek's reverie. "The Rezwyns keep their most precious things close to the earth." He glanced at Radek's quizzical expression and leaned in further. "Closer to the gods, they say. The throne room is the heart of this castle, in its depths. Wherever we are going, that isn't it."

The implication that their diplomat had never been here before struck Radek like a blow. "Remind me again how often you've graced these halls?"

Paqe hesitated. "The last time Emperor Nio Beumeut took an audience, I was thirteen."

"Great," Radek said more calmly than he felt.

He focused instead on the hallway. Arched windows lined the right side. They showed the city below, consumed by night and glinting with firelight. Dark mountains rose in the distance, sharp shadowy shapes cutting into the clear and dazzling night sky. The hall itself stayed unchanged. It was just one stretch of gray stone and muted firelight, but it curved so Radek couldn't see far ahead. Eventually, Izra started to slow. The bend evened out, and at the end of the hall were two oak doors.

No guards flanked the doorway.

Radek sucked in a breath and leaned over to Mirakel, breathless. "Is this it? Are we being introduced to the emperor?"

"How should I know?" Mirakel twisted up her face at him. "Only thing he's said to me tonight is 'follow.'"

In front of them, Izra was doing something to the door. Apparently, it wasn't as simple as pushing against the wood. He stood murmuring, making strange signs with his fingers. They glinted copperish in the candlelight. Radek saw the tips of his left fingers were covered in something like molten metal. Was this a form of prayer, an act of supplication? A nervous habit? Radek stared at those fingers, wondered about the size of them, and flushed at his own thought.

A spark zipped along the wood, and part of the cast iron uncoupled, slithering back the way a snake would react to fire. Unlocked, sound crept through the seam between the doors. Voices, muffled chatter. Radek couldn't pick out the tone of it, couldn't quite tell if it was joyful or mournful or some Rezwyn in between.

Radek went a little cold. Paqe approached slowly. "Heed this. If it is the emperor—the True Commander—you must treat him with the utmost respect."

Radek opened his mouth just as the grand door gave a yielding groan. The intricate iron lock had snaked apart and now rested in curled bud-like shapes near the doors' hinges.

Izra looked at them over his shoulder. He took the time to smooth down his hair and readjust his cloak. Then he did something peculiar. He offered Radek his arm.

Radek stared at it, uncomprehending. Was Izra was showing off? He wasn't even flexing, and the bulge of his bicep stared at Radek, a tempting, over-inflated invitation.

Radek swallowed. "You want me to . . . ?"

Izra blinked. A half-choked wheeze accompanied his claim that, "It is customary."

Radek stared down at the extended arm. He looked back at Paqe, his one lifeline. Paqe simply shrugged. Useless.

Radek turned back and wrapped his hand around Izra's bicep. Like Radek's touch burned it, Izra flexed instantly, muscle hardening beneath Radek's hand. What an odd custom. He gave Izra a weak smile. "Yes, very impressive."

Izra stared at him. His cheeks and nose were burning, but he kept his face blank.

"No," he murmured. "You are meant to . . . to take my arm. To be guided by one guided by the gods."

Radek let go. He heard Mirakel behind him struggling to breathe. "A lovely, lovely custom." Radek slipped his hand casually onto the commander's arm, and refused to turn around when Mirakel prodded his side.

If the gods were real, they were fucking cruel.

Thankfully, the doors opened to a flurry of movement and sound. Radek craned his neck. Colossal walls dwarfed him. He spied columns that bloomed into fan-style vaulting on the high ceiling. Radek's eyes fell to the empty wooden throne in the center of the wall. Drums and horns and grating stringed instruments played a jaunty tune. Marble tables bedecked with food curved around the room. A few people lounged on reclining seats, but a good hundred stood. People danced and clapped already, and Radek was overwhelmed by the unfamiliar shapes of their clothes and shoes. He saw both men and women in chophines, a shoe he'd only seen once before in Ostijan, where a young woman had worn them to walk through muddy streets. It was a platform shoe with a ridiculously high sole, and here they were decorated in furs and beads. They skirted daintily over the marble floor. Most women sported boxy headdresses lined with gems and veiled with silk. Thick strings of beads framed their faces. Priests wore beaded head-coverings and slightly embroidered versions of their dreary sacks, but they all lurked on the hall's edge with skulking expressions.

The men, Radek was happy to see, were not underdressed. The fashion of this court seemed to be based on thick, embroidered fabrics, with most men attired in oversized cloaks or jackets embellished with contrasting embroidery and appliques. Radek fell quietly in love with one man who wore a knitted rib coat that, from the back, folded in decorated flaps to resemble a moth. He got caught up in the new textiles, the style and weave of them.

Roped lanterns had been strung end to end across the high ceiling. Everything below them bathed in their warm glow. At the far corners of the hall, two trees loomed, pruned in a way that they bent towards one another. Beneath the lanterns, they looked like they burned. Nothing like Usleth's stately, controlled feasts—the empire seemed full of life and chaos.

Izra leaned toward an old man with a horn, whispering in his ear. The herald gave a stern nod, blared his horn—which drew no one's attention—and loudly proclaimed, "Commander Izra Dziove of the Uxbuh, the True Army, Blessed by Suoduny, guiding . . . several companions."

The people closest turned to look, but Radek's announcement barely turned heads. He hadn't even warranted a name-drop.

"Rather lackluster," he murmured under his breath, and by everything in him, he swore he heard Izra laugh. Fine. The empire appeared determined to ignore him. But they didn't know him yet. He forgave them.

"Come," Izra said. He led Radek to the left, avoiding dancing bodies with quick footwork. Izra escorted the Uslethians to tables close to the wall where servants scuttled behind a few seated people. Radek didn't know what to think of them. They weren't lords and ladies in the Uslethian sense. They were military men and women, or descendants of priests. Many had weathered faces puckered with scars or sunspots. Even if they dressed beautifully, there was a distinctive difference about them that made Radek feel like a foreigner.

Izra deposited them by a table, bowed low to Radek, and departed. Mirakel plopped herself down and hastily poured herself a glass of wine.

"I wouldn't," Radek cautioned, taking a seat beside her. "It's a lot."

"Good," she said, and drank. She did not choke. "Oh, that's good snake."

"This is a welcome feast," Paqe said. He looked confused. Radek followed his line of sight to the empty throne.

Radek felt himself growing tense. He put a staying hand on Mirakel's shoulder. "Stay sober," he told her, to which she huffed. In truth, nothing about this felt safe. They were lone Uslethians in a foreign court; a familiar court was dangerous enough. The Rezwyns on either side of them were paying them no mind, and they'd been sequestered away in a corner. "If this was a welcome feast, wouldn't we be . . . welcomed?"

Radek watched in real-time as Paqe's eyes shifted from a wondering awe to a hesitant gray.

"I fear we are not the intended guests." Paqe indicated across the hall, to a central table packed with men, women, and genderless others all dressed in silver and blue livery. They weren't soldiers. They were regional governors, marked so by beautiful, embroidered maps on the backs of their coats, indicating which city or province they were representing.

"Really was hoping you weren't going to say that," Radek said. He shifted uncomfortably in his seat. "I was hoping you'd say I was stupid, and it is empire custom for grand guests to be put in a corner, and not announced to the feast held in their honor."

Paqe said, "You have no idea how much I wish I could tell you that, Oren. Especially when. . ." he grimaced. "When sides are being drawn."

"Meaning what?" Radek asked. He squinted over to where Paqe had gestured.

"Blond one. See him? Longish hair, small nose? That's the Lord of Veprak. The True Commander had arranged a marriage between him and the Dziove, who snubbed him. Whole scandal—anyway, look at him."

Radek looked. The Lord of Veprak was animated in his gestures, throwing back drink after drink, laughing loudly. At some point, he'd shrugged off his outer jacket. His arms were bandaged. In fact, they wrapped up his whole trunk. Blood seeped through the back. Paqe stared at Radek like the point was made, but Radek had no bloody idea what that meant.

Paqe sighed. "Worshippers of Borviet self-flagellate. And all those wounds are fresh."

"So he's on the side of the man who was executed?"

"Not officially," Paqe said. "If so, he would be dead, too. But if there are sides in this court, he is declaring."

Then, before any of them could speak again, the hall quietened. Some unseen signal made the drums stop, the dancing slow. People quietly moved behind the tables.

The great doors rumbled open. Everyone seated shot to their feet, including Paqe, who made an aggressive motion with his hand to get Mirakel and Radek upright.

A tall, muscular woman—really quite massive—walked in, flanked by two priests. She sported a red, beautiful long tunic with flared sleeves and tight-legged pants in the same color. Her cuirass shone in the firelight, marking her as a devotee of Borviet. Pale, near-translucent skin, long jet-black hair, and a mess of kohl around her eyes, relined with red. She didn't need to get close to Izra for Radek to know they were related.

"Odrica Dziove," Paqe told him. "She used to be ambassador to Usleth before King Zavrius ascended. This procession is called the Emperor's Guidance. They interpret visions and counsel the emperor in the ways and wills of the gods."

There were ten priests in this council, two dedicated to each of the five main gods.

Radek noted Commander Izra Dziove took up a place near the rear of his sister's procession. To his right stalked a short young woman with a shaved head, strapped into a glinting cuirass. If it was stamped with a god's symbol, Radek couldn't see from this position. Behind them were a dozen or so soldiers of the Uxbuh, whom Izra commanded.

Radek nodded then jumped as the former ambassador opened her mouth and began a deep-throated, sharp-breathed song that echoed in the hall.

Radek had seen a similar ceremony two years ago, when the Rezwyns had sent a representative to congratulate King Zavrius's ascension. Odrica Dziove finished her song—or invocation—and moved to the side, accompanied by her two priests.

In the silence, a final woman entered. Though she dressed akin to a priest, there was no mistaking her importance. Where the others of the caste wore drab sacks, this one wore an ankle-length silk dress in white, sheer enough her pale skin looked like fog beneath it. A stiff mantle had been made for her in oknum and white wool, shaped to be an overcoat of sorts that rounded at the neck, flared at the shoulders, and tapered into two thigh-length tails. Incredibly detailed gold embroidery depicted the main five gods of the pantheon. Her headdress served as more a facial covering; a tasseled and beaded sheer silk that covered her mouth and tied into her mousy-brown hair but left her eyes exposed. Smoky kohl lined them. Without a doubt, she was a High Priestess.

The procession settled with this final entry. She settled in front of the throne so that its flared back, which rose from each side, formed a frame around her. Arches of stained glass rose on either side like wings. Each depicted the same five symbols, the main gods of the empire's massive pantheon.

The human-boar hybrid was Borviet, the war god, and most lauded of the empire's pantheon. Ognmoksh was the goddess of the hunt, a deer struck through with arrows. Next came Suoduny, a strange depiction of three floating heads, all veiled. After that, Zimsmrt, a tree shaped like a woman suckling a baby, who symbolized death and winter. Finally, depicted by a torch, was Zeljia, a strange, amalgamated god of sex and medicine.

The High Priestess turned and spoke in Doskorian. Filled with ceremony and weight, each sentence ended with a gesture applauded by the hall. Both Radek and Mirakel turned desperately to Paqe to translate, but even he was frowning.

"She is speaking of provinces on the outskirts. Of Ostijan and Elkar, near Usleth, and then some others to the east. They've gone astray, she says." Radek noticed Paqe visibly swallow. "She wishes to send priests into them. Remind them of the empire's true cause, its lifeblood."

Radek stared at him as a cheer went up. Some in the hall clapped politely whilst others howled their agreement. The Lord of Veprak, in particular, made his presence felt.

Ostijan and Elkar were two of the three cities Radek had been allowed to enter for trade.

Proximity to Westgar and distance from the central control of the empire had resulted in an inevitable cultural bleed. The fact that the empire consisted of city-states only exacerbated this. Decades before Radek was alive, the whole west of the empire had either been free states, or else a part of old Usleth. The empire's expansive urges, as ordained by their gods, had subsumed them.

Radek had warehouses in both cities, and they weren't

Doskor. There was none of the rigidity or the stiffness, and any faith there rung far truer than this sterile castle.

Paqe grumbled something—Radek could have sworn he started praying—and pulled Radek close. "She's talking about stamping out any dilution of the Rezwyn ethos . . . and burning those cities free of foreign influence."

Radek held his breath, but it didn't stop Paqe's words from destroying the last vestige of hope he'd stored deep in his heart. Radek had thought he was here to increase Uslethian presence, to deepen their culture's ties. The hall went quiet. Radek stilled, half expecting someone to propel him from the room and promptly 'disappear' him for his crimes. But no one was looking at them.

Izra Dziove had stepped forward, bowed before the High Priestess, and told her something that had brought her to silence. The quiet overwhelmed and Radek could hear the clinking beads of the priestess's headdress as she turned, eyes seeking them out in the crowd.

When she did, all eyes turned toward them as well.

"My dear guests," she said in Uslethian. She spoke well, the cadence in her voice changed with the language. She sounded altogether sweeter, and more actively unhappy. "You must forgive me. I was under the impression you were still unwell, Lord Radek. I am the High Priestess Neala Beumeut, blood of the emperor Nio Beumeut, the Great One and True Commander. My sister—" here she gestured to the bald general by Izra's side, "—is General Neve. We welcome you to our great empire."

Suddenly, Paqe was in the middle of the hall on his knees. He said, "It is a great honor to come before the Emperor's Guidance. We have brought gifts for the True Commander, to thank him for the audience that was promised to us."

No noise rippled through the crowd. Radek found himself slowly standing, body half inclined to run, and the other half on dragging Paqe away.

It took a long time for the High Priestess to speak again.

"I am very sorry," she said, somewhat quietly. "You must understand that much has changed. In the wake of a horrible attempt on his life, we celebrate my father's robustness and enduring strength. We thank the gods for their blessing and watchful eye. But he will see no one. Not his daughters, not his strix, and certainly not cizalecs. It is my solemn duty to inform you that tomorrow morning, by his command, you shall return to Usleth."

Radek's grip on the back of his chair made the poor wooden thing creak. He flashed a look to Paqe; the diplomat rose from his prostrate position unsteadily and did not turn around. The only person whose eye Radek could catch was Izra's; Izra, hair framing his head like a cowl, who had herded them somewhere they were not supposed to be.

The High Priestess stepped down from the throne. "Please enjoy this evening. It will be your final night in Doskor."

CHAPTER SEVEN

"Don't."

Radek flailed out of Paqe's weak grip. "Don't tell me to—"

"Here." Mirakel thrust goblets of wine into both their hands and downed one herself. They were huddled together in the furthest corner from the throne, well away from the dancing and the feasting.

Of course, Radek knew they'd have eyes on them. He tried earnestly to fake a smile but figured he'd failed by the way Mirakel winced. She nudged the wine up to his lips. He didn't drink.

"At least try to blend in," she said. "You're about to throw up from fear, Radek, I can smell it."

It was rich coming from her, especially after her obvious concern in the hallway earlier. But now, with the snake wine in her stomach, Mirakel's fear ebbed out of her. It astounded him. Despite having no bodyguards, despite being only a royal purser, she maintained her composure. Perhaps she coped through apathy, or perhaps she only stressed in situations that required her to spend Usleth's coin. In any case, her easy confidence was making Radek's anxiety settle. But he didn't want it to settle. He needed the adrenaline and the nervousness, or he would get complacent, and then drunk and then dead.

"The emperor has sent us away," Paqe said. "It is unfortunate, but I will not be responsible for any diplomatic upset. We must go, Oren."

"You cannot tell me your last night in Doskor wasn't at least a little bit unsettling." Radek folded his arms.

Paqe said nothing.

"Please!" Radek went on. "It was not said in good faith."

Paqe put his hands up. "Calm down. Surely murder isn't her intention. We must always consider the barrier of language."

Radek scoffed. "Barrier? What barrier? She's fucking fluent!"

"Tomorrow, we go back the way we came," Paqe said firmly.

"As failures," Radek added.

Radek slid his eyes to Mirakel, who shrugged. "I have enough money to last a handful of weeks in Doskor's court. But in truth, my real job is to get you back to Usleth spending as little of that coin as possible." She clicked her tongue. "Leaving has better odds."

"Screw you both." Radek had the beginnings of a tension headache creeping in at his temples, but he wouldn't—and couldn't—leave this place without doing what he came here for. He would have an audience with the emperor. He would.

He made to step away, and Paqe stopped him. With surprising strength, the diplomat held him there, hand on Radek's wrist. "Oren Radek," he wheezed, voice low. "Whatever you're thinking of doing, don't bloody do it."

Radek wrenched himself free. "I can't go back. Not yet. We came all this way, and you are entirely too trusting, Paqe. She is giving orders without the emperor's consent. He is nowhere to be seen. So no. I will not go."

Mirakel rolled her eyes. She made a gesture toward the king's seal around Radek's neck. "If this is about your boyish crush on King Zavrius—"

"This is about making Lord Oren Radek a name that is remembered," he said snappishly. He probably sounded like a child, but he didn't care. Mirakel was a royal officer of the treasury. Paqe had been born the seventh son of some lord.

They were settled. They were satisfied with their lot. And Radek would never be; there was an itch in his blood, and he would be proving himself until the day he died.

"If you do something that you shouldn't, I don't know if I can protect you." Paqe spoke so earnestly Radek couldn't even laugh. The sincerity twisted something in him, made him frightened.

"From the king's wrath? Or from our hosts?" Radek asked, but Paqe only softened his gaze and let him go. Radek whispered, "I am nothing without this trade deal. I must find a way to speak with the True Commander."

Paqe hesitated, but he was ultimately unable to stop his expression from slipping into pity. "You are not nothing, Lord Radek."

Radek grimaced and looked out at the dancing Rezwyns. "Fine. Start packing. If the emperor tells us to leave to my face, we leave." He looked back in time to see Paqe smother an expression of relief. "Happy?"

"You know I am." Paqe let go of him entirely. Radek nodded at him, then to Mirakel. "Accompany him, will you?"

"What?" she barked after him, but Radek had spun on his heels and pushed himself into the crowd. Radek hardly thought himself a confident dancer, but it would have been much easier to sway aimlessly through the dancing Rezwyns than to do what he did: skirt awkwardly around the outside, squished between tables and twirling feet ready to kick him off balance. He made it to the far wall and surveyed the crowd.

Izra Dziove stood unmoving to the far right, practically an ocean away. He wasn't looking Radek's way. But he had been the one to lead his little party here, and that marked him as close to an ally as Radek was going to get.

"What are you doing?" Mirakel was behind him, hissing into his ear.

Radek swore aloud. Then, "What are you doing? Where's Paqe?"

She gestured to the doors, but Radek said, "Disobey me again, and—"

She laughed. "Oh, you'll what? I answer to the king, numbnuts, not you."

"Fine," Radek said. "I'm going to talk to our chaperone." He took her arm and was about to step once more into the swirling crowd when a voice behind him called his name.

"Enjoying the party?" Odrica Dziove called. She gazed at them from the corner, two priests on either side of her. She had a cup of wine, but she looked too stiff to have drunk much of it. The priests on either side of her were uncannily still.

"Having the time of my life," Mirakel replied with a strained grin. Radek elbowed her lightly and kept smiling.

"The party is lovely." Radek bowed. "It's an honor to meet you, ambassador. I've heard only good things."

"I have heard my brother has upset you. Have you come to complain to me?"

Without thinking, Radek said, "What?"

"That one." She pointed behind them to Izra. "The one who guided you."

Radek's gaze hovered on Izra's back. Some unremarkable soldier had engaged him in conversation, and Radek watched as Izra laughed, shoulders heaving. Radek tried to imagine how joy sounded on him, then struck the thought away. Odrica knew Izra had gone to collect them. Radek slid his eyes over the priests and ignored the questioning murmur leaving Mirakel's lips.

"Yes," he said, faking tonal outrage. "I'm absolutely appalled. I think there's a true, diplomatic crisis brewing between our nations."

"We cannot have that, Lord Radek," Odrica said. "Let us discuss this immediately."

At a click of her fingers, the two priests peeled away. After a beat, Odrica beckoned Radek closer.

Leaning close she said, "You are far too obvious in your curiosity, Oren Radek, to survive the Rezwyn court."

Radek tried not to visibly tense, but his muscles contracted anyway, the implication of danger causing him to flinch.

Mirakel folded her arms and scoffed. "What are you talking about?"

"Ignore my servant," Radek said, as Mirakel barked her outrage. "I would be less curious if we hadn't received such mixed messages from your True Commander. First, we're welcomed as trading partners. Next thing I know, all negotiations are broken off without any explanation? How does this reversal benefit either of our nations? I only want to plead my case before the True Commander, that is all."

He could hear Mirakel's erratic breath beside him as she stood unmoving, the slight slosh of wine against the cup as her hand shook.

Odrica was statuesque. She had all the power, of course, and she knew it. Radek could have announced he planned to kill her, and she'd still look that serene and relaxed. Though perhaps threats from soft merchants weren't anything to be afraid of.

She tilted forward at the hip. Curtains of black wavy hair fell from her shoulders and framed her face; she loomed above the two of them with a dark look in her eye. Her thick accent punctuated the Uslethian. "You want to see a man blessed by the gods. A man who has chosen not to attend this evening?"

Odrica said nothing, just held herself unnaturally still above him.

Radek strained his neck to get closer to her. "We both know nothing good will come of this subterfuge. A priest was executed today for an attempt on the True Commander's life, and the True Commander is absent. Now his daughter announces her plan to re-educate the wayward city-states. Could she have also been the person behind the sudden revocation of the agreement between our nations? If that's the case, then shouldn't I be addressing my arguments directly to her?" Radek was banking on too many unknowns. Only an idiot would have asked that question so openly.

"You know what, Oren Radek?" Odrica began.

Radek's mouth ran dry. Mirakel grabbed the fabric at Radek's back. She anticipated a violence Radek hoped wouldn't happen. He felt Mirakel press against him, readying herself to yank him out of danger.

In the interim while Odrica decided whether or not to hurt him, Radek tried to think of some excuse for overstepping. Could he claim to be joking? Possessed? Actually an idiot?

Then Odrica slid a hand onto his shoulder. "You are exactly what I expected." Her expression did not indicate whether this was a good thing or not. "I want to show you something, though . . . I think it best your purser stays here."

"Wait," Mirakel spluttered. "I have coin. Don't hurt him." Which was sweet coming from Mirakel, until her lip curled off her teeth in a scowl. She really hated spending money.

"I will not hurt him." Odrica smiled at her, then turning to Radek she said, "Follow."

Odrica led him out of the room and down a narrow stairwell in complete silence. The halls were buzzing with servants. Radek caught glimpses of cowls in various colors and styles. Some had their entire faces covered, though these were few. He watched one barely-covered servant press herself to a wall to make way for another in a veil. The similarities to the priests' headwear startled him. But all he saw were people dressed in gray, a color he assumed none of the main pantheon adopted. If the headdresses were anything to go by, servanthood existed as another caste here in the court at Doskor—another ladder to be climbed.

The long staircase descended farther than Radek imagined it could. For the life of him, he had no idea where in the castle grounds they were. It should have been darker. It should have felt heavier. Yet the depth did nothing to squash the feeling: the catacombs were somehow lighter, airier, filled with lit sconces and fine candles.

Water dripped throughout the entire corridor. The air filled with the scent of night. Carefully pruned moss and a vine with small glowing flowers sprouted from the stone. Servants stood, even at this hour, trimming them, spritzing them with water.

At the end of the hall, two massive wooden doors ran from floor to ceiling. But before that, five nooks split open in the corridor's walls, all of them streaked with moonlight.

Deep underground, this startled him. Radek ducked his head in one as they passed. The nook housed a shrine. An unfamiliar idol perched on a pedestal, surrounded by candles, coins, and various offerings. A lone figure knelt before it in prayer. Radek rocked back on his heels. This kind of supplication unnerved him. For some reason, he thought of home: of himself as a young man in Awha Stad, hawking a raggedy bit of silk as something fine and worth having. He'd made wishes in his head, begging forces to push passersby to him. This worshipper seemed just as devout and desperate as he had been.

Was that all gods were? A face to wish to?

Moss and plants filled the nook, and small white moths flittered about. The basin cliff formed the back wall. He looked up; had to squint to see it, but an oculus had been made by splitting the stone at the very top.

It was terrifying architecture, really. Nothing in Usleth could compare to it. How these worshippers were meant to deal with the cold and snow of the empire's winters, he didn't know. But then Radek registered that it wasn't cold down here at all. Heat radiated from the ground, a comfortable warmth that relaxed him instantly.

Odrica answered the question in his eyes. "The earth is naturally warm. This place is closer to divinity, the very life-source of everything living, and where everything must return."

She stepped in, whispered a quiet word to the supplicant, and he shot up as if burned. Bowing profusely and stumbling over himself, they were alone within seconds.

They both stepped inside. The offerings and flowering plants brimmed in such abundance, with a few lines of water dribbling down the stone, that it bordered on claustrophobic. That feeling grew worse when Odrica knelt before the idol. It depicted a malformed human; a twist of boar-like features flowering over a cheekbone, an eye, the nose. There was a raw and primitive essence about it, as if he looked too long, pure violence would bleed from it.

Borviet, God of War.

An anger that wasn't really his, bubbled in him—how many had killed in the name of this thing? How many foreign lands were soaked with the blood of the innocent? Radek turned his face away.

"I can feel your contempt," Odrica muttered from her place on the ground. "It is not welcome here. Especially not when you look at a god like Borviet, and think it a simple thing to name him evil. Through conquest Borviet brings an end to petty wars." Radek held his tongue. He hated that she'd read his face so easily. He had to control himself. Trade with the Rezwyns would bring King Zavrius a certain stability. The promise of peace with their massive and powerful neighbor might settle the inevitable and ever-present grumblings of the nobility that still questioned his rule.

Radek briefly closed his eyes. "Forgive me, Ambassador."

"No need. Come." She slipped around the idol and pushed against the vines and moss on the far wall. The rock had moved inward. Radek had blinked and stepped forward, just as the floor began to tremble slightly.

The door opened onto a dark, damp corridor; like the dripping insides of some massive beast's gullet. Water trickled down the stone. No light lit the way except for a single burning torch flickering weakly at the corridor's far end.

Radek crinkled his nose and hunched forward, grimacing at the musty smell pervading the space. He dragged the flare of his beautiful tunic closer to his body. Grime like this destroyed good fabrics. Really melted into the fibers.

The wooden door they stopped by appeared plain, but the lock was an iron complexity, an interwoven knot joined in four different places. A lock so strangely combined there needn't be any guards—just like the one in the room he'd awakened in.

Odrica fumbled for something in her pocket and then raised her hands. Something resembling silver thimbles covered the tips of her fingers on her left hand. She began to make those same fluid motions Izra made before the feast hall, and like before, the lock yielded, snaking away into the corners of the frame.

"I am a poorer lock breaker than my brother. And he will know this is broken."

"What?" Radek said. "Know what's broken?"

"I owe King Zavrius my life. This is how I pay that debt: I am giving you your wish, Lord Radek. A chance to address the True Commander." She smiled glumly and patted his shoulder. "You will have as long as it takes for Izra to find you."

Immediately, he panicked. It felt like falling. "Ambassador—"

"When he comes, invoke my name so he does not kill you, yes?" She shoved him in with one forward push. He stumbled over the threshold and the door quickly closed behind him. He heard it reseal with a metallic rasp.

Radek braced himself, body suddenly weighty with apprehension.

Radek exhaled and turned to take in the room, only to choke on the sight. He was briefly overwhelmed with light, and then by the expanse of a sprawling underground chamber. Stalactites jutted down from the ceiling and glowed.

This might be a trap. Had Odrica brought him here so he could be discovered, and his entire party killed? Perhaps. But she also might be telling the truth. Radek wasn't about to squander the only opportunity he had. He would not return to Usleth without this trade deal, and not even Izra Dziove, empire giant, could stop him.

He readied himself. He stepped forward. With his heart in his throat, he reached out and peeled back the curtains.

Thick, overbearing heaviness struck him. His skull felt raw.

A bed hung with curtains the height of small waterfalls filled the center of the chamber. Its headboard formed the sides of a large, upturned boat, its bottom hollowed out so the stone wall could be seen. The panels had been carved with scenes of a battle, deep grooves resembling tiny men jabbing forward with spears. Five looming figures, no doubt gods, had been carved in much greater detail overlooking the scene.

And a man was on the bed.

"No," Radek said. Out of habit and fear, he glanced over his shoulder. "No, no."

The emperor. Radek knew it by the jeweled wreath wrapped around his head, and by his unnatural age . . .

really, incredibly old. Radek stepped back, frightened of waking him. He could smell something, unpleasant and lingering. It made everything in him tense. The emperor lay prone, unnaturally pale, but breathing—Radek made sure, watching the irregular and slow rise of his chest. But close to death. He'd seen crude drawings of Nio Beumeut before, but they'd all been drawn with the war in mind. To Usleth, he had been the wild, untamable leader, a force able to bring the dynasty to its knees. All artistic representations of him had made him monstrous. Now—old, skin wrinkled and thin—the monstrosity was in his feebleness. He was on the precipice. Any moment, he would slip off it, and be gone.

The assassination attempt had failed, but they had clearly been close. Radek could see no open wound, no raw and bloody flesh. Whatever the now-executed priest had done to him, it couldn't be seen on the surface.

Radek glanced again over his shoulder. He had no time. If Odrica was right, the commander would be rushing down now to apprehend him. So Radek was here and helpless. What was he meant to do? King Zavrius had given him an order, but that had been under the pretense that the emperor was awake and functioning. Not this.

Radek cursed. He leaned over the blank, barely alive form of the emperor. Hands shaking, he peeled back a sagging, translucent lid. A dead-eyed stare met his, this cloudy gaze that seemed disconnected from the world.

Radek couldn't break away from it. He felt himself drooping forward, lulled somehow by the unsettling eyes of the unconscious emperor.

Then, an image.

Implanted in his mind, for one bright, sharp moment, Radek saw snow. A blizzard over a night sky, a chill that made him shiver. All at once, Radek felt ill. Something inside him twisted. His mouth ran dry.

Radek pulled away, gasping. A garland of light bloomed in his eyes; a tessellating prismatic sheen that looked vaguely familiar.

Shivering, he dropped to his knees, and stayed there struggling to catch his breath. Prismatic light—only one thing shone like that. It was the flickering remnant of arcane ichor drawn from a gedrok—the huge exanimate colossi from which the paladins of Usleth powered their amazing weapons. How could that be here? He heard something; movement, shoes on stone. The noise seemed to come from every direction. Two hands scooped beneath his armpits and pulled him up and through the open doors and out into a new rocky corridor filled with fat stalagmites. And then he was shoved against one.

His head snapped against the damp rock. Radek cursed as pain bloomed through his skull and down his shoulders. The sharp point of a knife nestled uncomfortably against his jugular. Radek could feel it when he breathed, a scrape against his skin. He tried to breathe more shallowly, but when he looked up, he lost his breath altogether.

Izra Dziove had pinned him against a pillar and raised a knife to his neck.

Radek exhaled, throat expanding onto the blade's edge.

"Oh, Izra," Radek sighed. He tried to keep the jitters from his voice. "Fancy seeing you here."

Izra shook him, one arm firmly crossed against Radek's chest. He growled, "What did you do?"

"Not a thing beyond looking!" Radek calmed himself. He breathed deep and slow. "I was guided here by Ambassador Odrica." Izra paused, frown sitting low over his eyes. Radek saw the question in them, and tried to answer, as much for Izra as for himself.

A flush began to burn on Izra's cheeks. "The True Commander's chambers are not to be breached. She would not jeopardize her position like this."

"She would for the True Commander. Just like you jeopardized your own position by bringing us to that feast. You wanted me to know something was wrong." Almost drunk with the vision, he suddenly found the whole situation quite funny. He gave Izra a wink. "You Dzioves like me. Don't try to hide it."

Izra's face shifted at that. He dropped his eyes from Radek's face and drew the knife away slowly, standing to his full height. Over his shoulder, Izra stared at the open chamber doors as if he expected some great, terrifying creature to materialize inside.

"Where is Odrica now?"

Radek frowned. "I don't know. But I've seen what I was meant to see. What I want, what I came here to do . . . is hopeless." He gritted his teeth. "We should go back to the party. I'll start for Usleth in the morning."

"Be quiet," Izra growled, and then, with regret softening his features, "Please. You do not know Doskor. You do not know this castle. And you most definitely do not know what is happening right now. I am escorting you back to your chamber."

CHAPTER EIGHT

Izra meant to get Oren to safety before he hunted down his sister, but found her calmly waiting by Oren Radek's chambers. She had Izra's halberd with her, which unnerved him. The other Uslethians weren't in the corridor, and neither were any guards or priests. At least not yet, anyway.

"What happened?" his sister asked as they got close. Her question yanked him from his tumultuous reasoning, and re-stirred the anger in him. He pushed her into Oren's chambers.

"What happened?" Izra asked, incredulous. Izra moved his focus to his anger and his fear, both of which were burning pits in his belly. "You transgressed, sister. You breached a sacred barrier. If the True Commander ever learns a cizalec saw him in such a state!"

And Odrica said, in Uslethian, "I'm counting on it." Then, to Oren, "The priesthood, the Emperor's Guidance, his daughters—they deny the emperor is lost. They want to keep him in the astrok-mer while they implement their backward-looking plan. Borviet guides us toward creating the rule of law for all people, not in trying to prevent the rightful future from coming to pass."

His sister's words were sacrilege, and they were true. A knife in Izra's gut.

"So, you allowed me to see what has happened so that I will do what? Ask King Zavrius to assist your side in this internal struggle?" Oren murmured. "How tactical."

"You have a keen mind, Lord Radek," Izra said, stepping past his sister. Izra wanted to go to his knees before Oren and beg him to leave. Once High Priestess Neala discovered that Odrica had leaked the information about the

True Commander to the Uslethians all their lives would be snuffed out.

Oren looked at his feet. "I felt ill when I was near the True Commander. I felt the arcane. I saw the prismatic light of gedrok ichor."

Izra flinched. Gods, Oren had no tact. Izra tilted forward and put his forefinger against Oren's lips. It seemed unnaturally long against Oren's face, squashing the tip of his nose upward—adorable.

"It might be better if you don't speak," Izra whispered.

Oren frowned. "Better?" His soft lips brushed against Izra's finger with the word.

"Safer," Odrica said behind him. "For everyone here."

Oren nodded. Izra pulled back, the tip of his finger grazing ever so slightly against Oren's lower lip. He was well and truly teasing now, but he could not help it.

Izra saw something calculating in Oren Radek's eyes then, something that seemed assessing in a cruel and stripped-back way. It hurt Izra to look at, but only when he forgot to remind himself how far ahead he was in longing for his fated man. Oren Radek had only known he existed for one day. Izra thought about this, and then forced himself to stop thinking about it when he felt his cheeks flare. But if Oren's distrust meant safety, then so be it. If Oren stayed, and if Neala learned what he had seen, then the only solution was violent retribution. And when Izra thought about this, Oren dead before he learned what he meant to Izra, he panicked. He said very suddenly, "You must leave the castle. You and the other Uslethians."

It made Oren stiffen, but he did not relent. "Tell me this first, Dzioves. I am here to tie our nations together. Not everyone wants that, but do you?"

Izra grimaced. Once, he knew that had been the empire's aim. He knew what the man Nio Beumeut was, and what he used to be. A corrosive force, burning through other cultures, assimilating everything. Izra could feel his part in those wars, the visions that had been gifted to him and what the army used them for, etched into his skin. But it could only go so far. Eventually, the crumbling grip the True Commander retained on the furthest colonies, and the impossibility of extending that territory, had made itself apparent.

Odrica answered, “Yes. The emperor’s vision for us changed.”

“Well,” Oren snorted. “Good for us all, I suppose.”

Izra couldn’t bear his resentment. He briefly felt the clash in him, of his morals and his duty, something that once felt carved into his soul. Then—pain stabbed his temples, firm and sharp. He keeled forward, hand splayed to stop him from kissing the floor with his face. Izra groaned, vision blurred and spotted.

He felt his sister’s hands slip beneath his arms and start to drag him across the floor.

“Fire,” he managed. “Fireplace. . .”

“I know, I know,” his sister said. Her voice sounded muffled and far away. She dropped him near the fire and stepped away.

Oren said something. What’s happening, Izra thought. Odrica replied, yet her words lacked clarity. The fireplace detail blurred into a wall of orange and heat. He felt disconnected from himself, fading away. This vision was the most obvious Suoduny had given him in years. “Show me,” he stuttered, “what you want me to see.”

Red strings appeared in his vision. One glowed bright and dragged him forward. Izra’s mind detached itself from the cumbersome body; weightless, it zipped along the fated line, to a convoluted knot. He saw a dozen beating hearts, the Emperor’s Guidance arguing, the presence of several governors from cities near Ostijan and Elkar, governors angry at their neighbors’ brewing revolts. Talk of war circulated amongst them, but so far no one had taken direct action—enough knew better than to act against the True

Commander's wishes. But in her heart of hearts, the True Commander's daughter still wanted the option. Izra felt certain.

The vision buckled in an unsettling way, fanning out into fractured possibilities. He caught snippets of each, flashes of violence and blood. He saw the outcomes of Neala's cleanses and knew it for what it was: eradication.

More closely, a more certain future: Izra felt the knot of beating hearts within the Emperor's Guidance stir as they came to some decision. There were guards amongst them, blatant traitors already siding themselves publicly. A coup, then? He could not quite parse what Suoduny wanted him to know.

Suoduny did not elaborate. Just showed him panorama of spruce, fir, and flat stretches of land. Distant mountains loomed as a backdrop. A river. Izra struggled to place it. But he recognized it as somewhere safe—or safer than the dissent he could no longer navigate.

Suoduny was giving him direction.

Izra opened his mouth, intending to shout that his god had told them to leave. But when he came to, shouting had already broken out.

"You killed him! Izra Dziove is a traitor!"

Izra's mind snapped into focus, and he sat up. Odrica had drawn her sword, but barely had any room to use it. Oren screamed something about privacy. And the door to Oren's room had been swung wide. Someone was standing over the threshold and shouting—at Izra. Accusing him of murder.

"Guards! Guards! I have him!"

Izra sat up. The shadow on the threshold resolved into none other than the Lord of Veprak, his once betrothed,

He had no time to ask what was happening. As soon as he staggered to his feet, the traitor accosted him: "You, once great strix. You have murdered the cuvari! You have murdered the diplomat!"

And Izra did not know what else to do other than take the end of his halberd and slam the butt into the Lord of Veprak's head.

Odrica visibly swallowed and lowered her greatsword. "Brother, what is—"

"Suoduny was trying to warn me," Izra said in Uslethian. "I am—being framed."

Oren frowned and asked, "For what?"

Then they all fell silent.

Outside the room, someone was crying.

Oren froze. The three of them moved quickly to the door—whatever was happening, Izra knew they would be fools to stay here.

Izra moved out into the hall and put his halberd in position.

He studied the corridor. The stone arches. The marble floor. The warping shadows that stretched and flickered as some mass moved before the light. He readied himself and breathed deep. Another great wail cried out before it muffled and hushed.

The figure rounded the corner, and became two—Kew came stumbling out, hefting Oren's friend over his shoulder. He jolted awkwardly at the sight of Izra, then broke into a hobbled run.

"Mirakel," Oren said breathlessly. He ran to her.

She thrashed in Kew's arms, words incoherent and drowned in tears. Kew shakily put her down and she swung bodily, decking him squarely on the jaw. Kew staggered and she shoved past him, rushing back into the corridor—but Kew was fast. He grabbed her and hauled her forward. Mirakel choked, her words muffled and lost until Kew tried to calm her. That only set her off.

"Paqe," she wailed. "Paqe!"

Oren wrenched her from Kew's chest and spun her. Vibrant blood speckled her face.

Over their heads, Kew found Izra's eyes. He looked at him, stricken. "Commander. . ."

"Oren. Oren, I am so sorry." Mirakel's face crumpled. She sucked in a wobbly breath. "Paqe is dead."

Oren reached a shaky hand to his forehead. He looked as if he could not quite understand what had been said.

"He's not dead," Oren whispered, to no one in particular. He gave a breathless, disbelieving laugh. "He was—he was fine. He . . ." Now Oren seemed to register the blood, and his frown deepened. He swallowed thickly and pushed weakly away from Izra, moving towards the Uslethian official.

"He's a diplomat. No one would kill him. No one would. That's. . . that's an attack on the crown. On our king. And Paqe is a good man."

The purser fought for control. Her eyes were wet, but they had such a hateful gleam in them Izra knew she wasn't allowing herself to cry. Everyone else kept silent.

Oren made a low noise of despair. "Who was it? Who killed him?"

Mirakel glanced back at Kew for support he could not give and stuttered out, "A priest. I don't know. We were just—in the corridor. Being led to our rooms. And he just . . ."

"Who? Kew, report." Izra demanded.

Kew went soldier-stiff. "I kept an eye on the Emperor's Guidance like you ordered, Commander. One left the High Priestess's meeting to return to the party. I did not think to . . . I hesitated. When I finally decided to follow, the Uslethians had been led away, and the diplomat was dead. But sir. He was not the only one killed. A cuvari was with him. I think they had been talking, but about what, I can't be sure. Not that it matters, in the end, because they killed him, too."

Izra froze. He glanced over to Odrica, who in turn glanced back towards the door. "We need to leave now," she said.

A cuvari and a foreign diplomat—both killed.

And Izra framed for their murders.

"Ready the horses," he told her. Odrica nodded and went.

Something had happened whilst he and Oren were in the True Commander's chambers. Something that had gotten the diplomat and the cuvari killed. Something with enough of a dangerous effect for Suoduny to send him his first proper vision in months.

If they were going to live, they could not stay here.

"I need to see him," Oren whispered.

"You do not." Izra had to rush forward. He bundled Oren up, held fast as the other man pushed uselessly against Izra's shoulders. There was no time to feel this.

"Please," Oren said against Izra's neck, voice cracking. "I need to see him. I need to make sure he's dead. If we leave him here—"

"Oren, I am sorry. We need to go *now*."

"You're not sorry!" Rage cracked through his despair. Oren thrashed, kicking hard until Izra relented and let him go. But instead of running he dropped, sliding to the ground near Izra's feet.

"I should have listened to him," Oren muttered. "I should have, and then everything'd be . . ."

Here he turned to Mirakel. She had stopped crying, some resolve settling over her. Oren looked at her, imploring, "Are you sure?"

Her brows came together, and she looked away, but not before she nodded.

Izra went to his knees, too. "We must go."

"I . . ."

He trailed off, but Izra understood. A great weariness settled in his body, an exhaustion like his own soul had wailed and mourned and tired itself to the point the body felt heavy. Izra grabbed Oren around the shoulders instead, pulling him along toward great door at the end of the corridor. Kew and the purser followed close behind them. They reached the door swiftly. Odrica had already opened the intertwining iron lock. Wind screamed into the corridor. Izra shielded Oren's face with his wolf cloak.

"Go," Izra told Kew and the purser. Oren stumbled out into the snow, and Izra sealed the doors behind them.

Chapter Nine

By the early dawn light, they rode east, towards Usleth. It was more a dirt path than anything else, with a thin, winding river running alongside it. Mountains rose in the far distance, but this part of the valley lay flat, filled with fallow winter fields. No one had slept. Radek no longer knew where they were, only that Izra promised safety.

But who knew what that meant. Or if it was even true.

Radek felt unfocused and floating, the five of them propelled by the terror of their frantic departure. After the adrenaline had ebbed out of his body, Radek had slumped off Deina's back and crawled into the bushes to heave, and after he finished Izra had helped him stand. He tried not to breathe, worried about Izra inhaling the smell of vomit on his breath. That only made him want to combust. Guilt swarmed him. Paqe was dead and he was thinking of a man. Paqe was dead, and Mirakel wasn't meeting his eyes, and Radek deserved everybody's ire, not Izra's overly familiar, overly kind hand on his shoulder.

A sordid feeling sat in his empty stomach, clipped by a growing desire to do something unthinkable and erratic. Radek was the type of person who, when confronted with really awful shit, would rather fuck the feelings away than sit with them. This was particularly difficult given their current company and location. The nausea didn't help either.

"Come," said Izra. "Back in your saddle."

Radek let himself be lifted this time, if only to once more feel the pressure of Izra's big hands on his hips. Once seated, and with most of his anxiety giving way to exhaustion, Deina's smooth gait easily lulled him.

They were moving generally northeast, back toward the more familiar provinces of Elkar and Ostijan. Another few minutes on Deina, and he slumped forward into her russet mane, only to be awoken however many minutes later by Izra scruffing his neck as if he were an animal.

"Oren?" Izra's voice carried through the chill of the morning.

"I'm awake." He looked at Izra, looked into his eyes, and something about the soft look in them made Radek's body expel pent-up obligation. "I need to tell the king. I need to write Zavrius. And my warehouses in the empire—they'll need to evacuate."

"We will." Izra's hand lingered on Radek's back. "I promise you. Once we get to where Suoduny is guiding me."

Mirakel openly scoffed at this statement. Though exhausted and unable to comprehend the arcane or the gods, Radek still had enough sense to tell Mirakel to shut up. Her body went rigid, skin taking on an ashy hue. Dark circles rimmed her eyes. Her fury was clear.

"I'm sorry," Radek whispered to Izra, without pulling his eyes from Mirakel. "Would you excuse me?"

He slowed his horse before Izra responded and dropped back to Mirakel's side. She turned away from him.

"Don't," he spat.

"I—"

"Without Izra, we'd be dead. Like Paqe," said Radek sharply. "Least you can do is respect his religion. He's leading us to safety."

She laughed mirthlessly, tongue running along her teeth. "You're a fool, Radek. We're not being led anywhere. We are following a madman's whims."

Radek felt fire in his belly and quelled it with several deep breaths. They were tired. Their companion had died.

"Tell me what you're really thinking," he told her.

"Fine. King Zavrius sent me to accompany you to Doskor," she muttered. "And to Doskor you were fucking accompanied. You've gotten one man killed and wrapped us up in a coup. Any coin you spend now is Usleth funding a sightseeing tour. Ridiculous. A waste of money. I don't know why I'm here."

"You want to go. Is that it?"

She didn't reply, but anger flared in her eyes, stronger than before. Grief and failure dripped from her. Radek could see it, a reflection of his own.

"What do you want?" he asked, as gently as he could.

"Oh, I don't fucking know what I want, alright?" she spat, shifting in her saddle. She glared at him, eyes puffy and dark. "You got me. But I know I'm angry, and you're the only one here I can take it out on."

Radek grit his teeth. Small fires were popping to life in farmsteads across the landscape, and he turned to look; at life continuing.

He murmured, "I promise, I will sing your praises to the king for years to come. Give you a few bolts of my best fabrics, too."

"Yes, you will." She didn't look at him. Now that he'd said it, the offer felt weak and wrong. It wasn't what she wanted. She wanted some sense of agency or a plan to follow. Even Kew and Odrica seemed concerned when their eyes fell on Izra. Weren't those two supposed to have faith in visions? If even they were questioning him, then maybe Izra's behavior signaled true madness. What constituted lunacy when you were a strix, anyway? He didn't know.

Radek collected himself the way he would his cards; slowly, careful not to damage the paint. There was a tactic he could deploy somewhere in all of this, if he were a smart man. Radek looked out at the horizon, watching the pink and purple creep of sunrise as it crawled over the distant mountains. Izra had to understand that he wasn't the only person in this party. Izra had been accused of treason, but all of them were his co-conspirators. They needed to regroup and make a plan that they all could follow.

Radek rode up beside Izra and tried to parse his mood. Exhaustion and trepidation weighed heavily on them all. Radek sat tense, poised in the saddle with an unnecessarily firm grip on those reins.

Izra must have felt Radek staring. He turned and they locked eyes. Radek stuttered and said, "We Uslethians aren't, uh, used to this way of deciding our course. We normally try and talk amongst ourselves and not rely on . . . visions so much. Do you mind telling me what you saw?"

Izra blinked at him, brows buckling. "Mostly blood."

Radek went rigid. ". . . huh."

"Beyond that, not saw so much as felt," Izra said, which only made Radek more concerned. "Neala is planning to attack us. And I saw a place away from the castle, alongside a river. The Serpiz River.

Radek grit his teeth, worried about the guidance of Izra's god. "He's told you to wander up and down the Serpiz River looking for what, exactly?"

Usually he wouldn't mind some lovely empire exploration, but this blind travel was more than a little unnerving.

"Suoduny is a force," Izra said, ignoring Radek's tone. "Not a man, not a woman, not any gendered combination. In Doskorian, we would use ion. For you . . . it, or they, or if Uslethian has another genderless term I am unaware of it. Think of it more as a primordial force, not something contained to flesh. But in any case, you do not have to worry. I know where I am going—to Suoduny's temple."

Radek perked up. Finally, a location. "Which is where?"

"For now? Kiriz. I think."

"You think?" Radek frowned. "It's your bloody temple, isn't it?

Izra smiled like Radek had said something sweet. "It is not a fixed place, Oren Radek. It is not a building. Suoduny's temple is a people, a moving force. I will find it. I have a connection to the sacred objects."

Radek tilted his head. "It's nomadic?" That was interesting—as a concept, if not in practice. How were they meant to find this place in good time if it had a pair of restless legs?

Izra had closed his eyes. His body twitched as if in dreaming, but nothing else looked out of place. He was just a man. Very attractive, and broad, and smudged in kohl, but a man.

Right now, Izra was being led by his god—and whether Radek understood the religion or not, he would respect it. But he'd also show Izra exactly what he had to offer.

"This is what I see. We need a better understanding of what is happening. Forgive me—perhaps you know the ins-and-outs of the empire's current inner turmoils, but I don't. What's clear is that we both need the emperor awake and well. But first, we must avoid dying and find somewhere safe. We need someone we can trust, and if your god is pushing us in this direction anyway, perhaps he means to push us to my contact?"

Izra cocked his head. "You know someone this deep in the empire?"

"Would I be any kind of grand and famous merchant if I said no? I have contacts to the west of Doskor, my good man. You can bet your pretty head I have contacts to the east."

Kiriz as a city wasn't exactly the pinnacle of empire values, which was of course the reason Radek knew anyone there.

Radek swiveled to Mirakel, and to Odrica, who was translating the whole exchange to Kew. Radek decided he wanted more than their approval. He wanted a consensus, a coming together of this party.

Mirakel was still unhappy, but buried beneath the scowling and the hurt, was a resolve to stay. Whether that was a stipulation from the king, fear of traversing the hostile empire alone, or loyalty to Paqe, he couldn't be sure. But it existed.

Odrica and Kew were a whole other beast. Odrica was devoted to her brother, and to her country, and Radek supposed the same of Kew. He could only read Kew's body language, not his words, though that was enough to indicate his devotion to Izra.

"Thoughts?" Radek prompted.

"Suoduny has guided us to each other, and you are bound to my brother's fate. It would be foolish to turn away from this," said Odrica.

Radek wasn't about to poke holes in her reasoning, though the thought of being bound to Izra in any sense did make his stomach tingle.

Before that thought could go anywhere fun, Kew mumbled something Radek assumed to be assent when he dipped his head to his commander in reverence. When Radek finally slid his eyes to Mirakel, she made her eyes bulge out of her head, as if her answer were obvious.

"How are you lot meant to eat without coin?" she said, and nothing else, though Odrica had coin of her own, and Radek had no idea what her orders stipulated. She could technically leave now without question. Radek decided not to provoke her and took the answer at face value.

"Well, Izra Dziove," he said, grinning at Izra. "Will you partner up with a cizalec?"

A small smile crept onto his lips. "Suoduny is not only my god. It is fate itself, and even you cannot escape that, Oren Radek."

"Then it's settled," Radek said. "We go to Kiriz."

Odrica exhaled noisily. "Gods be good. I hate that grimy city."

The city of Kiriz lay to the northeast, closer to the border but not as far along the path of Uslethian depravity as the more eastern Ostijan or Elkar. These upstanding Rezwyns still feared the name, however.

Izra's second Kew heard 'Kiriz' without context and he barked in fear. Izra had to comfort him, and even he had a look of distaste.

"Scared, are you?" Radek teased Izra afterward, trying to find amusement in the way the Rezwyns shriveled at the city's name.

"Not if it is fate," said Izra. "Not if it's with you."

So they followed the river northeast alongside trees and shrubs crisp with frost that speckled the landscape. Kiriz lay in a hilly basin to the west of a wide, navigable river named the Serpiz. Because of its proximity to so much timber, early Rezwyns had centered their shipbuilding there, and fleets had sailed from it several times. But it was more a bastion for the lost now, and didn't have a notable export.

There was nothing exactly wrong with Kiriz, except that it was a bit of a cesspit, and a city for the unconventional. Radek had never been there, but had considered it for a warehouse, before deciding Ostijan to be the safer and more lucrative option. Kiriz was only accessible through the Serpiz River, which would only add more time onto an already excruciatingly long journey. However, his research had revealed that Kiriz had a tendency to attract defiant artists, or waywards who had denied the caste of their birth.

The empire's caste system meant that children inherited the profession of whichever parent wished to bequeath it. Many in the empire accepted the inherited caste of their family, and the child would learn the path of their parents. Some defied their caste, and formed new ones. Some lived wandering lives centered in Kiriz and other port towns.

Radek had never chafed as much as he did during those five days on horseback. He managed the first three without much trouble, and then, all at once, he reached his limit. Each trot burned, but the Rezwyns made no complaint, and Radek's vanity kept him upright and smiling every time Izra Dziove glanced his way.

Something about those backward glances kept Radek wound tight. Determined to impress, Radek pushed on even when the riding made him haggard, and his groomed beard became less so. The other tension was, of course, the fear of soldiers. Of being pursued. They each kept watch at night even at small farmsteads, worried about Doskor's banner appearing in the fog. On the fourth day they spotted the first of Neala's officials; armed priests of Borviet riding southeast, plain new banner of Borviet whipping in the wind. Izra and Odrica folded themselves over their horses to conceal their height, and the whole party rode stiffly, ready to bolt.

But luck was on their side. Or, according to Izra, fate.

They arrived at Kiriz late at night. The town was all candle-lit windows and glimmering wooden houses, which from the hillside—and in their exhausted state—made it a haven. And for Radek, it really was. It tasted much closer to home. Without much of a defining empire presence, it had gone perfectly astray from Rezwyn snootiness. Where soldiers lined the streets in Doskor, there was nothing of a military presence here. The regional governor had a reputation for being lenient and corrupt. In a sense, Kiriz had been abandoned and those who came to the city were left to their own devices.

As they crept further into the city's bowels, Kiriz opened for them and showed too much of itself. The streets reeked of fish and stagnant water. The skeletons of old abandoned ships had been converted into buildings, their bowels scooped out and replaced. People laughed and drank. Doskor seemed so docile in comparison.

This was only accentuated when they passed an alley and Radek caught sight of two grinding silhouettes. He thought nothing of it—sex was sex—until he wondered about the Rezwyns. To him, the empire felt prudish. Not in a snobbish way but in a fundamental divorcement from the body. Gods and magic and the arcane all seemed something outside the human, where, for many, pleasure was rooted in the flesh. He looked back expecting that he'd see the heat on Izra's cheeks even in the dark. But Izra made no reaction—until he did.

The grinding figures cried out, screaming names Radek had never thought he'd hear cried out in an act of fucking.

Izra pulled on the reins of his gelding and the poor thing whinnied, affronted. Izra waited for the next blasphemous moan and dismounted. By the sound of his ragged breaths, he was flushing all the way to his ears. Radek quickly dismounted after him, but the others stayed mounted, watching.

Radek flung a hand onto his shoulder and wrenched him back.

"I think you need a drink in you, and a good night's rest," Radek said.

Izra had the strength and size to barrel him—Radek half-expected to be flattened—but Izra put up no fight and let Radek walk him against the alley's wall. To their left, the huffed, half-choked sounds of sex echoed, and to his right Kew and Odrica looked at them both like they were mad. Radek heard Izra curse.

"Did you not hear?" he hissed at his sister.

"Come on," Radek patted his chest. "Let's leave them to it. Odrica, do you know where an inn is?"

She gestured up the road, where the faint nickering of horses could be heard. "Along the river's edge. There is a stable up ahead. Inns will not be far. We will find the temple tomorrow."

Radek nodded. "Then let's go."

"No." Izra shucked the halberd from his shoulder. Radek crinkled his brow at him, and felt utterly powerless to stop him. It had been a very long day, and he couldn't stop feeling jealous of whomever was having the time of their life in the alleyway.

"Izra. What are you doing?" he said carefully. For his own peace of mind, he made sure Izra had no murderous intent for the act itself. "If you have an issue with sex or night walkers or whores, Izra, we will not get along."

A new heat burst along Izra's cheeks. "No, I—" he choked. Briefly, language failed him. "It is not the desire. It is not the act, not the public nature of it. They mock the emperor. They bring an exalted man to his knees in a back alley—"

He stopped abruptly. Radek looked at him with neither pity nor judgment, and not quite understanding. He did not have the history Izra had with the emperor. Radek only had war.

"Don't think too much of it. Maybe they just don't have homes to go to," Radek reasoned. "Everything will be better when we wake up."

"Not Paqe," Mirakel said. Radek stopped in his tracks. His stomach dropped out of him. They looked at each other for a very long time before Mirakel shrugged, rubbed her eyes, and nudged her horse into a trot.

It was unkind. It was true. He couldn't feel anything but exhaustion when Mirakel cantered away.

CHAPTER TEN

After the incident in the alley, Izra walked in a haze, but Oren refrained from saying any more on it.

They found beds in a tiny but colorful lodge and left the horses in a stable shared by three similar-sized inns. Once inside, they took three rooms between them, and Mirakel—still lost somewhere in the haze of death, eyes never quite refocusing—apparently had forgotten her earlier anger toward Oren, since she attached herself by the hip to him and stole a place in his room.

Izra had a profane and nonsensical reaction to that, made only worse when his roommate ended up being Kew, who installed himself in the inn's dining room with hadic snake liquor, and kept ogling any woman who had the misfortune to be in his line of sight. He would be drunk and snoring later that night.

Odrica was the lucky one; having traveled extensively she knew this game well and grabbed a key out of the innkeep's hand for herself.

Izra gave one longing stare at Oren's door and went to find the temple.

He could have waited for morning light, but Izra needed to calm down. He needed to put aside both his horror and disgust at what he had seen—treason, and everything at Doskor—as well as his sense of total love for a near stranger. He might have seen Oren in his dreams but that did not mean he knew anything about the other man, or even about the fate that they shared. He hoped it would end well but dread welled up from the very core of his being that the destiny they shared might be tragic.

More than that, he wanted to see Selvik, the priest of Suoduny's nomadic temple. Izra would pray there, be calmed, and then interpret Suoduny's guidance tomorrow with a clear head.

When he asked the innkeeper where he could pray the wiry woman gave directions to the relevant district. She handed him a hooded lantern and wished him well.

Shrines were not hard to come by in Kiriz, but chaos reigned. Doskor had an order to it; five prominent shrines were designated for prayer to the main pantheon, while smaller house-like structures were set up for the worship of the smaller gods. In Kiriz, Izra found clusters of shrines at every corner, with no real sense of order, no ceremony. There were no shrine-keepers shadowing supplicants' every move. There were only the shrines, their burning candles, and the occasional person in prayer. Once or twice, though, Izra rounded a corner and could have sworn the curled ball of a person at the shrine's foot seemed more drunkenly unconscious than in meditative orison.

In a corner of the terraced wall, overlooking the Serpiz River, Izra discovered the first shrine to Suoduny. The priest who cared for it was there even at this late hour; they bowed, form mostly lost in the shadow.

Izra dipped his head in return and said, "Suoduny, Who Guides Our Fates, has led me here. I am after Selvik, of the nomadic temple. My visions led me to Kiriz."

"Izra Dziove," the priest said, and Izra froze instantly at the over-familiarity. Hearing his name in the open like this unsettled him. He gripped the halberd at his side, but the priest only raised a hand in concession. "Forgive me. The priest Selvik told all Suoduny's priests in Kiriz to watch for you. Selvik received a vision. He waited for you, as long as time allowed, but he has gone."

"Gone?" Izra whispered.

"Left. The whole temple, a day past. There have been . . . priests sent from the capital, though they are not pious individuals. They meant to detain Selvik, for his association with you. So . . ."

The priest trailed off, gesturing the natural conclusion that the temple had to move.

"They went east," the priest supplied weakly, at the exhausted look on Izra's face. He went to his knees and the priest patted his shoulder. "Pray. It will do you good."

So Izra prayed. But instead of praying for the temple's location, he found it impossible to think of anything but the events at Doskor. Meeting Oren Radek. The fate of the emperor. The coup instigated by the True Commander's own flesh and blood.

Suoduny's idol was made of wood, as it should have been. Most idols were pole-like, with many faces carved in detail at its end. Sometimes there were three, sometimes as many as five spread in all directions for omniscience. Carved like a standing human, the idol had five heads stacked upon one another.

Dozens of nooks were carved into the shrine, and each housed a small clay jar of dirt. He went to his knees and dug his hands into the earth and felt for their communion. The shrine lit up with red, a beautiful tangle of string; he found Doskor's soil preserved, and from there every shrine across the empire he had ever visited. Seeing the grand tapestry, the interconnected web of every act of worship of his life, grounded Izra.

It was like this, bowed and half buried in the dusty Kiriz street, that Izra Dziove began to pray.

"Suoduny, my god, I am outside myself. I am a Dziove. I am a strix to the emperor. What am I now that he is lost?" And then, almost with the same breath, "Lord, you were right. I feel it in me: Oren Radek is mine. But he does not know me. I am afraid . . ."

He had the rest of his sentence lodged somewhere deep and let it go, because he had already said the hard part aloud. Then he lapsed into silence and let himself feel every moment in his history, relearning who Izra Dziove was, and startled at the realization that everything came back to the empire. He had channeled Suoduny every day until the god filled his lungs until reaching out became as natural as breathing. He had done that out of love for his god, and out of love for the True Commander. Izra flinched. The world began tangling up, growing complicated and messy and he closed his eyes to the myriad of scenes. He had left the emperor alone. He had abandoned his duty to ensure Oren Radek made it back to Usleth alive. Success in that was by no means assured, but his mind sped forward nonetheless. What should he do afterward? Would the True Commander understand his treason? Would he be forgiven?

Would the emperor even wake up?

In the last show of desperation, Izra asked: “Will you show me?” Begging overshadowed his prayers. “Will you show me what I have to do to get him back?”

But Suoduny stayed silent, and that night Izra dreamed of nothing at all, not even his fated man.

The morning after they arrived in Kiriz, Izra informed the others of the temple’s leaving. For both the relative safety of the temple, and whatever next shred of guidance Suoduny might show him, they would have to travel further east.

But Oren’s contact was in Kiriz, so Izra accompanied Oren to locate his business associate, who he described as “a vexing woman with a ridiculous memory for old grudges and a dislike for nobility, so let’s just say you’re my bodyguard.”

Izra had agreed and covered his silver fingertips with a glove.

When Oren inquired about her, locals directed them to what could only be described as a very upsetting amphitheater, or what might have been a century ago. A distinct smell of mold and sweat had settled in the walls and was now being sweated back out of them, fouling the air.

It seemed to be a collective of sorts. Sailors and artisans intermingled, smoking and drinking in its many halls. This center room had once been used for prayer, and then performance. Its windows were stained glass spirals, dotted with hidden holy symbols. A series of once-beautiful light fixtures hung overhead. A few were limply hanging on, their wax melted and crusted over their cast iron sides

This is where they found Hapina. She had sinewy ropes of muscles in her shoulders and arms swarmed by puckered scars. She was also missing an eye. It had been replaced with a prosthesis that glinted in the socket. Without touching it, Izra could not be sure what it was made of. But he could guess. Animal fat, tar, and a poorly-mixed yellow paint meant to be gold. It made her arresting.

Izra found her Uslethian origin most intriguing, as she appeared to come from the far and rocky west of the Ashmon Range, her skin a mellow, dusty fawn. Whatever had led her to settle here he was not sure, but the empire had made its mark on her in two ways. The first: she had the symbol of the sea god Muripej inked into her exposed shoulders, a balanced reflection meant to keep the seas calm. The next mark of the empire was this: she had been a Rezwyn soldier once. She had an embroidered patch with her rank sewn into her outer coat, as if ripped from the uniform.

Hapina had hidden neither her surprise nor her disdain at the sight of Oren. Something about a bad job, or a lie. Izra was not quick enough to parse the argument, but it settled quickly when Oren said the words "exclusive deal."

Rows and rows of benches had been placed around the circular stage. They seemed perfectly suitable for sitting, but Hapina brought them to a tiny table framed by two chairs. She directed Izra to select his own from a stacked pile and bring it over. The seat he had selected proved to be so tiny and unstable he had to keep shifting every few moments to avoid something serious in his spine dislocating from its correct position. This, he was sure, was not something the big, silent Rezwyn bodyguard was meant to be doing. So he sat there, hoping his discomfort translated into a daunting presence.

They were playing Gulek Des, an Uslethian card game, and she kept answering Oren's questions with an open glee that Izra found suspicious.

Strangely, all the cards were torn slightly like something sharp had split through them, but when Hapina had asked Oren, he had only puffed out his chest and said something about his unrivaled tactical skills in close combat.

Izra thought this was very cute, and decided he would not question it.

"Used to cushions or something, big boy?" Hapina winked at him.

Oren didn't even look up. "Stop flirting with my bodyguard. Tell me what's the news here?"

"They say the emperor is dead, and some old and unnatural arcane power has preserved his flesh. And apparently, someone has slaughtered the entire Uslethian diplomatic party." A snort, the creaking of a chair as she reconsidered her words. "Though since you're sitting here, that one might be false."

Hapina owned ships; not quite a merchant, Oren had said, but certainly an agent of trade. She had ferried many of his goods out of Awha Stad, his hometown in Usleth, to the port towns Ostijan and Elkar and farther north. Often, she made runs to the western frontier. Oren had been hoping to snag space in her shipments for his own goods, whenever the trade deal passed, though any hope of that was now waning.

"Apropos of nothing, you have enough ships that, theoretically speaking, would have enough space to ferry, say, five odd bodies to . . . Banonok?"

Banonok, a port town, lay just a stone's throw away from the northern region of the Westgar province in Usleth. Oren had mentioned he had a warehouse there, as he did in many of the empire's eastern coastal cities. The three Rezwyns could lay low in it whilst Oren and Mirakel found a way to cross the border.

"Alive or dead?" Hapina grunted without looking up from her cards. She was not dismayed by this question.

Oren made a noise as if thinking on this. "Alive."

Hapina snorted. "Not possible. Not even theoretically," she clarified with a jab towards Oren's face the instant he opened his mouth. "Listen. My ships leave Kiriz through the Serpiz. Where it connects to Barveck Bay, I can technically get to Ostijan, Elkar, Banonok, whatever coastal town you want. But I can't get you there without you lot being caught. Or, uh . . . these five living bodies."

Oren pursed his lips. Izra could tell he was unhappy with her answer. Oren tried one last time, looking at Hapina with a very wide and very innocent expression. "But you could get there?"

"There's a blockade at the mouth of the river, Radek. They're searching every fucking crate like it's packed with assassins. It's simply not happening."

"Fine," Oren grunted. He flipped a card from his deck and put it down; Hapina groaned with something like true despair as she yanked two of her cards and abandoned them in a sad and growing pile by her arm. Izra didn't know the rules, but figured she was losing.

Hapina slapped down a card that made Oren hiss in surprise.

"Now it's my turn," she said.

Oren crossed his arms and settled into his chair. He crossed his legs, the back of his knee momentarily grazing Izra's thigh. Oren did not notice. "Go on then."

Hapina's lips burst apart like rotten fruit. "Tell me why you're really here. The details, Radek."

Oren sighed. "Sick of the foreplay already?"

"I'll leave the foreplay to you and your—" Here she paused and stared at Izra with that golden eye that seemed to bore into his very soul. "—your man."

"What?" Oren barked. He shifted, glancing at Izra before ripping his eyes away. "No. He's—he's not my man."

That stung. He did not know, he was not god-touched like Izra, but it stung. Izra could not help but look at him

"What is he then?"

Radek laughed. "Oh, use your imagination. He's massive. What do you think he is?"

In the deadest of voices, Hapina said, "A top."

"I—" This sentence broke Radek in some basic way. His cheeks browned and he stared at his contact for a very, very long time. Then he opened his mouth and said in a way that enunciated every syllable: "He is my bodyguard."

Hapina only rolled her eyes. "Radek, I don't have all day. You can go back to your childish flirting in your own time. But you're eating up good hours of the day, and I want to know what you're here for."

Something changed in Oren's face. "You know I love you, Hapina—"

"Oh, fuck off," she snorted. "What are you trying to say?"

Oren ignored this. "I need to get to Usleth. But I might be slightly wanted."

She stiffened suddenly, spine straightening until she stood almost as tall as Kew. When she spoke, she jutted out her chin, defiant and mirthful. "I am no criminal, Radek.

I've built myself from the ground up, and I'm not going to sully it with unscrupulous business practices."

At this Radek frowned. "You always consider unscrupulous business practices, Hapina, that's how I know you. You've only been half decent since working with me."

She deflated again. "Fair point." Her body was in the doldrums suddenly, a ship becalmed, very unhappy. It did not matter. She chewed her cheek and nodded her assent at him. "Why? What have you done?"

Minutely, Oren relaxed. "Nothing, except bear witness to the fact that the Emperor's Guidance killed the Uslethian ambassador in cold blood."

Hapina went quiet at this. She moved her lips as if sucking food out of her teeth. Then she shook her head. "I told you, they're searching all ships."

"The Emperor's Guidance means to purge our ilk from the empire. Foreigners. Anyone with ties to Usleth, anyone who might dilute the empire. I shouldn't need to beg you, Hapina. Have some decency."

This swayed her. She sighed and rocked to the side, leaning her weight on one thigh. The chair creaked beneath her. "The blockade at the mouth of the Serpiz means I cannot ferry you out of here. So what do you propose?"

"A letter. Just send it to the warehouses, and one to Usleth. I will write an account. I will stamp it with the king's seal. Everyone will know they murdered Usleth's diplomat, and—"

"—and you will plunge our countries into war," Izra had the good sense to say. Oren had frowned, but not with anger. He looked profoundly sad, and Izra knew that he understood but still hated it.

It was the first time Izra had spoken, and it broke the harshness of the spell settling over their shared communion. Hapina turned her bright eye on him again, and for the first time really looked at him. "He speaks."

Oren said, "And he speaks truth."

"What about the emperor?" Hapina asked. "Is that true as well?"

Izra shook his head, refusing to reveal the intimacies of the True Commander. "No, the emperor is only suffering from a mild illness."

Hapina sneered and bared her teeth. "The fucking emperor—"

The sound of Izra leaping to his feet cut that profanation short. Oren did not turn to him, but his hand slipped out from under the table and gently patted Izra's thigh.

"The emperor is not to blame," Oren said.

Hapina gave Izra a long, blank look, which Izra returned levelly. If rumors of the True Commander's fragility were confirmed, then half a dozen or more city-states might decide now was the time to take their independence. Whether it would be their generals going rogue and claiming power, or a city-state refusing to pay their taxes, it would all spiral once they understood the true instability of the throne.

It did not matter how far the empire's reach was. The farther they were from Doskor, the less inclined those people were to consider themselves Rezwyns. The old solution had simply been to push the boundary further and further, to subsume everything in the filmy cover of Rezwyn ideology. Only it meant more soldiers being sent to the front, a military presence knitted into every city-state and region to keep it all together. It was not sustainable. At some point they would simply run out of soldiers to hold it all together.

But beyond this, a more internal, selfish reasoning, Izra did not want the world to realize the emperor's mortality. They knew, of course—he was a man, he was flesh—but he had a presence spanning years and a history annexed onto his name.

"But it is true that right now the feeling in Doskor is that foreign influence must be expelled," Izra said. "You are not safe. Even if you cannot take Oren Radek with you, you should withdraw from this town."

Hapina spat over her shoulder at that—a Rezwyn habit she must have absorbed. "And abandon my own little empire? Not bloody likely. But as for those letters . . . not Usleth. I will not be the one to rouse Zavrius to war."

"King Zavrius," Oren amended, but he accepted the rest of this with a gentle sigh. He leaned back in his chair. "Ostijan and Elkar, at least. For the warehouses. Banonok might be far enough from the initial fallout to evacuate." A ray of sunlight hit the stained glass and split into multi-colored spirals over his face. "You know I can pay. Either with my coin, or the king's."

A pause stretched where no one spoke. Hapina looked like she had wandered into a snake pit and was staying still in the hopes of not getting bitten. Oren exhaled. Under the table, Izra saw him clench and unclench his hand. Fanning his cards out, then snapping them closed again.

"Who am I really talking to?" Hapina looked Izra in the eye as she scoffed and said, "What is this, Radek? The emperor's not a bad guy—the line doesn't suit you."

Before Oren could say anything, Izra leaned forward and edged out his medallion of Suoduny. He did not explain it. He did not need to. Hapina had lived here long enough. She widened her eyes and tilted forward to scrutinize Izra's face.

"You're the strix. Aren't you?" She drummed her fingers on the table, eyes darting from Izra's face to the chain of office, and back.

Izra nodded. "And my power has shown me blood. Neala is targeting Kiriz and any city charged with Uslethian debauchery. If you do not go—"

"Oh, I have enough imagination to guess the rest," she muttered. Hapina collapsed back against her seat, forefinger and thumb pressed to her lips. She wasn't looking at either of them. Oren used this lull to unfasten a small sack of coin from his side. The purser had counted out every coin for him, so Oren had stored a sack of his personal coin in case his contact needed more to be swayed.

Oren tossed it toward Hapina. The sack landed on the table with a satisfying clink. "There's enough coin in there to pay passage to Usleth. I'm not asking for any of it back. Just get word to my warehouses at Ostijan and Elkar, and any other foreigner you can think of. And . . . once you're in Barveck Bay, there's no blockade, right? You're already out of the Serpiz."

Hapina's eyes narrowed. ". . . I might have said that. Why?"

Oren breathed deeply. "My biggest warehouse is at Ostijan. You could get them to the border."

Hapina outright groaned.

"Please, Hap," Oren said. "The empire is no longer safe."

Hapina held his gaze for a long moment before she folded. She pocketed the coin and nodded. Then she was good enough to procure two slips of parchment for Oren to scrawl his letter ordering his people to close shop and return to Usleth. He gave no explanation so that even if the letters were read, Hapina would not be implicated for sedition. He seemed to consider using the king's seal to press them both closed but decided against using such a recognizable mark, settling for his thumb instead. He hissed as the hot wax stung his skin and handed them back to her.

"There's a rookery," she told them. "You might be able to send a letter to the palace from there, if you're trying to contact your king."

Just as they made to leave, Hapina stood and stopped them. She severed two locks of her own hair.

"If you know anything . . . terrible is about to happen, tell him to use his power to warn me, all right?" Hapina handed one of the long locks to Oren.

Oren cleared his throat to fill the uncomfortable silence. "His . . . power?"

Izra nodded down at the locks. "As a strix, I am connected to things. Anything of a similar ilk, same make, same location, I can find it."

"Exactly," Hapina said. "So you keep that one, and I'll put this one someplace I won't mind being scorched. That's how you'll do it, isn't it? Scorch a warning?"

Izra glanced at Oren, and then regretted it when he met the other man's startled gaze. "I . . . can do that, yes."

"Wonderful. So, warn me. And if you decide to get further inland at all, that I can do. I have connections. Just think on it," she said. "And keep my damn hair safe."

Chapter Eleven

They left the half-crumbling amphitheater just as sunset bled over Kiriz. There was a fragile and awkward sense of accomplishment—not quite the safe departure Izra had wanted for Oren, but a step forward, nonetheless. They meandered back toward the inn through the back alleys, which were cramped and claustrophobic. In the center of town, Kiriz's buildings were a haphazard pastiche, all strange amalgamations of brick and wood and mismatched stone. They leaned precariously over the roads, half-blocking out the red-orange sky. But Izra preferred the relative safety of the smaller, cramped thoroughfares. Sounds drifted into the backroads; trotting horses, chatter, already the slightly tipsy revelry of another end of day.

Oren held Hapina's lock of hair with both hands as if were something delicate and expensive. Within a minute he tried to proffer the thing to Izra.

Izra grimaced. "I do not want to touch it."

Oren waved it at him as if it was a stringy piece of flesh. He mistook Izra's cautiousness for squeamishness.

Suoduny was gifting him visions again, but they lacked order. He usually only had them in dreaming, but Suoduny had warned him of Neala's betrayal when he was well and truly awake. He did not think he could manage it if he touched Hapina's hair and saw every one of her potential futures.

Oren sighed and waved it at him weakly. "Well, I hardly want it." And then, in his sweetest voice, "Please?"

Adorable. After seeing Oren look at him like that, Izra barely hesitated, just threw open his coat and offered the breast pocket in his leather tunic for it.

"Aren't you sweet," Oren whispered as he deposited the lock. He had to lean in close to do it. Izra felt his warm breath against his neck. "Such a darling."

They had to duck out of the backroads to get to their inn, which was squashed in a little square with three others and a stable. Without the protection of the cramped buildings, Izra tensed immediately and tried to use the bulk of his body to block anyone's view of Oren. If they were being followed, they were far too conspicuous a pair; an obvious Uslethian, and an obvious Dziove. For a brief moment on the main thoroughfare, with orange glare obscuring most of his view, Izra could only see the back of Oren's head. Everything else—the carts, the few horses, the gaggle of party-goers ready for nightfall—fell away. It was only Oren.

They were thrown into shade and quiet the instant they walked into the square. Save for a few travelers and the quiet nicker of horses, the square sat empty. Some quiet chatter filtered out through the inns, but it was still too early for any real tavern ruckus.

Kew waited outside their inn. When he saw them, he perked up like a dog and pushed off the wall to intercept them, which made Izra worried.

"What happened?"

"You first," Kew prompted. "Can we be rid of the Uslethians, or. . .?"

"Anything? Any priests snooping around?" Oren asked in Uslethian. Kew had been their lookout, but he shook his head.

"No priests," Izra said, relieved. "But we should not linger. If Neala proclaimed her desire to guide rebellious city-states back to Doskorian ideals, she may very well start with the worst offenders."

Oren rolled his eyes. "You have such disdain for Kiriz, Dziove. If I didn't know any better, I'd say you hated Usleth. But then surely you would be a lot less kind to me."

Izra looked at him, and before any bit of logic could stop his heart, he said, "You are far too pretty to hate, Oren Radek."

Oren flushed. "And you are far too pretty to be saying those things to a man like me." Then he knocked his head towards Kew, who had crossed his arms and watched their exchange with an expression of pure contempt. "He, on the other hand, does not seem a fan of Uslethians."

"He is Rezwyn through-and-through," Izra said, by way of explanation. "You are also not his type, you see, which makes it harder to appreciate you."

"Not his type?" Oren clarified. "But yours?"

Izra did not answer that, for fear of saying yes, by all the gods, you are. But Izra could feel a smile stretching over his face all the same.

After that, Kew caught wind of their flirting and put a stop to it. He stepped bodily between them and raised a brow at Izra. "Your sister and the purser are deep in their cups, commander. I cannot have you getting all lusty—stop trying to deny it—I know that look. Now let's get inside. I want to know what happened."

Oren thankfully made no other comment as Kew led them through the bar. The inn's lower floor had only a few benches pressed against the wall and two smaller tables in the room's center. The décor featured bright maroons and reds, signaling a departure from the empire's blue-and-silver, but not much else.

Izra looked around the inn. It was different by daylight, both in what he could see and the people who lingered here. There were not many; a few pairs swapping stories, or individuals ready to drink. But there was a group that gave him pause, because they were as motley as theirs.

Rezwyn man, Uslethian woman. Three children. A family, of course, was usually nothing to stare at, but this . . .

And Izra felt foolish for his appraisal of Kiriz. Dirty, lawless chaos at worst, or unconventional barbarism at best—

nothing in Izra had allowed for Kiriz to be anything more. But here it was, a true melting pot between the extremes of Usleth and the empire. A place where three children could grow without the watchful judgment of the Rezwyns, or the fearful whispers of the Uslethians. They were not here having abandoned their duty, or as fugitives. They were here because they had been born, and now could not exist comfortably in the extremes of their heritage.

"Everything alright?" Oren whispered to him.

Izra made a non-committal sound, which Oren clicked his tongue at. "You're scaring the children, Izra. Look away, come on."

Izra swallowed and turned and let himself be led away. But the realization sat heavily in him like a stone. How good it felt to be proven wrong.

Though it only made the horror of Neala's intentions worse.

Odrica and Mirakel were half slumped in a booth. Izra cursed and slid in next to his sister.

"Fool," he hissed at her near-unconscious form. "What are you doing?"

"Eavesdropping. Sleuthing. Nothing so fun as drinking," she muttered back. She peeled her face off her arm. She had wiped it free of oznak velraj, the paint she normally wore. "I am not such a fool now, am I, brother?"

Mirakel sat up straight as well. "I really could use a drink now, of course. But I can tell you . . ." She made a series of hand gestures that were plucked from the Rezwyn military—Izra slid an eye to his sister, wondering at what else she had taught the Uslethian—and Mirakel revealed she had counted eight visitors from outside. Mostly people here for food, but one she believed to be soldier caste, by the scarring and the careful way he sat.

"Impressive," Izra told her.

She gave a languid shrug as if it were only natural. "Patterns and numbers. It's what I do. Still. Very boring when I don't know a single word of the language."

Izra barely contained a snort. "Well then, sister. Hear anything useful?"

Odrica shrugged. "Complaints about searches. Shipment times expected to double." She paused and looked to Oren. "I assume your contact told you much the same?"

Oren's gaze was fixed on the rest of the bar as he delivered the news to his purser "Mirakel, my dear, I'm terribly sorry to tell you this. But we aren't going home any time soon."

There was no outburst from Mirakel beyond a defeated slumping headfirst onto the table. "Why?" she asked, voice muffled by the wood.

Oren relayed what Hapina had told them. They would not be able to escape via the river and would have to travel over land. "And I haven't even managed to get a letter to the king yet."

"If your king knows how vulnerable the emperor is, then it is dangerous for both the empire and the dynasty." Izra could not help himself but say it. It unnerved him, even with Oren's faith in the king.

Oren sighed. "No one wants war, Izra, especially not Usleth. It is no secret that the king had to fight for his throne. If you think even now there are no threats to his reign, you are a fool."

Izra cocked his head in the silence. "Then what are you planning next, Oren Radek?"

Oren did not answer immediately. He craned his head, waved down the barman for a round of ale.

While waiting Oren shuffled his cards. It seemed more an anxious habit than anything else. He certainly did not offer to play a round with anyone, or even explain the rules.

Instead, Izra watched him breathe deep and pull one out, only to scrunch up his features at it like it disappointed him.

Izra did not understand this game. Quickly surveying the cards showed him beautiful, but often violent, scenes—which were made more-so by the hole stabbed through most of them. Oren kept pulling some out, rearranging others, and Izra suddenly could not tell if this was a game governed by rules or luck.

Oren bade them all to come closer and dropped his voice to such a low whisper they were forced to strain harder.

"We can't run," Oren said in a low whisper. He folded most of his cards away but kept one on the table between them all. It was upside down and took Izra a moment to translate, but it read RESISTANCE HOLDOUT in golden letters, which seemed ridiculous declaration for the grim scene it depicted. Over the ruins of a city, several soldiers brandished swords. Oren continued, prodding at it, "But neither can we sit here and let Neala purge her way through this empire. So, a question for you Rezwyns. What will happen if we attempt to eliminate the threat instead of running from it? Try to ruin High Priestess Neala, perhaps?"

Izra frowned. He glanced out at the tavern, worried one of the few people here would overhear. "What do you mean?"

"I don't know," Oren said with a sigh. "I just know people. Uslethians, at least. I have a good sense of how they'll react as a group, as a country. Perhaps even as a mob. But the Rezwyns . . . I haven't grown up here. I don't know what you'll stand for, what you'll die for. Just answer me this. If somehow everyone in the empire knows Neala is a usurper, will she be praised for her initiative, or damned for it?"

Izra felt the pull of a stare and turned to find his sister's eyes on him. Her lips were pressed into a careful line; she approved. But, of course, she would. All devotees of Borviet preferred to be always on the offensive.

He did not know what Oren planned, but he doubted it would be easy to achieve. He thought once more of Neala and her puppets. How she had comforted him as a child. How sweet she could be, how compassionate. It would be difficult to reveal her true nature.

"Neala's position is a strong one," Izra explained. "Not only does she have the blood of the True Commander, but as High Priestess, she holds favor with each of the five gods of the main pantheon. It is why she is so readily believed, when it comes to the gods and their will."

Oren did not seem swayed by this.

"You will be putting your life and legacy on the line," Izra told him carefully, still glancing around to make sure they were alone. Oren had no birthright in his blood. He had fought for his title, for his place in this world, and Izra needed him to be sure of what he was saying. "If it comes to war between our countries, King Zavrius might very well sacrifice you to stop it. Depict you as a rogue agent."

"You do not know my king," Oren murmured, lips soft around the possessive. "You only know emperors, Dziove."

It was a naive statement. It was said with love. They were each other's mirror image, defending their leaders as if they were gods, and ignoring every fault.

"One day, perhaps you will teach me," Izra told him. Oren blinked, flushed, and turned away.

Odrica spoke next. "He is right. Neala intends to teach a lesson in obeisance to Doskor. Places like Kiriz will not survive. She will come in, and she will remind this place who is in charge."

Mirakel shrugged. "So what is your plan? Start shouting in the street about how the High Priestess is shit? I don't think that one will catch on."

They bickered back and forth, while Izra translated to Kew.

He stared glumly back at Izra. "She will make him impotent and rule with the fumes of his memory."

"Yes," Izra said. And in Uslethian, "Yes, that's it."

"What?" Oren asked.

"We already know it. Neala will have power if the city-states believe she has the True Commander's support. She has his blood. Our focus must be to wake him, if we are to refute her claim."

"We need a vision," Odrica said. "Have you had any more since the warning in the castle?"

Izra tensed. He opened his mouth and almost told her that he had prayed in the cold beneath his god's shrine, that he had begged and been ignored. Instead, he just shook his head.

Her face hardened. "Then we must take you to Suoduny's temple and induce the vision ourselves."

Silence stretched. Izra's eyes slid unbidden to the Uslethians. He could feel the purser's disdain wafting off her, but Oren guarded his feelings about the gods more carefully.

Oren spoke into the silence, shifting the direction of their conversation. "There's a rookery here. I need to go there anyway, to send the king my warning. I might as well send letters throughout the empire, too."

Odrica frowned at him. "To what end? If you claim the High Priestess is a usurper and seal it with King Zavrius's mark, we will be at war in no time."

"Well, I won't be the one sealing it, will I? I'm not a nonce, Ambassador," Oren said.

Odrica bristled, but Oren just jabbed a finger in Izra's direction. "He bears a medallion with Suoduny's mark. If the strix of the True Commander writes those letters, it will have a different effect."

Everyone stayed quiet. As soon as Kew caught up, he made a panicked noise and turned Izra's way.

"What are you going to do?" he asked. Kew glanced at Oren. "I know he is your fated man, but you do not know what kind of fate Suoduny has in store for you. He could bring about your ruin, Izra. He could—"

"I will do it."

Kew shut up.

Oren was right, after all. Empire was all Izra knew. And it had come with war, and too many gods-given images of gore and death and pain. But that—he looked again to the other table, where the mixed family sat—could be empire, too, one day. A natural progression of peace between their two nations. One that Neala would gladly destroy.

How could Izra think himself a good man, and sit by to let that happen?

Izra repeated in Uslethian, "I will do it." He looked over to Kew. "My friend, there is no returning to Doskor with Neala in power anyway. Besides, Oren is right. We cannot run forever, and Neala and her wishes are not something we should be running from. We should be stopping her."

Odrica briefly broke and put her head in her hands. Then she straightened and nodded. "Then it is decided. We disrupt her efforts as best we can. But after that, brother, we must focus on the True Commander's cure. It is the only way each one of us gets what we want."

"Agreed," Oren said.

"Agreed," Mirakel echoed. "Though this business about the gods—"

"Agreed," Izra said, cutting her off.

Kew held his gaze for a very long time, but eventually relented. In thick Uslethian he said, "Agreed."

And that was that.

They bought parchment and wax from the inn and Mirakel briefly vacated their shared room for Izra and Oren to write their letters by candlelight. Oren wrote to the king, and Izra a short message to the rest of the empire. It read:

High Priestess Neala acts without the True Commander's leave. She defies both his wish and his command for the Rezwyn future. She means to usurp him. Resist her.

This is the emperor's command.

Izra Dziove, strix to the True Commander

He pressed the medallion at the end of his chain of office into each one. They rolled them all up to be carried by the birds. It took hours. Odrica came and told them Mirakel had been so tired she had collapsed on the floor of her room, which thrilled Izra up until the moment they finished with the letters. His plausible reason for lingering alone with Oren Radek evaporated suddenly.

When they were done, it was well into the night. Likely past midnight, Izra thought. Oren looked exhausted. Izra could see it in the way he held himself. Oren always carried himself with a surety, even if he clearly did not always feel it. Confidence gilded his stance, an easy charisma that wafted off him, that made his energy bright. But tiredness muted all this. Gone was the dynamism; he seemed softer, more accessible. He slumped himself, half-leaning against the table. Oren let his eyes close, and his body unwound, drowsiness seeping in.

"I will go," Izra said, standing. "Sleep well, Oren Radek."

Oren jolted from his dozing state and cleared his throat. "Wait."

Izra froze. Izra waited. He felt himself flushing for no good reason, so he only glanced back at Oren over his shoulder.

"Tell me what you can do," Oren whispered.

Izra frowned. "I do not know what you mean."

"You—well," Oren made some obscure gesture that helped his point in no way at all. "Somewhere in the Dziove line, there must have been an ichor-infused ancestor. Something that lets the arcane flow in your veins."

Izra's flush vanished. He turned around bodily. "That is the power of a god, Oren."

Oren flinched. Izra saw him fight a roll of his eyes and he stepped back with a taut and quiet despair.

"You do not believe me," Izra clarified. Oren said nothing; fine. "As you say, Oren Radek. But I will make a believer out of you one day. A godly man. That is a promise."

"I—apologize. I do. You certainly have power. We would not have made it out of Doskor alive without you. I am indebted to you, honestly, and I keep asking things of you." Oren paused there, as if expecting Izra to speak.

Izra could not. He would say something sweet and overly familiar, like "you could ask anything of me, and I would do it. You are the man tied to me by fate."

"Never mind," Oren said with a smile. "I overstepped. I just meant . . . one day, I hope to learn more about you, Izra. If you'll let me."

"Yes," Izra said, very quickly. "Yes, that would be nice."

Then he spun and left and walked as calmly as he could to his room. He punched the air as soon as the door closed. This felt like victory. The same glorious rush that came after winning a fight flooded him; his head pulsed, his heart raced. Every part of his body felt good.

But the feeling quickly became muted. What was to come was a battle. The High Priestess against this resistance. Even with Suoduny on his side, Izra lacked the foolishness to think it would be enough to destabilize Neala's hold. She had swayed governors already. She would claim direction from the gods no matter what Izra said, and every priest whether they received visions or not would agree with her.

He steadied himself. If it came down to it, would the general betray her sister? Would the general choose the empire over her sister? He hoped so. But if she could not do that, Izra would have to steel himself for the inevitable.

There were good fighting men and women in Doskor's army. If some could be swayed to Neala, there would be many others who would fight alongside him. For the True Commander. For the camaraderie they shared as soldiers. For his own connection to fate.

Enough of the army would follow him, if he needed them to.

So that was it. Izra confirmed it with himself. If this battle needed to be won, he would win it.

CHAPTER TWELVE

Radek woke with the kind of splitting headache you only get from squinting for hours by candlelight. The others were already awake; Deina and a gelding had been loaded up until their satchels were near bursting with letters, and the other three were packed with supplies.

Once the letters were sent, they would be on the road again for Suoduny's temple, and whatever fate had in store for them there. In the early morning, Kiriz shone with beauty. It reminded Radek of Awha Stad, his home, if only because of the persistent smell of the water and the way no one ever seemed to sleep. The main difference was the cold; both he and Mirakel kept sneezing and Radek decided to grow a proper beard if just to cover more of his face.

The rookery loomed above all the other buildings, an ugly gray tower impossible to miss. The others chatted, but Izra's mood had shifted south. Radek couldn't quite tell why; they had left on perfectly amicable terms the previous night. "What is it?" Radek asked when the fourth minute of walking passed without a word from him.

"Nothing," Izra said, and then immediately after, "only that I agree with your plan for Neala, but worry about the letter to your side." Radek grimaced. He'd thought the business of the letter to King Zavrius had been put to bed. "Telling your king is dangerous," Izra continued. "You must admit that much." Radek doubted admitting it would do anything to assuage Izra's fears, but he wasn't silly enough to imagine there was no risk involved at all.

"Well, of course it is," Radek said. "But so is never telling him. If the king doesn't know what might be brewing here, if he doesn't know Paqe is dead, then I can't imagine he'll have a good reaction when he does find out."

Radek made to walk back to Mirakel and start some other conversation. Izra spun. His strong hand clamped down on Radek's arm and held him there. Radek froze beneath the weight and grip of the other man. Radek's calm wavered. The stark differences in their loyalties seemed bluntly revealed.

He felt compelled to say, "What? You can be loyal to your leader, but I cannot be loyal to mine?"

Izra jolted and flushed with naked shame. His grip on Radek's arm softened. "Forgive me. To the True Commander I am like a dog. I always heel to him, even now."

There was a chilly comfort in this admission. "There is nothing I want less than war. I promise you."

Izra said nothing, but gazed upon him so glumly Radek wanted to embrace him and squeeze out all his worry.

"That surprises me," Odrica said from behind him.

Radek ignored the eavesdropping and shared a glance with Mirakel who said, "It does?"

"Of course," Odrica shrugged. "Usleth poses a threat."

Mirakel's lips began to upturn in a surprised smile. She gave Radek a meaningful stare; as far as Usleth understood, the empire was a beast, ever-hungry and ever-waiting. It expanded for the principle. Usleth was a secluded peninsula, one last holdout. What threat could they pose?

"Oh, sure," Radek murmured. "If we could take back the long-lost plains of Banonok, we'd have all the manpower to beat you. Although I hear sheep outnumber the people there six to one."

"You think too literally, Sweet Oren."

Sweet, Radek thought. That was a new one.

Izra looked to Odrica, who nodded her assent, then said, "One city falls, then it is a state. From there, half the empire is lost to rebellions. The guard fractures, either when they are split and sent to the various fronts, or some decide the gods are on the side of the priestess. There is no emperor there to guide them. It seems to me—" he audibly swallowed, and grew angry in his movement, "—it will collapse and then nowhere will be safe for anyone."

Radek tried not to react to this with any surprise. Uslethians had little understanding of the precipice and how close the empire was to toppling over it. This type of information was—sensitive. It surprised him that Izra gave it so freely.

"I thought you were concerned about vulnerability," Radek said softly, as if anyone in the crowd found them interesting. "You're being very naughty telling me all these things."

Izra did not hesitate. "I cannot help myself around you."

The other man's honesty surprised him. Mirakel did something suggestive with her eyebrows and distracted Radek to the point he could only stutter out, "I . . . see."

"It is not like that," Izra said. "It is instinctual. I look at you, and my body—" He pulled a face. "I do not have the words. Let's not linger here." He nodded vaguely at their destination and sped towards the tower.

Odrica choked on a laugh and muttered something to Kew, who made the same noise only much louder.

Radek let the topic go. He wanted to be quick. Though it felt less intense outside Doskor's walls, he had the unrelieved feeling of being watched. At the very least, sending these letters would relieve Radek of the feeling of doing nothing. He couldn't bear to be useless.

According to a faded paper poster near the tower's entrance, the rookery sat in a circular stone room at the top of a thin tower. Radek and Izra left the others at the base with the horses, and Izra heaved the heavy satchel onto his shoulder.

Amateurish portraits decorated the narrow stairwell. It felt like they were climbing up to someone's home, though no attendant could be seen. At the very last step before the rookery itself, Radek paused at the great and upsetting creaking of their weight on the boards. The wind moved through the room and made it groan.

Together they peered inside.

The rookery had a tall dome roof. It was cold and draughty; none of the windows had glass in them, ensuring the free comings and goings of the birds. Several feathers littered the floor, but it was surprisingly clean, with none of the fetid, sharp smells that usually accompanied birds. Pigeons cooed, waiting in their cages.

Radek craned his head, and caught sight of two people a young woman and a middle-aged man. The woman lay face down on the carpet. Bright crimson blood pooled from a cut on her neck so fresh that Radek could still see the steam rising from it. The man stood over her, holding a knife. His deep green robes were stitched in gold with the mark of Doskor.

Five spots in an arch. The five main gods of the empire.

Izra dropped the satchel, threw open his cloak and hefted his halberd away, drawing instead a short knife.

"Get started. I'll handle him," Izra told Radek.

The priest launched himself at Izra with a knife. Izra dodged, returning with a quick swipe of his dagger.

Radek was transfixed for a moment, but there was no time for this. He had to move quickly. He spotted a writing desk, and ink—he stumbled over and dumped the satchel—but without a damned bird to carry them, the letters would be useless.

A mighty crash sounded behind him and a wave of affronted squawking started up. Radek yelped as several birds fluttered overhead. One or two swooped out of the nearest windows. Pigeons screamed and cooed, flapping wildly in outrage. He caught sight of one of them, wings spread high. It revealed a densely painted mark on its belly; a seal stamped with the design of the city Myrtrana.

Perfect. Each one was marked with its home. He had to hope a pigeon here could be sent to Usleth—and that it hadn't just flown out the window. He turned to the cages and started opening them. He found birds marked with the seals of Ostijan and Elkar, then towns and regions so north he'd never heard of them. Cage after cage he checked for Usleth, heart speeding.

Something cracked to his right. Radek spun in time to watch as a beautiful table covered in bird-related trinkets split down the middle as Izra fell against it. The priest didn't relent. He raised a fist and threw himself towards Izra's face. Radek heard another crack. Blood poured from Izra's nose. Without another thought, Radek spun, pulled a pen from the writing desk—hand-spun glass, beautiful—and ran. When the priest reared up for another punch, Radek stabbed him in the armpit.

It shattered immediately, the long glass end snapping cleanly in half in Radek's hand. But the nasty sharp end stayed buried in the priest's armpit for a few agonizing seconds. The man howled and thrashed. Blood oozed through his green robes, a dark wine stain. He fell into a table and fumbled behind him, hauling anything his fingers curled around. Radek dodged as a brass pigeon flew at his face. Izra moved. He straddled the priest and within seconds had stabbed him cleanly in the neck.

It killed him, but it was not slow.

Radek exhaled. "Izra . . ."

Izra did not move away. Instead he prayed, one sweet, melodic sound. When he was done, he leaned down and kissed the priest's forehead.

"Suoduny was cruel to you," he told the dead man. "Sending you here to face me." Then he rose and looked back at Radek. "If Kiriz is like this, most places will also be unsafe for us. Neala's already sent her priests. If not for us, to consolidate the empire. We must go."

"The letter . . . I cannot find a bird for Usleth." Radek trailed off. He felt himself going into shock. This was altogether too much death for him, and in too few days.

Izra did something unexpected. He first touched Radek's shoulders, and then the back of his neck in a firm and familiar grip. "Which one are you looking for?"

"A lute-harp. After the king."

"There won't be one for King Zavrius," Izra said. With his other hand, he tapped Radek's forehead. "Usleth."

Radek blinked. "Ah—the rampant gedrok."

Izra nodded and scanned the cages until he found the symbol; Usleth's cat-serpent colossus. "Ready the notes."

Radek stumbled over to the writing desk. He rummaged through the satchel for the one addressed to the king, and when Izra said, "I have the bird," he could have kissed him.

He attached the letter to Usleth and let the bird go. He watched that beautiful thing fly until he couldn't see it anymore.

With haste, Izra started to attach the other notes to the birds' legs. They rushed, but there were still a dozen letters in the satchel when shouting echoed up to the tower. Izra tipped himself over the tower's large window and cursed.

"Kew spotted another priest. There will be more on the way—we must go."

Radek nodded and threw the rest of the notes out the window. They scattered, floating down amongst Kiriz's populace. For some reason the act made him want to cry.

~~~
~~~

They left Kiriz in a hurry after that.

After hours on the road, Radek decided he had had enough of all the silence. The chatter had dwindled into a sort of miasma of fatigue that he needed to dispel.

Unfortunately, the question on his mind would not spark light and easy conversation. But Radek decided to say it anyway, because it had been eating at him for some time.

Radek shifted in his saddle—he urged Deina forward until he and Izra rode abreast and said, "Who is the natural successor to your True Commander?"

Izra swallowed. He turned back to Oren and said in Uslethian, "He never named one."

Radek's brow twitched. "That . . . is unwise."

A quiet beat that stretched. Odrica was the one who said it. "Why would an immortal require an heir?"

"What?" Radek said.

Izra spoke before she could answer. "Why are you asking this, Oren Radek?"

Radek closed his mouth and swallowed. "Indulge me. If it were to happen, who would become emperor? Is it you—since you command the Uxbuh?"

Izra went so pale Radek thought he would faint. The other Rezwyns shared the same look of startled horror—it was, apparently, a horrifying suggestion.

"Blasphemy," Kew rasped.

"Thought you didn't know any Uslethian," Mirakel shot back.

"I cannot," Izra said quickly. "Why would I? Besides, I am a Dziove. We have not been rulers for centuries. Our place is by the True Commander's side. And I am just—I am close to nothing now. If we fail in this, my name is wiped from the annals. The cuvari will destroy my memory. If we do manage it, then the emperor lives, and your point is moot."

Agitation pricked at Izra. Radek watched him squirm in place. There was something underneath all this, making him twitch. Radek reached and gripped Izra's arm; the staying motion seemed only to make Izra more alarmed.

"Don't mistake me," Radek whispered. "I didn't mean to suggest you should usurp him. Only that Neala is not fit to rule, and General Neve . . ." He trailed off, uncertain.

Izra shook his head. "My role has only ever been strix. I am to give the emperor visions. I am to aid him with help from fate itself." He swallowed. "The last vision I had, the one guiding us, started with a dozen possibilities. All bloody. They used to be clearer. Suoduny . . . I am not sure what I am meant to do."

Radek frowned. He couldn't quite conceive of what Izra was saying. The visions, the strings of fate—he could only grasp this by assuming Izra or his ancestors had been exposed to ichor, granting them these abilities. The gods were as real as flesh to Izra, and belief held immense power. Radek didn't understand it. He didn't have to.

"Help me get closer to your way of thinking," he said. "Your visions are growing muddled?"

Izra exhaled as if embarrassed to say it. "Yes."

"But you saw Neala's priest when they were about to attack the True Commander," Radek said.

A frown, a slight shake of his head. "That is different."

Radek grimaced. "Not good enough. How?"

"A premonition is not . . . a vision," Izra said. His voice began to strain.

Radek touched his forehead. "So what exactly is wrong with your—"

"Because I have been having visions of you," Izra said, nearly shouting, "and they are disrupting anything else from coming through."

Radek froze. Every member of their party seemed to freeze with him. Odrica stared. Kew looked between the siblings like he could parse Uslethian from their expressions. Radek could feel Mirakel's gaze boring into the back of his skull.

Radek could focus on none of it. He swallowed. He clenched his jaw. Anticipation burned through his body in a way that made his heart sting.

Radek opened his mouth, voice cracking. "Of me?"

Izra looked pained. Radek could hear the conversation behind them coming to an end and glanced back to see Mirakel straining in her saddle to hear. Kew gave him a concerning thumbs up that Odrica echoed with a nod.

When Radek turned his gaze back to Izra, the other man was squeezing his eyes shut. Radek aborted three attempts to speak into the muggy silence before he managed to say, "What does that mean?" He shifted suddenly, hugging his arms to his chest. "When you say . . . of me."

A beat passed before Izra responded, an expanse where he simply considered Radek with a soft gaze. Then he said, "Do you not feel it?"

Radek paused again. He wanted to glance up, to scan Izra's eyes and confirm he wasn't just hearing what he wanted to hear. He felt—

Attraction, more than anything. A pull he felt when around appealing men, as he had always felt. Something that might easily dissipate after sex: something purely physical he needed to get out of his system.

But if it was that simple, why could he not look Izra in the eye?

Then he had waited too long. Izra glanced away. "I—apologize."

"For what?"

"Making you uncomfortable."

You didn't.

Radek should have said it—but he seemed to have lost his voice. Izra's words sounded like a chant in his mind. *Do you feel it, do you feel it.* Radek looked down at his hands, at the cards he'd started to gather up. That phrase had enough power in it to render Radek's mind quiet, and in his book that meant Izra had successfully won a round against him.

"I—" Radek squeezed his eyes shut, then made sure Izra was looking at him. "I don't know the gods. I don't know what you dream of, or who you see. But if you think we are—connected in some way, I . . ."

"Not in some way," Izra said numbly, "We are fated to be together."

Radek flinched. He thought about making some quip, to lighten the weight of it. To pretend it meant nothing to him to hear that. Instead, he said, "You sound so sure."

"I am sure. It upsets you?"

"It's just a bold and still unproven statement." Radek could laugh. To be wanted—who could be upset by that? But also, it was absurd. They lived in entirely different countries—different realms of existence, even. Assuming Izra's belief was correct, assuming he accepted his desire, they still didn't make sense. Why should they—no—where could they even be together? The court at Doskor? Radek's manor house in Usleth? The only place they could breathe the same air was traversing this road as fugitives and Radek didn't intend to stay on the run like this for his whole life. To have built himself from nothing, to have fought for the position and the reach that had landed him here, how could he relinquish that to wander alongside this very strange, albeit very attractive man?

Radek said none of that.

Izra dipped his head to the side, black hair falling to frame his face.

"I really will make a believer out of you one day, Oren Radek," Izra whispered. "Even if you cannot feel it now. I will wait."

Radek's lips twitched toward a smile, and he tried not to be rendered senseless. He felt the intense stares of the other three boring into his skull and refused to turn around.

In Usleth, the arcane was a great display of power. Ichor could be deadly, both in its raw form and when ingested. All the elements converged and erupted out of the bearer's hands. It could compel in the right hands, but often it could be a weapon. Almost always you could see it. Izra's hands used it altogether differently—he made it a silent, creeping thing, like fog clinging to trees. The insidiousness of it should have made Radek shiver. But it was beautiful. Quiet. Izra opened his eyes and said, "I know where we have to go," and Radek didn't prompt him or question him because when he saw the strength of the conviction in Izra's eyes he found himself believing. Or if not specifically believing, accepting that he would, for the time being, follow Izra's mysterious yet accurate intuition.

Chapter Thirteen

A day later, they rode until thick mist rose vaporous from the frosted ground, so dense it submerged half of Deina's flank. It was disorienting. If Radek stared down at where the ground should be, a dizziness overtook him. He half expected the fog to be a conjuration. The pine trees had become so dense that they obscured everything around them, causing Radek's view of the blue-tinged mountains to suffer. His sense of direction had vanished. Even the daylight was muted here; an overcast afternoon, all light eaten by the fog pit at his feet. He didn't want to imagine what it would be like when the sun sank.

"How much longer?" Mirakel hissed to him. "I can't fucking stand this. This forest—"

"Patience," Odrica said, head snapping back around to them. She said it in a way that bared her teeth; a terrifying sight, given that with her muscular build, she could easily snap Radek in two. Her straight black hair flared wild around her face.

"Not too much longer," Izra said with a smile, in great contrast to his sister. "Suoduny carves us a path."

Radek kept carefully neutral. The more he waded into the empire, the more Radek realized that arcane power was not something confined to Usleth.

Moreover, Radek understood that the Rezwyn gods, whatever they were, did exist. In some capacity, at least. And he might not have had the most solid of grasps on their exact nature—were they true gods? Strange watchers in another realm? Primordial forces? —but Radek had to admit they weren't imaginary.

On this point, the scholars of Usleth were completely wrong. Suoduny, at the very least, deserved little of Radek's cynicism. He had been warned of an attack, guided through the empire, and was now following a road of mist, a moving temple to receive visions of the future. He had no damned right to call it nonsense.

Besides—Izra believed. Who was Radek to question that?

One thing was certain though. When he returned to Usleth he would provide a full, first-person account of all of this to the scholars and diplomats at King Zavrius's court at Shoi Prya. He would take great pleasure in letting them know how wrong they'd been. Really, the gall they had to send him off with barely any accurate knowledge on the ways and habits of the Rezwyns—the strix in particular. Imagining the shock on their dull, pinched faces actually cheered him up.

Radek glanced at Izra. As far as any Uslethian scholar was concerned, a strix did little more than act as an advisor to the emperor, with a shamanistic flare that was often brushed over. The Uslethian skepticism towards the Rezwyn gods meant the role of the arcane was greatly overlooked. However, a strix played both the roles of advisor and prophet and couldn't be easily separated from divine power. Izra's connection to Suoduny indicated that all his visions for the emperor were a direct warning from the gods, with no intermediary.

Izra had influence; not only over the emperor, but with the people. Radek couldn't afford to upset Izra Dziove with his failure to understand the gods. He needed an ally: a proper, solid, dependable person he could rely upon.

Izra could be that man. For now, at least.

"Hey, Izra Dziove," Radek called.

Izra turned in his saddle, great weight of him shifting, his hair glistening black.

Radek nearly died.

"Thank your god for helping us, will you?" Radek grinned at him.

Izra's eyes softened and he broke into a smile. "Oh, I would be very happy to."

Satisfied, Radek reined Deina in and dropped back to ride alongside Mirakel. She gnawed at her lip. If her outburst could tell Radek anything, she was edging towards complete misery.

She rolled her head towards him when he sidled up next to her, eyes sunken and forlorn. "What was that about?"

"Morale," Radek returned.

She ignored that, lip curling over her teeth as she made a non-committal sound. Mirakel looked over her shoulder at the dense, unvarying lines of pines floating out of the mist.

"Fucking hate this place," she muttered. "It's . . ."

She wouldn't say it, Radek thought. Scared wasn't part of her character. Radek said it for her. "Not what you signed up for?"

She grunted. "I followed an order here, Oren Radek, not my heart."

Radek sighed, reaching out to pat her shoulder. "Listen. I know you hate it. But I just—wanted to thank you. For sticking around."

She opened her mouth. Radek could practically hear the king's orders sitting on her tongue, but she didn't speak. She cleared her throat. "I suppose it's frustrating for you as well . . . being in a forest with nowhere to spend money."

"That's the spirit," Radek murmured with a smile.

She said nothing, staring out into the moving gloom. Mirakel's breathing was just as uneven as his own. Together they made a breathy percussive beat for the horses to trot to. Then she tutted and swung towards him. "I didn't handle what happened to Paqe. I should've handled it. I've seen bodies before. I've paid for their return to Usleth. And I've left his body there. I should be—I don't know. I'm doing a shit job, Radek, and—"

"So, I shouldn't sing your praises to the king?" Radek asked.

"Bastard. I've been dragged kicking and screaming into fighting for what appears at this point to be the losing side of a battle for succession. If we live through this, you better commission a bard to sing songs of me at King Zavrius's court." Just like that, Mirakel fell back into place. A wink and a grin made her familiar again. He sighed, relieved. It didn't matter that it wouldn't last long. Radek had gotten her into this, and if that made him her lifeline, something to tether her to her acerbic personality, so be it. He'd much rather that over her apathy.

"It's not certain that he'll lose," he murmured—more to himself than anyone.

Abruptly, their party had stopped. From the mist, someone approached. Radek tensed immediately, looking to Izra for his reaction. But the other man called a greeting—it was a sentry, who smiled up at Izra with familiarity. She was young and sinewy, bundled up in furs, with red hair braided and twisted into a bun. A bow and quiver full of arrows were slung over her shoulder. Without comment, Izra handed her the reins of his horse. She silently took them. From the fog emerged several others—Radek almost screamed—who came and took the other horses' reins. In silence, they were led into a complete whiteout.

Radek could see nothing, but he could tell the sun was being eaten quickly. Final sunrays leaked through the congested fog—muted bleeding lights. But after minutes of silent walking, they, too, disappeared.

Sudden and total darkness consumed them. The cold and the silence made Radek nervous. He leaned forward into Deina's mane and kept his eyes trained on the large silhouette of Izra Dziove.

"Scared?" Izra murmured, turning back to him in an echo of Radek's earlier question.

And Radek said, "Not with you."

Even in the darkness, he could see Izra smile.

Then the mist fell away and Radek saw they were in a clearing. The attendants returned the reins and Radek nudged Deina forward, woozy with shock. Lanterns were strung about the clearing and broke through the gloom. He could see them staked in the grass: wooden poles with glass lanterns that buzzed with fireflies, defining the camp's perimeter. The camp swelled with tents, wagons, people—Radek didn't know where to look first. Kew and Odrica looked as lost as Radek felt, which was a welcome relief. The unfamiliarity of the place engulfed them all. Suoduny was Izra's god, not theirs.

Radek dismounted when the rest of the party did, but slowly; something about the way the firelight blurred in the dark, and the bustle of the camp, stunned him. He moved as if drowsy, all his tension having given way to an intoxicated disorientation. The sentry called out to the camp, and the chatter changed in tone, turning bright. Izra was a welcome surprise. With another whistle, two young men came and gently took the reins of the horses. Radek watched as great blankets were thrown over the horses' backs as they were led away further into camp, towards the sound of nickering.

Izra moved up ahead, being led further into camp and contending with a great many welcomes, but he still glanced back at Radek. Without the trappings of the castle, and with a slight relaxation of his shoulders, Izra looked very different. More youthful. Perhaps happier. He gave Radek a bright and dazzling smile that had the same effect as someone sticking their entire hand into Radek's stomach and wiggling their fingers. Radek picked up the pace just to be nearer to him.

The tents were large and triangular A-frames, and made from canvas pulled taut over decorated wooden frames. An elaborate set of animal and human heads was carved into the tent pegs; some wolf-like, some that multi-faceted depiction of Suoduny. A glimpse inside one of them showed him furs, lanterns, wicker tables and low seats—and the interior floor appeared somehow elevated to be just slightly off the ground, Radek realized. Radek stood there for long enough that Izra came back for him, looping his arm through Radek's and pulling him along.

"I am happy you are here, Oren Radek," Izra whispered, his smile warm and true. Radek turned, forgetting how close their faces would be. Izra's green eyes were speckled honey golden. Their warmth comingled as Radek felt Izra's firm grip on his arm, and he felt a pull, an urge in his stomach to lean even closer, gazing up. The Rezwyn's lips—red, as if faintly stained by blood—were parted, quirked in a wondrous smile. He could trip, if he wanted to. Izra might bend low to catch him. And if Radek aimed correctly, as he fell into that embrace, their lips might just—

"Happy to be here," Radek managed.

Izra swept him through the rest of the camp. Small campfires speckled the open glade. People hunkered over them, tending to pots and dishing out food. A great deal of the people here were children.

The older ones recognized Izra; some whispered to the younger, and others peeled off in a swarm to rush around him and chat. Standing next to Izra Dziove, strix to the emperor, made Radek invisible. The children thought so too. They quickly maneuvered Radek out of the way with their bustling to get at Izra.

When Izra managed to detach himself from the swarm of children, the sentry guided them further along. A fat wooden column stood in the center of it all, covered with moss. Rot had eaten away much of the detail, but Radek could see faces had been carved into it, making it a panoptic idol eternally surveying the temple and its people. Something physical made to contain a god. At its base were smaller stone structures, covered in candles and dried flowers. He watched someone suck the meat off a bone and place it in an osseous pile at the idol's base with a low bow.

As they passed Suoduny's column, Izra whispered a prayer under his breath.

Just past this column, Radek could see a massive red tent. Torches burned on either side of the tent's entrance, and two guards in garish ceremonial armor stood with halberds.

Their helmets were shaped like Suoduny's shrine. Bulbous faces protruded from three points, all of them off center so Radek couldn't be sure which way the guard's heads were turned. A mane of black horsehair crested the helmet and swept down their backs. Heavy black robes drooped from their arms, exposing heavily gilded vambraces underneath. They both wore cuirasses with the same mind-boggling detail, and greaves with more strange faces protecting their knees.

Radek glanced back around. Mirakel stared at him, not angrily, but focused; a warning flashed in her eyes, urging him to stay vigilant. Odrica and Kew had their heads low in deference. Just as Radek was about to turn back around, Izra's arm slipped away from his shoulder entirely, and Radek felt the absence keenly. He turned back around, feeling rigid and exposed without the protective arm of Izra Dziove.

The guards each nodded to Izra as he pulled back the tent flap to allow Radek and the other members of their party to enter. People and light filled the space. It swelled with priests in black robes and long-fringed headdresses that swished with every step they took. Beads and glass jewelry glinted in the candlelight, hanging low over their dark robes. Low tables spanned the carpeted floor, each one filled with enough food for a feast, as if they'd known Izra was coming.

But the sentry led them to the right, where a small ceremony seemed to be taking place. Radek balked, slipping back to stand beside Mirakel. Both Odrica and Kew hovered at his back as Izra stepped forward and watched with reverence. In front of a carved wooden chair, a priest stood half naked. They were striking, and ambiguous—androgynous in a way that was completely foreign to Uslethian understanding, but something Radek knew to be quite common in the empire. A feathered blue-and-black cloak draped over their pale forearms like they were waiting for the moment to throw it back on. Bindings pulled taut over their chest. They had a severe, thin face. They wore the shortest headdress Radek had ever seen, just enough to cover their eyes and frame the rest of their face. It exposed sharp cheekbones that seemed to grind against their skin. Their long hair had been constrained into several loose braids, secured at the back by a bulky silver ring.

Three other priests were on their knees around the standing figure, garbed in drab gray-black cloaks and on their knees. Two watched as the other took a knife to the standing priest's skin. Radek jolted to a stop at the sight. Raised, white scars speckled the priest's torso, but they weren't wounds. None of them had the jagged lines of something acquired in battle. The scars were dainty, fine-lined. The priest stood unmoving as the knife opened their skin.

Mirakel shrunk beside Radek, but the Rezwyns all appeared unfazed. This was normal, then. Radek risked a look at Odrica. He moved closer, kept his voice low. "Who is that?"

"The High Priest of this temple," Odrica said. "He is Selvik. He wears lines of fate on his skin."

Radek noted the use of he and wondered at the fluidity of the priest's appearance, and then at his age.

"Change in leadership?" Radek asked, ignoring talk of the scars. "He's young."

"He is twenty-three and has been the priest for a decade now." Odrica smiled, predicting his frown before it creased Radek's face. She patted his shoulder. "Sometimes wisdom comes from age, and other times it is breathed into us by the gods."

Priest Selvik rolled his shoulders forward, throwing the feathered cloak onto his body. His head turned, and he faced Izra for a long moment. Radek wished he could see Selvik's eyes, if just to parse the emotion in them.

Selvik beckoned Izra forward.

"Will you translate for us?" Radek whispered, just as the priest began to speak.

Odrica mumbled to them in soft, accented Uslethian. "Izra Dziove. Suoduny, Who Weaves our Fates, has guided you to us once more."

Izra raised his head. "Nje."

The priest sighed and sat in the single wooden chair. Odrica translated.

"Tell us why you are here—and who you have brought," Selvik said.

Izra introduced Kew and his sister, first. Both bowed solemnly when their names and stations were mentioned. But when it came to Radek and Mirakel, Izra looked uncertain. His eyes hovered on Radek for a long while, as if the words wouldn't come. And instead, Izra turned to Mirakel with his arm outstretched. He whispered Selvik's question to her in Uslethian and translated her answer.

A companion for Radek's journey, was how she referred to herself.

Radek's stomach dropped like an anchor in the ocean after that. Mirakel had played it safe. A treasurer carrying the Uslethian king's coin in her pocket was a target. Radek felt his body tense as he considered where he was. Declaring himself as an envoy of King Zavrius hadn't served him in Doskor, and though Izra trusted these people, how could they be sure none of them sided with Neala?

He looked at Izra and wondered what would benefit him. And given Radek needed to ingratiate himself to Izra in particular, he slipped forward wringing his hands together and nudged himself between Mirakel and Izra.

"I don't know what to say," he whispered to the Rezwyn. "But speaking a certain king's name aloud seems . . ."

"Dangerous," Izra whispered back. He kept his face light, but he seemed to agree. There was no telling who could be trusted. But this was Izra's world, his people. He had studied here amongst them, learned to love his god amongst Suoduny's worshippers.

"I won't have you lie to someone you respect," Radek said. "I'm sorry to even ask it."

"We do not have to lie," Izra said. He slung his arm around Radek and turned back to Selvik with an abnormally large smile on his face.

"Suodovikmuh," he said.

Selvik raised a brow. A pair of scrutinizing eyes raked over Radek, but he looked more amused than doubtful. Radek tried on his best smile and nodded.

"Oh, gods," Odrica laughed.

Radek craned his neck back toward her. "What? What was the word he used?"

"Fated," Odrica's impassive face cracked, and a smirk flowered on her lips. "Oh, Oren Radek," she said, patting his back. "You're so lucky."

Lucky? Well, fate as a concept confounded him, but the sweet attention from a broad, tall man like Izra was, admittedly, very nice. Radek stared down at Izra's large hand, which patted Radek's dismal right pectoral with an overfamiliarity that made him shiver. He felt himself unconsciously leaning into Izra's body—really, was it such a bad idea to leverage Izra's fondness and play the part of the fake lover? Surely that would be safer than admitting he was an Uslethian dignitary.

And Radek really could use an ally long-term.

Radek mustered every ounce of businessman charm he'd been neglecting and grinned at Selvik. He grabbed Izra's arm and squeezed, felt Izra tense, then relax, then tense again, and Radek's heart pounded thinking about how massive Izra was; how easily he might be thrown around. Which wasn't the sort of thing an impartial businessman should be thinking.

Odrica made a satisfied noise behind them which was accompanied by an actual slow clap from Kew. Radek turned slowly around to stare at him, because what kind of reaction was that?

Kew gave him a happy thumbs up.

Selvik turned to Izra and said something in Doskorian.

"Suoduny wills it," Izra whispered for Radek's sake. "Suoduny has made it so."

Izra's arm disappeared from Radek's shoulders. He went to Selvik and bent the knee, taking the young priest's hands in his own. He made some impassioned plea—the truth of the matter, Radek suspected. But when Odrica pulled him aside, she told him different.

"Izra is not explaining what has happened to the True Commander," she said. "He is explaining what has happened to him. His visions are erratic and come unexpectedly. He worries something is impeding his connection. Now, Izra is asking to be reconnected to Suoduny, in hopes a vision to cure the emperor will be revealed to him."

Mirakel edged away from the conversation with her arms folded. She hated talk of gods and fate—a woman in charge of her own destiny.

Selvik and Izra spoke for a few minutes more. The conversation ended when the priest reached out and cupped Izra's face affectionately and nodded. Something had been decided.

Odrica explained a ritual would take place, something to reconnect Izra to Suoduny's heart. But for that Izra would need to fast for the night and consume a slow-brewed concoction an hour before the ceremony. It could not happen until tomorrow.

Suoduny's priesthood welcomed the strangers with open arms. As guests, they were lined up behind a table, sitting cross-legged before a meal of crispy roots, rice-gruel and greasy meat. The tent filled with others with exposed faces, both old and young. Learners, Izra told him, or worshippers. Whoever had had a calling to Suoduny could learn the god's ways from a temple, and many made pilgrimages to worship at the god's likeness.

The priests here were different to the ones in the castle. Doskor's priesthood was intense and focused, seeming slightly beyond human. Radek supposed that's what they were, in a way: conduits for powers beyond the physical. But Suoduny was intricately a human god, Izra explained. Fate and destiny did not control the plants or the animals, but the humans. Suoduny would not exist without the humans that attempted to propitiate him, and without fate and destiny, humans would be untethered, left to worry and wonder.

"Is that how you see Uslethians?" Radek asked. "Are we chaotic to you because we have no god of fate to herd us?"

"Why do you think Suoduny cannot see you, Oren Radek?" Izra said with a laugh. "You were led here, after all. To me."

"I don't think so. No fate controls the King of the Merchants." He spoke breezily. "I am Lord Oren Radek. I don't accept being rendered down to someone without even free will."

Izra's face fell: this shattering collapse of that bright and genuine smile.

Radek nearly bit his tongue off. He shouldn't have said anything. Though Izra liked him, Radek continued to make blunders.

Mirakel and Odrica sat on either side of him, with Kew and Izra several spots away at the end of the table, near Selvik. Music played softly; a fat, long flute and a hollow box beaten like a drum. The sound they made could barely be called music; it was the sound of wind through the forest, a haunting cry of someone lost amongst the trees. It made it difficult to whisper. Even with the distance between himself and Izra, Radek tried to keep his voice down as he leaned Odrica's way.

"What is it, Oren Radek?" she said through a mouthful of meat. She washed it down with alcohol—another biting, poisonous thing Radek refused to let touch his mouth.

"I have a question."

"Evidently."

"It's just. . ." Radek swallowed. He'd piqued Mirakel's interest, now; could feel her staring at him with that curious expression of hers. "I have to ask. Your brother—Izra. He's, well. . ."

"Handsome?" Mirakel chimed behind him.

Radek swung his hand to slap her beneath the table. Odrica side-eyed the display, lips quirking.

"Your brother . . . is a nice man. Far more so than I first expected."

Odrica stared at him. "What is your question?"

Radek tilted closer again. "How do I get him to like me?"

Odrica's hand flew to the cup of alcohol again. "He does like you," she murmured as she drank.

"No, well—" Radek sighed. "I mean to say, I hope to make a long-lasting contact in this country. And your brother is in a unique position to be that person. As you say, he likes me. That's good. I like him too. I find him very amiable."

"Oh, bloody—" Mirakel mumbled.

"But how do I . . ." Radek said very loudly over Mirakel's exasperation before he trailed off. He felt his hands itch for his cards. He always felt better at talking to people when he could fidget with them, shuffle them. They made him feel like he had the upper hand. And usually, he did. He wasn't someone who regularly got flustered—as a merchant and a salesman, talking to people was simply what he did.

So why did speaking about Izra make his tongue completely useless?

Odrica handed him a cup of the cursed alcohol. Radek hesitated for half a breath before he snatched it from her hands. He gulped most of it down. Disgusting wasn't the word for it. It tasted downright offensive, both bitter and scorching, so the flavor was more a feeling than anything else.

"Shit, this is bad," he groaned.

"It does the job," Odrica said, plucking the cup from his hands. "It will do enough to keep you calm."

"I am perfectly—"

"You want to make a good, long connection with my brother? You want to secure him as someone to rely upon, and you want it to be reciprocated?" Odrica said all this with a rhetorical air, throwing back the rest of Radek's drink. She had a look about her like a wily cat. "You are not looking to take advantage of him, but you are interested in using his position to your benefit. No—do not back off now. No shame in that, Oren Radek. But is that what you want?"

Radek exhaled. "Yes."

Odrica considered him, then shrugged. "Fine. I know what you should do."

By the time she'd finished explaining it, a false calm had settled into his muscles and relaxed them.

Radek stood shakily and slipped out from behind the table with a knife slipped up his sleeve. No one paid him any mind, the revel continuing loudly around them.

He stumbled out into the frigid night, mind running wild—this was perhaps a silly thing to do, but he would do it properly. He passed a few guards who nodded at him, and then he lurched to a stop and craned his neck. The wooden idol of Suoduny loomed above him. Lanterns blazed around it, and Radek stared up at its panoptic gaze. Up close, he could see long, red strings had been lain over hooks jutting out of the wood. But Odrica had told him not to touch those yet, so he lowered himself to the dewy grass at its base. His gaze flickered down to the offering bowl leaned against it, filled with bone and hair and blood.

A shiver ran through Radek, not of revulsion but fear; fear that truth lay in, and that somewhere, somehow, his destiny was marked. But doing this, at least, was his decision. He would make Izra Dziove an ally, truly.

Radek slipped out the knife from his tunic and paused. Around the base of the idol, little flowers glowed iridescent in the moonlight.

No, not iridescent—prismatic.

Radek breathed deep. Only ichor glowed like that, the substance that drove all arcane power in Usleth. He grazed his finger against one and shivered at the contact. Usually, the arcane terrified him, but Radek found the thought of ichor—a substance at least somewhat familiar to him—was comforting when knelt before the idol of a god.

"Well," he said aloud, picking up the knife. "This is what gods are for, right? To ask for things you need?" He took the knife and cut the back of his hand until blood dripped from it and into the bowl. Then he craned his neck to stare up at Suoduny's many faces. "I need a friend."

Radek got to his knees and, following Odrica's instructions, took some of the blood in his fingers. Before he reached for the thread, he pressed his bloody fingertips against the wood.

And his mind opened.

A flash of something filled his vision—a man, himself perhaps, two eyes staring up at him and gasping in recognition.

Radek yanked his hand away from the column.

Absolutely not. He would absolutely not be doing whatever that was.

"Alright, thank you," he said, terrified, and if this was real, he wasn't about to offend a god. And if this was the effect of ichor, then he had just experienced a hint of madness.

In either case, he was a businessman. He knew how to deal with uncomfortable situations. Radek made an awkward little bow, reached up, and took a thread from a hook.

Then he wrapped it up in his fist and ambled back to the party.

Kew and Izra were laughing and drinking, chatting together in Doskorian. Radek felt like a child as he stood behind them. Awkwardly, he cleared his throat.

Izra turned, smile fading. "Oren. Is everything alright?"

Radek swallowed and nodded. He unfurled his fist. A line of red string dropped between his forefinger and thumb.

Izra stared at him. "What?"

Others in the tent noticed the action. The flute-player choked on air and gurgled out a strangled note. Conversations died. For one achingly long moment, everyone stared at him.

Radek looked at Odrica. What cruel joke was this?

Then Kew started laughing, a brassy roar he brayed into Izra's face. He slapped the other man on the back three times before he vacated his seat to Radek. The music started again, a rapid, jaunty tune—or as close to one as could be managed on the airy flute. Kew made a few very excited gestures to get Radek to sit.

"Chy," Kew swore, hand over his chest. He gripped Radek's shoulder and pointed firmly at his face. "Surprising!"

Radek laughed with him, trying to suppress his sudden unease like some bloated snake trying to shed its skin. He was not particularly successful.

Izra looked flushed. He whispered into Radek's ear. "Do you understand what you're doing?"

"Absolutely. I've agreed, haven't I?" Radek picked up a goblet and motioned for Izra to do the same. The big Rezwyn had a shake in his hand, but he reached forward and lifted his goblet high. Radek weaved the red string between their cups. "Once we . . . put things right in Doskor, I hope our friendship will remain. I'd like it to. I'd . . . like to depend upon you in the future."

"You can have anything," Izra said breathlessly. "Anything at all."

Radek grinned. That felt too easy. "I mean to say, that even when all is said and done, I want us to have a good relationship. A solid one."

Izra laughed. "Of course, we will. Suoduny wills it so. You are here with me, I am here with you. That is a good and solid start."

Radek could agree to that. He nodded, leaned forward, and drank from the cup, just as Izra did the same.

A small cheer went up in the tent as they put their goblets down. Izra's gaze fell on the red string wrapped around their cups, and his eyes went soft. He played with the end between forefinger and thumb.

The priest Selvik called something out in Doskorian that made another cheer go up.

"We dance," Izra told him. "The whole temple will celebrate."

Radek frowned and tried to smile. "Funny to have everyone onboard," he said.

"Why is that?"

Radek looked around the tent and shrugged. "A cizalec and a Dziove declaring—"

"Oh, no, they love this," Izra said. He took Radek by the shoulders and squeezed. "Cizalec or no, it does not matter. It is about Suoduny, that fate has bound two people together. You acknowledged such a thing. It . . . makes my heart warm."

Izra looked at him, eyes shining, and smile warm. It was such a lovely way to be looked at, Radek felt himself flush. He had no idea what to say.

Izra squeezed his shoulders again. "I told you, Oren Radek. I will make a believer out of you one day."

"Well, you shall have plenty of days for it. Once the High Priestess is deposed, we can get down to business," Radek said, giving the table a playful slap.

Izra went redder at that for some reason. "Of course. We must focus on the nation. The real celebration can come after."

Izra stood and offered his hand to help Radek stand. "One moment," he said, bowing slightly before Radek. "I must present Suoduny with an offering. But do not worry—I will be back soon."

Izra slipped his hand out of Radek's and threw open the tent flap. Radek stood with the eyes of a dozen Rezwyns staring at him. Kew raised his own goblet and nodded happily. An old woman started weeping. Many were looking at him like he'd just done something quite profound.

Mirakel came to stand by his side. "Radek, what the fuck is—why is that woman crying?"

"I have . . . absolutely no idea."

"Are you dying?"

Radek balked. "What?"

"You just participated in some weird Rezwyn bullshit. You could be a sacrifice, you know. An offering. Didn't I just hear the big one say something about an offering?"

"I'm not—" Radek said, voice growing loud. The old woman wailed a little louder, so he dragged Mirakel to the side. With his voice hushed, Radek tried again. "I'm fairly certain I've not been poisoned."

"Pretty shit odds when we're talking about death."

"I know you're enjoying yourself, but you can stop. All I did was . . . well. Odrica," Radek hissed, leaning around Mirakel to get the other woman's attention. "What exactly did I do again?"

The ambassador grinned up at him and raised a glass. "You made a companion out of him, Oren Radek. A lifelong one at that."

"Right. Friendship ceremony. See?" Radek said, turning back to Mirakel. "I've gone and secured a Dziove as my contact in the empire."

Mirakel's looked wholly unconvinced, but she gave him a long, slow clap. "Well done, King of the Merchants. Very well done to you."

CHAPTER FOURTEEN

"Cannot say I was expecting that one. A cizalec binding himself to you. Without so much as a kiss, too, eh?" Kew threw back another cup of wine. "Dismal nuptials, Izra. When you turned down the Lord of Veprak, I always thought you would aim a little higher than a—"

"Careful what you say next," Izra murmured, letting real venom seep into his tone. "That is my new husband you are talking about."

He knew Kew was teasing him, but in that moment, it was immaterial.

Kew put up his hands and laughed. "As you say. Your fated man." He leaned forward and offered Izra a shot, nudging his shoulder. "But not even a kiss?"

"In the face of our destiny, that is such an inconsequential—"

"You are telling me your fated man is celibate, and—"

"He is not celibate! I think. It is just—he wishes our focus to be on our mission." Izra tried to stop himself from becoming defensive. In truth, Kew's rambling could do nothing to dislodge the feeling in Izra's chest; the deepest, most unfeigned joy he had ever experienced. He took a breath to steady himself. "Until we stop Neala, neither of us wish to lose ourselves in one another. It would be . . . far too distracting."

Kew made a face and kept drinking. "Mm-hm."

Izra tutted. His body ached. Izra had spent the night in vigil before the raised idol to Suoduny. Not quite the wedding night he had dreamed of, but Oren had the right idea of it. With the True Commander unanchored somewhere in infinity, and his daughters ready to take the Rezwyn Empire backward at least a hundred years, how could either of them devote themselves fully to one another? But this act, this tethering driven by Oren, was a pledge. A promise of devotion.

Izra had been waiting for years. What was a little longer?

He looked around the temple's camp. Gone was all the revelry of the previous night. A godly and reverent ambience had replaced it in the morning. Many people were in the forest, foraging or hunting beyond the camp's bounds. The emptiness made the temple seem mystical and secret, like Suoduny was a god of the earth, more so than a god of its people.

Izra sighed and stretched, standing. He shook out his cramped legs and peered back at Kew. With a drink in hand, the man lay sprawled on the ground. Kew, despite the gravity of the emperor's health, was not often a serious man. But a drink? Izra shielded his eyes from the morning light. "You know the sun is out, do you not?"

"What is your point?"

Izra put a hand over Kew's cup and forcefully lowered it. "My point is just that: the sun is out. I need your help today. It has been years since I have been exposed to the cajudsan, and my body may not react well."

"What?" Kew scoffed, but then his smile slipped. "You think you'll end up in the astrok-mer with the True Commander?"

Izra grimaced. He knew Kew had said the most impossible, outlandish thing he could—that Izra's soul would be ejected from its mortal flesh by the force of the ancient magics he would ingest.

"I have no words for what might happen," Izra said, stretching. "Only prayer."

He craned his neck and took in the looming presence of Suoduny surveying the temple grounds. Frost and dew covered the wood, seeping into the old, wrinkle-like cracks that ran through the idol. One day this wood would rot, as fate would have it, and another would be erected in its place. This one would be planted where it decayed, in the last campsite of the temple. Cajudsan would sprout at its base, a gift from the force of destiny for those who worshipped it.

Izra leaned over the wagon to place his bare hand against the idol. He could feel his god in everything: every passing moment, every dream and whisper of the future that came with each breath. But sometimes he wanted something tangible. Something he could touch.

Though soon enough, he supposed he would have Oren.

"Gods," Kew scoffed. He slapped Izra's shoulder, making him jerk away from the wagon. "You should not lie about prayer."

Izra's cheeks ignited with shame. "I was not—"

"Ah, you can't fool me, Izra. Nothing pious in your eyes right now." Kew crossed his arms. His tone shifted. "You want to kiss him."

Izra scoffed. "Of course, I want to kiss him. He is—well. Do you think me blind?"

"Good morning."

Izra's body went stiff before he whirled around.

And there he was. Oren Radek, his fated-man—and husband. Oren stood haloed by rays of the morning sun. His russet skin lit up in a way that made his face seem outlined in gold, specks of gold leaf accenting his black beard and hair. He had changed out of the garish tunic he'd worn to the party. Odrica had convinced Selvik to hand over something of his. He had given Radek a kaftan. Black and sleek, it dropped midway down Radek's thighs. Izra stared at the junction between the kaftan's end and the form-fitting woolen tights that hid Radek's skin. This looked good on him; like it was made for him as much as Izra's old, familiar wolf-pelt was meant for the shoulders of a Dziove. Oren wore fine things well. It was in his very blood to be this handsome.

Izra's eyes dropped over Oren's face and lingered on his lips. Gods, he was a commander and a strix, and—charged with the greatest duty he would ever need to fulfill—he was thinking about a man. Meanwhile, there was Oren, a cizalec determined to stabilize their nation before indulging in things like kisses. Clearly, Izra had something to learn from him. They had even been so chaste as to sleep in separate beds.

"Good morning!" Izra grinned and cleared his throat. Kew snickered behind him. Gods, Izra was grateful Oren did not know his tongue. "How did you sleep?"

"Oh, well enough." Oren looked about the temple grounds. He looked—sad, Izra thought. Worried. But then Oren turned to face him, and despite it all, his eyes were calculating. He had something to say.

A heavy wave of fear washed over Izra, drowning the anxiety of the ceremony to come, the dangers of the astrokmer. Instead, he thought of the night before; the binding Oren had initiated, the words he had said. Morning always made men sober. Perhaps in this new light Oren had regrets.

Izra turned just enough to catch Kew in his periphery. "Leave us," he ordered. Kew heard his tone and slunk away like a disciplined dog.

As soon as his second left, Izra spun back to Oren. He tried—truly—to let Oren have the first word, but dread sat in his throat like bile. He had to speak.

"You regret it," Izra said hurriedly. "The binding. Last night."

Oren frowned and cocked his head. "The binding?" His eyes widened. "No. What is there to regret? On the contrary, I was hoping . . ."

Breathlessly, impatiently, Izra repeated, "Hoping?"

But this was not a talk between two married men. Oren was not hoping for a kiss, or a touch—he needed something from Izra Dziove, strix, Commander of the Uxbuh.

"I was hoping the binding would give you more confidence in me. That you would feel comfortable sharing it with me. The truth, I mean. Of what's to come."

Izra frowned. "The truth?"

"I don't worship any gods, Izra. It's not in my nature. But I know the power of the arcane." Oren paused. This would be it, Izra realized: the greatest bit of tension between them. Every part of Oren would resist a world where the gods were real. Either it terrified him, or it made no sense to him—but in both those cases, to Oren Radek, Izra and this country was mad for what they believed. Oren sighed and continued. "And I'm . . . worried for you. In Usleth people can easily go mad from contact with it."

Izra stepped forward and gripped Oren's shoulder. The other man dropped his eyes to the touch.

"I won't go mad," Izra said. "I promise."

Oren made an odd gesture with his hand before he stepped forward and clamped it down on Izra's shoulder. "The ceremony—I don't know much about . . . well. How to act."

That surprised Izra. There was a confidence to Oren, an easy charm that should have meant he was well-liked and well sought after—by men, or whomever took his fancy. Unless Izra had misunderstood, and just like him, Oren had to battle his restraint.

He clarified with. "Do you mean to say . . . you have never touched a man?"

Oren's eyes went wide. "I—I. Wh—sorry." He took a breath. "What?"

Izra could not read him. He took a breath.

"Izra Dziove." The voice echoed out over the empty, misted campsite. Izra swallowed his words and craned towards the voice.

The priest, Selvik, leaned out of the large tent with his arms folded. Izra could not see his eyes, but he felt their severity boring into him even from this distance. The priest was a serious, devout man, but when Izra had first met him, Selvik had been a willful girl, thrown into the priesthood by a vision. The previous night, when Izra had told him of his fated man, even the headdress failed to cover the shock on Selvik's face. It had been years since they had spoken. They had had a youthful interest in one another. But Suoduny had disrupted it; thrown them both onto their true paths. Even if Selvik nursed a small wound this morning, he would never do anything to overstep a god.

Izra nodded his head back to the priest's tent and patted Oren's shoulder. "There is a plant called cajudsan. A special thing. It favors the ground where Suoduny's old idols are placed. We priests make a tea from it."

Oren peered past him at Selvik. "And it's brewed?"

"It is ready," Izra nodded. "Will you come with me?"

Oren scanned his face and pressed his lips together. Izra tensed, expecting him to say no. But Oren nodded his assent.

As he walked, Izra's stomach twisted, half with nerves and half with joy. Izra had always had a strong connection to Suoduny. The dreams he had been gifted always showed him the way forward. But they were not always what Izra needed. The gods were beyond this plane. They were forces more so than agents: primal concepts affecting the world, not at all like people. The brew would guide Suoduny's vision to what Izra needed to see.

When he woke, he would know how to mend the empire.

Selvik held the tent flap open. The priest wore a simple black robe, loosely belted around his middle. Today's headdress covered everything but his lower face; Izra could only just see the severe, pursed lips behind the fringe.

No one else was in the tent besides the three of them. The space had transformed from the night before. It had experienced the same pious spell that had settled over the camp and stamped out all the revelry.

The floor had been cleared of long tables, but Selvik led them toward the far-left corner, where last night big furs had been strewn about. Now there were only heavy mats meant to keep the cold from seeping in. A single pillow lay ready and waiting for his head.

Izra glanced back at Oren, who smiled at him, eyebrows furrowed.

All the warmth and comfort had been stripped away. Izra knew it was for the best—he needed a simple space to connect with a god, someplace free from the clutter of the material. But a shiver went through him as he stood there.

Selvik told them to sit. He went to get the tea.

Oren leaned over and nudged him. "You told me to trust you, and here you are, unable to trust yourself. You look positively terrified."

Izra wanted to tell him he had every reason to be scared. He had been told the dangers of the astral plane as soon as he was named strix. But how could he say that to a man who had just promised himself to Izra?

He said instead, "Sometimes viewing what fate has in store is not that pleasant."

"It must be hard for you," Oren said. "But I'll stay here with you, if that's what you want."

They were so close. Izra dropped his gaze to Oren's lips. He studied them, saw the color; a rosiness to them, a nectar, ripe and sweet. He could not help himself. He tipped forward and kissed the other man.

It was chaste, and quick. Izra had a moment of self awareness and pulled back—Oren had told him they were to wait. But then Oren's fingertips hovered over his chin, his lips parting against Izra's for a moment longer. There was a pureness to it, a sweet joy. Izra knocked his forehead against Oren's. He thanked his lord for everything, for the perfection that was Oren Radek.

The floor creaked. Selvik had returned, so both of them flinched away from each other like embarrassed adolescents. They said nothing about the kiss.

Selvik knelt and decanted the tea into a small iron cup.

Izra held the cup in his hands, felt the hot elixir warm the metal.

Perhaps a month ago, this would have been easier—when Oren was a blurred dream and nothing more, when his fated man had not made a promise and bound them to each other. Izra's eyes slipped from the priest and fell like an anchor on Oren's careful gaze.

And he told himself, then, he would not be lost. He would not allow it. Izra would claw and scrape and drag himself back to his body, back to the physical world. Whatever it took to return to his man—he would do it.

Oren seemed to notice his new anxiety. He reached out to Izra, placed a comforting hand on his shoulder and said, "For the future of both our peoples."

Izra nodded and sculled the tea.

Chapter Fifteen

Izra did not wake for two days. Radek remained beside him, out of a strange obligation. Mirakel and Odrica took turns keeping him company, and Kew often came to sit in silence, before the Rezwyn grew so tired of doing nothing he went outside to wave a sword around. But Radek simply stayed.

Both nights, Radek laid down beside Izra and stared intently at the faint rise and fall of his chest, that mark of the living, that tiny tether to this world. The first night, Radek managed to force most thoughts away and sleep. But the second, he could do nothing but think. He watched Izra, the sweat on his brow, the sheen to his already too-pale skin, and longed to touch him.

It was becoming undeniable that something brewed between them. Radek could pretend it was only his own attraction, but when he had touched Suoduny's idol, he'd had—a vision. Someone had stared out at him from the mess of fate and destiny, and that someone had not been Izra Dziove. Radek's insides squirmed, because the arcane was a terrifying and confusing void to him, but Izra believed.

Believed they were fated.

So Radek thought again about the dewy iridescence on the cajudsan flowers. Ichor, to his knowledge, was something drawn out of a gedrok. A rare substance. It wasn't—on flowers. This of course meant Usleth was, once again, woefully underinformed. If ichor abounded naturally in the empire, then everything Usleth understood about the arcane was wrong.

It always came back to the arcane, and sooner or later, Radek would have to swallow all his discomfort and accept that something profoundly upsetting was happening.

That perhaps he had a destiny after all. Perhaps he could change the course of Rezwyn history. Before he slept, Radek reached out and grazed his fingers against Izra's. A jolt went through him—fate? Or simple attraction?—and with his heart racing at the intimacy, at the softness of the touch, Radek slept.

On the morning of the third day, Radek woke from a fitful rest to a howl of rage. He stumbled out into the camp, watching as Odrica threw back the flap to Selvik's tent and hurried out. She looked a mess. Kohl-stained tears ran in furrows down her cheeks, parts of her hair seemed suddenly matted. She took her great sword from her back, stalked to the edge of the forest and kicked the nearest tree trunk and let out another inarticulate shriek.

"Ambassador!" Radek called. He knew she heard him—her shoulders stiffened in recognition—but she did not turn. Odrica hefted her sword and stalked off further into the trees.

Radek heard a noise behind him and looked back in time to see Selvik, lingering at the entrance of the tent, staring out after Odrica's angry retreat.

A terrible premonition came over him. Odrica was a calm and level-headed woman; emotion did not destroy her resolve. This outburst was uncontainable, the kind of pain that would have burned through her heart until screaming became a necessary release. She was in pain. She was scared.

Izra had still not awoken. Would he be waking up at all?

Horror split open his lower belly. He staggered toward Selvik.

"What did you tell her?" he demanded.

Selvik's fringed and beaded headdress clacked together as the priest turned to face him.

Selvik made no reply.

He couldn't understand, Radek realized, he didn't know a lick of Uslethian. He tried a different tactic. He reached out and took Selvik's hand.

"Izra?" he whispered. He squeezed Selvik's hand, hoped he could convey every worry and every bit of pleading with a name. On an inspiration he held up his arm to show the red cord, the symbol of his bond with Izra, as if it were proof that he had the right to ask. "Izra?"

Selvik's face changed, expression melting towards concern and apologetic sorrow. It was the worst expression Radek had ever seen. It meant that he was right, that Odrica had wept and screamed for her brother, because something was going wrong.

"Tell me. Show me." Radek shook Selvik's hand, tugging him down. "It's Izra. It's Izra, isn't it? How long does this usually take? How do you know something is going wrong?"

Selvik yanked his hand free from Radek's grip, but instead of moving away Selvik put his palms against Radek's face and held him there. It was not a demanding action; it was comfort. Radek exhaled, hoping to expel the fear and the worry, every complicated and messy feeling broiling in his chest. Selvik knocked their heads together. Radek stared at the swaying beads, at the refraction of light off the stone. He saw his own face warped and distorted and knew by the way Selvik held him that the solution was to let go. He was meant to let this run its course, even when that meant letting Izra slip away.

Well, that wasn't going to happen.

"No! You have to wake him up." Radek ripped Selvik's hands from the sides of his face. He all but dragged the priest back into the tent where Izra lay prone. Radek bent closer, put his mouth near Izra's ear. His breath stirred across Izra's eyelashes. "You have to come back," Radek whispered. "Out of the astrok-mer, back to your body. You have to come now."

Selvik had no words for him. Radek's eyes fell on the bronze kettle Selvik had poured from two days earlier and went to his knees before Selvik in supplication.

"Izra said one day we could walk the astrok-mer together. So it's possible. I can go in, and I can find him. Let me drink," he said. "Izra said we were fated to be together. This can't be the end. Let me find him—I will bring him back."

Selvik did nothing. Radek looked at the kettle. It might have been empty. It might have contained something else entirely. Radek launched himself up anyway. He snatched the kettle and drank from the spout.

Selvik screamed in surprised horror, but by then it was too late. The mixture—the cajudsan—had a vile, bitter taste. It burned Radek's throat. He made an involuntary sound as he swallowed. "By the Bones, that's even worse than snake wine."

He moved clumsily to where Izra lay prone.

"Izra." He reached out with his hand—and froze. He wanted to touch him, but Izra seemed locked in a moment, frowning and fighting but awfully still.

Radek keeled forward and rested his head on Izra's chest.

Izra's heartbeat fluttered weakly beneath his touch. Moments later, Radek felt his own heartbeat slow. He felt as if his body were submerged in tepid water. A weight filled him; he couldn't keep his head above the flood.

Someone came and tried to pull him off Izra's chest. Radek looked up. Odrica loomed over him, real wrath contorting the flesh of her face. "Whatever you are doing, you will stop it. You will kill him."

"Let go of me." He could barely breathe. His limbs were heavy in the rising waters.

Sudden and ripe anger enveloped Odrica. Her pale face turned a brilliant vermillion. "You do not order me, Oren Radek. And you do not harm my brother. Stop whatever you're doing at once."

There was a quiet word from Selvik, a hand on Odrica's shoulder—it all started to blur. Radek became vaguely aware that Odrica's hands were back by her side, but the force of her grip lingered.

"I can't," he told her. "I can't. I drank it. I am not asking you. I am not asking for your permission. I am telling you—I am going after him."

Odrica's jaw pulsed. She turned to Selvik, and sighed. "Oren Radek, you are a fool."

Those were the last words Radek heard before he went under.

He was thrown violently upward, and then like being caught in a wave, tumbled over and over until all sense of direction disappeared. When the turbulence stopped, Radek vomited what tasted like seawater onto the ground.

Radek lay in the tent and recovered his senses, and in recovering them realized he was not in the tent at all. He lay below deck on a ship. Above, he saw evenly spaced cross-beams, and he could feel the sway of waves beneath him. The ever-present creaking of the ship's hull sounded around him, near-haunted in its lurching.

Oren Radek sat up, and was thirteen again.

When the Rezwyns had invaded, the port town of Awha Stad, the whole city had loaded up into ships and lived on them for years, to flee the invading forces. Radek never experienced a battle, but this cabin was something he longed to forget.

The cabin was small and cramped. It had two narrow berths—one for himself, and one for his mother. The sum of their worldly possessions was packed into a small trunk that doubled as a table. And in Radek's hands, when he looked down, were the first cards he had ever owned.

His father's deck, originally. Too big for his hands, and block printed, lacking the beauty of his current hand-painted set. Nostalgia made him nauseous—and then sense came back to him.

He was in the astrok-mer, and his duty was clear. He was here to bargain with Suoduny and ask the god to give Izra Dziove back to him. An air of great unease settled on Radek. He'd expected to arrive in a temple, perhaps gazing up at a multi-faced figure as tall as the sky, not be shifted back onto the ship where he'd lived as a refugee.

And what was he meant to do? Play a round of Gulek Des?

He supposed so. Radek looked down at the cards and drew one.

His hand quivered. He had drawn 'ULTIMATE DESTRUCTION,' a trump card, one that could obliterate nearly half of the opponent's forces. This card was stamped with a snowscape and something he had never before seen depicted on these cards.

The rampant gedrok.

The ship around him collapsed. It all fell away, wooden panels tearing off and spinning into nothingness, and when Radek blinked he was somewhere else entirely.

Barrows of snow covered the ground, flakes of it whipping through the air. It turned oddly red as it refracted the grim dusk bleeding on the horizon. Radek looked up at the sky. Red as dark as venous blood spilled across it. A storm was gathering; gray-tinted clouds swirled together with a rumble. The air was thick with the scent of brewing petrichor and half-cooked meat. An edge of rot crept into Radek's nose. It took a moment for him to make sense of the shadows moving in the snow, for him to understand that the ambient droning was battle, death cries, and triumph.

This was war.

Across the freezing, snow-covered landscape, chaos and noise rumbled up toward him. Bodies lunged at one another. Corpses and severed limbs lay unmoving in their own gore. It was a battle in its death throes. Exhaustion and desperation occupied the tired limbs of these fighters. The snows were covered in blood, and were swamp-like with the viscera, a sludge of entrails and death that made for poor footing. Half the battle seemed staying upright.

He scanned the horizon, saw the ocean in the distance, the stretch of plains, and realized where he was.

This was Ostijan. This was a Battle of Ostijan—but which one? Usleth and the Rezwyn Empire had fought over this strip of territory for centuries.

And then there was the roar. It was a call drawn from the depths of old and creaking lungs, something that felt wholly wrong to hear with human ears; a droning cry, from something colossal. From something old.

A gedrok.

It was a colossal beast towering four men high, with a muscular, cat-like body that winnowed into a serpent tail. Tumorous knobs of bones protruded along its spine as if spikes had half grown and then abandoned their attempts. The head was earless and smooth, with an eerie glossiness to it, and its jaw was dense and thick. Great teeth sprung from it as it roared, and moss and plants grew within the cavity of its mouth. With its roar, the air filled with the thin smell of brine as if it had brought the sea with it. A wound was open on its chest but it was corpse-like and bloodless. Along the bellflower curve of its haunches, white scales had fallen away and exposed the translucent skin beneath, but in other areas where the pearlescent shine of its scales were evident, strong muscle still moved beneath.

And life clung to the gedrok like mildew, a kind of rotting approximate. But Radek had only seen a gedrok skeleton and heard rumors of a crystallized other. What he saw now was altogether something else.

It stormed out of the snowy haze, tearing into the Rezwyn army. Screams and choking cries, a flurry of motion—Radek watched the gedrok stampede, crushing bodies in its wake. The Rezwyn line broke and fled. Usleth was winning. It meant this was six centuries ago, when Usleth had first taken Ostijan as its territory.

And he stared because the gedrok was not alone. It was mounted.

Someone was riding it into war.

Radek didn't understand. This was centuries ago, not thousands. The annals of Usleth made it clear that the gedroks had never walked in the time of humans. They had been unearthed, discovered like preserved fossils. This—whatever he was seeing—simply wasn't possible.

The figure sat mounted on a striking red and black saddle that fitted around the massive bulk of the beast's torso. It also fitted deftly around the spikes that protruded from the gedrok's back—there was no doubt this saddle had been hand crafted specifically for this creature. Radek squinted, eager to see who this brave figure was.

The man riding the gedrok had russet brown skin, kohl-lined eyes and golden jewels through his nose and ears. He had thick shoulder-length hair, and he looked furious.

Radek cast about at this haunting of long-dead ghosts; this ancient tapestry. He breathed deep and focused. Six centuries ago—who could it be? If that king bore the power of the gedrok, he must have been Gedrok Ach Meedin, one of the first recorded kings in Uslethian history, the dynasty that preceded the Dued Vuuthriks. It was he who gave his name for the unearthed colossi they found in Usleth.

And Radek's mother had always said they were descendants.

Radek stumbled closer. He saw threads, pearlescent, like reins of ichor strung about the gedrok's mouth. Its eye was glassy like it was not alive at all. And it wasn't. He saw the gedrok's chest had been carved open. Could Gedrok Ach Meedin be puppeting the gedrok's corpse? But how?

On instinct, Radek looked down. His cards were still clutched in his hand, lightly dusted with snow, and they seemed so incongruous in this scene that the simple impossibility of their being here moved Radek to draw another.

His brows crumpled.

SCORCHED EARTH.

The card depicted a barren landscape, flames and smoke rising in the distance.

It was a card Radek was always wary of drawing; or rather, it made him wary of those who played it. It was the card that represented brutal military tactics; a retreating army turning the land desolate. Burning crops, destroying infrastructure, poisoning wells.

The mark of brutal wartime decisions.

And in answer to Radek's question, the scene shifted from the battle to show him exactly what Gedrok Ach Meedin had done.

Radek saw something fleshy, an organ being hauled from the gedrok's corpse.

A voice asked the king, "Will it work?"

And Gedrok Ach Meedin touched the organ, the heart, and then lifted a vial of ichor to his lips. "Yes."

He drank with solemnity because this was his duty. But underneath it all, Radek could feel a thrumming desire that wasn't his, but the king's; the urge not only to win this battle, but to make it hurt.

His actions here were prompted by something deeply personal.

Radek thrust that thought away as Gedrok Ach Meedin reacted to the power he had ingested into his body. There was no telling how many times he had done this; if this was the first, there was no ceremony to it beyond a sense of obligation. And if it was the third, or the fourth, or the fifth, then by now, the king must truly have been mad.

Gedrok Ach Meedin rocked forward with a groan that suggested the ichor was corroding his insides. But very quickly, he suppressed the pain, waving away the invisible attendant Radek couldn't see.

Then, it happened.

Sprouting from the very veins of the gedrok itself were threads, iridescent and in the dozens, and power called to power. From the king's hands they grew, and from within the gedrok they reached, liquid smooth, until a weblike knotting had formed at the interval between the threads emerging from the king's fingers, and those unfurling from the gedrok itself. A kind of netting. The king pulled his hand back and the heavy paw of the gedrok lifted and thudded into the ground.

Gedrok Ach Meedin screamed. The hand he had moved convulsed, but he swallowed the pain and rolled his shoulders back. Sweat shone on his brow.

But something else had happened. Radek could see, with vision perhaps lent by Suoduny itself, that in taking part of the gedrok into his body, the king had also returned some. A bloody bandage was wrapped around a forearm, and suddenly Radek could see the severed piece of human flesh in the gedrok's gullet; Suoduny's vision had made it momentarily translucent as if to tell Radek: this came at a price. Or at several. The ingestion of ichor, the inevitable madness that came with that, the sacrifice of his own flesh—and pain.

Gedrok Ach Meedin howled with it and then bit down on his own cheek until blood flooded his mouth. And the gedrok howled with him, ancient throat opening to scream.

Radek stepped back in horror.

Why? Why had he done all this? Why tie yourself to a primordial creature you could never understand? Why drink the ichor, why risk it?

This time, Radek drew no card; it launched out toward him, levitating in the air.

TENUOUS TRUCE.

Two hands reached toward each other, one of them armored, the other unarmored, meant to symbolize a willingness to trust. It was the card you played to initiate a parley with the enemy. To form an alliance; to potentially reconcile. But there was always a risk in playing this card. Always a chance the trust would be undermined for a surprise attack.

Then the card dissolved and a new scene appeared—a parley, the meeting of Gedrok Ach Meedin and another before the battle. The Rezwyn Emperor looked so much like Odrica and Izra that Radek had to double-take. This was centuries ago—centuries!—but that pale otherworldliness had come from someone with a set of very strong genes, apparently.

"You have desecrated your own body," the Rezwyn told Gedrok Ach Meedin. "You have invited something infernal into your flesh, and it is corrupting you."

A dismissive laugh.

The Dziove frowned. "You are mad. And you won't stop."

"No," Gedrok Ach Meedin whispered. "This war was born from the empire's selfishness. You breached the sacred division between our nations. You breached Winigari,"—Radek recognized this as an antiquated name for Westgar—"You stole hundreds of our women."

This moved Dziove to speak. "You know they went willingly. The gods moved them! They willfully renounced their Uslethian citizenship—"

"—for food. Land. You bribed them."

"And you?" Dziove shouted. "Were you bribed each time you crawled into my bed?"

A chilly silence filled the space. Radek could feel his own heart straining; the king referred heartbreak.

"Those were mistakes," Gedrok Ach Meedin whispered, "that will never be repeated."

The Rezwyn man's face grew very still. His lips became a thin line, and all blood drained away. "I cannot let you do this."

Gedrok Ach Meedin raised his chin. "Then we will fight to the death."

"Why are you showing me these two?" Radek asked aloud.

The deck shifted in his hand, and another card sprang out, held swaying in front of his eyes.

CONFLICT'S LEGACY.

The image on the card was divided in two; one side, the dilapidated ruins of a hold, and on the other, the same hold in pristine condition. Radek breathed deep.

Conflict's Legacy was another trump card, meant to acknowledge how past events had played a role in the current conflict. In game, it simply gave the player an advantage the following turn; a double action, to represent how lessons of the past had prepared your army for the present conflict.

But in the astrok-mer, it seemed Radek would be learning about the conflict firsthand.

The snowstorm whipped up again, and Radek was back at the Battle of Ostijan; only it was he who was now mounted on the gedrok. He was Gedrok Ach Meedin, trampling a hundred Rezwyns to his victory.

And there was nothing sweet about it. Nothing good. It was carnage and brutality for the sake of it. No honor drove Gedrok Ach Meedin as he mangled the enemy. No honor, and no necessity. Nothing but rage.

Something punched through his chest. Radek gasped. He spluttered warmth—blood, blood all over his hands, his organs indiscriminately spraying themselves onto the gedrok's back. An arrow had pierced his heart. In shock, Radek thrust out his hand. The gedrok reacted and thrust forward too, tearing into the man who had shot the arrow, throwing the body to the side. Half unconscious, Radek slipped from the gedrok's saddle and fell beside his attacker's broken body. He looked over and saw, in horror, that it was Izra—but when he blinked it was that ancient Dziove, blood pouring from his lips.

The battle continued around them, but Radek could look nowhere else. Both kings' guards surrounded them, weapons drawn, but Dziove raised his hand.

"Record us," he croaked out. "Cuvari, I order you. Record us."

"Don't be stupid," Radek said—Gedrok Ach Meedin said through Radek. "What's the point?"

Someone emerged from the guards and scratched away on a stone tablet. Dziove reached out to Radek and intertwined their bloody fingers; pearlescent ichor shone in the blood where the king's met the emperor's.

"So we can know what happened," Dziove murmured. "I know we can try again. I've seen the possibility in the astrok-mer."

Radek's body tensed involuntarily. Gedrok tried to pull away, but Dziove's grip was firm. A pool of blood settled into the snow between them and made it steam. Radek's eyes dropped to it and the way it shone. Gedrok's voice rattled out of Radek, saying, "What have you done?"

"There is one life where we are happy," Dziove whispered. Izra's eyes bore into Radek, exhausted and determined and *loving*, and Radek flushed at the intensity of his gaze, and the knowledge that Emperor Dziove had loved Gedrok Ach Meedin immeasurably.

Enough to do this.

"That's not what I asked," the king said. "Tell me what you have done."

"I asked Suoduny to keep us."

Radek's heart lurched. Gedrok said, "What?"

"Our blood is united here, in the place where we will die. Our essences have visited the astrok-mer before. So all that is left is this. Let's commit our souls to Suoduny, and let fate keep us until the time we can reunite."

Gedrok shook, not with anger or fear, but with relief. The kind of anxious relief that breaks you, that shatters all bulwarks and walls and makes one instantly vulnerable.

"You still," he whispered, just loud enough for Dziove to hear over the dying battle and the murmurings of their guards. "You still love me."

Not a question, but not a statement, either. A hopeful whisper.

"Always," Dziove said, and slipped from inside his cuirass a red cord, as if he had planned this, or hoped for this moment. He bound their hands together and whispered a prayer, and when he reached again into his cuirass and pulled out a cajudsan blossom he began to chew. Then he leaned and put the other against Gedrok's lips, like a kiss, like a farewell.

And both chewed until they slipped into oblivion.

Or into the astrok-mer.

Radek sat up, heart pounding; he was in his own body again. He stumbled away from the death, leaving behind both the battle and twilight of two rulers, unable or unwilling to fully comprehend what he was seeing.

Then he spun back to the body of Izra dead on the ground. This wasn't his Izra. Radek needed to find him.

He squeezed his eyes shut and raised his deck high. "Show yourself!"

He drew a card stamped with a forest scene. A thick

wooden pole erupted from the fog of pine trees painted in the card's background, a pole with multiple carved heads. Izra's god. Suoduny's eyes were closed.

And in silver accented letters, the card declared itself to be FATE'S EDICT.

Radek stared a little longer at the closed-eye god, nervous and approaching angry. Then he said, "You've kept Izra long enough. I'm taking him back. Now."

The eyes in the card snapped open, so alarmingly they strained in their sockets.

Without warning, a force dragged Radek forward. The card expanded rapidly, unfolding map-like in the way it tumbled open, and dropped unceremoniously in a forest not dissimilar to the one his body lay in. Izra sat propped up against Suoduny's idol, and when Radek looked up at the carved heads, all their eyes were human. He could see the jelly whites of their eyes luminescent with light that wasn't there. And they followed him, straining, struck through with bursting capillaries, as he dropped by Izra's side.

Radek hesitated, then shook Izra. He expected sweat, the same fever burning through his flesh outside the astrokmer. But he felt cold. Not just cold—freezing, as if left out in the snow. Radek couldn't quite feel his clothes, as if the texture were somehow foggy, but he felt the cold. And that couldn't be good.

He shook again and Izra stirred with a mutter.

Radek jolted, glad, and said, "You have to come back with me."

"But I have not found the right future," Izra whispered. "It keeps leading me to the same one. The wrong one. And it cannot possibly be right."

"Izra," Radek said, desperate. "You must come back. Please. We will—figure it out. The two of us. Just wake up."

"Wicjezst," Izra said, in wonderment. What was that? A place? Radek had no time to ask, because Izra looked at him suddenly. "All this has happened before. To the other us."

Radek thought of the war, of Dziove and Gedrok Ach Meedin dying, at the hope that they could try again. He leaned close to Izra. "That doesn't mean it has to happen again."

He rummaged through the cards, fingers running, until they pulled free from the deck that first card. ULTIMATE DESTRUCTION. The pinnacle of demise. Death without meaning. It would not happen again.

Radek reached for the card and reversed it.

The astrok-mer spit him out.

CHAPTER SIXTEEN

Izra was in the palace at Doskor, though every time he tried to leave, he would be guided hastily back to the throne room where the empty marble seat sat taunting him. He had no concept of how long he had been doing this; staring at the throne, turning on his heel, opening another door only to find it led straight back here.

It frightened him because it felt like blasphemy. As if Suoduny were urging him to sit in it—which was treason, and upsetting, and something he absolutely would not do.

This was no fantasy of his. This was closer to a nightmare. The True Commander would wake and would reclaim his throne. There was no future, in Izra's mind, that would ever lead him here.

So he traversed the maze of the castle, whipping open doors, turning in circles for many hours. Eventually, he came to a window. Izra tried to stare out of it, but the sun glare was too intense. A silhouetted figure stood in the distance, his fated man in a corona of light, only he was not walking away from Izra.

Oren Radek stalked toward him.

As soon as that thought crystallized, the window threw itself roughly open, and Oren's voice carried up in a shout. "You have to come back with me."

Izra turned back from the window to find he was once again in the throne room. No. This was not right, and he told Oren just as much.

Oren pleaded with him. "We will—figure it out. The two of us. Just wake up."

And behind Oren, the scene resolved into a snowscape, a rural mountain town, and an insurmountable gate locked tight by magic. Izra's heart twisted. He had seen those gates before, seen the town. It was Wicjezst. He had been there once before, under the orders of the High Priestess Neala. He had committed a crime then—to try and bring the True Commander back from the astrok-mer. Was he to return there? Was he to face his crimes?

"Wicjezst. All of this has happened before," Izra whispered, terrified by the implication.

"That doesn't mean it has to happen again," Oren said, and then the whole room tilted.

Oren disappeared, and Izra was on the ceiling, clutching the window frame to keep himself from dropping. But this was childish, now. Suoduny was telling him what to do in no uncertain terms.

There was nothing left to do but drop.

Izra let go, and the room righted itself. He dropped slowly to the ground and climbed the steps of the throne. He ran his fingers over the cold marble, felt the smooth hardness of the seat. He shook, his body hating every moment, anxious with blasphemy. Izra Dziove lowered himself onto the throne with his heart in his mouth, and waited for punishment; for Suoduny to curse him for the wickedness of his overreach.

Instead, he heard his name booming around the throne room, an invisible crowd cheering, a circlet heavy with the burden of a nation coming down on his shoulders.

"Emperor Izra Dziove," he heard.

Izra gasped awake.

Pain bloomed along his ribs, an ache of neglect and inactivity. The same discomfort curled over his hips and burrowed close to his spine. Every part of his body felt stiff. With his soul floating in the astrok-mer, he had not even twitched in his sleep, and the disuse made him ache. He gasped for air. His lungs creaked as they inflated, and the air scorched his insides. It felt like the first time he had ever breathed.

"Gods." Odrica came to him and smoothed the hair away from his forehead. He felt it stick, his skin slick with sweat. "Chy, brother, you took your time."

"Sister—"

"Izra." Oren stood beside him. "What did you see?"

He was dressed like a Rezwyn, in a heavy overcoat meant for the cold, a deep red embroidered in silver and trimmed with brown fur. His beard was longer than it had been. Two silver beads tied off the ends of his mustache. He had slicked his hair back behind his ears and wore a thin line of kohl beneath each eye.

Izra frowned, not comprehending.

A fire crackled beside him, the heat making the air dry and his skin warm. No tent arced above him, but a flat daub roof. And he lay on a bed, not prone on the ground.

The strong sense of Suoduny he had in the temple was absent, too.

He had been moved.

The room lacked much decoration. It took Izra a moment to process that it was not a room at an inn. The open doorway behind Odrica revealed a massive wooden structure, filled with rows and rows of fabrics. Nearest to the room were rolls of it, or treated specialty pieces, and on the opposite side he could just make out stairs leading to a lower level.

"Where—"

"Ostijan. Or, more specifically, my warehouse in Ostijan. Fine Uslethian textiles! You won't find better." Oren said hurriedly. He clutched a bowl in his hands, which he put down on the bedside table. Kew and Mirakel were there too, both standing with folded arms on either side of a window. Izra squinted then, because side by side they were near comical in their differences. Kew was tall, lanky, pale, his red hair growing long over his eyes. Mirakel was short with tawny skin. She had managed to keep her hair short, though it was cut haphazardly as if she had gone at it herself with a knife. Kew's relief was not quite palpable, but grudging; he held himself rigidly. Only his eyes told Izra a different story.

The cream curtains were drawn tight. They were safe, the lot of them.

But Ostijan? Ostijan was to the east and a port—a port a merchant like Oren would have visited often. Still, the distance made no sense.

"How could we be?" Izra said, coughing. He pushed himself onto his elbows. "It would take days—gods, nearly a week—"

"It did take a week," his sister said.

Izra frowned and turned to Kew. "What do you mean?"

But it was Oren who answered. His husband patted his head with a warm cloth, clearing his forehead of sweat. "Izra, you've been out for days."

Izra tried to keep calm. A week in the astrok-mer—it was nothing short of divine intervention that he had made it back into this flesh. And whole, too.

Izra shook his head. "You were there, too," he clarified, and Oren nodded. "You made it out without me?" Izra was desperately surprised, and relieved, that Oren was standing and functional, and not missing half his soul in the astrok-mer.

Oren shrugged nonchalantly, as if it was an easy thing to do and not a holy miracle. Izra wanted to press him on it—how had he managed it?—but in the end, what did it matter? All Izra could feel was relief, the calm unfurling of every tightly wound muscle in him. Oren was alive. Oren had made it out.

And Oren had been Izra's guide, too.

"You were my only anchor," he murmured in thanks. "But—we left the temple?" Then, because he could think of no other reason that would make them leave, he said, "Were we betrayed?"

"No. We made the decision." Odrica leaned down to kiss Izra on his forehead. As she pulled away, she murmured to him in Doskorian. "Your man did something very stupid, brother. He went after you. He downed the cajudsan and walked with Suoduny to find you. You told us where to go. Wicjezst." Izra said nothing, only stared. His sister nodded at his expression. "He is brave when he wants to be—and equal parts stupid."

He lay there for a small eternity processing this stupidity. Then his eyes shifted to Oren, his beautiful, stupid man, and rage became dismay. "Selvik allowed this?"

"Of course not," Oren said. He did not say it softly, or particularly kindly, but there was a matter-of-factness to it. "But I was faster than him and he couldn't stop me. In situations like this I've always thought it's better to apologize than ask for permission."

"You are impossible, in too many ways. If you had died, I would have—I would have—" Oren clearly did not comprehend the sheer impossibility of it. He could not understand how close he had come to death—and all for Izra.

Oren stared at him, poised with his warm cloth but otherwise unmoving.

Mirakel pushed off from the window. "Floppy, unconscious dead-weights forfeit their right to complain. We had to drag your body here. Know how much it costs for a cart that can fit your massive body in it? More than I wanted to spend! Not to mention that I had to put up with this anxious wreck the entire time." Here she jabbed an accusatory thumb at Oren. "So perhaps a thank you is in order. The priest, whose opinion you seem to care so much about, was fairly convinced you would have drowned in there without this one to anchor you."

Izra recalled Oren calling for him from the window. Like the cord they had bound each other with, a mark of communion—Oren was already proving his devotion. Izra bit his tongue.

There was much unsaid, and perhaps too much to say.

Odrica shot Mirakel a dark look when she muttered something Izra missed. Her face had been cleaned, scrubbed of the oznak velraj she wore daily—her war paint. He rubbed his eyes and they came away clean of kohl, too. All of them were waiting for him to get up.

He held his head and swung his legs over the side of the bed. Oren leaned away to give him space, and for a moment their shoulders touched. Izra caught Oren's eye, and realized his own chest lay bare. Oren's eyes drifted, and after a gratuitous glance downward, he glanced away.

"Should I ask who has been washing me?" Izra murmured. Oren swung back to him immediately. The man tensed, damp cloth in hand, but otherwise kept his face blank.

"Same man who's been pressing sugar water to your lips, so your body doesn't die," Oren muttered. "Though I could have easily let you sweat, or wither to a husk. Either option would have made this place foul to be in, though." He stood suddenly and dumped the cloth back in its basin.

"Thank you," Izra said. Oren folded his arms and nodded. The moment stretched between them, eaten at by an uncomfortable silence and three sets of eyes staring at them.

Odrica muttered something—chy, Izra thought—and shook him by the shoulder. "Are you hungry, brother?"

"I—" Izra started. Then hunger hit him like a well-aimed blow, and with it everything he had gleaned in the astrok-mer. A chill went through him; the chill of snow and wind from the mountaintops. He tried to stand. The shock of verticality after being prone for so long wormed itself into his head making him dizzy and ill. Izra groaned and sat back down, blinking away white spots.

Odrica's voice strained. "Brother—"

Izra raised a hand to stop her. "Leave me," he murmured in Doskorian. She hesitated, lips pursing in disapproval. She always worried for him, underneath it all; the bearish look to her, the stern way she carried herself. Odrica Dziove was full of passion and life, and gods, he loved her. But right now, he needed to be alone—as alone as he could be with the man he was bound to. Izra grabbed his sister's hand and squeezed it, nodding ever so slightly to Oren next to him. "Leave us, please. I have to speak to my husband."

He thought he saw a brief flicker of shock cross her face; not a feeling of betrayal but surprise. But whatever her feelings, his sister quickly smothered them, locking them beneath the façade she usually reserved for cizalecs. She peeled her hand away and nodded stiffly.

"Ocinje," she ordered Kew, who seemed dismayed to learn Izra's request referred to him, too. He jerked back as if he had been struck, unfurling his arms and standing tall over Izra's sitting form, full of outrage.

"You are sending me away?" he whispered.

"Never," he said. The look on Kew's face made his heart twist. "Only for a moment. I need—"

"You have been gone a week and you want him?"

Izra pressed his lips firmly together. He had much to say to that; much to interpret in Kew's jealousy. Odrica gave Izra no chance to reprimand him. She hooked an arm around his neck, whispered something low and guttural in his ear, and gave him a hefty shove toward the door.

Odrica half turned towards Mirakel and nodded her way. "You as well, lady."

Mirakel scoffed, shoving off the wall with a bitter kick. "You should know by now I'm not a lady," she seethed. That one was hard to read, Izra thought, and even harder to keep track of; though Odrica fixed the skulking form with a small smile.

Oren gestured for Odrica's attention. "Meet us downstairs. Don't go far." He said it almost like a command. Brave of him—or stupid; Izra tilted his head toward his sister, expecting some incensed refusal. She never took orders.

But something had changed in these last few days. Oren's energy felt different. More secure, more confident; like all of them were playing by his rules, now. Still, there was none of the smug overconfidence that sometimes accompanied authority. Oren was gentle and caring. Odrica seemed to know it too. She nodded at him, and the door clicked shut behind her.

They said nothing.

Oren moved to the center of the room and wrapped his arms around himself. The Rezwyn style suited him. Izra knew it to be a disguise, an attempt to covertly exist beyond the prying empire eyes. But he looked good—achingly good.

Izra swallowed and glanced away. "You look beautiful dressed in our colors."

Oren jolted. He did not meet Izra's eye.

The silence hurt. Watching him made Izra's heart as heavy as the world and as full as its oceans.

Eventually Oren moved to the window. He gently peered beyond the curtains. "You're not hungry?"

Izra laughed. "I am starving. And I have much to tell you. But first I—"

"No," Oren said.

Izra blinked. "What?"

"No, actually. I will speak first." Oren turned away. His sharp expression bore into Izra. "Because I have spent the last week watching over you, unsure if you'd be lost forever, like some empty living corpse, and I—"

"Oren."

"Don't you speak over me," he snapped. Then he fell quiet and sat down on the bed. He looked away. Izra could have filled the silence; was eager to, burning to do it. But Oren had claimed this moment. "I thought you were gone."

"I heard you calling out to me," Izra whispered. "And I saw you. You came to me, in the ether."

Oren inspected his hands. He kept gnawing at his lip. It looked like he was at war with himself; Izra noted the anxious tap of his foot, the flush of his cheeks.

"Yes," Oren said eventually. "I was right there with you. You kept saying you were trapped. I . . . hallucinated. Or had a vision."

Izra perked up at this, but Oren kept talking.

"You know, I find you very confusing. And terrifying, honestly. I don't understand your religion. I am scared of fate and destiny and everything you think of as natural. I watched for a week and every day I thought it'd be the end. That you'd end up like the emperor. I was worried. And I thought it was because you are a good man. That you are kind, that you're fighting against something bigger than yourself, at the risk of your name and your life. But it is more than that. It's just . . . you."

Cautiously, testing the waters, Izra put out his hands. "Do you not feel it?" he asked again. This time, Oren's face crumpled. Izra thought he might be crying.

In a hushed whisper, Oren said, "I believe you. I don't know how to reconcile it. I saw . . . something. I think, long ago, you and I—a different you and I—knew one another."

When Oren next met Izra's gaze, his eyes were wide. Then he exhaled and all the nervousness in him vanished. He reached out and grabbed Izra's hand. He looked so serious, so ridiculously serious for a man before his husband, that Izra started to smile. They squeezed each other's hands, and just that little bit of intimacy made Izra's heart pound.

Izra took his chin between his fingers. Oren stilled. Izra drew him close enough that he felt Oren's heavy, warm exhale against his lips in the moment before they kissed.

That instant felt perfect: fate and fortune and desire colliding in their kiss.

Izra only pulled away to whisper, "I missed you, Oren Radek," and Oren answered by crashing his lips against Izra's once more. Oren unwound; every tightly coiled part of him laced itself over Izra's body. And then it did not end. Izra slid his hand down Oren's back, cradling the shallow divot of his hips.

They tumbled back into the mattress. He could feel years of practice in these kisses, these touches. The bed creaked under their combined weight, and they shuffled awkwardly through breathless bouts of laughter until Izra's head hit a pillow. His hunger vanished. Panting, Izra ran a fond hand up Oren's thigh. Then he grabbed the fabric of his tunic and dragged him back down. Oren kissed him again, and only kissed him, like someone nervous and demure. Izra would have believed it, if not for the hungry look in his eye and the firmness of him against Izra's leg.

Izra pulled away, breathing against Oren's lips.

"You said you had a vision," Izra said, voice curling around that word. Vision. Too long it had been something spoken about him, or on the rare occasion his sister. To hear that his fated man had experienced something close to what he had, made Izra feel seen.

Oren hesitated. He raised his hand and slowly settled it against Izra's cheek.

"You know, I have spent so long thinking I was—undesirable. Not bodily," he clarified quickly when Izra opened his mouth, "but fundamentally. I have fought for everything I have ever had. This title, this business. My place in the world. And it's been upended by your god, Izra."

Oren told him. He said the name Gedrok Ach Meedin, but Izra did not quite grasp the implication. Though there had been a week to ruminate on this, Oren spoke cautiously, keeping the details sparse as he told Izra he had seen two souls in the astrok-mer, two lives that were somehow connected to him. Even if Izra did not quite comprehend it, he knew about faith, and if it meant Oren understood their fated nature more easily, who was Izra to question it?

Izra pushed back the hair from Oren's face, finger skimming along his cheek so he could roll the bead in his beard through finger and thumb.

Izra said, "Thank you for telling me. I know the arcane confounds you. Scares you. I know you hate it. But if Suoduny had a hand in your life, it was only to guide you to me. Everything you did, you did yourself."

Oren glanced away and sighed softly. Izra could not end it there. He said, "I cannot have you thinking I only want you because fate made it so."

Oren took this with a small smile and nothing else, so Izra kept speaking.

"Listen. A soul is not. . .You do not have to share their life, if you do not wish it. You do not have to like me. And if you decide you do not want me, then I will not hold you to it."

But Oren's eyes only softened, and he kissed Izra's lips.

Izra wanted to feel Oren's hot skin, to be done with all this carefulness and tiptoeing—he had wanted Oren Radek for years, had dreamed of this for years, and no other man had ever been enough. All the pain and the discomfort of his immobility dissipated, wiped from his mind by the heat and desire flooding his lower belly.

"Take it off," he whispered.

Oren made a shaky, hopeful noise. "Are you—"

"Take it off," Izra growled, more a command than a request.

Oren threw off the long coat and ripped his tunic over his head. The instant Izra saw Oren's naked his chest, he flipped him, pinned him down by the wrists. He leaned forward, brushing his lips against Oren's ear, and said, "I am going to ravish you, Oren Radek."

Oren spread his legs—

—and the door burst open.

Oren yelped. Every muscle in Izra's back tensed, fighting to keep still. He rolled his eyes and fought to keep a guttural moan of frustration caged before he glanced over his shoulder.

Kew stood there, stupid, wide grin splitting across his face. "So not celibate then, eh?"

"No," Izra murmured.

Kew cocked his head and peered around him. "Pants still on, though. So, you have not consummated—"

"If you leave," Izra said, irritated, "I just might have a chance to."

"I cannot do that."

Izra swung half off Oren to fix Kew with a scathing glare. What sort of friend—no, what kind of man would wedge himself between Izra and his husband?

Kew's eyes dropped low, quickly darting off Izra's obvious arousal.

Good, he thought. Let him feel shame. Perhaps then he would leave them alone.

"Izra," Oren said beneath him through gritted teeth. "What's happening? You need to bloody translate."

Izra turned back, gripping the headboard for stability, and whispered to him in Uslethian. "Just a moment. I am sorry—very sorry." With one hand on the headboard, Izra swung back to Kew and pulled his chain of office taut with his thumb. Kew's eyes dropped to the heavy chain and exhaled heavily as Izra said, "See this? Recall what it means? Commander of the Uxbuh, strix to the emperor—and I am ordering you to please, please, leave us alone."

Kew blinked at him, mouth agape. "Are you really pulling rank to have sex?"

Izra frowned and let the chain drop against his chest. "Yes."

"Admirable," Kew said with a laugh, but he still did not bow nor back out of the room. Instead he cleared his throat and had the decency to look apologetic as he whispered, "There are priests here."

Izra nearly snapped the headboard in half. He clenched his teeth and swung back to Kew. "There are priests everywhere."

"Neala's operatives," Kew said hurriedly. "Priests with Doskor's mark." Then, when Izra said nothing, Kew added, "Your sister thought it best we retrieve you."

Izra let out a heavy, disappointed sigh. "Go," he ordered Kew. "I will be ready shortly."

Kew shut the door and Izra crumpled hopelessly against Oren's chest. Fingers ran through his hair, and Oren's heart rate began to slow. Izra could still feel Oren's arousal firm beneath him.

"I'm guessing we have to postpone this," Oren whispered.

Izra said nothing, letting a whiny noise of complaint speak for him. It earned a snort out of Oren.

"It's probably for the best," Oren said. "You haven't eaten anything solid in a week. A bit of meat, a bit of wine, and you'll be back in fighting form."

Izra raised his head to meet Oren's heavy-lidded gaze. "Is that how you like it?"

Oren's heavy-lidded stare met his. There was weight behind it, a lustful depth. "Very much so."

Izra bit back another grin. He peeled himself off Oren's chest and ran a hand over his face. "Well, you will not like this," he said, as he told Oren of Kew's message.

Oren looked alarmed, frustrated. His hand clenched in a fist. "They're not here just for us. We just got here. They are following Neala's plan: she did as she said she would, and sent priests to every settlement." And then, "But there has been talk about Westgar."

"What about Westgar?" Izra said as he rose from the bed. Standing hurt, made him dizzy. Perhaps Oren was right—food and drink would do him good.

"Agitation on the border," Oren whispered.

They stared at each other. Izra sighed. He pushed out of the room—an office, perhaps—and found a little table right outside with cold cuts and cheese. He managed to point at it and waited for the first motion of Oren's assent before he dug in. Gods, he was hungry. Nausea gave way to ravenous hunger. He sat down at the stool and Oren took the other, and was very polite about the way Izra stuffed himself. "Your letter to the king?" Izra asked, licking his fingers.

Oren sighed. "Perhaps? As far as we know, a small group of Paladins have arrived in Westgar. I think if Ostijan and Elkar decide to make a bid for independence . . ."

"Usleth will support them." An outright act of war. Neala would not stand it. It might even be enough to sway General Neve. "What did you tell him?"

"About Paqe," Oren whispered. Then, "I had to."

"I know. But we have to move fast. Allying with the True Commander and reviving the relationship between our nations is our only hope," Izra said, looking back at his husband. He could not blame him, but nor could he justify lingering here; not with priests searching, or Usleth growing agitated.

Oren sat straighter, running a hand through his beautiful hair. He rested his chin against his knee. "You mumbled Wicjezst in the astrok-mer. But Odrica called it a shipping village, and Kew got agitated about it. Didn't want to go there without your explicit say-so. Hence," he gestured around his warehouse. "We've been sitting here."

"No, you were right. That's where the vision showed me." He tried not to sound so guilty, but Wicjezst was synonymous with Izra's great failure. He thanked Kew silently—nothing would have shaken him like waking up in that frigid village. Izra needed to be conscious for that journey. "It is north from this port. I was thinking we might call on your contact."

Oren's expression twisted. "What?"

Oren had given Hapina enough coin for a trip to Usleth. She had even offered to get them further inland, if they needed. And now that they had arrived at Ostijan by land, Hapina would not be caught ferrying fugitives through the blockade. Besides, Izra needed someone he could trust—or at least, trust more than a stranger.

Izra reached out and grabbed his hand. "Do you have Hapina's lock of hair?"

Oren blinked at him and stood, rummaging through Izra's discarded tunic. He turned back with it in his hands and gingerly handed it over. "What will you do?"

Izra showed him. He scooped ash from the fireplace and knelt on the ground, arranging the hair in a messy script until it read, as best it could: Come to Ostijan. Then he let Suoduny take over. It was an easy spell, usually so simple he could blink and be done with it. But power felt hard to grasp now, as if behind a fog. It took a long time before the hair began to burn, but then it burnt the wood. Somewhere in Kiriz, Hapina had received the same message.

It scorched the wood; in Kiriz, Hapina's second lock of hair burned with the same message. On average, it would take a day from Kiriz to Ostijan, including the time from the river to the ocean. But there was no telling how quick Hapina would be—if she complied with his request at all. In the meantime, Izra would have to keep them all out of trouble.

They dressed. Oren helped him into a new set of trousers, and a tunic. Izra tried to keep his face impassive, willed the blood away from his cheeks as Oren's fingers brushed his lower back. Oren explained the types of materials he had in this warehouse. Silk, cotton, and an Uslethian material called oknum. Black was inconspicuous in Doskor, and in the dead of night; but Ostijan, being a port town and closer to the border, had embraced Uslethian culture more wholly than most of the empire. Black was glaringly Rezwyn, here, not color.

So Oren had dressed Izra in green.

"I look hideous," Izra seethed, standing in front of the room's mirror.

"Nonsense," Oren said. He patted down Izra's shoulders, grinning at him from behind his back. "Not in my fabrics, not ever."

There was something changed about him. He seemed more the man Izra had hoped him to be; more soft, more open, and Izra hated himself for thinking that way. Before they were pulled into the chaos outside, "Even if we consummate our marriage—"

"Sorry, our what?"

"Our marriage."

"Marriage?" Oren stared at him blankly. Then he rocked forward in awkward revelation, shoulders deflating. "Oh," he said. "Oh!"

He stared at Izra. He said nothing else. He flushed to the tips of his ears.

Izra nearly bit his tongue off staring at him. He could die in that moment and be grateful for it. "You did not mean to marry me."

"I meant to—well, I meant something like that, I suppose, looking back. Your sister probably thought I meant—"

"So she did put you up to it." Izra turned dizzily, fingers pressed to his mouth. This was too much after waking. "I'm so sorry."

Oren grabbed him by the arm. "You're acting like I said I wanted to end it."

"You want to—try?" Izra said, stilted. He looked at Oren—really tried to look at him, because there was this great, gnawing fear in him that Oren Radek was just too kind to say no. That the insanity of marrying Izra so quickly would catch up to him. Izra tensed himself, growing nauseous with his worry.

Oren said nothing with his words. Instead he stepped forward and, on the tips of his toes, kissed him.

"At the very least, I want to try you once," Oren said.

Then he was out the door.

CHAPTER SEVENTEEN

Kew had not gone far, which surprised Izra; Kew usually wandered, and Izra would have leashed him if he could. When he spotted Izra, Kew gave an insubordinate waggle of his eyebrows that made Izra furious, until he recalled exactly why Kew had interrupted them. Then his second turned and conspicuously pressed his face against the glass.

"Like fucking ants," Kew grunted, waving a finger at the window. "Crawling all over for a meal."

Izra clapped him on the shoulder and peered over it, resting his chin against his friend's sturdy muscle. The outside chill and Kew's breath had fogged the glass. Firelamps strung along the docks glowed softly and split the night gloom, showing Izra the undulating black void of the sea. An open square sat to the right of the warehouse, lit by lanterns. Izra pressed further along the windows until he had a better view of it—and jolted to a stop.

Cloaks fluttered below. In the dark, they had turned the color of blood—but they were priests of Borviet, two of them, passing a pipe between themselves. A priest of Zimsmrt stood there too, in the stark white of winter and mortality. But that was all he could see—only three. This must have been no focused search, just scouts. Neala truly had scattered her priests across the empire.

Kew knocked his head against the glass and sighed. "What do you think? Why is she making her move so blatantly? Has the True Commander passed on?"

A vicious fire ensconced Izra's heart, then, with a growl that rumbled in his throat. "No. No, of course not."

The Borviet priests finished their pipe and crossed the square to, thankfully, some other building. A misted rain had started, hazing the light from the lanterns strung between the buildings. Izra ground his teeth as he watched them.

"I should not have said that," Kew whispered.

"Now it's planted in my mind," Izra agreed. He pushed off from Kew's shoulder and whirled around, where he found Oren staring at him. To have come so close to a paradise with this man, and minutes later be reminded of his own simple mortality, Izra could cry. He wanted to go back to the room. He wanted to have Oren beneath him. Izra pressed two fingers against a blossoming tension in his forehead.

"Come on, you green giant," Kew said. He put a hand on Izra's shoulder. "Let's sit and eat and not dwell on this."

The tavern Kew brought them to had three levels. A set of rooms sat at the very top, then a landing with a scattered mismatch of tables, stools, and benches, in assorted colors and styles. Dried herbs and flowers bound with twine hung from the rafters. A woven carpet in red and cream wool covered the floor, and pendulous lamps made with colored glass shipped from the empire's north, hung on long chains from the ceiling.

Ostijan was an interesting city. Whereas Doskor could be said to be representative of the empire's ideals, and Kiriz a direct rejection of them, Ostijan was a melting pot; an empire city with a uniquely Uslethian flair to it. It had belonged to old Usleth, once, as most of the Western empire had, but a century on from its annexation and it had become something more altogether. It did not quite fit Usleth anymore, but neither was it wholly empire. The port city had become an amalgam of both their cultures—and this inn had attempted to embrace Usleth.

There was music, too; a guttural throat singing, accompanied by a drum and some round-bellied string instrument he assumed was imported. A set of shrines to the gods filled the far-left wall, cavities in the stone packed with candles and offerings.

The sheer overabundance was a shrieking ode to Usleth, but the presence of the gods still relieved Izra.

Izra's gut churned. There were so many people, loud and rowdy—which he hoped would give them cover if those priests wandered in—but he worried his sister had planted herself on the lower floor. Neither himself nor his sister were particularly unmemorable, even dressed so casually. But this was probably doing her a disservice. Odrica did not have the same military training Izra did, but she grew up in wartime, and even without the experience of a soldier, she knew the necessity of blending into crowds. If those priests came in, they would deal with it.

Odrica was not on the ground floor, which relieved him somewhat. Oren led the way with confidence, which made Izra wary only in that it suggested the lot of them had been doing a fair amount of drinking without him. The second level was more dimly lit—good—with only a few hanging lamps and a single hearth along the back wall, and packed full of customers.

Odrica and Mirakel were at a table very close to the fire. He spotted his sister easily. She had a presence about her, even stripped out of her leathers and armor. They had changed, apparently, because now Odrica wore—a skirt, he realized, which made him nearly keel over and fall like a stone. Oren must have dressed her, and Mirakel too. Odrica wore a long, wide-pleated skirt, covered in a cross-hatched red pattern. A broad belt encompassed her waist, and the rest of her bulk had been buttoned into a high-necked black shirt she had rolled up to the elbows, exposing the thick muscle of her forearms. To Izra, this only made her stand out more. Odrica did not dress like this. But she wore it like she had never worn anything else. Mirakel wore a blue and yellow dress with a red shawl across her shoulders. She had the shawl gripped so tightly in her hand that her fawn skin was turning a sickly pale white.

"I outfitted them with the latest fashions," Oren said beside him. "Though convincing them of it was like gnawing at my own arm."

Izra clicked his tongue. "Your charm is otherworldly, Oren Radek, if you have managed to dress my sister as such."

"I do hope my charm is otherworldly enough for other things, too," Oren gave him a wink and slapped him on the back, hand lingering softly in the following moment, which drove Izra almost instantly mad. "Shall we?"

Izra clenched his teeth as he went to the table. The floor boomed with laughter and cheers and discordant singing; a chorus of empire accents, from Veprak, and Myrtrana, and Doskor—which stilled him, until some sense kicked in and he registered these men were soldiers. Or had been. He chanced a look over his shoulder as he sat: there were perhaps fifteen of them, most of them the burly and stocky types that had filled Doskor's vanguard army. Izra ducked his head as he looked and realized with horror that several of those men had served under him.

Odrica flagged down a server as they approached, and ordered three more of whatever she was having.

"The priests have not come inside yet," Odrica said, head tipping towards the door.

"Good," Izra mumbled, turning back around. "But Suoduny is punishing me for something, sister, because those men behind us once called me 'Commander.'"

Everyone stared at him. Kew cursed his own obliviousness and quietly gestured to Mirakel to swap seats, so his back would also be turned.

Oren did the one thing you are not meant to do when attempting to remain inconspicuous, and turned around almost fully to stare at the soldiers. Izra whipped out his hand to grab the back of Oren's head, as if to redirect his husband's gaze.

"Very silly, turning around like that," Izra said.

"They're partying," Oren murmured. "They are in Ostijan. No one with a pious stick up their arse would party in Ostijan. No offense."

Izra frowned. He was certainly pious, but the other part? "I do not have a stick up my arse."

Mirakel, voice muffled in her drinking cup, said, "Not yet."

"Enough," Odrica mumbled, reaching for her ale. "It's true, brother. You likely pissed off your god. But no one has seen you yet. Do not cause a commotion."

Izra shrugged like he was done with this, though he very much was not. There was a basket of steaming bread in front of him. He grabbed a handful and ate without manners, too hungry to feel shame. "If it is not the priests, it will be one of these men who recognizes me." He paused to breathe and chew, ravenous, before his concern and paranoia resurfaced. "We should not have left the warehouse. Perhaps we should not stay in this place at all."

"Look at you, you are starving," Odrica snorted. "We will go soon, once you eat. Now, before these priests inevitably ruin our night, tell us what happened in the astrok-mer."

The server came and placed fat jugs of Uslethian ale on their table. Izra scrunched his nose as he drank it. Weak, paltry thing. He sculled it anyway.

"Give me the rundown, first," he said. "What's changed? I know of some movement in Westgar, but what about the empire?"

Odrica shifted, uncrossing her legs and arms to get closer to him. "No news on the True Commander. But it is clear the priestess's focus is on the east. She worries about Usleth; there have been rumors that she has recalled many priests scattered about the empire to Doskor, before sending them out again."

"With a new objective," Izra said. "She's talking about stamping out any dilution of the Rezwyn ethos . . . and burning those cities free of foreign influence."

Odrica made a face. "There was some commotion in Kiriz. A priest was killed—another one, not the one you dealt with."

Izra swore. Hapina might be stuck there, unable to come to them.

Odrica continued, "Other reports of general resistance to the west, though those are few. A lot of these rumors have apparently come from apostates. They have refused Neala's orders, and in turn she has stripped them of their titles."

Izra hated this. At this rate, there would be no stopping a civil war.

Neala's methods to take control deeply unnerved Izra. Of course, she had been brazen before, but this? He rocked forward against his hands and started drinking from Oren's flagon, as if this watery ale would be enough.

Izra could not voice that fear aloud so instead he said, "Suoduny showed me the mountains at Wicjezst. There is something there. A Uslethian god. An exanimate body."

Oren jolted. "What?"

"The gods who are natural to your country," Odrica said, not comprehending the significance. "The palace at Cres Stros was built around one. Though I did not. . ." She was unnaturally scared as she said it. She had not known of this one's existence. Guilt burned in Izra's throat.

"A gedrok? Here?" Oren hissed. He looked like he was ready to faint. He hunched forward as if to huffing the fumes of his drink. "Oh, for—"

"Fuck's sake." Mirakel finished for him. She downed her ale and accosted a wandering server for another. "I fucking hate the arcane."

"How did it get here?" Oren pressed. He looked vaguely ill. "That is—gedroks are rare and precious. The king wishes . . . to safeguard them all."

"One of them must have fallen into its eternal rest beyond your border," Izra said. "In any case, Suoduny has shown me it as the way forward."

Oren's chair creaked as he moved. "Really?" He looked pallid. "You're certain?"

"Izra," Kew prompted. "You must translate for me."

"A moment," he said, trying to keep the obvious desperation from his words.

Thankfully Mirakel spoke over Kew's next plea.

"What could a creature from Usleth have to do with any of this?"

Before Izra could say anything, Oren leaned forward and added, flustered, "Their power is volatile. We have seen the effects of it. What were you thinking? Why would we go there? I—" he abruptly cut himself off.

"Are you alright?" Izra whispered.

"Yes. No. I—" Radek touched his forehead. "I just worry. That it's a bad idea."

"To follow Suoduny?" Izra clarified. He had thought something had shifted with Oren in the astrok-mer but braced himself for the old skepticism.

Instead, Oren let out a deep breath. "No. No, that's not what I meant," he mumbled into his ale. Then he drank and did not elaborate.

The table fell silent. Izra could feel Kew's gaze boring into his skull.

Izra stood rapidly and beckoned for Kew to follow him. Nodding to Odrica he said, "Think on what we will need in the mountains. We will gather it tomorrow before we leave."

He dragged Kew closer to the wall, where a few shrine nooks sat, like proximity to the gods would save him. He made them both turn to them as if they were praying.

"You aren't telling me something." Anger tinged Kew's voice. "I am completely unserious, Izra, until it comes to this: my friend not telling me something he will share with cizalecs."

"Kew," Izra tried to reach out, but the other man moved away from his touch. Izra sighed. "I am telling you more than I am telling them."

"You would tell me more than you would tell your husband?" Kew's eyes narrowed. Defensively, his shoulders crept up closer to his ears once more. "What did you see?"

And what could be said to that? Izra wished to smash his head against the wall. Instead, he rubbed his face. "Suoduny showed me the throne."

Through the gaps between his fingers, Izra watched Kew turn red. "What do you mean?"

"You know what I mean," Izra whispered, as if his speaking softer could mollify the truth. "I saw myself on the throne."

"Shut your mouth," Kew snapped. His hands shot out, twisting in Izra's tunic. He flinched at the loudness in Kew's voice, and the man quickly adjusted his volume, but not his vitriol. "That's treason. How can you stand there and speak those words?"

The accusation—that this was his fault, that he had abused his position to essentially poison the True Commander—hurt Izra as truly as a direct blow.

"I," Izra said, "did not know. Suoduny—"

"Neither you nor your god is innocent." As soon as he had spoken, Kew slammed his mouth shut. He covered his lips with his hand. Izra thought it must be shame. Speaking of the gods out of turn like that . . . but then Kew looked up with wide, horrified eyes.

"Was taking the throne your goal all along?" he murmured.

Izra's stomach dropped. A great heavy shock—Kew really thought him capabale of becoming a traitor. But his stupor did not last. Anger, as bright and hot as the fire sparking in his belly, burned in his throat. Who was Kew to speak to him like this? Him, Izra Dziove, strix and trusted man of the True Commander, blessed by the gods? He grabbed Kew by the chin. "You cannot possibly think I—"

There was a sound of surprise downstairs. Izra turned. He saw a flash of white, the sweeping drift of a robe. Zimsmrt's priest stood mere feet from them, flanked by two priests of Borviet.

The sounds of the bar continued, too boisterous to be felled by the commonplace sight of priests, but a few at the door who had a view of their backs—and the arched symbol of Doskor—began to fall quiet.

Izra swore and dragged Kew further away.

"You must trust me," he hissed to Kew. "Please."

Kew scanned his face, eyes wider and more questioning than Izra wanted them to be. Kew's faith in him should have been instant. Theirs was not a blind, nor baseless trust. They had years of friendship. So why was Kew looking at him like he was as unrecognizable as an Uslethian?

Then, pitching loud over the raucous disorder of the tavern, came the chilling voice of the priest. He spoke the same words three times, until every soul in the place had quietened, and each time Izra's body shuddered at the sound of his name.

"I am looking for Izra Dziove," said the priest. "Traitor to the empire.

CHAPTER EIGHTEEN

So far this evening, Radek had kissed a Rezwyn, been pinned beneath him, and been thoroughly interrupted—and that was before a trio of damn priests had put a target on Izra's head.

There were three of them. The man in white—for death, Radek recalled—had a long grey beard decorated with beads. The other two were plain-faced, practically indistinguishable from one another. None of them looked like much, but then again, Radek's first impression of Doskor's priests had been an execution. Dull-looking or not, they were here to absolutely ruin his night. Potentially his life. He gritted his teeth and tried to look as inconspicuous as possible, though part of him vibrated with an urge to start a commotion. The rage felt raw, and his grip on it brittle.

"Don't," Mirakel whispered to him, eyes locked on the table. She'd seen right through him without even looking; knew something stupid and foolish stewed in his head. "Don't you dare."

She was right, of course. What was he going to do? Push them down the stairs and slide down the banister?

The tavern had gone quiet, this tense pause that hung in the air, suspended on a collective drawn breath. Radek wanted to turn around. Somewhere behind him, Kew and Izra had been talking. But he stayed still and watched as other tavern-goers pulled back from the priests. For some, there seemed a reverence to it—though many didn't bother to contain their disdain.

Someone shouted something short and sharp in Doskorian, most definitely a curse. Laughter sounded; incredibly dismissive. Several people went back to their conversations.

Odrica kept drinking as if she hadn't heard the priests at all.

Remarkable woman, Radek thought—all stoic calm when it really mattered. But even she had hunkered forward. She tugged free the ribbon that had tied her hair. As it spilled across her shoulders, she dragged half of it over her eyes.

Radek noisily exhaled and stared down at the remains of his ale. Shit, he wished he'd had something stronger. Something to blunt his nerves and keep the fear out of his face. Agitated, his leg started to bounce.

The priest shouted again, a hint of frustration clouding his voice. Doskorian was a harsh language without anger tinting the words. He could only understand one thing: the name Izra Dziove.

But then another string of Doskorian quickly followed, and Radek blanched when he heard his own name.

In thickly accented Uslethian, one of the priests—Radek had his head down, refusing to look up—repeated for their benefit, loudly: "He travels with a Lord Oren Radek."

Because of course. If Suoduny was real, if fate had any hand in this, it must really hate Oren Radek. Had the god taken offense at Radek's reversal of the ULTIMATE DESTRUCTION card? He hadn't meant to defy a god—but screw the ultimate destruction of anything. Oren Radek intended to live happily and well, not as outright defiance. Could a god be that petty?

A crippling sense of dread poured into his stomach, which became so heavy it promptly fell to his knees. He made an abortive gesture with his head, fighting the urge to canvass the room. How many other Uslethians were here? He saw a woman with the same russet-brown tones as him, a few with the fawn and taupe of Cres Stros and Westgar. In Doskor he'd stood out like a sore thumb, but he'd had the misplaced belief Ostijan would be a haven. It wouldn't take long for the priests to sort through the Uslethians here and determine his identity.

The silence stretched. Radek wondered if the people here would help or hinder the investigation. Would they have loyalty to Doskor? Ostijan was a commercial hub, less rigid than other places in empire territory. Uslethians weren't the only foreigners, either. He could tell from their fabrics alone. So was it possible that they might help him? And what about the soldiers Izra used to command? Would they take a side if it came to a fight?

Carefully, and ignoring Mirakel's warning look, Radek slowly turned his head.

Shrouded in shadow and illuminated only by the soft glow of the candles, Izra had pressed himself near the prayer nooks. Kew stood beside him.

Very quickly, grabbing Kew's arm and staying low, Izra moved back over to their table. He went down on one knee, put a hand on Radek's thigh and said, imploringly, "We have to go."

"Where?" Radek murmured back. It wasn't like he wanted to sit here and let the priests find them, but they were on the second floor of a tavern with only one door.

Shit. Shit.

One by one priests started gripping people's shoulders and swinging them around to inspect their faces. Outrage and noise started up. One or two angry Rezwyns got to their feet. But they were cautious. Neither of them ever raised a hand to a priest; an unspoken rule, as if their proximity to divinity made touching them dangerous.

It came to him, then, like the worst hand of cards he had ever been dealt. Fear: a genuine stab of it right in his heart. But, for the first time he felt this terror not for himself, but for Izra. Every muscle and sinew in his body was tightly wound, but his heart strained at the bit. The anxious beating of it smothered any hint of logic left in him. They were going to find Izra. And what then? What then?

Radek couldn't deny the pull he felt to the other man—could not ignore what he had seen in the astrok-mer. And in the end, did it matter? Whether it be the gods or raw attraction, Radek knew then that he could not let these priests discover Izra Dziove.

So he turned around and made direct eye contact with the first ex-soldier he could. He had a skin tone that was slightly warmer than Izra's, so Radek assumed he hailed from the eastern part of the empire. His body looked powerful; he had a slight paunch, and a square build. His beard and hair were neat, brown struck through with a hint of grey, which surprised Radek, because this man looked quite young, only a handful of years older than him.

The soldier returned his gaze curiously. Radek made an open-handed gesture toward Izra.

"What are you doing?" Izra mumbled, clocking the motion immediately.

"Showing our position to your former soldiers. I think it's a better option then letting the priests find you," Radek said as he started to stand.

"Oren," Izra said. He wasn't alone—the others started grumbling, too—but by that point, the ex-soldiers had started to rise, too.

The man moved out from behind the table. Radek was surprised to see he had a limp; he relied heavily on a cane that was, without a doubt, a gorgeous piece of craftsmanship. It took the bulk of this man well. However, he dressed quite conservatively. Upsetting. He had such beautifully broad shoulders, Radek could think of ten ways to dress him.

Having reached their table, the soldier took a seat, arranging his chair in a way that shielded Izra from the sight of the priests. "As I live and breathe, it's you."

Izra dipped his head. "Squadron Leader Luan Zek."

Luan Zek grit his teeth, shifting his weight uncomfortably. He looked over the banister and mumbled, "Not anymore."

"Luan," Kew said with a big grin. He reached over the table to shake hands, rather than risk being seen, but he had to awkwardly splay himself to reach. Luan laughed at this, seemingly amused, and they exchanged a few words in Doskorian. Nothing overly joyful—Radek didn't get the sense this was a particularly heartfelt reunion, which Odrica confirmed when she gave Luan a curt nod of recognition, and nothing more.

Luan turned back to his group and barked an order. Radek assumed it was meant to quiet one of the men who was still laughing, but instead of shutting up, the young soldier stood with a cackle, slipped his boot off, and whipped it over the banister at the priest.

Radek spun with a surprised noise just as a priest of Borviet dodged it and shouted back. Two others from Luan's party stood from the group and start clapping and cheering; they slipped out and went to the stairs and shouted to the lower level. They sang, then, some drinking song, something that demanded they jump up and down on the stairs in a percussive beat.

After that, everything slipped very easily into chaos.

Luan appeared tired; he slumped deeper into his chair, whilst most of the other ex-soldiers ran amok, hurling food scraps at the priests and each other. Radek laughed; it felt impossibly like a pantomime, or some ridiculous show, but it wasn't just the drunken mercenaries that started hurling things. He heard glass smashing, some more raucous laughter, the sounds of people aggressively screeching out the words to a song—very, very badly. They were, all of them, trying to make noise. Trying to drown out the priests' request. Completely and utterly reducing what little reverence existed for their authority to ash.

A single message pervaded: Ostijan did not bow to Doskor. Ostijan was not Neala's to command.

The priests were trying to hold their ground, but not doing a particularly good job of it. A look of feral surprise made all their mouths downturned and open beneath their headdresses, and Radek got the sense they were, fundamentally, surprised. No one acted this way against them. Now, they didn't know what to do.

Good. The longer they were struggling, the more chance of them giving up and leaving.

Radek opened his mouth to comment just as a cheer went up. It was warm and victorious, a relieved howl that echoed in the voice of every tavern-goer. Izra got to his feet, so Radek did, too. He had to squeeze himself between two whooping soldiers to see the three priests were giving up. They turned tail and left quickly, not brave enough to confront the crowd who so obviously resented them. Now the music turned jaunty and fast, and almost immediately all the space between the tables was filled by dancers.

"Welcome to Ostijan," Luan called over the ruckus of his party.

Radek moved closer to Luan for two reasons. The first being that he had an allure about him; charm leaked out of his pores, sure, but he was also so physically intimidating Radek got a little shiver out of being so close to him. The second was that Izra looked at Luan strangely. There was a hesitation and a caution that was out of character. He was treating Luan carefully, and perhaps if Radek squinted and was insecure enough about it, tenderly. And this outlandish and unfounded stretch made Radek extremely jealous.

Kew patted Luan on the back and went whooping toward the shoulders, tackling a man in a warm hug. The partying crowd quickly enveloped him. Odrica sat, and Mirakel took the empty seat beside Radek with a look that said she regretted everything that had led to this moment. Their party was shielded from sight by the depth of this level, and then by the standing ex-soldiers—who were probably a lot less drunk than Radek had assumed. They were following orders right now.

Izra sighed and leaned onto his knees, rubbing his hands. He spoke in Uslethian and said, "I thought you went back to Veprak."

"To die? Or to wallow?" Luan scoffed. His voice was deep and lush, with a slight edge in it; a gruffness that sounded buried. He settled back in his chair and folded his arms. "No. But I assume that belief is why you sent your letter to Hulik and not me."

They both turned to a man Radek assumed to be this Hulik: he was a skinny, unhinged-looking fellow. He'd climbed onto a table and at some point in the last few seconds had removed his shirt, which he waved above his head. Kew quickly followed suit.

Izra sucked his teeth and shrugged. "Hulik's been in Ostijan for nearly a decade. I was certain he would get the warning."

"He got the warning," Luan agreed, "then sat on it, thinking it was bullshit for a week too long. Not that he would ever leave this place. Not even if Neala had the army behind her." He turned his attention to Radek next. "Lord Oren Radek, I presume?" When Radek nodded, Luan nodded back. He gestured to the lot of them. "Two for two. What is stopping me from standing up and rushing after those priests?"

A lot of things, Radek imagined. Luan hadn't hesitated to shout orders to shield them the instant they needed saving—but pointing that out seemed petty, and not what Luan wished to hear.

"Because the letter is true," Radek said. He recalled the warning now. It had been a simple statement of facts. "The High Priestess has sent this lot and many other priests across the empire. For re-education. To stamp out dissidents. She has cut off trade with Usleth. She means to isolate you, subsume everything back under Doskor's rule."

Luan shrugged. He seemed tired, in a vital way. There was no shock, no panic, like all of his reactions were being filtered through fog. He calmly said, "Well. Ostijan will not stand for that."

Radek swallowed. "She also tried to kill the emperor."

Luan glanced up.

"Ah," Radek said, satisfied. "Got your attention now."

Luan made a strange movement with his mouth. "Not sure I like you. Who is this Oren Radek to you, commander?"

"My husband," Izra said.

"Sorry, what?" Mirakel murmured, but Radek just quietly patted her leg.

Luan didn't bother to hide his disbelieving glance and a good moment of scrutiny. "Are you sure?" Then—because apparently Izra told everyone and their dog about his fated dreams—Luan choked out, "Not the one you abandoned the Lord of Veprak for?"

Izra smiled. "Who else?"

Radek shifted. He'd known Izra had refused to marry the lord. But he hadn't known the reason. Radek glanced over at Izra, who had said "Who else?" like it was easy, like Izra hadn't made a life-changing decision before ever meeting Oren Radek in person.

Radek took a deep breath and held it.

Something happened in silence that Radek couldn't parse. Luan shifted, seemingly uncomfortable again in his chair, and nodded solemnly, like he found the whole thing unfortunate. Like Radek was a downgrade. Which wouldn't do. Radek was very unused to not being liked.

"You may call me Oren," he said, putting out his hand. Luan stared at him, then his hand, and tentatively shook it. "Very noble thing you've done by shielding us. I'm actually a merchant, you know. Warehouses in Ostijan, Elkar—and since all of you are beautiful men—"

"Oren," Izra murmured, cautious.

"—what? The women, too, but come now. My preferences are obvious."

Luan snorted here, which Radek counted as a win.

Oren continued, "Point being, I have some very expensive bolts of oknum and linen from Usleth just for you and your crew. Or outfits. A few tailors would jump at the chance to style those shoulders."

Luan smiled now, in a considered way. He raised his flagon, quite reservedly. "You do not have to impress me, Lord Radek."

"Nonsense, I make it my business to impress everyone," Radek said, seriously. With Ostijan so clearly on the brink of rebellion, and with Izra the face of a brewing civil war, Radek needed to do what he did best: get people on his side. But in truth, he really was grateful. "You've done an honorable thing for us. It is the least I can do."

Luan smiled again, more warmly. "I was never going to let Commander Dziove be dragged out of here by those priests. Besides him being the most holy man I know, he is also an honest one." Now he looked to Odrica and raised his cup to her. "And there is no way Ambassador Dziove would let her younger brother ruin her reputation at court without good reason."

Odrica snorted at that.

Luan turned back to Izra. "What are you planning on doing now?"

"The emperor is sick," he said quietly. "His daughter takes advantage. I have direction, from the gods. And I plan to cure him."

Luan nodded. "He seems a different man in his old age." There looked to be more he wanted to say; he opened and closed his mouth, shifted again, and brought his cane to rest over his lap.

"No longer someone who would have sent a thirteen-year-old like you to war," Izra murmured. "No longer someone who would ask the ten-year-old me to prognosticate death and violence."

Neither of those were questions. They stared at each other and shared in something Radek could never hope to understand. For him the war had been mostly displacement; months at a time on ships, waiting for it all to end. He hadn't fought it the same way these two had.

"Never thought you would admit that the emperor is not infallible," Luan whispered.

Izra opened his mouth, then closed it. Radek slid a hand over his back—his very firm back—and said to Luan, "It can be difficult to admit when we're wrong. I recently had to admit the empire's gods might be a teensy bit real."

Luan's lips edged towards a smile. "Ah. So you are handsome, savvy, and psychologically flexible. Now I see what Izra sees."

"I can be flexible in more ways than one, too," Radek said with a wink, because he couldn't help himself when looking at those shoulders. Luan laughed loud at that.

Izra motioned Radek close and whispered, with something close to jealousy, "Are you flirting with Luan Zek?"

And Radek, who wouldn't miss an opportunity to tease Izra, said, "Do I seem like the kind of man who would do that in front of his husband?"

Pink prickled Izra's cheeks, but Radek pretended not to notice. Then he grabbed the nearest serving boy and proclaimed loudly that he'd had just gotten married and was buying drinks for everyone in Luan's party to celebrate. Everyone cheered, save for Mirakel, who practically screamed her dismay. Something about a budget—Radek refused to listen.

It didn't take much after that. The lot of them were already tipsy, save Luan, who stoically sipped on probably his first ale of the night. But once Radek announced he'd bought the lot of them drinks, and told the others about his promised pretty outfits, the party gladly told him all about themselves. Naturally, he pulled out his cards. He met old lieutenants and learned all their names. He learned most were mercenaries now. Then he got a good chance to learn all their strategies. Luan, whose leg had been injured irreparably in a battle, acted as something of a consultant to them—begrudgingly, by the look of it. He did not seem satisfied with his current exploits.

Mirakel, surprisingly, immediately got along with them—and then got drunk enough herself to wax lyrical about all the similarities between working the royal treasury and warfare. Apparently keeping Radek's expenses under budget was war in its own right.

The party was fun, a chance to relax, to drink off the buzzing relief at escaping those priests. But then it dragged. And the alcohol took effect on Radek's sense.

It had been hours since he had been pinned underneath Izra, and even with all the commotion of the night, Radek could feel a latent heat throbbing in his belly every time he looked at him. So Radek did his best not to look at him. He felt like everything he did—had ever done and ever would do—was entirely inadequate. Radek, who often loved being seen, could suddenly hardly stand it. Without his tunics, without the beautiful draping layers of expensive material, what was he except a man?

Izra was complicated, a man of faith and loyalty and virtue. How terrifying it felt to be seen by a man like that. Radek thought: He hasn't even seen you yet. Not all of you. Suddenly Radek's desire, which had always been native to his body, to his very core, scared him.

It was made worse by his time in the astrok-mer. Desire had become complicated, and Radek could not separate what parts of it belonged to him and was something latent, left over from another life. He still felt like himself. His own agent. If he'd managed to retain his skepticism, it wouldn't have affected him at all. But Radek felt unstable with his convictions now. He could not pretend there was nothing divine or pointed about Izra Dziove. Whom he was now staring at.

Could it really be true that he and Izra were those two long-dead men?

Very suddenly, Radek realized the chatter had the table had diminished. Someone stared at him. Luan Zek cleared his throat and shifted in his chair.

"I believe your husband wants your attention, commander," Luan murmured with a smile. He raised a brow at Radek's obvious staring. A few of his men snickered. "Yeah, he does," and, "a lot of it," were said through drunken giggles, once again, in Uslethian. Just to embarrass the shit out of Radek.

Izra settled the weight of his gaze on Radek. "What is it?"

But screw embarrassment. Radek had been a good boy. Radek had waited. He'd even gotten married! And all that had done was make his desire stronger.

So now, Radek patted Izra's chest and he brought his voice low, "You know, we still haven't sealed the deal."

Izra only frowned. Radek had a brief, uncomprehending moment of pure fear, but he waited for Izra to acknowledge it—to give any indication he'd either liked what he'd heard, or at the very least understood. Then Izra cocked his head and pointed at himself.

"Did you mean—"

"Our marriage," Radek nearly shouted. He felt the flush in his cheeks and keeled forward, head in his hands. "Shit. Fucking embarrassing."

Comprehension lit Izra's expression. "It is not embarrassing—"

"It's pretty embarrassing," another voice said.

Radek practically crumpled when he saw Mirakel grinning at him. Here, Radek nearly walked out into the night and into the sea to drown. It was one thing to persuade Izra's subordinates to throw them a party, quite another to endure Mirakel's teasing over his clumsy and sincere lust. But endure it he must. He straightened and rolled his shoulders back.

"Oh, you be quiet. I just won us these fantastic people as allies." A cheer of agreement went up. "I think I deserve—"

"—a cock?" Mirakel offered, and Luan's entire party turned against him with their laughter.

"A drink!" Radek hissed. "A drink. We are talking about drinks now."

Radek jumped; Odrica loomed behind him. She offered him his cards in a neat stack, and either fate or she had arranged them so the card titled NEEDED RESPITE sat on top.

"Oh, aren't you wonderful," he murmured. "Now, we can't stay here."

"It is probably for the best." She nodded her head to the front of the tavern, where a new swarm of people had entered. Word had spread of the grand celebration underway, Radek surmised. They should withdraw while the ebb and flow of people was still high. But they were missing a member.

"Where's Kew?" Radek asked.

Izra deflated a little. "He . . . said he needed to breathe. He will meet us outside."

Odrica folded her arms. "But now we know the priests are searching for Oren Radek as well, we can hardly return to your warehouse."

"Where, then?" Radek said a little snappily—he didn't want to think logistics. He just wanted a bed. Wanted a certain someone in that bed with him.

"Ours," Luan called. He raised his cup in an almost salute, and gestured to a soldier half-slumped on the table. "Take them to ours."

CHAPTER NINETEEN

"Ours" was a house to the east of the city, away from Radek's warehouse and the water. Said house was painted a strange peachy color, and looked like a family home, not a base for ex-soldiers. Inside, though, had the classic mercenary marks. A single dying plant drooped in a corner, and the rest of the décor boiled down to scattered chairs and half empty bottles of liquor.

Luan's mercenary led them in, and Radek had a moment to panic about sharing a room—he couldn't do that, not when he was feeling so feral—but he said there were three rooms available, and that most of the mercenaries would likely pass out in the tavern.

"And if not," he said pointedly to Radek, accent thick, "the doors have locks."

After pointing out the rooms, the mercenary stumbled out and back toward the tavern. Everyone watched him go.

"I think it is best we retire," Odrica murmured, not unkindly. She didn't look away from Radek as she said it. Mirakel turned her head towards Odrica and shouldered her lightly.

"Come on, you oaf," Mirakel said, grabbing a fistful of Kew's collar. "I think something disgusting and sweet is about to happen."

Radek mouthed the word disgusting back at her with false outrage as Kew interpreted what was happening. He waggled his brows at Izra just as Odrica yanked him around the corner.

Radek and Izra stood there politely smiling at each for a moment, before Mirakel rounded the corner once more, alone, and hissed at Izra. "You take care of his heart, empire scum."

"Oh, bones, please don't," Radek whispered.

Izra looked too startled to say anything, but now that Mirakel had spoken, she seemed unfettered. "That thing is more well-kept than any of his other enterprises. And by well-kept I mean, of course, completely hidden away. He is not a man to offer his heart to just anyone."

"Alright, alright, you can absolutely leave now," he said, practically shoving her back. Out of earshot of Izra he whispered, "We're not talking about my heart. Just my body."

She stared at him for a moment and quirked one eyebrow, wholly disbelieving. "Sure," she said, before she left.

And then it was just Izra and Radek.

Izra glanced back at the bar. "Do you want to. . ."

"Yes," Radek sighed. "Whatever you're about to say, it's yes."

Izra snorted and offered Radek his hand. Radek's heart swelled as Izra's fingers—callused, warm, strong—wrapped around his own.

As they walked toward the door to their assigned room, Radek's heart became an anxious, thudding stone in his chest.

It made no sense. He had done this before—many bloody times—but never in such a slow, careful way. Without the thunderbolt passion driving him from room to bed, Radek could think. And thinking made it all that more deliberate, and less about his body, in a way. Izra wanted him. All of him. Not just the unchecked desire. It was enough for Radek to realize what an abominable condition his heart was in. What a mess it was.

"Tell me why I feel nervous," he whispered as Izra pushed a door open.

"There is no need for that," Izra murmured back. The small room felt near claustrophobic, the bed crammed against a wall with just enough space for a bedside table and lamp. An old, well-trodden carpet peeked out from under the bed. And that was it.

Izra closed the door and Radek's body stiffened. It was obvious enough for Izra to turn to him.

"Oren." Izra sounded almost exasperated. He unslung the halberd from his back and placed it carefully against the wall. "We do not have to—" he stopped, searching for the word, "—continue what we were doing. We can just—"

All the nervousness in him sparked, red-hot and bright. Radek laughed and rubbed his hands over his face, sound muffling and morphing into a groan. He gasped and stood tall. "Izra, I have wanted you since I saw you. I think if you had wanted me then, I would have mindlessly done whatever you wanted. I think I still might. And maybe that is desperation, and pitiful, and maybe it's something left over from another life. I don't think I care anymore. I have never done anything with this body and a man that wasn't purely degrading and carnal, and I want—" Radek gulped and choked on the rest of the sentence. Then he forced himself to speak. It was integral that he said the rest, that he spoke it into the world, before Izra and his god, exactly what he wanted. "Izra, I want you. Every part. Your body, your mind, your soul. Every terrifying thing about you I can never hope to understand. But if it is just my body you want, then I will take that too. I will take the scraps if that's all I can get."

Radek had split open his chest and showed off his bleeding heart. Izra responded with an abysmally short sentence.

"Where is this coming from?"

Radek flushed. He threw up his hands. "Do you know how fucking awful it is to—to like someone?"

And now Izra unraveled. "Gods, you are a fool. Did you think I wanted anything less?"

Of course, Radek wanted to say. It was all anyone had wanted before. And in some cases—he felt the king's seal cold against his skin, as frigid as rejection—not even that.

"You made an oath, and I accepted," Izra continued. "And besides, I have been haunted by you in my dreams for years. Every night I tried to sleep peacefully, and Suoduny would seek me out with visions of you, drive me mad with you, until it was all I could do to dream. Until every waking moment I was praying to dream of you again. I never even saw your face," Izra laughed now, breathless, closer to a sigh, "and I knew I wanted you."

"That was—a promise. From a god. Not the reality."

Izra held his hands. "Then let me say this now. A new oath, to you and you alone. No gods, no eternities; not until you want them. I want you, whatever that means to Oren Radek. Let's just start here."

Radek let Izra slide his hand around his back. His palm felt strong, the pressure veering away from mere support to something hungry. Radek could feel it in Izra's fingertips; desire bleeding through the skin. But still Izra moved slowly. He ran a hand to Radek's neck, thumb grazing his jaw, running through his beard. Strong fingers tilted back his head and Radek—who remained acutely aware of the size of Izra's hands, of the calluses and warmth of his right and the cold hard metal of his left—raised his chin with eagerness. Izra leaned down, painstakingly slow. Warm breath bloomed up Radek's neck.

"Where," Radek whispered, lips brushing against Izra's as he spoke, "do you plan to start, exactly?"

And Izra's eyes gleamed, a wild, happy rush flaring through them. Wolf quick, Izra's palm flew to Radek's shoulder and shoved him roughly backward. He rammed Radek against the wall. All the air knocked out of his lungs in an unsteady exhale. He gasped—and with it escaped a surprised, airy laugh. Oh, he thought, as the nervous raw feeling in his body became something else entirely, Izra is that kind of man. An anxious search flared in Izra's eyes—a need for approval, for Radek to show this was what he wanted. So Radek obliged, craning his neck and sliding his arms high above his head. Izra didn't wait for anything else. His grip was viselike around Radek's wrists, the pressure firm, warm, burning. Izra leaned in to kiss him, but Radek wrenched his head away.

He tutted. "What kind of pious man are you," Radek mused, wriggling closer to Izra's body. "Here I was thinking your godliness would make you demure."

"You thought wrong," Izra whispered back. He never broke eye contact, not even as he wrestled Radek's legs apart with a kick and stepped between them. "My godliness means I do not shy from worship. And I have wanted to worship you in filthy ways since the first time I dreamed of you."

Izra's lips brushed against Radek's neck. Instinctively, Radek tried to press against the grip around his wrist, but Izra was strong—and Radek was resolutely pinned there as Izra's other hand ran down the length of Radek's torso, feeling over the tunic. Radek arched towards each touch. The noises coming out of his mouth were small, reflexive things—embarrassing, uncontrollable. He wanted this. He'd known he wanted this. But until now, until this very moment when Izra touched him, Radek hadn't understood quite how much. And perhaps Izra hadn't either. Radek's quiet, sighing moans seemed to drive Izra mad. Eagerly, he ground hard against Radek's body, so firmly the ribs of the wood-paneled wall dug into his back.

And Izra barely waited. His hand cupped the tenting bulge in Radek's pants. A clipped, involuntary gasp slipped from between Radek's teeth. He couldn't help his hips. They twitched towards the warmth of Izra's hand. Now, with more urgency than his earlier testing, Radek tried to free his hands. He wanted to touch Izra, wanted to grip his hair, to haul him closer. But Izra was pure strength, muscle. He towered over Radek, this colossal man, eyes burning with desire. Radek spread his legs even further.

The eye contact was a mistake. Abruptly, warmth flooded Radek's groin, and he went from half-hard to aching against Izra's palm.

Izra blinked, ravenous wolfish grin splitting his lips apart. Without warning, he dropped Radek's wrists, moving to Radek's hips. With a single heave, Izra spun Radek to face the wall. He crashed against it with both hands splayed, gasping, and not a breath later Izra drove close, erection hard against him. The layers of clothing between them did nothing to soften it. It was then Radek realized how long it had been, how much he fucking wanted this—needed this. He groaned and arched his back against the contact.

Febrile fingers ran underneath his tunic and up his skin, scraping over his nipple, clasping around his throat. Radek's answering moan was met by one of Izra's, as hot as flame against his neck.

Radek didn't have the patience for this. "Fuck me," he said. "Like this, or the ground, or the bed. I don't care. But fuck me."

Izra's laugh made him feel desperate. "I am getting around to it."

"Izra," Radek whined, half pleading.

"Take it off." More a command than an ask. The weight disappeared from Radek's back, and he keenly felt the absence of Izra's warmth. But he didn't need to be told twice. Fingers shaking with barely contained desire, cock twitching in his pants, Radek hurried to shed his shirt. A soft thump sounded behind him as Izra's heavy cloak dropped to the ground. Radek kicked off his shoes, reached for his pants—and a powerful hand whipped out to stop him.

"Ah," Radek exhaled. The grip was tight. Slight blissful pain shivered up Radek's forearm. Stifling a moan, he obediently dropped his fingers away from his pants. Surely now Izra would touch him with more focus, with none of that awful teasing. But then he forced him toward the wall again. Frustrated, he dropped his forehead against it with an agonized groan.

"Izra, I swear," he hissed. He tried to twist against the force holding him there, reaching his arm around to lace through Izra's hair. This was permitted; Izra moaned into his neck as Radek tightened his grip. So Radek canted his hips, managed a few eager, indecent bucks against Izra's erection before the other man crowded him so closely to the wall he couldn't move at all. Izra ignored his impatient eagerness.

Izra kissed his neck, raked his teeth along the exposed length and down his back. Which was all very nice, but every muscle in Radek's body was taut with want. He jolted and shivered. "You are positively killing me."

"You waited all night," Izra whispered, hands trailing across his stomach. "You can wait a little longer."

The wait had made Radek's need impossible to ignore. It was in his skin, his limbs, his bones. He gave another desperate buck backward.

And all at once, Izra's slow, insistent patience imploded. Both hands flew to Radek's pants. His used his left to steady Radek's hips as the right tried to yank the damn thing off. Izra's usual precision vanished; he fumbled at the laces, breathing clipped and eager as Radek thrust upward, trying to graze the tip of his cock against the edge of Izra's hand.

"You are not helping," Izra growled.

"I can't help it," Radek said, "I need—"

Finally, Izra undid enough laces to slip his hand into the trousers. Izra's hand wrapped around Radek's cock.

Radek's whole body jolted. A long, protracted groan escaped his throat. He knocked his forehead against the wall, hips stirring minutely into Izra's grasp. Izra put a firm hand against Radek's hips, stopping the movement and rendering him helpless. And then Izra touched him slowly, without rhythm—another fucking tease.

A sound strangled in Radek's throat. "For fuck's sake, you bastard, please."

Izra's movement halted completely. He made a low noise against Radek's neck. "Say that again."

"Please," Radek panted, hearing his voice devolve into desperate begging. "Please, please."

Izra groaned like he was already inside Radek; he ground forward once, erection firm in the cleft of Radek's ass. Shit, Izra hadn't even kissed him on the lips yet, and Radek's desire was uncontainable. He arched his neck, cock jumping against Izra's palm—and then Izra let go of him, pressure slipping away entirely. Radek practically sobbed, heart racing with want as Izra spun him around and—finally—crashed their lips together. The two of them inhaled sharply in time. Roughly, Izra wrenched Radek's trousers down and off. He barely had time to step out of them before Izra jostled him away from the wall and shoved him onto the bed.

The mattress creaked as Radek scrambled onto his elbows, watching eagerly as Izra stripped the rest of his clothes off.

There was a jumble of emotion in Radek's belly; something close to fear, an eagerness that was almost swallowing him, that was making him nauseous, and heat keeping him swollen and aching. Naked, Izra stood over him. His eyes raked over Radek in the same starved way Radek inspected him. Izra was—in every way—big. His shoulders, his arms—Radek watched the rise and fall of his panting chest, each breath accentuating the defined muscle. His skin looked inlaid with silver and ivory; scars running across his skin. Radek wanted to trail his fingers over all of them, to learn every pattern and path across Izra's body.

Radek's eyes dropped. The sight of Izra's cock made his stomach flip.

"Gods," he whispered.

Izra leaned forward. "I told you I would make you a godly man, Oren Radek."

He mounted Radek with a fierceness, but when Izra kissed him, it was all sweet and soft. Then he inhaled and deepened the kiss. Radek spread his legs unthinkingly, letting Izra crawl forward between them. Izra's knee glided along the inside of Radek's thigh, warm and insistent. The heat from Izra's body curled over him, and Radek arched, hoping Izra would react. But he didn't. Radek chanced a look, just to see Izra staring down at him, one hand reaching out to run his thumb across Radek's jaw, to press into his lips.

"This is all very nice," Radek grunted, momentarily taking Izra's thumb between his teeth. "But I'm really quite desperate."

"I know," Izra smiled. "I quite like the sight of it."

Maybe Radek could have stood the teasing, if it hadn't been months, if this wasn't the first time Izra was going to fuck him, but his body was practically throbbing now. So he coaxed him. Radek pulled Izra down into a kiss, tongue and teeth grazing across his lips, body rocking up. Radek slipped a hand down Izra's torso, curving his palm around Izra's cock. Izra opened his mouth against Radek's lips in a sigh.

Gently experimenting, Izra slid one hand around Radek's neck. Radek gasped as cold metal fingers pressed against him, flinching and tensing as Izra's other hand dragged down his skin to his groin. Radek threw his head into the pillow with a sigh as Izra's knuckles grazed the underside, making his cock jump.

"Pant pocket," he managed weakly. "Little glass bottle. It's an oil for—"

"You came prepared?"

"Always am," Radek said.

Izra's grip hardened. "Always prepared to be fucked?"

Radek froze. He tried to sit up, but Izra's sure and firm grip around his throat kept him still. A delicious quiver of fear shot down his back at the look in Izra's eyes, at the quirked lip and raised brow.

Defiantly, Radek smiled back. "Yes. I always want it. Or to fuck someone. Or to do whatever they want—" The last word was a strangled moan as Izra pressed against the side of Radek's neck, other hand starting to work him. He knew he was slick with precum. Izra's finger grazed over the head, and a rush of feeling trembled up Radek's body.

"Jealous?" Radek whispered.

Izra's eyes flashed to his. "Very."

He could barely stand it. Radek squirmed and raised his hips high. "Then what are you going to do about it?"

Without any more teasing, Izra's hands left their current tasks. Radek's frustration spilled out of him with such excess he couldn't help but groan—and then his arms were yanked roughly over his head as Izra intertwined their fingers together and pushed him down for a deep kiss. Radek closed his eyes as Izra ground against him. Then the pressure disappeared momentarily as Izra ungracefully lifted himself from the bed, scooped up Radek's pants, and roughly tore into the pockets. Radek opened his eyes and watched Izra standing there, cock hard, face twisted in frustration as he eagerly rummaged for his prize. Then, in his right hand, he lifted out the small bottle; a lovely, scented oil that hadn't gotten nearly as much use as Radek would have liked.

"Here," Radek sat up as Izra approached and wrenched the bottle from his hands with a kiss he quickly stole, teeth dragging Izra's lip away from his mouth.

The bed creaked as Izra slid onto it, propped up on his knees. Radek looked down at the bottle, but could feel Izra watching, his hungry gaze burning into his naked body as Radek opened it and let some of its contents trickle over

Izra's cock. The moment Radek touched him, Izra jerked forward, eagerly thrusting into Radek's strokes. And the view was mesmerizing. Radek could look nowhere else but Izra's eyes; the heavy-lidded stare fluttering closed, the quick rise and fall of his chest, the arch of his hips into Radek's hand.

"Touch-starved," Radek commented

"Speak carefully," Izra's head lolled forward. His eyes opened, the look in them severe, wanting.

Radek rocked forward and ran a pointed tongue along Izra's jaw. "Or what?'

Izra planted a hand on Radek's chest and, without any effort, shoved him onto his back. Radek laughed and kept his legs apart, watching and panting as Izra reached for the oil to coat his fingers. But Radek knew he would die if it didn't happen soon.

"Don't fucking bother," Radek hissed, reaching down and urging Izra's cock-filled hand to where he wanted it. The look on Izra's face shifted, and at first Radek thought he was concerned or hesitant. But then Izra's hand snaked up to his jaw, his mouth; his thumb forced Radek's mouth open and he grated the skin of his thumb against Radek's teeth. His other hand hefted Radek's right leg up to his shoulder and, tilting back, Radek obediently offered the other one to the air. Eyes locked on one another, Izra leaned forward and pressed inside.

They moaned together. Radek's voice went high and shrill; he felt his eyes roll back as pleasure and pain ripped through him. Izra thrust again. Radek felt so untethered from himself he had to knot his fingers through Izra's hair, to hold on as Izra drove into him. At first it was heavy and slow, two bodies unraveling and readjusting and finding a tempo, but then Izra seemed to know what Radek wanted. He pulled out and rammed him—hard, fast—and Radek clenched his quivering legs around Izra's hips. Every impact slammed Radek's eyes to the back of his skull. Izra yanked him into an open-mouthed kiss and swallowed Radek's next full-throated moan. As the pace accelerated, Radek couldn't even manage moans—just weak, staccato grunts or half-formed begs. He was seeing stars, seeing every god of Izra's blinking brightly in his mind.

Izra folded forward, still thrusting, and groaned against his neck. Then he whispered to him in Doskorian; guttural, husky words, all senseless to Radek, but enough to make him buck. His grip was tight in Izra's hair, the other a claw down his back.

Radek knew he wouldn't last much longer. All of him ached. He thrashed back against the pillow, reaching down for his swollen cock—and Izra caught his wrist, wrenching it high over his head. Frantically, Radek tried to twist free.

"Please," he breathed, half pleading, trying to rub his cock against Izra's belly. "Please."

"You are suddenly so polite," Izra murmured. Still thrusting, he shifted so Radek's ankles were laced behind his neck. Radek's cock throbbed in the air between them.

"Izra," Radek pleaded. Tears pricked the corners of his eyes. "I want to come."

Izra caressed his cheek, then tilted Radek's chin up for a long kiss. He pulled away only to say, "Then come for me."

He splayed his silver left hand on Radek's stomach and let the other finally curl around his cock.

Radek couldn't help but surge toward him, canting desperately into Izra's warm grip. He buried his hands in Izra's hair. And Izra plowed into him, the two of them grunting and moaning and grinding, lips sealed together. Radek heard himself panting, whining, and each high noise encouraged Izra to thrust harder, hand tugging in time at Radek's cock. The momentum built until the final, potent tremor jolted through Radek's body. He arched, mouth open in strangled release, his eyes unseeing and fluttering as Izra kept pace.

Pleasure washed over him, so intense and blinding he barely registered the halting, gasping moan Izra made. Then his head was shoved against the crook of Izra's neck, buried against the slick, sweating skin. Shivering, twitching echoes of pleasure rocked through them both.

For a moment they lay together, exhausted. Izra exhaled a sweet, satisfied moan into his ear and started to pull away—much too fast for Radek's liking. He tightened his thighs around Izra's waist and held him, nuzzled into his neck. Locking his fingers at the base of Izra's head, Radek leaned back just far enough to kiss him; a slow, languid thing, but he was still out of breath by the time Izra tugged himself away. Then Izra pulled himself out and collapsed next to Radek, turning to give his forehead a strangely reverent kiss.

They stared at one another through half-closed eyes, lying in sweat and cum and tangled sheets. Radek sighed and burrowed against him, letting himself be held, to relax into Izra's arms like this was something familiar. And when sleep came, it was lulling and peaceful, and lured the both of them into a deep slumber.

Chapter Twenty

Izra woke aching, and it was the most wonderful feeling a man could feel.

Izra had made love before, but he had never felt like this in the sobering morning light. Any sane man might have woken in this cramped bed, noted the filthy state of the room and faint scent of unwashed mercenaries seeping through the walls and thought: fuck. Carnal want always seemed insurmountable in the moment, and then absolutely silly when you were spent. And it was only worse when you woke up in bed with the wrong man.

So to wake and see Oren Radek was nothing short of bliss.

Suoduny was like the ocean, in a way. The god and its power was every unsettling thing that moved beneath the surface. Everything unstill. Ever moving. Exposed to that constantly, feeling the fated threads linking both the hypnotic minds of the living and insensate objects, should have been exhausting. And it was. It had been. Only Izra had never noticed, not until this very moment waking up in Oren's arms and realizing all of it had stopped.

Suoduny had not gone—that god existed in his very blood—but the noise, the cacophony of fate screaming at the edges of his mind, had grown quiet. There was only Oren Radek. Everything about Oren Radek.

Once, the thought of being beholden to someone was like having his free will wrenched out of him and destroyed. Now it was everything he had ever wanted. And how funny it was, to have known for years what his life would be like—what it should have been like—and now, finally, to be living it.

"You're staring," Oren mumbled without opening his eyes. His voice sounded husky, as if sleep had caught in his throat.

A smile tugged at Izra's lip, impossible to stop. "Am I not allowed to stare at you?"

"Do you know how terrifying it is to wake up to that?" Oren mumbled. He shifted and rolled onto his back. "Let alone by a man with your kind of arms."

"What is wrong with my arms?"

"Not a thing," Oren grinned. "Only they're positively massive, and if you wanted to, you could crush all my insides. Turn me to stew."

"And why," Izra said with a laugh, "would I want to do that?"

"Well, you wouldn't, I hope." Oren stretched his arms above his head. He tensed, muscles stretching taut as he arched. Izra could not help but reach out and thumb a nipple. Oren made a noise and caught Izra's wrist. "I thought the sex was quite good, actually. Good enough not to be crushed in retribution, anyhow." Now he turned to Izra with a heavy-lidded smile. "But if you didn't like it, I'd be happy to try again."

"I hated it," Izra said as seriously as he could manage. "Terrible. You need a lot of practice."

"Oh, really?" Oren rolled into him, voice close to a purr. "How much practice?"

"A lifetime's worth."

Oren shuddered at that. He pulled away slightly. "A lifetime?"

Izra shrugged. "Perhaps that is wishful thinking. But as long as our bodies can handle it, I wish to do that with you. In all its variations."

Oren grew very quiet. Was he shy again, Izra wondered? Or did he feel what Izra did? Was he considering every possible configuration of their union, spread out over their lives together?

Oren rolled onto his back again. "That is . . . a long time to be wanting me."

"Then I'll prove it," Izra whispered. He reached around his neck and unclasped the chain of office that marked him strix and commander. It bore an amalgamated symbol of Borviet and Suoduny; multi-faceted boar, the True Commander's symbol, for fate and expansion combined. "Wear it, and for this lifetime, I will always be able to find you. Fate will always lead me back to you."

Oren looked at it, then at Izra. "Are you sure? Are you sure that I'm—worth it?"

And Izra smiled, because gods, Oren really did not understand how beautiful he was. Izra felt deeply, gravely affected by it. He wanted to shake sense into him; kiss him, fuck him, laud him before the gods. Whatever it took for Oren Radek to realize his beauty. His soul's perfection.

"Did you think I did not want you all this time?" Izra asked. "Body and mind?"

And the door burst open.

Kew stood there with his mouth open, ready to speak, and promptly turned a paler shade of white at the sight of the two of them tangled in the sheets.

"Oh," Kew said. His eyes dragged to Izra. "Good job."

Izra felt himself flushing. "I swear to every god both named and unnamed, you idiot, unless someone is dying, you have got to learn to knock."

Kew suppressed a laugh and half turned back to the door. "Right. Yes." He curled his hand into a fist and weakly rapped against the pane. "Like this?"

"Izra," Oren hissed beside him.

Izra cleared his throat. "Kew, turn around."

Kew spun around to face the empty corridor without another word. "Your sister plans to gather the supplies today. I'll be going with her. And you . . .? Well. Are you staying in bed?"

Izra frowned and cleared his throat. "Do you have something to say?"

With more attitude than befitted his second, Kew said, "You slept well past dawn you know."

Izra bit his lip. When had he started allowing Kew to get away with such impropriety? "I was tired."

"Well. Physical exertion will do that. Commander." Kew walked out and left the door wide open.

Oren sighed and rubbed his face.

Izra shuffled closer. The mattress groaned with the weight shift, bowing a little inward. Izra wondered if there had been some irreparable damage to its structure, but he grew distracted when Oren leaned against his chest as if on instinct. Izra's heart thudded loudly. "You do not have to get up today, if you are tired."

A snort. "You flatter yourself."

"I meant—because of the last few weeks," Izra said. He ran a hand down Oren's back, and hoped somehow that the gentle touch of his fingertips would transfer his concern, his care. "Would be best to remain out of sight, anyway."

After a beat, when Oren's face did not rise from the coffin of his hands, Izra nudged his shoulder. "Lovely thing, why are you sad?"

Muffled through his hands, Oren replied, "I'm not sad."

"No?"

"No," came another stifled reply. "Just eternally embarrassed."

Izra frowned. He flashed a look at the open doorway. "Over Kew?"

Oren's head shot up. He had mussed hair, all wispy and disheveled. It instantly reminded Izra of last night—and that thought was enough to send heat to his groin.

Oren continued, blissfully unaware of Izra's shameful body, and all its minute reactions to him. "Over how you saw me. Last night."

Izra fought the urge the squeeze him, to envelop him until every stupid fear evaporated. "Oh, Suoduny save me," he whispered in Doskorian, and over Oren's questioning reply, Izra said, "You are ridiculous. It is not a bad thing. You are as filthy as me. Just as free."

Oren pounced forward and kissed him hard, arms laced around his neck.

"And just as fucking loud."

They broke apart. Hulik, seemingly still shirtless from when he stripped in the tavern, stood in the doorway.

"Oh, kill me now," Oren mumbled.

Hulik chewed on a bit of bread. He waggled it toward them. "You boys want breakfast?"

Izra sat there and was genuinely surprised by this man's bravery.

"Did you forget who I am?" Izra asked, not unkindly—just a soft prodding question.

Hulik stopped chewing. He stopped doing much of anything. "Just thought you might want to eat," he said, meeting Izra's eye. "Sir. Commander. Sorry. Uh—"

Hulik reached out and slammed the door closed.

"Incredible morning after," Oren muttered as he dropped into a squat to dig for his underclothes in the stream of discarded garments they had left scattered on the floor. The chain of office looked good on him, especially naked.

Izra's eyes raked over him, at the way his skin folded over his hips, the bump of his spine in his back, the softness of his body, muscle hidden.

"Stop looking at me."

"But you are—"

"—If you say beautiful one more time. . .!"

At this, Izra walked over to the muttering Oren and pulled him from the ground. He pulled Oren to him, let their soft, warm skin touch. Oren tensed until Izra slid his hands around his hips. "It is not my fault you do not believe me."

Oren said nothing. His jaw was locked; Izra could practically hear his teeth being ground together. So he kissed him. Izra tilted back Oren's head, fingers grazing the nape of his neck, and he watched a little gleefully as all that rigidity fluttered out of Oren as he closed his eyes and arched for Izra's lips.

There was no other word for him. Oren Radek was beautiful—and his.

"Good morning," Luan Zek called out to Izra the instant he set foot in the common room. It was late morning by the time Izra stumbled out. Shortly after dressing, Oren had found a reason to rip them off of him again, and was now sleeping off all that early-morning activity. But Izra wanted to talk to Luan.

The common room was empty, save for a few bleary-eyed mercenaries. Luan stood at the top of the stairs to the house's second story, so Izra spoke loudly, "Morning," and then, "I was wondering—I wanted to thank you. Again." Izra said, which was true but only partly true. The sight of the priests the previous night had unnerved him, and now that they had to lay low for a few days until Hapina arrived, Izra felt anxious about the state of Doskor. He hoped that Luan Zek had his finger on the city's pulse.

Luan stared at him, then nodded, pointing Izra toward a long wooden table scattered with papers and flagons. Then Luan began his slow descent. He moved slowly, trying and failing to keep the intense pain from his face. One particularly heavy drop made him wince. Luan was a big man, wide and strong, but his leg had been causing him grief for years.

"Stiff in the morning," Luan muttered. "This cold isn't helping, neither."

Izra hadn't seen him in years, but even at twenty-four Luan had had the tones of a jaded general, long-ago disillusioned with war. He was only a year older than Izra; at thirty-one, he sounded much older, much more tired than he should have been.

"What is it you are doing for this group?"

Luan pulled a face like he was not quite sure himself. "Consulting, I suppose you'd call it. Mentoring."

As if he were well-decorated; as if he had more experience than a handful of battles. Luan had been injured early on. Seventeen, eighteen perhaps. He had kept fighting for weeks afterward. Izra had never learned what had done it, in the end, whether it had been a fracture, or something that partially severed the muscles. But Luan Zek had not fought in battle since.

He had a keen mind, though. Good for strategy and leadership. Mentoring, though? Most of his mentees were face down on the carpet, sleeping off the evening's revelries. The few that were conscious stared intently at Izra and Luan, and made no attempt to hide their interest in the unfolding conversation.

Izra sat back in his chair and folded his arms. "Do you plan to do that for long?"

Luan grimaced as he dropped. "Likely not."

"Then what?"

A flicker of something crossed across Luan's face. "Izra. Not everyone has had their destinies carved out for them from birth. I can't see where I'll be a month from now, let alone a year."

Izra looked at him as tenderly as he could manage and nodded. "And the wife?" he ventured.

A choking snort sounded from an eavesdropping mentee, who tried to bury it with a cough and a fake conversation whipped up quickly with the unconscious man beside her. Luan refused to acknowledge the commotion, his gaze fixed on Izra.

"Asking all the wrong questions today, Commander," Luan said. It was not quite a warning, but even Izra's curiosity could not contend with Luan's expression. With some asperity, Luan shifted, moving his attention to his cane as he spoke. "I am a . . . very different man from the last time I saw you."

Izra wanted to ask something else, to clarify. Too jaded for love? He almost asked, before sense thundered in his mind. Not only was that unkind, but symptomatic of the early romantic bliss taking root in him. Luan should not have to bear the brunt of that. So he gave Luan a smile, cleared his throat, and got down to business.

"I wanted to know," Izra said, "about Doskor. I am not sure if you have been there in the past weeks—"

"We haven't. All I have are rumors."

Izra conceded with a shrug. "All I have are sporadic visions from Suoduny and my own paranoid imagination."

"So one up on you then, eh?" Luan said. He sucked his teeth and nodded, before planting his cane on the table between them. "Doskor is Doskor. It is the stronghold of the priesthood, and Neala knows it. But they aren't accepting visitors. The markets are dead. Anything coming in is scrutinized. Leaving the city is apparently impossible, too." Luan leaned forward. "Here things take a bit of an eccentric turn with the rumors, Dziove. They're all: The High Priestess is favored! And the High Priestess demands your faith! As if prayer is something to be directed to her instead of the gods. Then it gets downright insane."

Izra blinked. "Oh?"

Luan sighed and made an abortive gesture with his hands. "Anything from she is killing dissidents in Doskor itself or readying the army to massacre cities like Ostijan."

At whatever expression Izra wore—shock and disgust and fear, he imagined—Luan closed his eyes and grimaced. "Could be horseshit, commander."

"You do not believe it?"

Luan glanced away. "I don't want to believe it." He had a calmness about him, a way to internalize all this information in a way Izra did not. His eyes grew quiet, and when he glanced next at Izra, Luan shrugged, with nothing left to say.

"What about Veprak?" Izra asked.

"Fuck Veprak," Luan said, then seemingly regretted the outburst. He went to reach for a drink he did not have. "Forgive me. But I am done with that city. And as far as I know, Neala is concentrating her efforts to the west. Locking down border cities like this one before she turns to the western frontier. I shudder to imagine Usleth's response to all this . . ."

Luan sighed again and trailed off. Izra decided then and there to go—Oren had revealed that King Zavrius was mobilizing in Westgar.

"Thank you," Izra said. As Izra stood, Luan reached out and grabbed his arm.

"Commander. I don't have much sway," he said. "Not anywhere of great import. Even this crew finds it fine and good to mock the man saving their asses." He gestured with his head to the collapsed mentees. "But I'm giving you my thoughts anyway, Izra, because as far as I can see, your piety and your loyalty do not erase your rationality. You balance all of it together. All the empire's values; all its changing idiosyncrasies. Years ago, the you from the war—I don't know. I think that child might have been different from the man you are now."

Izra looked down at Luan's arm. "He had to be," he whispered. He could have said more, could have explained that had been justifying those gory visions for years. But by the time he found the words, Luan had let him go.

"Empire will need men like you," he said. "To lead it. To lead it well."

The sentiment made him nauseous, but Izra forced a smile. "The True Commander is still alive. No one should be thinking beyond that."

Izra left Oren to rest, and went to find Kew and Odrica, but Luan followed him, intent on dragging out the mentees who had passed out at the tavern. They split at the square, and Izra went from shop to shop searching for his sister and second.

In the afternoon light, Ostijan was alive. Dock workers hauled crated wares and food from the ships, but they were few and far between. Uslethian ships were conspicuously absent. It upset Izra to see, knowing Neala had ordered it in her father's name. But Usleth's king waited to send aid. Izra had seen revolts before, in his visions. Sobbing, screaming, blood. Never a quiet affair. It was a slow and broiling rejection. Izra thought Oren was wrong. This was not a revolt—but a simmering anger of a people who had forgotten what it felt like to be cowed. Ostijan had been a pluralistic place for years. There was nothing to revolt against; no sudden shift in empire values or Uslethian influence. Both existed here with equal amounts of respect. Neala could not see it yet, but Ostijan had been its own city for a decade. It would not let a draconian decree alter it—and why should it? There was no real homogeny in empire. There was no problem to be solved.

Neither Kew nor Odrica were to be found in the shops. At one point, he had seen a red cloak and frozen, only to chide himself upon realizing it to be no priestly garb. But he kept a look out after that. When he walked near the square from last night, he saw Oren's warehouse. A priest staked out the front, waiting for Oren's return. Furious, Izra slipped onto the docks to avoid walking through the square.

He found Odrica alone, Kew nowhere in sight. His sister had propped herself in the shade of a dockside warehouse, eyes straining and unblinking, staring at the water. There were no supplies around her, no food or drink. She had wandered out here and stood locked in a trance, and this was, very obviously, an indication that something was wrong.

"What's happened, then?" Izra said as he approached.

Surprisingly, she startled. Odrica kicked off the wall and flinched away from him.

"Brother."

She could not quite look at him when she spoke, which was odd. Izra wondered if it was about last night—if she had heard noises through the thin walls. But sex never made her squeamish or embarrassed, and she had seemed quite accommodating the night before. He grabbed her arm, pulled her back to him.

"What is it?"

She opened her mouth, lips half curling around a word—nothing, Izra imagined her saying, but then she just shut it and sighed.

"I had a dream."

Izra went still at that. Dzioves never had the luxury of a quiet, senseless dream. Divine touch always marred them. And now that he looked at her, she had tried in vain to cover the sunken darkness of her eyes with kohl. How long had she been awake? Had she slept at all?

"I saw you in Doskor," she said. "In chains."

Raw grief edged her voice, like mourning, but Izra could not understand why. They had lived with a kind of impotent knowledge of potential futures for years.

But his sister's sudden nervousness made him wary. Fearful in a way he did not want to recognize.

Odrica hugged her folded arms closer to her chest. "The number of supporters that Neala has already garnered has proven many in the priesthood that would oppose the True Commander. They would willfully question the gods."

She put a hand over her mouth. Izra's heart thudded. He was not used to seeing his sister like this. She was muscle and height, had a density to her body he had always assumed was the same for her soul. Seeing her unnerved made him violently ill. He stepped forward, half-wanting to ask the specifics of her dream, and half afraid to do it.

"There is no good in this," she said. "Our empire cannot continue like this."

"Odrica," he said sharply.

"This city is barely recognizable as Rezwyn," she said, gesturing around at Ostijan. In the daytime, the amalgamation of cultures was clear to see. "What happened at the tavern last night—the people rebelling against Neala's operatives—it saved our lives, but to openly defy priests of Doskor . . . I heard talk that those priests complained to the governor and she did nothing but offer a bland apology. To priests of Borviet!" She pounded the symbol on her chest. "Doskor's control is truly slipping. A weak hold might as well be no hold at all."

They looked at each other, and Izra tried to keep down the burning bile in his throat. He did not want to argue with his sister. At the same time, she was wrong.

"I disagree entirely," he said. "Not every horse runs its best with a strong hand. Some do better with free rein. Territories are no different. What is the point of having city governors if we do not allow them to make appropriate decisions to where they are? All Neala's decrees will do is drive them closer to rebellion."

"Your words border on blasphemy," she murmured. "But maybe that is how it needs to be. I don't think the True Commander will ever wake."

Izra's stomach twisted, and it took a moment for him to comprehend the enormity of what he felt; because the True Commander was a fixed point in his mind. Entirely immutable. Izra could not comprehend the empire without him, let alone his own life. And standing here now before his sister, he realized this had not been a good enough reason to unnaturally preserve his life.

He felt like a child, listening to her. Felt some childish defiance bubbling up in him. Dreams were his realm more than hers, and his were certain visions, not half-formed fears. Odrica had been the one to force him from the castle, to drive them all out and find a cure for the man lying suspended between life and death in the depths of Doskor's castle. To hear this shift in her, to see her shaken by a dream—Izra could not afford to think too long on it.

"Your god is not Suoduny," he reminded her, as gently and warmly as he could manage. "These are not visions with the same power as mine. You are not looking at a certain future, sister. It could only be your intuition."

She stared at him, eyes not wholly convinced. "I am afraid for you."

Izra frowned but made himself nod. "Then I thank you for the warning."

She smiled a little, the corners of her mouth wrinkling. He saw a little of her usual self in her, and felt confident that whatever this was, it would pass.

And sure enough, she slapped a solid hand on his back and drew him close into a side embrace, just long enough for Izra to feel her warmth seeping through her clothes. Then she stepped away. "You had a good night, I suspect?" she said. She always did this—making the subject about Izra to avoid talking about herself.

But he let her, half because he wanted to stop talking about her dream, and half because he was still feeling the afterglow of the previous night.

"Very good," he said. "A night I hope to repeat." And then, "Let's stop lurking, shall we?

Odrica sighed against him and let herself be guided away from this end of the harbor, and back toward Luan's place.

Then: commotion. Izra spun back around to face the way he had come. It sounded loud, violent; unfettered screams. Several dock workers and sailors dropped their tasks and sprinted toward the square. Izra hesitated, meeting Odrica's eye carefully. He prayed that Oren would sleep through whatever this was and turned back to Odrica. They nodded to each other and moved back along the docks, flanking the buildings, hugging the shadows cast by the overhangs to peer at the chaos.

A horn blared. The sound struggled out, weak and forced, as if from the mouth of someone who had never sounded one. When Izra edged himself to spy around the corner, he saw a priest of Borviet—from last night, headdress jingling as she moved—spluttering into the horn for the square's attention. She stood alone in front of the inn from last night.

Izra's stomach sank.

The other two priests forced everyone out of the inn. It was bad luck—Luan had returned to rouse his mentees and limped out now, ex-soldiers and mercenaries behind him. The inn's owner was forced to his knees, and some exchange happened between the priests and Luan—whatever they were asking, Luan refused. A tense moment passed where Izra expected a fight to break out. But Zimsmrt's priest simply made a gesture, and backed away from Luan's crew.

Then, behind them, the inn where they'd celebrated the night before burst into flame.

Zimsmrt's priest waited for his audience. The commotion had drawn a crowd. Several people ran shouting toward the inn. Luan barked an order that was drowned out. The priests were ignored as a concerted effort to smother the flames ignited amongst the populace.

"Gods," Odrica muttered. She watched the scene. "What are they doing?

"Retribution," Izra murmured back to her.

The gods were not on the side of these priests. Izra knew this in his heart, because Suoduny continued to help him. He felt fate and destiny burning at the edge of his mind, more vibrant than usual. He hunkered low and reached for his halberd—then cursed, remembering he had left it.

"Come away." Odrica dragged him further back. The crackling sound of the burning inn roared in his ears.

"Are we stopping them?" he asked. He pushed back against her half-heartedly. She held him. She knew his pain. Suoduny screamed in his ears. He wanted to kill these traitors. He wanted them to burn.

"No," Odrica grunted low. She shook sense into him by grabbing him by the shoulders. "They cannot die. If Ostijan kills them, it will be war. Neala will attack. Usleth will support the insurgents. It will be everything the True Commander is trying to avoid."

Izra paled. "Does the city know that?" he spat. Odrica pursed her lips. Izra pushed against her. "No. I will not leave them to seal their own fate."

"Then what?" she asked, incredulous. She was too much of a diplomat sometimes. He could not bear it.

"This is happening because all of those people shielded me from the priests last night," he said. "I must show myself."

Izra went. He hesitated by the corner of the building they were using for cover. There were so many heads, a whole sea of bodies. Many stood stock-still in fear.

Izra pushed forward. The priest of Zimsmrt was speaking. He heard only his name over the crowd; a summons he would not ignore.

Odrica did not follow him as he stepped out. The crowd was thick, but they let him pass. Near enough, and before anyone else could gain the courage to be killed, he shouted, "I hear you are looking for me."

Several people stepped away from him, exposing him to the priests.

"I am Izra Dziove, honest and loyal follower of the True Commander. The emperor lives, and these priests instead follow the whims of the High Priestess, who directly betrays his wishes." He paused and looked around. He made eye contact with Luan before he turned back to the priests. "I hereby condemn your actions here today. I name all of you traitors. Squadron Leader Luan Zek," he called, invoking Luan's old title. "These priests have committed arson and treason. Arrest them immediately! Bring them before the governor so she may enact the emperor's justice."

He said it all with conviction and with Suoduny at his back; the gods, and faith, and the deep knowledge that this injustice would not go unpunished. Luan Zek only had to say one thing, before the men and women of his crew descended. Old, conditioned behavior bubbled to the surface; they moved like soldiers in strong clean lines and led the priests away, neatly keeping enraged Ostijinians away.

Over the burning of the inn, cries and chants sounded in Uslethian, in Doskorian, in heavy accents and dialects Izra could barely parse. There was a language he did not know, perhaps one spoken here generations ago.

"Ostijan bows to no priests!"

"Izra Dziove! Protector of the empire!"

Izra stood there, recognized for the first time, and smiled.

CHAPTER TWENTY-ONE

It took another two days for Hapina's ship to arrive in port, and for those two days Izra was all smiles. The weight of what came next—what they would learn in the mountains, and the core of why Suoduny had bade him return—felt blurred beneath his joy. Firstly, by the distance they had to travel, and secondly, by Oren, whom was lodged in Izra's mind like a centerpiece. An idol.

On the morning of Hapina's arrival, Izra and the others stood on the docks as her crew unloaded and restocked. Oren stood staring at the horizon, illuminated by the sun. Even directly under its light, Ostijan was cold that morning, as if the sun's entire focus was on Oren, on making him glow. Which Izra could understand. Oren was a sight.

Though days had passed since the priests' arrests, the docks were still full of commotion. Some people were fleeing Ostijan, anticipating Doskor's retribution. Others crowded sailors asking for news of Doskor, or to spread the story of what had happened here.

When the last of the supplies were gathered from Ostijan's docks, Izra led them on board.

Several crates were stored on the main deck, but Izra imagined most of them were packed below. They were the only non-sailors he could see, and it was obvious when he scanned the four of his companions, which ones had experience on the sea, and which ones did not.

Hapina greeted them with a stoic nod, standing strong with her arms folded tightly over her chest.

"Your message scared the piss out of me," she called, by way of greeting. Then she kicked the deck. Izra dropped his gaze, just as her boot scuffed over an indent. No, not an indent—scorch marks. OSTIJAN burned into the deck, the result of Izra's spell. He searched her eyes for any hidden fury. But it wasn't quite his specialty the way it was Oren's. At the very least, Izra thought he could sense her respect.

"Alright, well, unfortunate placement," Oren muttered, mirroring Hapina's stance. "But to be fair—what a place to store a lock of your own hair."

"You're a dolt," Hapina said flatly. "I was moving it after the Uslethians vacated the ship when it started burning in my hand." Then she looked over at Izra. "Incredible. But terrified me."

"My coin should pay for the damage," Oren said with a bright smile. "And if not, I have a lovely brocade we could put down."

"Mm-hm," Hapina muttered. "Don't think that will work, Radek."

Oren looked genuinely stumped—Izra could not tell if he was being facetious. "True. It really won't match the décor."

Hapina punched Oren on the arm with a snort, and Izra had to calcify the urge to ask his husband if he was alright. He managed to graze the skin of his pinky across Oren's hand, which earned him a wink, and something else: a glint in Oren's eyes he wanted to reach out and snatch.

Once they were underway, Odrica slunk over to Mirakel, who had propped herself by the bow to stare out at the horizon. His sister usually liked being alone. After their conversation, he would have expected her to disappear somewhere quiet. So this felt like a development—perhaps in something he should have been aware of all along, but was too caught up in his own cizalec to notice.

Kew had seemingly disappeared, until Izra found him, looking ready to vomit. They had only cast off a few minutes ago, and already Kew had curled between a stack of barrels and crates, staring at the slight sway of the planks beneath his feet.

"Alright?" Izra placed a steadying hand on his shoulder.

Kew jumped as if he had been slapped, eyes flinching to Izra wide and uncertain.

"Y-yes," he said, swallowing back what Izra assumed to be bile. Then he turned toward the ocean, his pallid angled face taking on a look that seemed too dark for Kew; a look that had never before survived his humor. "Then again. Is it really 'alright'? What you have done?"

Izra considered him quietly. He withdrew his hand from Kew's shoulder then asked, "Which thing?"

Kew frowned. "You know very well what I mean." He shifted, rearranging his body so he was not so awkwardly slumped between the barrels. Kew got to his feet and gestured back towards Ostijan. "That—that performance. That theater! You shamed the holy men and women by dragging them away like that. You had no right."

Izra blinked rapidly, wondering if he had heard correctly. No one spoke to him like that, not on matters of the court. Certainly not Kew.

Incredulous, Izra said, "As a member of the imperial court, it is not only my right but my duty to enforce the law. And my prerogative to appoint whomever I wish to carry out my orders."

"And how much longer will you be part of that court, do you think?" Kew got close enough so that Izra could inspect the freckles on his face, the blue of his eyes, the anger in them. "How much longer can you get away with this?"

Izra loathed this conversation. Loathed this tone. He felt old, embedded dignity in him starting to rile. "Did you forget you are also here, carrying out what the High Priestess will label treason? You cannot absolve yourself from this, Kew."

"Maybe not. But you hold the most guilt." It was a low blow, and Kew followed it with, "Well? What of our destination? What possible reason could we have to return there?"

"We will know when we get there," Izra said and folded his arms. At least he hoped.

The anger he could justify. The lack of respect was a problem. But one Izra could address later—once the mysteries of Suoduny's guidance had been dealt with.

He patted Kew on the back and walked away before any more conversation could happen. He walked without thinking, but of course he was walking to Oren.

Oren had already drawn out his cards and started playing with a member of the crew. It made Oren happy to play it; or calmer, at least, more focused. Something about the sea air, and perhaps the incident at Ostijan, had made Oren seem more alive, and in a way more luminous, as if the salt and the brine and the waves were as much a part of his body as the flesh. Izra smiled at that and thought about the gods; thought how Oren worshipped without really realizing it, in his own way. The air whipped through his hair, sending his curls scattering about his face.

"You're a resourceful man," Oren laughed, gesturing to whatever spread of cards had been played against him. Here he turned and gestured for Kew and Izra to join him, but Kew somehow looked sicker than moments before, and Izra just wanted to watch.

"Voyeurism looks good on you," Oren said in response, and Izra did not quite understand, but was sure Oren was flirting.

Their course would take them north, directly up the coastline from Ostijan to a tiny, isolated port called Wicjezst. The ship would not get there for two days which gave Izra two whole nights with Oren—and he found, even when Odrica had planted a seed of uncertainty in his belly—that Oren was all he could think about.

Later, they ate in the mess but away from the crew, who resolutely ignored them like they were just another bit of cargo to be transported. Izra was grateful for it. He did not want conversation. He barely wanted food. He felt, scratching at the edges of his mind, Suoduny and the coming conflict clawing for his attention. For that night, for the liminality of this journey, Izra did not have to feel guilty ignoring them.

He watched Oren laughing at something Mirakel said, kept his eyes focused on the twist of his smile, partially covered by his beard. And when Hapina informed the others they had space belowdecks with the crew, Izra stood expecting to be told the same. But when she told them she had ejected the first mate out of his place for the voyage, Izra moved with a bit too much excitement, Oren in arm.

The quarters were cramped, but the luxury was in its privacy. Wood panels covered every wall. The room consisted of a bed short enough Izra knew his feet would be dangling over the edge, and a writing desk squashed next to it. The instant Oren shut the door, Izra wanted him.

"Oh, again?" Oren said, but he was laughing and slow to stop Izra tugging at his clothes. His eyes stopped on the bed. "That thing looks tiny. I'm not even sure you'll fit."

"There's an easy solution," Izra muttered into his neck. He inhaled the scent of him; dried sweat, caramel, the ocean, and wanted him to smell like he had last night, tangled up in Izra's arms and dripping from sex.

Oren's hands slid beneath Izra's shirt and squeezed over his shoulders, and then Izra backed himself against the wall and hefted Oren high.

He dragged Oren down for a kiss. "We simply do not use the bed."

Oren's eyes filled with lust. He spread his legs apart and ordered Izra, far too sweetly, what to do with his hands. They touched each other, and when they were done, they crawled into the bed to sleep.

And in sleep, it all came back.

Every terrible, overpowering link of Suoduny's started to burn through his mind: a kiss of wild divinity that was both brilliance and torture at once. Those golden threads encompassed him like a net and dragged him awake.

Izra put his head in his hands. An unnatural amount of sweat pooled on his forehead, beading onto his palms. He panted, gasping as if running, or drowning.

At first, he thought it was just the shock of reconnection. Hours had passed mutedly, with his focus on Oren and the night before. But here he was, spent again, Oren next to him, and every bit of Suoduny's power burned through his body. Izra sat up.

He saw Neala in one of the endless futures of this world. He watched as she drank the blood of Usleth's exanimate god. Had she kept some of what Izra had harvested for her father? To what end? He could not tell. But he saw this:

Neala was in the throne room, perfidiously sitting in the empty seat of her father. It rocked Izra to see her sitting there. She dressed in ceremonial wear; white high-necked robes, marking her as unclaimed by any single god, an empty vessel. And now she was taking another god's power inside of her, framing blasphemy in ritual to hide her sin from the empire's gods. Izra watched as she drank the iridescent blood. It stained her lips pearlescent, made the starkness of her pale skin more apparent. And then she looked up—at Izra.

Shivering surprise jolted through Izra as he saw Neala in his mind's eye, Neala grinning at him, using a power that was not hers.

She had found him. She had corrupted whatever latent magic sat in the exanimate's blood and twisted it, so she could step into Suoduny's threads and follow them back to Izra. It felt violating in the basest of ways. Forever, for as long as Izra had lived, this had been his realm.

Neala reached for him. Excruciating pain blossomed in his temples.

She wanted to render him down to nothingness; erase his mind, destroy the gods-given gift in him. Izra saw what was impossible for him to see: the connections in his mind, the brain, the golden threads that let him see fate. And Neala's hands were upon them, dirtying them, attempting with little more than the sharpened nails of her fingers to saw away at whatever she could, whether it be those golden threads or the brain itself. She wanted to destroy at once his power and his senses.

Izra retreated from the intrusion. He had no idea how this translated in his body, but in his mind he darted away from Neala's grip. The panic of waking like this had made him slow. But this was his realm. Neala might as well be a child with a new toy. She lacked the legacy of a strix, of a Dziove's blood, and she did not know how to call Suoduny to her the way Izra knew.

Izra did something awful. He had very little to work with. The throne room was a cavern, the throne itself a beautiful slab of marble.

He placed a hand on the wood paneling of the ship's quarters, he focused on the two thin trees that grew in the throne room's corners. It was a hard connection to establish—the trees were thin but alive, and the thick wood paneling long dead—made even more difficult by the insistent scratching of Neala, attempting to cut away Izra's mind. He had to steady himself with slow breaths, and he was vaguely aware his motion had roused Oren, but Izra could not afford to focus on his body. This was an attack of the mind.

He found the connection and urged those slender trees to grow. He found the roots beneath the stone and made them thick, crossed them over like latticework, made them unruly with life. They could not be contained. All at once, they split the stone. A great crack resounded in the throne room. Izra could have vomited from the shame of his treachery against the emperor, a sullying of his greatness. The base of the marble throne had split.

The sound made Neala jump. She looked down in shock as her stolen throne fragmented. It was enough distraction for Izra to sever the connection, block Neala from cutting away his mind.

By the time it was over, sweat drenched him. He had been violated. Suoduny and those threads had always belonged to Izra, had always been his realm and his alone. No one else could walk them. Shuddering, Izra raised a hand to his mouth. The hot burn of tears pricked behind his eyes, but the release never came. Nothing could have aided his resolve quite as much as Neala thinking she could use his own power against him.

"What happened?"

It was Oren; his voice sounded desperate, and Izra realized he had been asking that for minutes now. Izra finally turned to him, took his hand, and kissed the back of it.

"Neala found me. She drank the blood of an exanimate and gained power from it." Izra did not want to think on what that meant. The violation made him furious. "I severed the connection. I am alright."

"What?" Oren's brows buckled. He gripped Izra's hand more firmly and gave an airy laugh of disbelief. "But taking in that ichor will drive her mad."

"She is already mad," Izra said.

After that, he could not get back to sleep.

CHAPTER TWENTY-TWO

"I'm only waiting three days," Hapina told them when they landed at port. "I have my actual cargo to transport. And besides," she murmured, grimacing at the sight of Wicjezst. "There's always something nasty happening in isolated towns. I don't want to stick around long enough to find out what."

This was good motivation—Hapina was their only transport. But also, Izra did not want to linger too long in this insular town with whatever they retrieved from the mountains.

They had stopped only to purchase supplies for their trek up. The townsfolk were poor conversation. Izra had learned that the last time he had stepped through. A blanketing kind of superstition sat over them, and if any of them knew of the god in their mountains, they did not speak of it. They did not give it more attention, more thought, more energy—they worked hard to forget it. They worshipped Zimsmrt, or shadowy, altered versions of her. Death and winter, a barren cropless land. Whatever it took to propitiate such forces, Izra had deep respect for them. Their trust in the god kept them in this desolate place.

With as few words as possible, they used the last of Odrica's coin on heavy furs, dried meats, and fodder for their horses.

Since the arrest of the priests, and that outburst on the ship, Kew had said very little to him. It concerned Izra, fundamentally, that his friend had withdrawn. Did Kew believe Izra was in the wrong?

It took half a day to reach their destination. Soon the path became so rocky and narrow they had to abandon the horses; stake them down to keep them from wandering. Izra had lived this moment before; jutting shelves shielded the path on either side, two low overhangs that meant Izra had to duck a little to move forward.

But then they encountered a blockage—a gate. It was human made, reminiscent of Doskor's design, but wholly unadorned. The gate had a lock, one that would open only for the magic of the gods.

He had confronted this gate before, and still—something about the lack of flavor, the minimalism, made Izra uncomfortable. He was used to embellishments in these types of gates, but the grandness of this one spoke for itself. It loomed high and was aged. Moss crowded near the base. It looked like an untouched ruin, something from lifetimes ago, a relic still holding on, safeguarding what lay beyond. And it had a different lock to the ones in the castle. Odrica would not be able to open it. Most would not have the power.

Which was, of course, why Izra had been sent in the first place.

Izra raised his left hand. Power thrummed through his silver fingertips. Very slowly, he managed to open the ancient lock. It let out a whine as it grazed against the stone and other iron parts. He breathed deep and pushed it open. Stone rumbled on stone, announcing their arrival.

And then the path broke open into a flat shoulder and a gap between two ridges that continued out of sight, blocking half of the sky from Izra's view. It had not changed. Snow blanketed the ground and flecked the ridges. Kew stopped almost immediately and hung back by the path, unhappiness wafting off him. Odrica and Mirakel managed a few more steps forward than him, but Izra could not blame them. He took Oren's hand and moved forward, until the exanimate filled their view.

It had died between two ridges. Suspended in the air above them, the gedrok's body slung like some half-accepted offering to the gods above. It looked like it had died mid run and stumbled, head crashing down on the right ridge, back leg lodging it on the left. It hung between them, belly facing the snow, its cat-like head forced to sit at an awkward, upward angle on the rightmost ridge. Its maw stretched open, screaming silently at the sky. Fog obscured Izra's vision, but he could still see that the creature's eyes had a stormy, golden sheen to them. He shivered and stepped forward. On the other ridge, its tail drooped, limp and unmoving.

Bloated, enormous frame, but with sleek scale on its outside, this pearly bone color shot through with red, like veins—it was in its own way beautiful, but Izra preferred when gods were invisible to the human eye, something confined in the astrok-mer, or some other realm distinct from the physical. Seeing a god, and seeing one dead, felt unnatural and sickening.

Izra hated this place. How something could be so thoroughly abandoned by the gods and yet filled with the body of one, he did not know.

Oren said, "I have never seen one this intact. It looks . . . alive."

Shaken from his miserable mind, Izra turned his head. Sunlight streaked Oren's face. His beard had grown unruly in the past days, and the sun ran through its jutting ends and turned them gold-tipped. When the wind whipped through his hair and Oren shivered, Izra had to fight himself from stepping close and embracing him. He did not want to break this image.

Gods, as long as he lived, he would never forget the look on Oren's face as he stood there, basked in the iridescent glow of an eternal god. "Back home, they're . . . stripped to the bone. Used for armor, instruments. I've only ever seen the one at Cres Stros, and that was a skeleton. The face is really beautiful . . ."

Izra's face involuntarily wrinkled. Bile burnt the back of his throat—shot up from his belly not from disgust, but pure fear.

Oren continued, "There's a process that goes along with how Paladins of Usleth create weapons from them . . . a reverence for the power? I don't know. I never understood it. But only the Paladins are allowed to make arcane materials. Besides, without their plate armor, ingesting ichor can drive a person insane."

The wind whipped up, a barrel of snow and ice blasting over the lot of them. Like the gods were listening, like even mentioning this undead grave was blasphemy. Izra shivered and brought Oren closer to him, holding his waist, and growing slowly worried. Soon, Izra would have to tell them.

Would Oren let Izra touch him like this again?

The others moved close as well. Mirakel shivered and even Kew had a shake to his hands. Izra's second reached into his cloak and pulled out a flagon.

"Snake wine," he said, tossing it to Izra. "Calm your nerves and keep warm." Kew's eyes darted up at the exanimate behind Izra's head and he shuddered; Kew knew Izra felt guilty. Staying warm was not on Izra's mind when he took a swig.

Odrica grabbed it off him, and Mirakel drank steadily to keep warm. Even Oren was cold enough to drink from it, though he practically convulsed at the taste.

They stood together like that and turned as one to confront the dead beast, to truly consider why they were here.

The shame of returning sat stonelike in Izra's belly. When he had first come here and stalked up the side of the ridge to harvest the exanimate, he had been shielded from the shame by the righteousness of his action. His faith had blinded him to the peculiarity of the gods' request—why rely on a foreign god for a Rezwyn emperor?—as well as the ignominy of not receiving the vision in the first place.

Izra had been passed over in receiving it in favor of the Emperor's Guidance. But he had been able to justify it all away, so long as it meant he was the agent preserving the emperor's life; the empire itself. It had been his duty as a strix to do so.

And he had been wrong.

Now, Suoduny had made him return. And for what? To reinforce his failure? No. What Izra had done, what he had helped occur, was wrong—not only morally and spiritually, but fundamentally. Stealing immortality for a mortal man betrayed the emperor's destiny. The fate of all humankind. That was why the emperor was in the astrok-mer. That was why he would not wake.

Izra was here to correct his own mistake.

But how? If Suoduny wanted to communicate that extending the emperor's life had been wrong, why not punish Izra by making him end the True Commander's life? Why not place a knife in his hand and bid him to do what he killed the priest Semor for? And amongst all this lay the greater question: why block all of Izra's visions to show him only Oren Radek?

Izra swallowed. This was it: the time for honesty, the moment of his reckoning.

He whispered. "It was me."

A beat passed. No one spoke. None of them moved. The silence yawned heavy and aching, the wind whipped in his ears. Izra kept his eyes fixed on the exanimate, feeling ill as he said, "I came up here. I harvested the blood—the ichor in its bones—and brought it back to Doskor for the True Commander. He . . . consumed it. That's when he fell into the astrok-mer."

To his credit—or perhaps to his shock—Oren did not flinch. He did not question Izra, did not shout, did not utter one word aloud. And somehow that was worse.

Vaguely, Izra could hear the others—Odrica quickly gave up questioning Izra and turned her ire to Kew.

Mirakel was trying to understand. Izra did not care. Izra's focus stayed on his husband—his unmoving, blank-faced husband, who might never look at him the same ever again.

"Do you understand, Oren?" Izra moved around to see Oren's expression.

Oren's face was pinched and far away, as if frozen before an outburst. His eyes were distant—that was the worst of it—glazed over, stormy with sorrow.

Even horror would be better than this silence. "Look at me. I need to—"

"Are you serious?" Oren hissed. His distant façade broken.

Oren jabbed a finger in the direction of the gaping hole in the exanimate's chest and said, "You did that?"

Odrica grabbed Izra by the back of the neck like a dog, intent to hold him in place. "What have you done?" she screamed. "What have you done? You have condemned the True Commander! You poisoned him!"

Mirakel scoffed, muttering that she had known all along Izra was no good. Kew pulled Odrica backward. Tears burned through the dirt on her face; she could not conceive of Izra this way, as traitor and blasphemer, and Izra wanted to shout: I followed an order. But the words would not form, because his own heart did not believe it.

Izra opened his mouth, then closed it. Still, he avoided looking at Oren.

Seething now, Oren grabbed him by the lapels and heaved him forward.

Voice hushed now, but filled with vitriol, "We've spent weeks trekking this fucking nation for no reason!"

"That is not true."

"Oh, isn't it? You knew what caused the emperor's condition. You could have just told the truth."

"Really? Tell the truth? In the imperial court at Doskor?" Izra seethed. "I made a mistake. But I did not act at random. I listened to Neala and the Emperor's Guidance and did not think what the true fate of the True Commander was. What the fate of the empire was. I was only thinking—about my duty to keep him alive."

"You told me none of this," Oren said tersely. "None of it. Not for weeks. But you married me, and fucked me, and now you've brought me here, to face your mistake, with no plan and no where else to go, and for what? Because you needed someone to hold your hand?"

Izra felt himself flushing. He shifted, went to reach for Oren's hand, only for the other man to yank it away. Izra said, "We are here because... we need to do the right thing."

This was met with nothing but vitriol from the whole party. Kew laughed, this deep, insidious chuckle, as if he was absolved from all this. As if Izra had stalked up here intent on doing anything but preserving the True Commander's life. Odrica had fallen into an enraged stupor, hand flexing—she looked ready to draw her greatsword, but she was unable to decide if Izra was in the wrong. Mirakel kept silent and stared at Oren, and Oren—

Oren had this awful expression, as if Izra were a stranger.

"Which is what?" Oren yelled. He sounded furious, and terrified. "Why did you let this happen, Izra? Why have you dragged me into this?"

Izra blinked rapidly and glanced away. "Neala and the priests sent me here. The True Commander ordered me to go. I did my duty to him and watched his soul slip away when he consumed the exanimate's blood. Then what? What do you think I did? Do you think I sat there and whined and hid from what I had done?" His fist shook over his heart. "I confronted Neala, confronted the very gods themselves. I stripped myself bare and gave them my blood and offered everything to them for an answer. And in their silence, when I asked Suoduny, I only saw you. Over and over again, the answer was Oren Radek. Now here you are, and you see only the wrong I have done. So perhaps I am a stupid man. Perhaps I should have known Neala's designs and intercepted her from the start."

Oren exhaled and shakily rubbed his eyes. "No," he said, defeated. "No, of course you couldn't have known what she really wanted."

He spoke hoarsely and sounded tired—but that red-hot anger had dripped away. Relief flooded Izra's head and made him dizzy with it. His head swam with the feeling.

Odrica wiped her tears and adopted her usual impassive mask. "Why are we here?"

Oren perked up a little, frowning. "In the astrok-mer, you said you saw that we should come here. To Wicjezst."

Izra nodded. "That's right."

But Oren shook his head, as if this was not possible. "But it wasn't until we were on Hapina's ship that you felt that reconnection. Suoduny returned to you only a few days ago. So how could that vision have been from your god?"

Izra said nothing. Kew could not look at him. Odrica stared furiously. She saw him as a traitor. And Oren undermined him by suggesting that the guidance Izra had been given was not godly at all.

A chill went through Izra's body. He could have keeled over. Sudden exhaustion fatigued every inch of him.

"If not Suoduny," Odrica whispered slowly, "then who?"

Oren looked at him. Izra wished he had not met that gaze. The feeling in him, the feeling that something awful had happened, that he had been duped, filled him up.

Do not say it, he almost said.

But Oren spoke. "You were attacked on the ship, Izra. And it was Neala on the other end, trying to sever your connection. Because she did not want Suoduny warning you."

Izra spoke as if in a stupor, "The vision came from her."

Mirakel looked sick, which surprised Izra; she had no stake in this like he did. "But . . . why?" she asked quietly.

"For the same reason I was sent here before," Izra said with sudden, dizzying clarity. He turned back to the grand gates, the ones locked by a magic so ancient only the power in his blood could unlock it. That was why Neala had sent him last time—not because it was his duty, but because it was a necessity.

And now, again, she had guided him back here.

To unlock the gates that now stood open to the world.

"We have been tricked," Izra said, voice cracking. He backed up, feet sinking into the snow. Panic made it difficult to breathe, making the world seem slippery and unstable. He had to hold on. He had to breathe through it, and calm down, because if he lost control now, Neala would win. He had to—hold on—

"I don't," Oren said, slightly slurred, "feel well."

Once Oren said it, Izra became acutely aware that the blurring of the world had not gone away. Time seemed fragmented, as if Izra's awareness was fading in and out; he experienced each moment separately, distantly. Panic did not feel like this.

All sense, any grip he had on consciousness, seemed to be fading fast. Oren lay down in the snow. Izra blinked, and saw Mirakel was down there, too. When did she sit down? Odrica lowered herself and Izra joined her; verticality made him feel ill, and the snow was cool and comforting. He was going to sleep. He was going to freeze to death.

And then: Kew. His friend appeared like an agent of Suoduny, come to pluck the two of them from insanity, from death. Kew knelt in the snow and said, "Izra, look at me."

Izra tried. He squinted until his vision settled and Kew became clear. He fumbled in the snow, trying to reach for Kew, to make sure he was real and to steady himself. Kew pushed his hand away. Then he grabbed the other.

Izra became vaguely aware of being rolled over. Someone pushed his face into the snow, half smothering him. He made a noise. "Kew, what—"

"This is the end," Kew said.

Izra did not understand. He tried to sit, but everything in him felt soft and tired.

Kew said, "You have gone too far, Izra Dziove. You have acted blasphemously against holy priests. You refuse to take responsibility for your actions against the emperor. You now return to the scene of your greatest crime, and I know you will doom the empire's future just to absolve yourself."

Izra was slow to understand. Perhaps it was the horror of it, the great depth of the betrayal. He did not want to feel it, so his mind let him flounder for another minute before his sense kicked in. He became aware of what Kew was doing to his hands: roughly tying them behind his back. Izra flinched.

"No," he said. "Oren?" He got a muffled noise in response.

Kew did not answer. He finished tying and moved to Oren. It took every bit of remaining strength for Izra to raise his head; in the snow, he saw his sister and Mirakel similarly prone. He glanced back to the gates.

Izra's heart dropped.

He looked down and saw guards there, like a vision. Only it was not a vision. The gate to the exanimate had been thrown open by Izra's power. He had let them in. And now men and women he had once commanded were here—to arrest him.

When the realization came, it hurt. All of them had been drugged. Kew's canteen—that brief moment of camaraderie—had been betrayal.

"Kew," Izra said. "Kew, wait. You are my friend. You are my second. Please do not—"

"I have to," Kew said solemnly. "You are not the only man with a duty in this empire. I cannot let you destroy it all. Neala . . . may be an intense empress, but her convictions, her beliefs, they are all rooted in tradition."

Since when had tradition driven Kew? Izra resisted; his awareness slipped away from him. But he needed to stay awake.

"Kew, this is not like you."

"No," Kew agreed. "But I'm done letting you drag me into all your messes. I won't suffer for them anymore, Izra." And then, perhaps the core of it all, he said, "I want to go home."

Izra looked up. Kew met his gaze.

"I am taking you back to Doskor."

As he said it, the guards swarmed. Only one went for Izra—he was too weak to warrant any more force—and he watched in horror as the others went to the exanimate. They stalked up the side, walked the same path Izra had that first time. They knelt before the hole Izra had carved in its chest. Four of them reached in with long halberds to dislodge something from inside it. One of the blades came out corroded and was roughly abandoned in the snow. Then a great weight tumbled out of the beast and onto the snow below. It sank slightly as it landed. Heavy, weighted, fleshy—they were, for whatever reason, stealing its heart.

Izra flailed. Every limb felt heavy. "Stop. Wait." He glanced at Oren, precious, beautiful Oren, and said, "I know you will take me. I know you will take Odrica. We are Dzioves, it makes sense to return us to Neala. But the Uslethians are hardly involved in the empire's civil war. Leave them. Let it be up to fate whether they survive or not."

Kew smiled very softly. "Izra." He gently nudged Oren with his foot and received no reaction. "This one is too clever, and he likes you too much." Then Kew dropped into a squat, making sure Izra could see his face. And just as everything became blurry once more, Kew's piercing blue eyes were the only thing Izra could focus on. "Anyway," Kew said. "I can leave the Usleth official's life to fate but isn't Oren Radek a Dziove now, too? Since you married him?"

It was the first time Izra had ever regretted marrying Oren Radek.

Chapter Twenty-Three

They were shipped back to Port Sulvoy and a hideous, foul-smelling caged wagon had taken them to the castle at Doskor. Odrica had been ripped away shortly after. But Radek remembered very little of this. Days with poor sleep, no food, and a ration of water—on the back of his stress about Izra's omissions, and Mirakel's absence—made for a poor recall. It was funny how thoroughly corrosive loss could be, in all its forms. The ride back had been uncomfortably quiet, tension like a muzzle on all their jaws—of Izra's supposed duplicity, of Kew's definite betrayal, and of the abject sense of failure that was a weight in Radek's belly. Izra didn't try to explain himself to his sister. Radek had far too much time to imagine Mirakel freezing to death.

And now he had no clue which part of the maze-like castle they'd been carted off to, nor where Odrica had been taken. Izra said Doskor's prison was two dungeons, split by a vestibule. If they were in one, it stood to reason that Odrica was in the other.

"When we first met, I told you that you had the best empire prison of them all," Izra said, voice croaking. Radek slid his eyes over to him. He had to squint to see in this light. The vague shadowy mass that was Izra shuffled and pointed upward to the basalt ceiling. "You see what I mean now?"

Radek made a noise stuck between an acknowledgement, a scoff, and a laugh; this malformed thing that edged out of him and died in the shadows of their prison. His voice croaked thick with disuse.

Izra and Radek did not share a cell, but they were side-by-side, iron bars between them. Radek lay propped against the far wall, tunic spread out over the dusty, grime-covered stone. He was sure one of the other cells was filled, but whether its occupant was still alive could have been hotly debated. No one had come to see them. They'd been dumped there several hours earlier, then left alone.

Izra's hands had been bound. Radek had discovered this upon waking—they had put Izra's big, beautiful hands in rounded iron mittens, ostensibly to keep him from communing with his god.

Which to Radek meant there was something Neala didn't want them to find out.

"What do you think will happen now?" Radek croaked, clearing his throat.

A beat passed where Izra said nothing. Radek thought he must have fallen asleep, when suddenly the other man sighed deep and shifted closer to the bars. Izra looked a mess. Sunken eyes, knotted hair—he was a destitute man in that moment, not a strix commander. Not a Dziove. "It's hard to say. This is all my fault."

Radek rolled his eyes. This kind of attitude normally pissed him off, and now, trying to function on so little sleep, it made him frustrated immediately.

"You're right. This is, in every way, your fault but I think I've had rather enough of your silent burdens and unending guilt," Radek spat.

"Oh, have you?" Izra peeled back from the strip of light and reshuffled against the wall. "I do not think I am quite over them."

"Well, you'll have to be, if we're going to get out of this." And before Izra had a chance to tell him there was no getting out of it, or whatever his current mood would compel him to say, Radek said, "I want to talk about what happened. And you will talk about it with me—none of this avoidant whining—if you ever cared about me."

For whatever reason, that spurred Izra back to life. He shuffled back to the bars and pressed his face against them. "You are my husband."

Radek bit his tongue. A mistake he did not wish to be reminded of. "And?"

"And I care about you, Oren Radek. More than anything. More than—"

"Oh, enough. That's not what I want you to wax lyrical about," Radek cut him off, trying to sound firm. Though secretly Izra's words left him with a dizzying flood of relief. He wanted them to be true. Craved a world where they were true.

Radek gnawed on his tongue, finding his words. Heaviness filled his chest. He hadn't slept. Izra waited patiently in the other cell, watching him with careful, soft eyes.

"Izra," Radek said finally. "I take it Odrica didn't know what you took from the gedrok."

"You saw her. She tried to take my head. She will most certainly try again."

"That's a no then."

A sniffle, a stifled laugh. Izra sat up. "Only Kew. And you. I thought . . ." he put a hand on the bar to steady himself but fell quiet. Even in the dimness, Radek was sure of Izra's expression. They hadn't spoken of Kew. Mention of his name seemed to throw Izra into gloom.

Radek stared at the dirt and found himself once more thinking about their link; whatever strange and otherworldly power that had showed him the past. Gedrok had marched a beast into Ostijan, Dziove had killed the mad king of Usleth—and they had been fated to try again. It felt embarrassing; first that he could believe in fate, and then because he was somehow failing destiny.

"Get over here," Radek muttered. He took out the pearl earring in his ears and gestured for Izra to spin around. "These are ugly, and that's the only reason I'm taking them off you."

Izra gently sighed and Radek slipped the metal ends of the earrings into the locks on the ridiculous iron mittens. He was well out of practice, and tinkered slowly.

"What do you think happened," Radek said, "in our past lives?"

Izra glanced over his shoulder. He had a crease in his brow, a little furrow of incomprehension. "What do you mean?"

"Gedrok Ach Meedin. Emperor Dziove," Radek prompted. But Izra only gently shook his head. "Izra. It's obvious. We have lived in this world before. You have ichor in your blood, and when I gave my blood to Suoduny's idol before I married you, I saw Gedrok Ach Meedin. Before I was even in the astrok-mer. Some part of us has done this all before. Loved before—and failed."

Izra thought about this solemnly, and eventually all he did was nod. He murmured, quite sadly, "Gods, is that what I see, every time I dream of you? Before they died—it ended. I watch Gedrok Ach Meedin leaving Emperor Dziove. I watch the end of their love?"

Radek had no answer. He stared down at the iron mittens and tinkered uselessly. It struck him how easily Izra accepted this, how faith was inevitable in his eyes.

"Who knows," Radek said. "Here we are at the end, and I'm not sure what it was all for. Perhaps Suoduny got it wrong."

"We are fated," Izra said, soft smile spreading on his face. "I told you. You are my fated man."

Radek felt grimy. Shit, he really hated fate. It was lazy, and any immoral person would milk it for every excuse it could possibly cover. Radek glanced up at Izra. His chin and neck were scalded by the bright sun ray that split through the ceiling, casting the rest of his face in shadow. He looked hauntingly at ease with where he was, so calm Radek almost forgot they were caged like animals. He couldn't bring himself to say anything else.

"Do you know much about the war that our previous selves fought?"

Izra frowned. "I have spent most of my waking life interpreting visions for a future, and very rarely thinking about the past. Why?"

Radek wrinkled his nose. "Shit, I don't know Izra. Maybe it's a terrible thought to me that we are trapped in a cycle, and every thought, feeling, or action that's come to my mind might be scripted by a force I will never understand." He could hear himself getting angry but failed to contain himself. "I hate destiny. I hate the thought that everything I feel for you is only because it has happened before."

"Really," Izra shifted, seeming truly surprised. "I think it is beautiful."

Radek scoffed out of instinct, then sighed. "Of course, you do. You're that kind of person."

"We made an oath. Two, actually. I committed to you and you alone, no gods involved. No fate. No destiny. No past—only a future. I gave you the chain of my office—which you wear beautifully, by the way—because I always mean to find you. And—"

Radek rattled the shackles. "And I hate that it seems like I'm being forced to clean up my other self's mistakes. I want to make my own mistakes."

"No, you don't. Believe me. It's much better to be able to blame some distant past incarnation for your problems. Count yourself lucky," Izra said.

The clasp around Izra's left wrist popped open suddenly. Radek grabbed a fistful of Izra's clothes through the bars, forcing the other man to turn, and dragged him into a kiss. Cold metal pressed against his cheeks, and the angle didn't allow for anything beyond a chaste, closed-lip kiss, but Radek's heart still came alive.

"You make pithy remarks so easily," Radek whispered against Izra's lips.

"They come as easily as loving you does." Izra said, far too casually. He pulled back and smiled at Radek like he hadn't just declared something quite profound, and then he grinned. "If we ever get out of here, I could take you to the cuvari."

"The what?"

Izra struggled for the words. "Ah . . . a place. To find out about the men you dreamed of. Archivists, scribes, historians, philosophers . . . meant to preserve memory."

Radek cocked his head. "Whose memory?"

Izra flashed him a grin. "Quite the question. Usually the emperor's."

Radek nodded. But of course. What was he expecting?

"Do you think we did anything on the mountain?" Radek asked quietly.

Izra's face edged towards an apology. "All I did was open the way for Neala's guards to steal the exanimate's heart."

Radek ignored this. "They pledged their souls to the astrok-mer. After . . . Gedrok Ach Meedin rode an undead exanimate into Ostijan." He glanced up at Izra, whose brows furrowed.

"Now who's withholding information?" he whispered.

Radek grit his teeth. "I was worried. And when you said you'd seen a gedrok, and that was where Suoduny was leading you—I was terrified you would try to march it against Neala."

“I commanded the Uxbuh,” Izra said with a laugh. “I would not have bet on the exanimate against the whole of the empire’s forces.”

“I know, I just—” Radek cut himself off. This was a mess. When Emperor Dziove had reached out, mingled his blood with the ichor in Gedrok Ach Meedin, and committed their souls to Suoduny, had he hoped for something better than this? Radek said quietly, “Emperor Dziove thought they could try again. To be reborn, to bring peace. That’s what we’re meant to be doing.”

Izra glanced up at him, smiled, and kissed him. “So far, the only peace I have found is with you.”

Then, before Radek could say anything, two soldiers marched into the prison. In rapid, angry Doskorian, they barked an order at Izra that made him seethe. Radek caught the growled words—strix and Dziove—but they were dripping with vitriol that made Izra nearly recoil. He did not rise, refusing to even look them in the eye.

Radek whispered, “Are you—”

And was cut off by another bark to attention he didn’t understand.

But Izra did. Izra scrambled to stand. A moment later, Radek saw why.

General Neve had come to see them.

Izra’s heart nearly fell out of him.

General Neve stood before him, flanked by two soldiers he knew by name, had trained with, had once shouted orders to. And now he was caged, branded a traitor.

Rage and sorrow and every complicated emotion welled in his body.

General Neve’s eyes scoured over him. She squared her shoulders and jutted out her chin, cast her gaze upon the two of them like they were ants. She looked harrowed. She had not shaved her head recently, but the brown fuzz did nothing to soften her severity. Deep-set, sunken eyes, whites streaked with red, and with a slight pallid sheen to her skin—it was either sadness or anger that had made her that way.

Izra felt a deep shame standing there. When she looked at him like that, he almost expected his skin to begin sloughing off, scalded away beneath her glare. He might even have welcomed it.

"You may go," she said with a taut impatience to the soldiers behind her.

They hesitated. "Sir, he's a strix. A Dziove"

General Neve's eyes flashed. Her low, "I know," came out like a growl.

Izra strained against himself, careful to hold the clasp of the left mitten closed. They must have been fed the same lie; that Izra had willfully poisoned the emperor for his own gain. It was the only thing that made any sense—the only way such loyalty could be shifted.

General Neve raised her head and did not turn around to watch the soldiers slink away. She waited until their footfalls went quiet.

"Izra," she said by way of greeting.

The urge to explain himself bubbled up in his throat. He held it back the way he held back bile; swallowed it down and accepted the burn of it. "General Neve."

"Kew says he saw you kneeling before an exanimate, worshipping its body. That you exsanguinated the beast, collected its blood for my father, the True Commander, to drink."

"I wouldn't call it worship. More like a surgery." Izra pressed close to the bars. "And what about you, General Neve, why did you break your vow? You cannot let your sister control the army."

Again, the wrong thing to say—but this was vital enough that he had to risk the disrespect.

To her credit, General Neve controlled her anger well. "My sister and I will jointly lead this empire—"

"You and I both know that won't work!"

"—and we will put an end to foreign interference!" Here she cast her eye on Radek.

That stopped Izra cold. He shoved himself against the bars. "What interference? You call an interest in trade interference? There is a treaty. There is peace! For the first time in years, Sir, there is peace. And not just with Usleth. At home."

She scoffed. "You have been gone for weeks. Rumors have spread about us. News of the emperor's condition has only stirred unrest on the frontier. City-states wishing for their own autonomy."

Izra clenched his jaw. Expansion had for so long been the empire's purpose. But there was only so far that they could go without decentralizing. Neala craved an empire where once again people lauded Borviet as the most powerful god, and all decisions were made in Doskor—regardless of how untenable those decisions might be to subjects living in the roiling edge of the empire.

"Let them have it," he whispered.

General Neve went red. "Fine. And what then? What happens if I disband the army, send these people home with no purpose and nothing behind them except their training for an empire that no longer needs them?"

"What is the origin of this grandiose catastrophe you envision? Why disband? Our subjects will always need the army to protect them from banditry and foreign incursion. But we need not expand our empire any more. We have enough." Izra locked eyes with the general, feeling his own conviction running straight through the core of him. "And perhaps it will not be perfect, but new things are rarely perfect. The True Commander wills this change."

General Neve looked at him for a very long time. She kept clenching and unclenching her hand discreetly by her side. Eventually her features settled into a determined calm; not one that seemed altogether natural or correct. A clear façade.

"My father is dead."

Izra stared at her. His face twitched. That could not be right. He would have felt it.

"No," he said.

Again, as even toned and sweet as when she had first said it, "My father is dead. So his will no longer matters."

It was the way she said it, so calmly and certain as if it had happened months ago, weeks ago, but General Neve was wrong—could she not see that?—and Izra himself had been the one to stop the blade from slicing the True Commander's heart, and that threat had been hanged weeks ago, and he had promised the True Commander it would never happen again, that it was but a moment on the sea, that as things had been once, they would be again, and—

He gasped and backed away from the bars, and then lost all sense of what his body was doing. Vaguely, he knew he was moving, pacing about. He heard a keening cry, and knew it had to be his voice making that horrible sound. But all of this seemed to be happening to someone else, because if it was happening to him, then Izra had failed and the emperor was dead.

"Someone. . . someone got him," he choked out. "Someone, while I was away. I—"

"No, Izra Dziove," General Neve said. She touched the bars and met his eye, but he could not hold that strong gaze. He felt sick. Everything blurred and melted together, the world too much for his eyes to bear. "He simply died. In his sleep, as men sometimes do. Only whether it was age or the trauma of the astrok-mer, how are we to know?"

"When?"

"Two days past."

Izra shivered. He looked away. He had been with the exanimate then. He had been with some foreign thing when his emperor was dying.

"Izra!" Oren called next to him. "What is it? What's going on?"

Izra ignored him. He focused on General Neve, terrified that if she left here, both he and Oren would be forgotten to rot as war raged. "Do not choose Neala's cultural purification," he pleaded.

"I have made my decision."

She was leaving. She was turning, going to forget them here, or have them killed. He called out, "You will punish the people we subsumed because they did not break so cleanly? You would do that? General!"

She did not turn around. Izra stood there dumbfounded, Oren's voice drowned out by the beat of his own heart, and the knowledge that the emperor was dead, and nothing was ever going to be the same.

Izra was going to be sick.

He heard a high keening noise—his own cry, his own weak mind cracking—and Oren, sweet Oren, calling out his name. He could not say with certainty, but he thought he saw Oren reaching for him, in the corner of his eye—but Izra could not turn. He was trapped, fused to those bars and shaking, trying to keep the sick in his belly.

Then, unbidden, the dead priest Semor came to him. He stepped out of the shadows, elongated, rotting, spine jutting into his neck in a malformed, bruised lump. This vision of him, dragged from a cold, pathetic death; the echo of his broken neck ringing in Izra's ears—what was it all for? What was it all for?

Izra rammed his shoulder against the bars, screaming, frustrated.

"Izra!" Oren shouted. Then softer, more scared, "Izra, tell me. Tell me! What is it?"

No amount of screaming or wailing would be enough. A man who had raised him was dead. A man who had loved him was dead. Death was expected in the empire and so often welcome under the reign of Nio Beumeut that it should not have shaken him this badly. But how easy it was to conceive of the death of a stranger and how awful to feel it; to truly feel it. It was as if a bone had snapped from his own ribcage and been yanked out through his chest.

"My heart," he cried. "My heart." The shock that had locked him in place evaporated. Izra fell to his knees and vomited into the dust. Then he heaved, cried, lungs burning. He could barely hear Oren over the sound of his own distress.

Two fingers edged into view and brushed his shoulder, so lightly he could barely feel it through the thickness of his cloak. It was Oren. His man, his husband, the very heart he could feel dying in his chest.

Oren strained against the bars to touch him, face wet with his own tears; not from the knowledge of the emperor's death, but from Izra's pain. And that was enough. Enough to wrench Izra free of the pit for a moment.

Izra crawled to him. Oren put both hands through the bars and held his face. He said nothing. He just looked. And in looking, he saw, without words, what had happened.

"How?" he whispered.

Izra shook his head. Another surge welled in him. "Just death."

Oren frowned. "A priest?"

Izra shook his head harder, more firmly. "Just death," he said again. And then, "It would have been better if it was a knife. A wound."

"Why?"

"Because I could have stopped it. If I had been here. If I had been doing my duty to him. But death is—" he swallowed back bile, raised his head to the stone ceiling. Where had Suoduny been? Why had there been no warning, no pull in his heart? He had a link to the True Commander, did he not? Izra sighed, shook his head. "Zimsmrt took him. That is all."

It did not make it hurt any less.

Oren's hand dropped, thumb skimming over Izra's jaw. "I'm sorry," he said. He pressed himself close to the bars and kissed Izra's forehead, unhurried, just a moment of intimacy Izra could not help but lean into.

And then it all fell apart.

Those two guards returned to the prison. They were unannounced and unaccompanied. Izra froze and drew back from Oren, willing himself to stand. He braced himself for what was to come, whispering to Oren that it was alright, even when his stomach tensed with the knowledge that if they took him from here, he would not return the same.

But then the figure moved towards Oren's cell.

Izra slammed himself against the bars with a growl. "No!" he howled. "Get your hands off him! Bastard! Scum! Do not touch my husband!"

And Oren screamed back to him, struggling, saying, "Izra! Izra!" with all the high desperation of someone who believes you can save them. Izra shook the bars; Izra screamed.

He was an impotent failure.

All he could do was yell as Oren Radek was dragged away.

CHAPTER TWENTY-FOUR

Radek did his best to be an absolute nightmare. There was no way he'd let himself be dragged to fuck knows where. There was no way he'd go easily if they were taking him from Izra.

As soon as his assailant had him in the prison hall, Radek howled and writhed and wrenched. Two more guards peeled off the wall to help and nearly sprained both of his arms pulling them behind his back.

They led him down another corridor and pulled open a wooden door. Blistering cold instantly hit him. Radek went still, suddenly fearful. If they left him out here, he'd freeze to death. That would be the end of the King of the Merchants.

But moments later, the guards threw him bodily forward. Radek landed not in snow but on wood—a wagon. The floor of a covered wagon. He shoved upward, readying himself to launch back outside, to scrap and fight—but there was someone else in the wagon with him.

Radek went still, heart racing. The figure was hooded and ignored him entirely, uncoupling a fat purse from their side and lobbing it to one of the guards.

Then the wagon door closed roughly with a clank and when the hooded figure tapped the ceiling, Radek heard a whipcrack. Horses whinnied. The wagon jolted forward.

And he was leaving Doskor. Leaving Izra to rot in a cell.

"No," he said. He shoved himself against the wagon's door. "No, no." He spun back to the hooded figure.

Fuck this. Without waiting another moment, he reached out, yanked down their hood—and gasped.

Mirakel, or someone who had once been her, flashed around to stare at him.

She looked haggard. Bruised. A yellowing smudge brushed over her left eye. Dead skin had lifted on her cracked lips. And she glared at him, glared with such animosity; maybe the gods were real because she was here and breathing and not frozen to death on a damn mountain.

"You're alive," he whispered.

"Fuck you, Radek," she hissed. "Do you know how much that just cost?"

She looked more than a little disheveled; her shaggy hair was a mess, dirt was packed under her fingernails. Radek certainly wrinkled his nose when he caught a whiff of her. But she lived. "You're alive!"

Mirakel just stared at him. The wagon rocked unsteadily. The realization burst open in Radek's stomach. He glanced back at the wagon's window, at Doskor's castle growing smaller.

"Wait," Radek said. "Wait, what are you doing? What about Izra?"

Mirakel folded her arms and rolled her eyes. "Oh, yuck. Don't be ridiculous."

"Mirakel," Radek said slowly. He watched her face; she wouldn't meet his eyes. His stomach filled with uncertainty. "Mirakel, we have to go back."

And it all turned to dust in his stomach. Radek rushed to the window, pounding on the door—Izra was back there. Izra was rotting in a cell, awaiting death, and Radek could not leave him like that.

"Snap out of it!" Mirakel shouted. "Right now, Radek. Seriously—this," she opened her arms as if to encompass the whole empire, "is the Rezwyn's problem. It has nothing to do with us. No man's dick is good enough to die for."

Radek blanched, then felt heat pouring into his cheeks. But Mirakel wasn't finished.

"I don't know why they tricked you into that wedding. I don't know how they've indoctrinated you into thinking fate and destiny are real. But I promise you, no one in Usleth will make you honor that commitment. The king will stand by your side."

Radek said, very simply, "I am not leaving him."

Mirakel flushed and tried to pry him from the door. "If you stay here, you'll die like the rest of the Dzioves, and for what? Some drug-induced romantic fantasy?"

"Because I love him!"

Mirakel flushed. She stared at him, eyes wide, unhappy. "Shut the fuck up, you fool. Sit down and get comfortable. And if you so much as think of trying to get out of this wagon, I will tell the king you cost him the equivalent of three really good feasts. Got it?"

Radek felt something fundamental in his chest squeeze. He thought, maybe, he might die—he stared out once more at Doskor's castle, the tiny mark of it, and realized there was nothing he could do. He was powerless here. He could drop and roll out of the wagon, and what? Freeze to death on the road?

Slowly he sat down. He could feel the weight of Izra's chain of office around his neck, and he touched it there, touched the king's seal and this empire mark together, wishing he could have told Izra the extent of how he felt about him.

They sat in silence for a time. Radek didn't know how long. He settled into it, managing to force down a mounting hysteria, when Mirakel went and ruined his almost-calm with, "They would have killed you, Radek. You should be thanking me."

She was right and he hated it. Hated that he was running. But Mirakel clearly had a plan she intended to see through. He asked her, "Where are we going then?"

She glanced away. "Ostijan."

Radek shot to his feet. Ostijan? Fucking Ostijan? He turned to the wagon door. Screw it. Let him be killed on sight. It would take a week to get there. By the time he set foot in the city, there was a chance Izra would already be dead.

Mirakel stood too; hands pressed against the wall for support. "Stop and think," she spat. "There is nothing for you here but death. So we get to Ostijan. We investigate, see how easy it will be to get a ship or get over the border. Some of the army will still be in Westgar. We can get an escort back to the palace, and inform King Zavrius of the situation here. What to do after—whether or not he will intercede to assist city-states that seek independence from Doskor—that will be his decision. As it should be."

Radek sat, defeated. He hadn't even been thinking about the impending civil war. He had been thinking only about Izra Dziove. His husband.

"He would try to save me," Radek said. "I want to save him too."

"How?" Mirakel sat and touched his leg. "You go back there, and they'll kill you on sight, and whatever hope you have for saving Izra Dziove dies with you. Live to fight another day."

Radek looked at her, really looked at her, and thought: I have no intention of letting Izra Dziove die. But Mirakel was right, and even if she was just saying that to pacify him, to convince him there was hope of a rescue, he was glad for it.

"No, you're right," he said. "Few plans work with single actors, and even fewer rescues from imperial prisons can work like that. But who said anything about doing it alone?"

"If you think I can buy his way out the way I bought yours, think again. There isn't enough coin in the world," Mirakel said.

"That's not what I want you to buy." Radek gave a grim smile. "How much does it cost to buy an army?"

Chapter Twenty-Five

Ribbons of the afternoon sun breached the rocky ceiling of the throne room, sending long shadows crawling towards Izra's feet. It made the once godly place feel desolate; the cavern looked like the imposing maw of some beast turned to stone, its jaw split open and stretched wide.

In the cavern's gaping hollow sat the marble throne. It sat on a massive, flat boulder that raised it above the dirt; large cracks ran jaggedly through the base, broken by Izra's power just a week earlier. Blue gems were pressed into its domed back, and arches of stained glass flared on either side like wings. Neala sat upon it, beautiful, clean, dressed in all white. Empress of the Rezwyns. Traitor to them all.

A palanquin lay at the back of the room. It had carried her inside. Neala had deigned to be carried everywhere, Izra guessed, now that she was a so-called empress. Both General Neve and Kew flanked the High Priestess. Neither of them would give him the honor of their gaze. Beyond the guards and two priests of Borviet, no one else was in court. These two were the witnesses. And they would not look at him.

Izra was entirely alone, chained and on his knees before Neala. It had been days since Oren had been taken. How many? Two? Everything had blurred together and he could not recall.

Izra's hands were shackled behind his back. It was a deliberate attempt to sever his connection to Suoduny, and meant Izra could not thread fate with his fingers. But before being dragged away, Oren had managed to open the left mitten—and Izra held it closed now, desperate not to give his one advantage away.

"Izra Dziove," the High Priestess—he refused to call her True Commander—said. "For the crime of murdering a cuvari and foreign ambassador, for the crime of sedition and conspiracy, I hereby strip you of your titles, any and all privileges bestowed upon you and your family by my father and his predecessors, and sentence you to death."

There was no ceremony to the order of his death. She spoke it plainly, like fact. With certainty that it would come to pass.

Until this moment, he had not felt much fear. With Oren gone, what more was there to be afraid of? His heart had fallen somewhere numb and dark—until now. He felt with great certainty the twist of fate, the wrongness of this, the impossibility. This was not meant to happen. This was—not his destiny. A seed of panic began to take root and grow, but Izra pushed it down, letting it smother in the shadowy depths of his apathy.

The High Priestess spoke again, gracing him with the details of his remaining days alive.

"Until the date of your execution, you will remain in Doskor's prison under supervision. I am not so blind to your past deeds for the betterment of this empire. For all services rendered, you will be given a formal, public execution, complete with all burial honors. But should you attempt to engage Suoduny in any further betrayal against me as empress, then I won't hesitate to have you killed and buried in an unmarked grave."

He heard it all distantly. This was happening to another man. Not him. Izra Dziove was strix and commander of the Uxbuh. Izra Dziove was descended from the gods. Izra Dziove had a husband—had just started stepping into his destiny.

How could that man die like this?

The High Priestess shifted. "Do you understand?"

Izra could not bring himself to look her way. He looked to Kew—gods, why was Kew not looking at him? How could his best friend have abandoned him so thoroughly?

The High Priestess sighed. In Izra's periphery, she made a dismissive gesture with her hand. "So be it. Return him to his cell."

Izra felt nothing as two guards approached. They looped their arms beneath his armpits and dragged him out. And there was no point in fighting. His fate had been sealed. Izra Dziove had been reduced to nothing more than a stain in the empire's history.

Only when he was nearly over the threshold did Kew and General Neve finally turn to him. And there was nothing friendly in their gazes.

They looked upon him as if he were a stranger.

They returned Izra to the cell and dumped him there as if already dead. And he landed as if already dead; every feeling in him was suffocated and buried. He let himself hit the dirt and made his peace with it, grateful to rot, for the tranquility that came with nothingness. He lay there long enough that the sun began to set, with only the damp earth and musty dirt for company. But he could not fall asleep. He could not find any rest.

Izra's mind would not leave him alone. As much as he tried to lie there unthinking, something would disturb him. The sound of Oren Radek laughing. The smile he wore so well; upturned corner, beguiling, always amused. The glint in Oren's eyes when he wanted something; the way he arched beneath Izra's touch.

Izra wanted to be left alone; he wanted his thoughts to leave him alone.

But of course, he was lying to himself, and his soul, which had spent Izra's whole life craving his fated man, would not give him up so easily.

Izra sat upright. Anxiety overwhelmed him. Everything he had crushed down, flooded him. He felt panic, despair, a kind of excitement that could only be explained away by the severity of the emotion: his anxiety had nowhere to go.

The truth was that Izra did not want to die. It might have been easier to accept it; to lie there and wait for the execution he had been promised. But he wanted, more than anything, to live, and live happily.

And ultimately, Izra could not shake the feeling that this was wrong. Fate had been his constant companion; this was not his destiny.

"Suoduny, hear me. I need you. Let me understand why my fate has moved off course."

He crawled to the wall, left hand writhing out of its sweaty iron cage. He slapped his hand against the wall, feeling the coolness, the stone, the moss—and how good it was to touch again.

It was the only connection to the rest of the castle, his only chance at scrying, at trying to piece together the reality. Suoduny answered immediately. Golden threads emerged from the stone like roots and spread throughout the castle. Izra let his heart guide him, which was a mistake. It led him first to Odrica—alive, but haggard, in some other part of the prison. When he blinked next, he saw Kew, lying awake on a pallet, eyes to the ceiling. Izra's heart twisted fitfully—he could not see Kew and feel good. He thought briefly this was Suoduny's message: he was here because of Kew's betrayal. But then he blinked again and saw, finally, Neala.

She was at prayer in a room Izra did not recognize. Somewhere in the castle, certainly, but where? She knelt, dirtying that pure white dress of hers in stone dust.

Izra breathed deeply, solidifying the connection, and walked around for another view. He kept his hand on the wall, ensuring a tether to this scene.

He staggered to a stop. Neala was hunched over and whispering, but he had been wrong. She was not in prayer.

She was using magic. Izra was struck again by his complicity in all this. He had gone and carved out ichor from the exanimate, hauled it back—and Neala had drank from it. She had, in a cruel and ironic twist, ultimately been the person using the magic of Usleth.

Whatever she pored over had a dozen strands of prismatic light, connections sprouting out in long, eager tendrils. She violated it, tugging at the threads, manipulating them. She was trying to—control something. To puppet something, like she had when they were young; making puppets to keep Izra from losing his mind to war.

Against the swelling anger in him, Izra pressed himself closer, desperate to understand what he was seeing. What she was doing. He peered over his shoulder. And then he veered back in horror.

A weighty slab of flesh sat on the chair.

Izra nearly flinched away from the wall, but he held fast. He felt so close to understanding, and he could not risk losing the connection. He edged forward, closer still, until he could see more clearly this wretched, twitching thing Neala bowed to. It looked dense, viscous; red blotched over with a dead green-black. With mounting horror, Izra came to understand the shape of it. But he wanted to be sure. Writhing out from this fleshy mass were convoluted streams; a haphazard mess of stunning, prismatic light, lustrous as if trying to cleanse the revolting flesh it emanated from.

He leaned over and touched the light. His sense of space fell out from under him as Izra catapulted through space; his corporeal body became nothing, left behind as his soul vacated the vessel. Stepping onto the path

Neala had opened meant everything was a further degree removed from his reality; his eyesight was blurry, motion slow. But Izra saw the mountains.

And glancing down he saw feet, large and clawed, stamping through the snow. The vision was unfocused, but Izra felt the weight of each step, an echoed vibration that traveled back to his body.

The dead exanimate walked. Its chest had been carved open. The black cavity sat gaping to the elements as the undead beast was puppeted through the mountains. Empty, hollow.

Which meant what Neala had was—

—its heart.

Izra woke with a sudden, vicious fear. He screamed as his soul rebounded back into his body. At once he felt everything: the cold, the damp, the way breath ran down his throat. He had to lie prone for minutes before it all felt familiar again.

She had kept it. She had sent those guards to cut the thing out on the mountain for a reason—a reason Izra could not comprehend.

What was she doing? Manipulating something like that—a foreign god!—and for what? What did she mean to do with it?

Then Izra recalled what Oren had told him. His husband had seen something similar in the astrok-mer. Gedrok Ach Meedin had puppeted an exanimate into Ostijan, had massacred Rezwyn forces. And now Neala, after drinking its blood, was doing the same?

What was Izra's place in all this?

He was trapped here, unable to stop Neala. Desperately, Izra pushed back to rest against the stone.

"Suoduny," he murmured. "I do not know what I am meant to do. I have no power here. I am impotent. Trapped. But my husband—Oren. Oren will help. Let me send to him the knowledge the way you sent me knowledge of him. Let me into his dreams, lord."

Izra closed his eyes and prayed. And waited. Prayed again.

Please. Please. Answer me now.

But the god did not answer him. Izra collapsed and barely contained a scream. He had promised Oren that he could find him, if the other man wore Izra's chain of office. But Izra was scattered, exhausted, fearful, and his magic would not come. He needed a stronger link. He had nothing.

Izra felt ready to slip into oblivion, then. A primal despair filled him; he had never felt so useless in his life. The first soul wrecking sob surged up his throat—and a noise made Izra choke on it.

A clank, then footsteps. He had a visitor. Several, by the sound of it. Izra first replaced his left hand in the mitten and then tried to gather the will to stand, to meet them face on, but the lower, more base part of his mind fought him. What was the point?

He was met first by a lone figure: Kew. And then by two cuvari, which was a unique form of torture. They had come to record his life; he was a strix and commander, and even as a so-called traitor, his was a life meant for the annals. But Izra hated them. Hated how they might twist his life, everything he had done and suffered for this empire, to fit Neala's truth.

The cuvari waited in the shadows as Kew stepped forward.

Kew's face had no pity, no apology, but rather a kind of thirst; like Kew had been craving to speak to him. Something like hope spiked in Izra, and he had a difficult time fighting it. He looked to Kew with enormous anticipation, silently praying to whichever god that this was Kew, his old friend, and not Kew, agent of Neala.

"Kew," Izra whispered.

Kew glanced away immediately at the sound of his name. He pulled back his shoulders, clasped his hands behind his back, and turned to inspect the dripping, moss infested wall. "Before the cuvari attend you, I thought I would inform you . . . that they've set the execution for a week and a half from now." He gave Izra the honor of meeting his eye, then. To report clearly and calmly the date of his death. "They are giving all the governors a chance to visit, even as far as Veprak. To pay their respects to the strix at his death."

Izra had nothing to say to that. No thanks to give, no anger. It was beginning to feel inevitable; that brief surge of fight had shown him only Neala's further betrayal. He could not contact Oren. And the *cuvari* were here. This was their chance to record his life, mark him down in the annals. Izra Dziove would forever be marked a traitor to the empire.

All this meant, without question, that Izra really was going to die.

Kew's gaze turned unsettling quickly, when Izra said nothing. Then Kew scoffed and folded his arms.

"It's an honor, Izra."

Gods. Izra slid his eyes to Kew. "It does not feel honorable."

"Well, after what you have done, you hardly deserve it." Kew signaled to the two cuvari, who happily stepped forward, slates out to ruin Izra's memory.

Kew turned to leave.

"Wait!" Izra stood then, surging towards the bars. They rattled as he crashed against them, hands still behind his back. "Do not be a fool, Kew. Think about it. She calls an audience not for me, but for herself. We watched her cut the heart out of the exanimate on that mountain. What do you think that was for?"

Kew hesitated. He half turned, enough Izra could see the sharp descent of his nose, but he did not speak.

Izra's eyes flashed between the cuvari and Kew, worried about what they would overhear—but gods be good, what other choice did he have? "She's raised it," Izra said. He heard his own shock ring out. "I have seen it marching across the mountains. I do not know what for, except that Neala will use that god nefariously. And whatever she does with it, she will blame it on Usleth. She will start a war on no grounds. Please—"

Kew spat, "She will be empress. *Empress Neala.* You will address her with respect."

"Look at me!" Izra screamed. He crashed against the bars, furious, desperate. "Look at me. I have done everything for this empire. I won us that war. I let so many Uslethians die; I saw all their deaths. I would never ask you to betray the True Commander or the empire he built. But what Neala plans to do is its own betrayal. You know this. You know this, Kew, and the general knows it, too."

"Izra," Kew said, very softly. "You have been sentenced to death."

As if Izra had forgotten; as if that rendered everything else a lie. "Then leave me here. This is bigger than me. You need to stop this, Kew. Find Odrica. She's a child of Borviet; she will think like Neala thinks. She will know where Neala is storing it. She can help you get to the heart. And you can destroy it, you can stop this war before it starts."

Kew glanced back at him. Then at the cuvari. "These two will record your life now, Izra Dziove. For the records of the empire, under Empress Neala's order."

And Kew walked away.

"No, Kew. Kew!"

The jail door banged closed, leaving Izra alone with the two cuvari; cretin scavengers, come to pick at his body. They unfurled from the shadows, sweeping forward with their slates to scratch his history down. They were the older woman, and the genderless one who looked about Izra's age. Their young male counterpart had fallen already to Neala.

"I did not kill your third," Izra said; felt compelled to say, as if the truth might keep them from destroying his name. "Nor the foreign diplomat. But given that it is your job to know things, I hope you know I speak the truth already."

"You are Izra Dziove, formerly strix and commander of the Uxbuh, favored of True Commander Nio Beumeut. Now traitor to Empress Neala. We have questions—"

"You know I speak the truth. You know why I was framed," he cut them off. Izra felt the open shackle at his wrist and thought: I am not ready to die. He was alone with these cuvari, and as much as they were meant to value truth, they were scared. But he could press them. Surely. Izra said, "You, or your third, he found something. Am I right? In the emperor's memories. And he was killed for it."

An uncomfortable beat of silence passed. The woman scratched on her slate—what she could glean from Izra's desperate rant, he did not know.

Izra could not stop. The other cuvari watched him, and though they were mostly impassive, something flickered in their eyes, a wobbly conviction, a dam creaking under weight. And Izra knew with certainty then that this horrid little order was his only chance. He needed an ally. Neala had killed one of theirs, too. Solidarity lurked beneath the surface. "You are scared of retribution. You are scared Neala will kill you, too. But I can help. I can help stop this—this future from unfolding. This is not right. Not what fate intended. I know that you can feel it, too."

"We cannot," the genderless cuvari whispered.

"Yulik," the woman hissed. She was agitated, kept shifting her weight. "Silence."

Izra pressed on, desperate. "She killed one of you. Like it was nothing. Why?"

The woman turned to Yulik immediately, but she was too slow. They were already saying, "Because of the emperor's will."

"Stop it," the other cuvari hissed.

"He deserves to know. And what of it? He's set to die anyway. The knowledge will die with him."

The woman pursed her lips, made them very small, and stopped scratching on her slate. She glanced away as if to say she would not be a part of this, but Yulik ignored her, and stepped closer to the bars.

Izra could tell they were cautious at being overheard. He strained closer, sinking into the brown depths of the cuvari's eyes, eager to know. The cuvari said, "The emperor had a clause in his will. It protected against . . . an unnatural death. And you would inherit the title, Izra Dziove, not his daughters, if he were to die like that. And . . . he added it just after the High Priestess's so-called vision: that the exanimate's ichor would extend his natural life."

"What?" Izra's stomach opened. His forehead kissed the bars as the weight of his head became too much.

The True Commander had not trusted his own daughter. The True Commander had craved immortality enough to try it anyway. And though Izra had retrieved the ichor, had presented it to the emperor in supplication, it was not Izra's fault.

"It is you who should be on the throne," Yulik murmured. "And the cuvari have the will to prove it. The written word of the True Commander Nio Beumeut."

Izra would inherit the empire. Izra was meant to be the True Commander. Suoduny's visions were not treason, but truth.

"Then prove it," Izra said in a whisper. Something sparked his chest, a momentary hope. "Is this not treachery? Treason? You have the will of the True Commander; you have the proof."

"And Neala has the army," Yulik whispered. They sounded quietly ashamed and glanced down at their hands.

That was the crux of it. Neala's power might not have been grounded in the emperor's will, but it was tangible. If she ordered the death of the cuvari, it would be done, as it had been for the first cuvari to die with Paqe.

But Izra could not wither here, not when he knew for certain fate had planned something else for him. So this was it: his chance to pull fate back in his favor. Suoduny was still on his side; and Izra needed to contact someone.

"You do not have to free me. You only have to free my mind. I will ask nothing else of you. And if I fail, then so be it. No one will know what you have done."

The woman made a soft, hissing noise of disapproval, and was resolutely ignored. Yulik stared at Izra, truly stared, like they saw into his mind, and were able to sifting through memories, desires, intentions.

Something softened in their gaze. Izra knew he had them.

"What do you need?" Yulik said.

And Izra thought only of Oren. Of how to contact Oren.

Oren Radek. His hope. The man he would gladly give his life for.

"A chain of office," Izra said. "I need a chain of office."

CHAPTER TWENTY-SIX

Radek woke in a grove beside the castle, a little protected forest of moss, rocks, and trees, and felt more at peace than he had felt in weeks. His vision softened; the details ebbed away, and any sense of time, space, or the impossibility of this—where was he? He was—in Ostijan?—was resolutely buried under a numbing wave of calm.

He wobbled to his feet and put one foot in front of the other. Moss touched the soles of his feet; soft and weirdly warm, otherworldly. He felt as he had in the astrok-mer, or sometimes between sleep and waking in Izra's arms; not quite in this world, not quite human.

The sun was rising, or setting—he had no sense of it, only the starburst bloom of orange glow flooding the grove. The stone of the castle turned bright in a cascade of light. Radek followed the ray, had to arch his neck to see a window glare suddenly when the sun hit it.

And there, just like that, was Izra.

All sense left Radek's body. He became aware of multiple conflicting emotions rumbling in his stomach; sudden, unstoppable energy, fear, relief. It propelled him forward, until he could scale the wall. If he could just—get closer, get nearer—if Izra would just smash the glass and lean down, then perhaps Radek could be hauled up.

"Izra! Izra!" Radek called. Izra stared at him and pointed down to the space at Radek's right. Radek craned up at him, and through the window he saw Izra press a card to the glass. It slipped through, absorbed, and popped out the other side, flittering down within arm's reach. Radek snatched it from the air. It was hand-painted as if from his own deck, but resolutely not. That damn card that had taunted him in the astrok-mer.

FATE'S EDICT.

Some invisible wind took the card from his fingers and Radek followed it without thinking, in that dream-logic haze where every action feels important and correct. The card flew over to his right and there, where it hadn't been a moment before, sat a piece of flesh.

Something in Radek recognized it immediately as a heart. It was the size of his torso and still beating madly, pumping nothing but squelching air, awful and twitching. And the deep, primordial part of him peeled away in horror; run, it said. This is a nightmare.

But Radek found he could not move, and shortly after, all fear in him ebbed away. He reached out. Some force compelled him to touch it.

For a split second, he held a memory in his mind that wasn't his. Fuzzy, indistinct: a gedrok walking, marching; dead and ancient, the same one from the mountain. The same gedrok—the same one—and somehow his touch made the whole giant body jerk. The gedrok stuttered to a stop, booming footsteps replaced by the soft rain of rock and snow settling at its feet.

Then the gedrok turned to face him. And in its eyes he saw reflected not his own face, but that of Gedrok Ach Meedin.

Radek woke with a start.

He shot up violently, head swimming, panting. Floorboards. A door. Inside, and warm—no snow around.

He was not in Doskor. He was nowhere near Doskor. Oren Radek woke in his pallet in his Ostijan warehouse, the same bed Izra Dziove had woken in. It had been a week and a night since he had left the cell in which his husband was rotting. Radek gripped the sheets and forced his breath to slow. He grounded himself, reminded himself where he was, and told himself it was just a dream.

Only the placation felt hollow.

And perhaps it was guilt making him think that odd vision had truth in it, or perhaps he was a lovesick fool—but Radek knew that hadn't been a dream. That was unlike any dream he had ever had. Months ago, he would have dismissed it, but that was a different Oren Radek—a man who hadn't managed to marry a damn prophet. He felt Izra's chain of office around his neck. Izra had promised him, after all, that if Radek wore it, Izra could find him.

So, no.

For the week's journey, he had been handling his emotions relatively well. They would rise, and he would beat them back—or Mirakel would—and Radek would once again fall into a nice and distant apathy, where nothing was bad, but neither was anything good. He had rendered himself unemotional by necessity. And this dream, or prophecy, had gone and ruined it all.

Radek felt again the same desperate urge he had felt in that wagon. He did not want to leave Izra. And Izra's timing was brilliant and focused; the day after their arrival in Ostijan, Izra Dziove had managed to give Radek a warning.

He needed to get back to Doskor. But he couldn't do that alone.

Radek stood and stumbled out of the small office shirtless. Downstairs he could already hear someone bartering with a fuller for some new fabric, and floorboards creaking with workers. Upstairs, he moved passed rows of bolts of fabrics. Mirakel was already awake, pressed to the glass.

She spotted him and nodded. "I'll head out to the docks today. Try to canvass the area, see if anyone's attempting to get over to Usleth. And if not there, merchants. Anyone who can get us close to the border."

Radek didn't say anything. He tried to gather the words, the arguments, the solid and immutable reasons that would make Mirakel understand. But this time she worked it out for herself. She looked at him, exhaled, and touched her forehead.

"No."

She had tried talking him out of it. An army would be too expensive, and mercenaries were too untrustworthy. To give his heart a rest, Radek had dropped the topic. But that vision—that message—meant he couldn't be silent any longer.

Radek smiled weakly. "We have to go back."

Mirakel made a face and crossed her arms, sitting back against the windowsill. She had a unique look of fury on her face; sadness and fear crept in behind her eyes to soften it. And she did not look at him when she said, "I don't know exactly when it was you lost your senses, but for the bone's sake, Radek, listen to yourself. How good was the sex that you'd throw your life away."

"Bloody good, but that's beside the point." Mirakel glared at him; wrong thing to say. He put up his hands. "I'm not throwing anything away. Ignore it: ignore how I feel for him—"

"Gladly," Mirakel scoffed.

"—but still listen to me."

She looked down at the boards, still not gifting him with eye contact. But she stayed quiet, and that was enough.

"If we don't do this, there will be war. Real war, worse than the last one," Radek said, moving closer to implore her. "Neala is not like Nio. There will be no treaty to negotiate. Only obliteration. And you know as well I do, Usleth is simply too small. We do not have the resources. We certainly don't have the funds."

That got her attention. She rolled her eyes and went to speak. Radek cut her off.

"No, listen. His Majesty is a good king. But Zavrius won't be able to do anything that doesn't destroy Usleth in some way or the other. The populace. The culture. The finances. Something will have to give. And Usleth will suffer for it, in a way it won't ever recover from."

"No," Mirakel said, definitively. She pushed off the sill, arms still hugged close to her chest. "It's not a good enough reason—and even if it was, what could the two of us possibly hope to achieve?"

Radek blinked at her. "Do you think me so daft I would suggest the two of us go alone?"

"Absolutely," she said, without hesitation. "It's definitely something you would do, especially if you think you love him."

Bones, she thought him stupid. Had she thought he mentioned an expensive army just to rile her? Radek gaped at her. "Well, have a little faith, Mirakel. I've grown as a person." Radek folded his arms and sighed. "We have a perfectly decent group of mercenaries getting drunk in Ostijan to petition. I still owe them those bolts of fine silk."

Mirakel scoffed at him, then realized his sincerity. "Luan's crew? Why on earth would they risk it all to save your husband?"

"Because Izra will be a far better emperor than Neala." Mirakel made a noise and Radek had to practically shout. "Listen to me. If it's not them, then it will be another mercenary crew. Money talks. We pay them, we rescue Izra, and we make the damn man the emperor. Don't say anything, just listen: he has a claim. He has supporters. And doing this will mean King Zavrius has a hand in securing the new emperor's place. Usleth will be more secure than it ever has been. Not to mention, Izra married me. I will be consort to the emperor—"

"Oh, Radek, for fuck's sake."

"—*and* Izra has no ill will towards Usleth. He had too much of a hand in the first war. He will not want another. So, how's that? Plenty of reasons for the empire and Usleth to get along."

Mirakel started pacing. She had been pushed too far, Radek decided—something in her mind cracked under the pressure. When she reached some conclusion, she snapped back at him. "It doesn't matter what I think, does it? You'll stay regardless."

"I have to," Radek said honestly.

She said nothing. Just looked at him, sadly, like she wasn't sure what to do, or like she'd lost him somewhere. Radek foresaw a potential future where she walked out the door and got on a ship and left him here. Which would be manageable, but not what Radek wanted.

And he was surprised to realize how truly he didn't want her to go.

"Mirakel," he said. "I know for certain there's a lot less chance of me fucking this up with you here."

She snorted immediately and glanced away. "Flatterer." She sighed, stood still for a moment, and then groaned. Mirakel viciously rubbed her face as if trying to erase it. From between her fingers, she grunted out, "I would need . . . money. More money than I have access to. Getting you out of Doskor, Radek, that cost *so damned much*."

Radek fought the urge to run forward and sweep her up in an embrace. That would be, most likely, her final straw. He glanced around the warehouse. The answer was simple. "I'll fund it."

Mirakel paused. "What?"

"What? Surely you didn't forget," Radek said. He spread his arms. "King of the Merchants. I have the funds for this, and I am authorizing you to spend as much as you bloody want to convince Luan's crew to come with us. Throw in some expensive fabrics if you need to. Just get them onside."

She clicked her tongue. "Radek. It will take a week to get back—"

He couldn't hear this, not right now. Couldn't let himself imagine the possibility where Izra was dead before

Radek could do a thing about it. "Then stop wasting time arguing with me and let's meet with Luan."

She looked at him for a long time, blinking rapidly. Radek wanted to scream, wanted to thank her, wanted to embrace her. But he just stood there waiting. She smiled softly. "That I can do."

They wasted no time. They had a man to meet.

"Well," Luan sighed, sucking ale through his teeth. "That's horrifying to learn."

They were back at the mercenaries' house. The front room looked cleaner, without empty bottles and passed-out drunkards, and there was enough difference for Radek to put distance between the last time he was here and now. Which felt necessary—he had been pressed against the walls of this house, touched, loved. Panic lurked beneath Radek's necessary apathy, though, because this had been the night he had really made Izra his. And this was where Izra had made a new vow to Radek.

No gods. No fate. No past. Just a future they might carve out together.

Radek had just poured out his heart, told the whole story. They sat at a table in the house's front room, packed with mercenaries eager to listen in. Most of them sat on the stairs and craned down, out of the way but obviously interested.

All of their reactions were noticeable except for Luan's, which seemed suppressed. Two men and a woman from his company flanked him, and the anxious glances they gave each other made Radek squirm.

"How long have you been back in Ostijan?" Luan asked, ignoring the silent exchange happening behind him.

"We arrived last night," Mirakel offered.

Luan nodded, drank again. "Right. Then you wouldn't know."

Luan pushed himself away from the table and made a two fingered gesture to someone on the stairs. The table before them had an abandoned card game Radek didn't know the name of. As Luan twisted in his seat, Radek got another chance to understand the size of him: wide as he was tall, muscle, fat, strength. His cane leaned against the table. Luan stayed facing away from Radek until two people arrived; one from the kitchen and another squeezing their way down the stairs. Another jug of ale was placed on the table, and as Mirakel reached over to pour, a young woman slapped something onto the table between Radek and Luan.

A letter. A letter Radek recognized.

He and Izra had spent hours writing these out.

"These are spreading like the pox," Luan said, shifting back to drill two fingers on Izra's sworn statement. "Copies of them are being made, too, so there's rumors the whole lot of them are fakes. Other people want to fight. There is," he paused, seemingly lost for words. "Ostijan has always been on the brink of a true rebellion. But Elkar, other coastal towns—people are starting to choose sides."

Radek was missing something important. Izra and he had sent the letters with this intention—to warn people, to let them form their own judgment about Neala. He glanced back at Mirakel as he said, "I'm sorry, I don't quite—"

"We expected Izra to call on us. With everything that's brewing, and with . . . what happened last time you lot graced Ostijan. We expected Commander Izra Dziove to ask us to join him in removing the usurper from the throne. But we did not expect you."

Radek shifted. He wished he'd paid more attention to how Luan played Gulek Des, because he felt something fundamental changing. Was Radek losing this negotiation?

"What, you don't believe me?" he said, too emotionally. "You don't think he's going to be hanged?"

"It's not that, Oren Radek. Or rather, Oren Dziove. I have no doubt they will kill him. What I doubt is what you ask of us—because following the orders of the strix and the commander is one thing. But opening myself and my company to accusations of treason is another."

Radek stilled himself. It would not be the end of everything if he lost Luan. But it would mean more money, and more time, spent on convincing another company. And Izra was waiting, and Radek didn't know how long they had. He leaned forward.

"Then let me ask you this. Do you believe Neala is legitimate in her claim to the title?"

Luan made a face. When he spoke next it was gruff, accent coming through thickly. "You do not really have to ask that, do you?"

"I do," Radek said seriously.

Luan leaned back in his chair. It creaked with his weight. "No. She is not the legitimate empress."

Radek exhaled through his nose, nodding. "Then the orders of Izra Dziove are still binding." He reached beneath his tunic, feeling the now-warmed metal of the chain of office. With deliberate slowness, he slipped the chain of office out from beneath his clothes. Witness it, he wanted to say. Follow it. Please. But he said, "The symbol of the strix, Commander of the Uxbuh, Izra Dziove. I bear it. And I ask on his behalf: join us. Remove the usurper and put Izra in her place."

Luan leaned forward with a proffered palm, and Radek had to extend his neck uncomfortably for the other man to get a hold of the symbol. Luan ran a big thumb over the many-faced boar embossed in the metal and glanced up at Radek. Then he broke into a smile, this dazzling, split-mouthed grin. "That's more like it." He clapped his hands together and leaned his elbows on the table. "What did you have in mind?"

They discussed, first, the money. A great deal of coin was agreed upon, with a further stipulation about all the pretty clothes Radek might have made for them. And time was of the essence, so Radek promised something he shouldn't have: a proper audience with Izra after it was all done, and some gifts only an emperor could offer.

Then the plan itself. They would slip into the city in small groups, rather than fight their way through, because they needed to attract as little attention as possible while they headed for the castle. Radek knew the prison sat somewhere in the castle's depths, but Mirakel knew where that side door was located, and that would be their point of entry.

It was a simple extraction, and a simple plan, but Luan spoke with a confidence; about where he would post mercenaries, about the codes they used to alert others. They agreed on the points they would stop to switch horses, and Radek promised to pay them extra for the hard ride.

"How long do we have?" Luan asked.

"No time at all," Radek said. "We need to leave today, and we need to ride fast. Is that—doable?"

Luan and Hulik snorted in time. "Compared to the Rezwyn army, I am sure this will be a luxury," Luan said. He uncrossed his arms and leaned against the table. "You have a deal, Oren Radek."

And Radek felt, for the first time in a week, hope.

Chapter Twenty-Seven

Up until the very moment Izra Dziove had a noose around his neck, he felt the days had passed long and terribly. But the instant he was there, he realized the time to his execution had passed in a relative haze.

Izra had risen from his disassociation in only a few bouts of panic—burning, rabid anger, a desperate will to live—but the inevitably of his situation kept luring him back to a quiet agony.

He had tried to contact Radek. But there was a particular skill to carrying information through Suoduny's threads, one that felt entirely different to scrying. Izra would have needed years to master it. He had no idea if it worked. So one night, instead of calling for Oren or trying to warn him, he had simply followed that thread to Oren. And Izra had seen his husband. Sleeping peacefully in Ostijan. Safe.

After that, Izra had stopped trying. He had blinked and the last week of his life had gone by without incident.

Now, he stood bound and waiting.

Izra shivered. The gallows loomed behind, a shadow at his back. Even with the sun out, the wind blew blistering cold. It cut across his cheeks, turned them red and raw. Before his feet, the crowd edged close to the raised platform, kept at bay by a circle of soldiers he had once commanded. None of them looked his way.

Locals, priests, and governors from the city-states dotted the crowd. Some had arrived as late as the hour of his death, having traveled from as far as Veprak or the Western Frontier. And of course his favorite vermin, the cuvari, were set off to the side of the gallows, slates raised, ready to record every kick and gurgled cry he made in his death.

There was a haunting happening, Izra felt. All this had happened to someone else; he had been executioner, waiting eagerly to punish Semor. And now the dead traitorous priest lurked here, waiting just beyond to revel in Izra's death. Izra felt his soul strain with how familiar this felt.

Panic rose again, slipping out through the carefully knitted calm that had been keeping him in check. But then onto the gallows came Neala herself, borne in her dark wood palanquin, flanked by Kew and General Neve—his friend, his confidant—and something in Izra snapped. His hands started to quiver behind his back, and it could have been fear, but it felt more like rage: a hot, jagged mess of anger and impotence forcing its way out of Izra's body.

Not much longer until Izra would feel nothing at all. Not much longer to go.

The door to the palanquin slid open with a grinding wheeze and two priests of Borviet came and offered their hands. Neala emerged, balanced between the two of them, and very daintily set foot onto the stage.

And she was a sight to behold. She had dressed very well for his death. Neala wore her long hair in two plaits down her back, held in place by a thick circlet running around her head. She wore, as was her custom, a floor-length white gown, but she bore a cuirass over it—emblazoned with the human-boar representation of Borviet himself.

She projected a unique and poised image; a deliberately confusing amalgam of holy stability, with the bloodthirsty craving of the war god she favored. Masterful.

Kew and General Neve moved behind her as Neala stepped forward, which put them closer to Izra. He chanced a look, but neither of them acknowledged his presence.

"Children of the empire," Neala called, and the ambient buzzing of chatter died instantly. Her voice carried; Izra could hear the distant reverb of the basin, the mountain walls calling back. "I am Neala Beumeut. Your empress, your True Commander, your High Priestess, daughter of Nio Beumeut, blessed by Borviet. And I have borne witness as this once great empire has begun to crumble. I have seen the taint of foreigners on our land. The way they twist our culture, infect our children, corrupt our greatness. No longer! It is now my solemn duty to ensure the Rezwyn Empire returns to its days of glory. That we conquer as Borviet intended!"

Most of the crowd cheered, most of what Izra could see. He closed his eyes to them and turned again to Kew. Who wasn't looking at him. Gods, why could Kew not even look at him?

Neala continued, "And the first act to rectify this wicked divergence is this: the execution of the traitor Izra Dziove!"

The next cheer from the crowd felt like a knife to Izra's gut. It had weight to it, a personal opening of his soul. He was going to die, and it was real, it was happening. And he had promised himself he would not scream, or fight—that shouting his innocence would be useless and degrading—but as the moment drew closer, all those nightmarish, convoluted feelings Izra had a handle on started to slip out of him. His body jolted. The soldiers tensed; Izra knew that body language, knew they were anticipating some rebellion, but the crowd swelled only with eagerness. A few soldiers turned to the general, and Izra let himself believe they were looking back for orders—the orders to attack. To free Izra Dziove. But General Neve made no motion to move.

"Izra Dziove has been stripped of all his honors, all his privileges, and all his greatness!" Neala shouted with barely contained glee, pacing back and forth like the gallows were her stage. "Forget what you know of Izra Dziove the strix. History will only know this man: a traitor, a fool, and bedfellow to the Uslethians. You have abandoned the path the gods laid out for you. And now you will be removed, cleanly and swiftly; a curse on the Rezwyn name to be stamped out."

Then she turned to him, with glee in her eyes. "Izra Dziove, I hereby sentence you to death."

The priests of Borviet moved to enact the order instantly, flanked by two soldiers. They shoved him roughly to the ground, put the noose around his neck. Izra broke. A bestial frenzy roughly pulled reason away from the forefront of Izra's: Izra realized he had made no peace with death. He wanted to live. His body twisted against his restraints, even as the rational, muffled part of his brain told him it was useless. Fear overrode it all. Fear, and desperate hope.

"I am framed," he yelled. His voice edged out raspy from disuse; it screeched in echo back to his ears. Hair whipped across his face as he fought against the ropes. "Neala lies! Please! Listen to me! I invoke the cuvari, who are impartial and nonpartisan. I am the rightful inheritor, and they have the document to prove it!"

This gave him a moment of respite from any jeering. The crowd was shocked, and they waited tensely for a cuvari to emerge, document in hand. Izra waited too, waited with hope. But the moment stretched, and Neala began to laugh, and Izra grimaced. Speaking had been foolish. There was no point in shouting.

Izra turned to Kew, and finally, *finally*, his friend was looking at him.

Kew nodded to Izra once. His expression was still unreadable, enough that Izra thought: this is Kew acknowledging me at the time of my death. This is the last honor he can bestow upon me, the last deferential nod, the last bit of respect he can afford me. Izra breathed in and held it.

Then Kew inclined his head to the crowd.

Izra frowned. He turned with careful anticipation to the sea of faces, the overwhelming stares. It was difficult to look at, daunting to have those eyes watching him, a dozen souls, a hundred, more. Izra wanted to glance away. And he would have, if someone in the crowd had not stood to their full height: had not pushed back their hood, let their long hair loose.

They locked eyes, and the shudder of hope that ran through Izra felt at once instantaneous and simultaneously slow—he turned back to look at Kew and wondered: how did you free my sister?

Odrica was in the crowd. Odrica was—

Something howled.

At once, everything stopped. Or rather, it felt like it did. Everyone in the crowd stilled, breaths held, gaze unblinking. Izra heard a wail, this great, gripping cry that echoed in the basin. Deep throated, inhuman, ancient. A cry buried in the lungs for a millennia.

The cry of an exanimate.

CHAPTER TWENTY-EIGHT

A bellow shook Radek to his core.

The horses whinnied, frightened, but Luan barked an order and everyone pressed firmly into their mounts' flanks—from the hill, Radek could see the gates of Doskor glinting at the bottom, the river cutting through the city, the castle sprawling to the city's left—and the speck of some massive thing bursting into the keep.

"Shit."

They had ridden hard for a week, but all that exhaustion evaporated from Radek's body as soon as he heard that noise.

This was it: the horrible confirmation that what Izra had shown him in that dream was true. Neala had marched the gedrok here. Something ancient and primal and possibly a god had been puppeted here—for what?

Whatever its true purpose, Radek knew at least this: it was tearing a hole in the castle. A terrible thought gripped Radek's heart. Was Neala executing his husband by having him *eaten?*

Luan led the party. They streamed down the slope, a cavalcade of galloping horses. Rows of buildings submerged the sight of the gedrok roaring at the sky; it sank below, in that open-throated howl, head raised to the sky like when Radek first saw its corpse.

Just before they hit the gate, which was swung wide—posts abandoned, no soldiers in the turrets—Luan yelled, "Clearly we need a change of plan!"

But the plan stayed the same to Radek. "We must get to Izra."

Mirakel blasted him with a cruel, "That fucking gedrok got him, Radek—"

And she resolutely shut up as they rounded the corner and saw, in a perfect mirroring of their first day in Doskor, a swollen throng of people, soldiers, priests, all yelling. Whatever neat group this audience had been in quickly deformed. Soldiers struggled to keep them in the square. Some spilled out and ran through the streets, heading for the gate. Underneath him, Radek's horse stamped and shuddered as the crowd warped and split around them—and then, when Radek looked, he saw Izra.

Noose around his neck. On his knees. Bound. Disheveled, knotted hair, beard, dirty. Radek thought his heart was about to burst in his chest. Izra was alive, but on the precipice, and the appearance of the gedrok had seemingly saved his life. The High Priestess stood poised on the gallows beside Izra, flanked by the general, the bastard Kew, soldiers, priests. She shouted something, but it was lost over the cacophony of panicked people pressing against each other. Uncomprehending fury flashed across her face, and from inside the cuirass she pulled out a thin vial. If it weren't for the sun bearing down on them, Radek might have dismissed it as any other substance. But the vial glowed prismatic.

Ichor.

Neala uncorked it and sipped, just a bit of it, before speaking again.

Then: sound. Clear and crisp, her voice carried to the edges of the basin with unnatural quality. Radek shivered and tensed instinctively. Neala used the arcane power she had stolen. Luan glanced at Radek and shouted to him in Uslethian: "She says: Usleth has declared war! They have set their infernal god on us! And the Rezwyn Empire will not fall to it!"

But as she spoke, a great boom echoed out. Then another. Another.

The gedrok was marching down.

Screams sounded all around them.

"We'll be crushed—we can't get to him," Radek screamed. Luan nodded and made a two fingered gesture. Several mercenaries rode forward into the throng. Radek caught sight of them—they were engaging the soldiers, trying to restrain them. But Luan was backing out and turning right, circumventing the suffocating, narrowing crowd through the tight roads of Doskor. Radek put his foot in his mare's flank and followed.

For what felt like forever, Radek was cut off from the sight of Izra. Only the sounds of the crowd told him anything, and theirs was a choral dirge; oscillating from panic to despair. It sounded like they were already dead, mourning their lives. The gedrok's descent gave all of this a percussive, thundering beat.

Radek emerged at the back of the gallows in time for a new, desperate scream. The general had turned toward them, and Radek thought they were caught, until he saw her craning upward, and he realized she wasn't looking at them at all.

"Nje! Nje!" she howled; broken, fucking broken. When Radek turned, compelled by the sheer woundedness in the general's cry, he froze.

The gedrok lurched above them. And in its mouth was a body—limp, green-white skin left untreated and unpreserved, the flesh dead. The whole torso drooped from the massive jaws and faced the crowd, so there was no denying for any who had ever seen him exactly who they were looking at. Even for Radek, who had seen him only once.

It was Emperor Nio Beumeut's corpse.

Various sounds overlapped then, as recognition registered in the crowd. A true mournful lament, further screams, the defeated, furious cries of General Neve who sank to her knees and beat the gallows' stage. Radek had to wrest his eyes away. Now was the chance. Now was the time to get to Izra.

"Go for the soldiers," Luan ordered those of his company that had followed. He drew his sword and stayed in the saddle. "Cizalec, the time is now!"

Radek dismounted in a hurry. Luan's mercenaries streamed past to gain control of the empire soldiers.

Radek didn't see it happen, but the instant he dismounted, the quiet bastion behind the gallows' stage broke, filling quickly as members of the crowd surged through. Suddenly Radek had to fight his way forward, shoulders aching as he shoved people aside. His line of sight kept dipping as he stumbled, but he tried to keep his eyes on Izra. Just push forward, get to the stage.

Get to your husband.

Someone roughly pulled his arms back.

Radek's heart dropped. He strained in the grip, but they weren't letting go. They had more muscle than him, they were obviously stronger, and all Radek could do was thrash about. He was so close. So damn close.

"No," he said, on instinct. He clenched his hand into a fist and readied himself for a fight.

"You took your time, cizalec," a voice told him, and Radek went still. He turned his head.

Above him stood Odrica Dziove, one eye swollen shut, other eye staring down at him with glinting intent. "Cut it very close."

Radek keeled into her. He wanted to yell, wanted to embrace her, and did none of it, because Izra was waiting. "How are you–? Never mind. No time to waste—there's a heart, it controls—"

"The exanimate, I know," she called back. She took him by the wrist and shoved him closer to the stage, forcing a path through the fleeing throng. Above them, a massive shadow moved. Radek craned up just as the gedrok opened its mouth. Its tongue, a frilly pink mass, curled up its throat and encompassed the corpse sitting in the bowl of its mouth. It threw back its head and swallowed. More screams sounded and the gedrok roared in response. Odrica ignored all this to say, "Kew told me all of it when he released me."

"Kew?" Radek spat, dropping his head down to stare at her. "Where is the damn bastard?"

"He *freed* me," Odrica said slowly, like Radek hadn't heard her.

"And who's to say he won't switch sides at the last minute if this doesn't go our way?"

As if in answer, the gedrok roared. They had no time for this. Odrica grabbed him, pointing to the stage, where Neala still shouted.

"The heart is in the palanquin," Odrica said.

Radek watched Neala's fingers, saw them moving slightly, the way King Zavrius's would move across a lute-harp. She was, without a doubt, using the arcane to control the heart.

It truly must have been in there.

Radek watched as Neala barked some order. The soldiers on the stage drew their weapons. General Neve stopped crying, got to her feet, and did the same.

What was she doing? Were they going to fight the gedrok? What was the point—it was dead.

And Radek realized with startling clarity that no one drawing a weapon on that stage knew.

"She means to kill the gedrok," Odrica shouted over the cacophony, coming to the same conclusion. "To show the empire's strength."

Radek could have laughed. "But she's puppeting the fucking thing. It's a farce."

Odrica didn't reply, not directly. All she said was, "Ready?"

Radek didn't ask 'what for?' He just nodded, and Odrica hoisted him aloft and barreled through the crowd. Odrica, with all the strength of a woman desperate to save her brother. Odrica, who had endured torture for both Izra's and Radek's sake. She stormed through and lifted him onto the stage, springing up behind him shortly after. Radek caught a glimpse of the crowd in the main square. Luan's mercenaries had engaged and made a perimeter around the gallows.

Kew rushed to their side of the stage to help him up, and Radek howled at him, just an unhinged scream that made Kew let go and stand stock still. Then Radek wound himself up and gave Kew the slapping of a lifetime.

"You bastard!" Radek spat as Kew's head whipped back in a satisfying arc. "What the bloody fuck is wrong with you?"

Odrica tugged Radek backward. "We really do not have time—"

"Oh, I know, but I'm just so—*furious!*"

Kew gripped his cheek and gave a weak smile. "Sorry," he said in cracked Uslethian. "Very sorry."

"Whatever," Radek said. And then, "Get the heart to me."

Odrica looked at him, confused, but Radek couldn't explain. He didn't know exactly what to do with it, but he wanted it out of Neala's hands.

He had seen Gedrok Ach Meedin's face reflected in the gedrok's eye. He had seen Gedrok command a dead beast to destroy an empire city in an ancient war. He had watched as the mad king had ingested ichor and threaded his power through the gedrok's heart to control it. And if Gedrok's soul was his, then surely, Radek had inherited that power. But first: "I'll get Izra."

Odrica turned without question and grabbed Kew. Neala's soldiers and priests went on the offensive—just as

General Neve moved to block a blow aimed at Odrica's shoulder.

Radek had no eyes for this, though. He crawled around and found—

—his husband. Izra, on his knees, wide-eyed, the most haggard he had ever been. And still when he saw Radek, he had enough in him to smile: dazzling and relieved.

"You came," Izra whispered.

Radek's heart convulsed, his whole chest seizing. He went to Izra, hands removing first the noose, grazing the thick beard, Izra's cheek, before he moved to the knots binding Izra's wrists. "You came to me first," Radek said, "in a dream." He met Izra's eyes as the ropes fell away from his wrists. "That's the most romantic thing anyone's ever done for me."

Izra surged forward and kissed him. Radek breathed deep and gripped him; realized how scared he was, how he had been scared since he'd left Izra. When Izra hugged him, Radek thought how it was the easiest thing in the world to love him.

Then the gedrok's colossal tail swept into the stage. Wood cracked and splintered everywhere. The gallows buckled and fell, and part of the foundations were smashed apart. Izra, squatting, was off-balance from the first vibration. Radek roughly followed. Izra's arms wrapped around Radek's head, muffling the screams and keeping him safe as the debris fell around them. By the end of it, only Neala and General Neve were left standing.

And Radek glanced over just as the general pressed a blade to her sister's neck.

The gedrok shuddered to a stop when Neala raised her hands. It stood above them unmoving, waiting for its orders.

"Are you alright?" Radek called to Izra, who nodded.

Radek quickly got to his feet. His head throbbed, but it had to be now. Neala was distracted.

He nodded over to the other side of the stage. Together, Kew and Odrica hauled the palanquin towards him. Neala stared at this act and screamed something primal, a rage lodged somewhere deep in her system, and only when she released it did she stop, face perfectly impassive, perfectly calm.

Radek knelt and opened the palanquin. He stared down at the heart. It was a deep red glinting iridescent; the ice had thawed and it looked fresh enough he almost anticipated it to beat. Then he put his hands to it, felt ill with the ichor, the potency of it. He tried to will the gedrok to move, but it didn't budge. He almost prayed to Gedrok, the memory of him, or whatever latent part of him remained in Radek's own soul.

It would not work. But why would it? Gedrok Ach Meedin had not had this power innately. He had sacrificed something for it: his mind.

Gedrok Ach Meedin, the mad king of Usleth. Gedrok Ach Meedin, who had consumed the ichor without protection, to punish the empire for its encroachment.

Radek stared down at his hand. It shone with ichor, viscous and pearlescent. His heart fluttered—this was insanity. This was necessity.

He brought his fingers to his lips and licked them clean.

Radek did not wait. General Neve and Neala's conversation was slow and tense, and there was no telling how long Neala would allow it. Did she still control the gedrok? What would happen if she ordered it to maul everyone on this stage?

Focus. Breathe.

Radek closed his eyes and felt warmth in his stomach, an unnatural prickling at his skin, the urge to breathe heavier. It must have been the early effects of the ichor. He tried desperately to control the gedrok, and nothing happened. But as he did, something else in him changed.

Radek found he could understand the general's thick Doskorian; the impenetrability of the language fell away in layers until he heard, "—and you treated this foreign god to our father. You traitor. You cur. I have loved you my whole life, sister, and until now I trusted you could change. Believed you good. And I am a fool for that."

Radek blinked. He was woozy; this felt like the astrok-mer, invited into a world that wasn't his. The crowd swayed, kept in place by Luan's crew.

Neala shook her head, in tears. "You will doom us if you do this. And you have forsaken me, as the gods have. They have abandoned me. Abandoned Doskor and the Rezwyns so wholly they would make that man emperor."

Beside him, Izra tensed. The same confused, defensive motion happened in the general's back. "What?"

There might as well have been no one else there. Radek swung back to Izra, checking his face, which was pinched in anticipation.

A sob bubbled high. Neala said, "I saw it. And it must have been wrong. I saw it in the astrok-mer, but it was just—a lie. I should be empress. I am his blood. I have the vision. I have the love of Borviet."

The realization made Radek's breath stop. He lifted his hands from the heart—the gedrok swayed then fell again into stillness—and looked over to Izra, whose lips were pressed together. He was not shaken by the truth of his fate.

Suoduny must have shown him.

Neala muttered something Radek did not catch. She flicked her fingers—in response the gedrok half-bent, keeling forward. No. It was going to fall.

"Stop it," General Neve said. "Sister, please."

Neala stopped it, but she kept her hand raised.

Radek swung back and replaced his hands on the gedrok's heart. He could not trust Neala, nor her whims. He had to control this thing. He had to, finally, step into his birthright.

Oren Radek had the soul of Gedrok Ach Meedin, gedrok-rider. And he would not let this creature of his homeland be corrupted like this.

He looked down at the thawed flesh, urging himself not to panic. Thread, he needed to thread it, to weave power into it if he had any hope of puppeting it—only now as he looked, he saw someone had already woven threads of ichor into it. Somehow, Neala had known to do this. He tried to tug her threads and found he couldn't—these were the marks of Neala's magic, her own netting to control the beast.

And at once Radek recalled that Gedrok Ach Meedin had been bandaged as he communed with the gedrok's heart. Blood had soaked it.

Because he had given a piece of himself to the gedrok.

Radek scanned Neala, saw no sign of a wound—but what did it matter how she had done it? The astrok-mer, Suoduny, fate itself had shown Radek what to do.

He got onto his knees and ripped Kew's knife from the sheath, and before anyone could stop him, he had stuck it into his forearm. Radek screamed and gouged out a piece of his arm.

Blood bloomed in the wound and over his skin, hot rivulets dripping onto the stage. He shakily dropped the knife, and peeled out the chunk of flesh before his body could register the pain. Shock numbed him immediately. He heard Izra scream, and the commotion drew Neala's attention. As soon as she understood what he was doing, she would try to stop it.

Radek couldn't let that happen.

Woozy, he got to his feet and stumbled before the gedrok. Suddenly, it keeled forward again, huge body balanced on the balls of its feet.

Radek glanced to Neala. She had her hands outstretched.

She spat at him and said, "Whatever you are doing, cizalec scum, you should stop it."

And motivated either by bravery or blood loss, Radek swung back and profferred the flesh of his arm up to the gedrok's mouth.

"I have the soul of Gedrok Ach Meedin," he announced to it in Uslethian. "Commune with me, and I will free you. I will wrest control back from the High Priestess. I will let you rest."

And on its own, the gedrok's mouth opened, and the fringed tongue unfurled for Radek's offering. It brought it back to its mouth. It swallowed.

Neala howled and let it drop.

Radek ran back to the heart, and as he did, threads of ichor bloomed from his skin. The tendrils reached, fingers searching, and new threads ruptured from the heart and sought Radek in turn. Neala's threads were dull by comparison; these were bright, strong, thick. And Neala's threads thrummed under sudden tension as they were yanked toward the crowd—the command that told the gedrok to topple forward.

Radek didn't even have to touch the heart. Without another thought, he yanked his own threads back like reins. The shadow of the creature edged off the gallows stage as the gedrok hauled itself upright. Dust and wood splinters whirled around its feet. Radek had stopped it, but barely, and the great weight of the gedrok creaked against its own joints.

Radek had it. It was a colossal beast, towering over them. It would have crushed them if it fell. But pulling on those threads made Radek's forearm ache. The tendons strained, burning with immediate overuse. They were stretched to the point of tearing—how had Neala done this so calmly?

Radek recalled Gedrok Ach Meedin sitting over the heart, testing his connection, and screaming with the pain of it. How had he combatted it? How had he ridden that beast to war?

Ichor.

The thought hit Radek unbidden. It was the same for Neala. Both Gedrok Ach Meedin and Neala Beumeut had consumed enough ichor to control these ancient colossi—and the price was their sanity.

She glared at him now, frowning, seething. She gave a few more impotent yanks on her own ichor threads and then tried moving towards him.

The general's sword had been slipping, but now she hastily repositioned it against her sister's neck. She seemed to come to some conclusion; from behind, Radek could see her shoulders settle. "You," Neve hissed brokenly, "have done all this—for a title the gods did not even want you to have? You have nearly killed Izra Dziove because you disliked what the gods decreed? How can you call yourself High Priestess? How did your greed corrupt you so?"

Her sword arm began to shake, not from the weight, Radek guessed, but from the horror of what she had to do.

Neala saw it too and relaxed minutely. "You will not kill me. You won't. You're my sister."

And Radek said, "But I will."

Neala reacted instantly. She jerked towards him, even if that meant pressing her jugular against Neve's sword. Neala reached, first physically and then in a way Radek's nerves could feel; this twisting, scrabbling probing into his skin, his soul. She had moved on from trying to control the gedrok. Now she was trying to control him directly. Radek, who had spent so long hating the arcane, struggled. But he resisted. She would not claw her way inside.

Radek closed his eyes and pressed Neala out of his mind. The scratching fell away as Radek focused on the gedrok, both its looming physical presence, and the ichor. Like Izra finding a link, Radek felt buzzing in the tips of his fingers. He felt the gedrok's mind like it was armor. He pressed against it. Pushed.

"Please," he said. "Gedrok Ach Meedin commands it so."

It gave. And then the gedrok opened for him completely. It was like a door swinging inward, a lock being opened; whatever Gedrok had done meant Radek had this power now. And once that first barrier collapsed inward, Radek found himself relaxing. Power flowed into him from his hands, and his mind sparked alive with ancient, long buried recognition. Prismatic light danced along his fingers from an old and borrowed source; Gedrok's power united with the ichor Radek had ingested, and something unlocked in his blood and his soul. This is how you do it, something seemed to tell him. This is where you put your hands.

It wasn't so much about control, nor propitiation; not the way Neala had puppeted it, or how the Rezwyns treated their gods. It was simply a matter of asking.

So Radek asked, "Would you get down lower for me?"

And the gedrok bowed low, with an almost eager speed; none of the creaking, fighting reluctance when Neala forcibly used it.

Radek called out, in Doskorian, "I am Lord Oren Radek of Usleth. Neala: you betray the empire so thoroughly that you keep the chosen heir from the seat of the True Commander."

In that moment, Radek thought Neala understood. A cloudiness came about her face, her eyes. She pressed her lips very thinly into a line and met the gedrok's eyes with anger.

Radek called out, "Usleth will support the new emperor. But first it will deal with the usurper: she who has murdered her own father to make her claim legitimate. She who has defied the wishes of the gods by attempting to execute their chosen emperor!"

Neala turned. Radek had the good grace to meet Neala's stare as he said, "For this, Neala, you die."

The gedrok moved, jaw cracking open with inhuman speed to encompass the body. There was no ceremony, no hesitation, no reluctance. There was no burst of ichor power, nothing to suggest she had ever held it in her blood at all. The presence of the colossus rendered the High Priestess utterly human, and the gedrok left nothing for anyone to mourn, or laud, or desecrate. The gedrok swallowed her whole.

The instant she was gone, General Neve discarded her sword. She turned back to stare at Radek, tears in her eyes, this deep anger he could feel emanating from her gaze. But she made no move against him.

The crowd erupted with more screams, more outrage. Officials Radek didn't recognize shouted and pushed against Luan's crew. The soldiers were split, in two minds—but they all looked to Neve. She made some motion.

Most put their weapons away. Those that didn't were encircled by Luan's crew.

Radek wasted no time. Some people stood in trance-like veneration before the gedrok. General Neve had chosen a side, but how long before others reacted? Radek reached around his neck, feeling first the chain of office given to him by Izra, and then the seal of King Zavrius. He slipped it off his neck and reached high into the air. The gedrok bowed forward and took the string delicately in its mouth. The gedrokbone seal swung from its teeth.

"Get up," he told Izra. "Get up, stand in the middle."

Izra sounded distant. "What are you doing?"

Radek yelled again,"Usleth hereby recognizes Izra Dziove as emperor!"

The gedrok shifted again and presented Izra with the seal. He took it from the gedrok's mouth, stared at it in his hands. And then Radek made a point of sending it away. This was Izra's moment; Izra's great acceptance of his destiny.

They were left in the gedrok's wake, staring at the snow-capped highlands as it meandered back to the castle under Radek's control. Each step echoed in the basin. In silence, the whole of Doskor watched it reverently as the gedrok slouched back to the castle slowly. Beside the great hole it had ripped, the gedrok stopped and nestled down to sleep. And when Radek would break the connection, it would sleep there forever, undisturbed. Radek had promised it peace, and peace he would give it.

But when the moment passed, Radek heard the crowd, the whispers, the confused and uneasy sound of dozens of bodies pressed together, of the remaining soldiers attempting to hold the peace. This was a foreign god, and it terrified them.

The silence was so uneasy Radek almost regretted sending the gedrok away. He had declared Radek emperor, and if this wasn't accepted, what then? Would he be Gedrok Ach Meedin, massacring Doskor? Would Radek become the mad king of the merchants in the annals?

Someone on the edge of the gallows came forward to Odrica. They slipped a thick roll of parchment from their tunic and placed it in her hands. Odrica took it and unrolled it. She read hastily in silence with a frown, glancing between her brother and Radek. Then she walked forward.

"Holy men and women! People of Doskor! We have witnessed Suoduny himself intercede on behalf of my brother!" It was a necessary step, and Odrica was uniquely placed. She worshipped Borviet herself. She could sway them. "By Neala's own admission, her claim to the title was based on a lie. But the gods themselves favor my brother–enough that the High Priestess would murder her own father for fear of the truth! Izra Dziove, strix and True Commander, favorite of the late Nio Beumeut," here she raised the parchment high and tapped it, "you have been named by him as emperor of the Rezwyns. Signed by the emperor, marked by his own blood, you as his inheritor. You alone bear this destiny. All hail the True Commander, strix, blessed by Suoduny, Emperor Izra Dziove!"

The moment stretched in surreal silence. Arcane power thrummed in Radek's blood, fear and unease and a growing anticipation blossoming in his chest. He looked at Izra and waited tensely for the Rezwyn Empire to react.

The first to bow was Kew. He went to his knees with a solid, fast thud, like something about being the first would rectify all he had done. But he did it with such earnestness, Radek had to smile. This motion made Radek move next, then followed by Odrica, paper still in hand. From there it was a cascade; the general, the soldiers, the whole crowd. Radek squeezed his eyes shut and brought a hand over his heart as the cry sounded, a chant like a prayer.

"*All Hail Emperor Dziove! All Hail Emperor Dziove!*"

Footfalls sounded by Radek's head.

Izra was illuminated in a glow, the bright light of Doskor behind him—the radiant emperor, a corona of light diffusing behind his skull.

"What are you doing?" Radek whispered, in awe. "This is—your fate."

Izra lowered himself and took Radek's hands. "No," he whispered, planting a kiss on Radek's forehead. "My sister was wrong. I do not bear this destiny alone. You married me," Izra reminded him. "So, stand with me now."

Radek took his hand, thinking, *this has happened before*, when it never had.

The two of them stared out, husbands, Dzioves, over the people they were meant to rule.

EPILOGUE

The world changed quickly.

Several things had happened. The first was that something like a reckoning had swept through the empire. Ostijan had been granted autonomy. Izra was in talks to allow the same of Elkar. Some city-states further east had taken to celebrating their governor as a pledge to the empire. But Izra had no doubt the empire would take months to settle.

The second was that the castle, too, had changed. A convocation of provincial priests had been summoned from across the empire for Izra's council. Odrica had been named High Priestess. General Neve commanded the army, a whole caste of people focused now on defense. Kew was given a not-quite exile; a governorship to the east, a technical honor that meant Izra would only have to see him when he wished. There was a soreness there, still, at Kew's betrayal—but so too was there a debt.

Most prominently, the giant gedrok had nestled against the castle's northern side. It had been laid to rest, heart returned to it, a new shrine symbolic of the union between two nations.

And finally: the emperor of the Rezwyns had signed a new treaty with Usleth, and trade and peace would follow. This third thing concerned Radek the most, because the emperor of the Rezwyns was his husband, and the sudden and overbearing truth of his situation terrified him.

On the day of the official coronation and grand feast of Izra Dziove, Oren Radek thought: "I have no idea what I'm doing," and nearly went insane with the thought. He had the soul of Gedrok Ach Meedin, a king, a bloody king, and all he had to do this time around was be the emperor's consort—but that role itself was enormous. Opportunities to fail abounded. Fear of doing something that would hurt Izra—hurt the whole empire overwhelmed him, and because he didn't know what else to do, he stumbled down to a great stone crypt in the catacombs of Doskor's castle.

The people here—the cuvari—had made themselves the keepers of the empire's memories. Izra had called it an organic library. When Radek whispered the names Gedrok Ach Meedin and Emperor Dziove, the cuvari grew very quiet. But one peeled off from the rest and led him further into the castle's depths.

This was a crypt of knowledge. Dozens of rows of bookshelves crowded this living tomb, and each one contained a stone tablet Radek had learned was filled with an event deserving of preservation. Other bookshelves kept the written notes of the everyday. Events, people, places. Every moment of the empire's existence was recorded here, in stone that would not fade and could not easily be altered—though Radek had his doubts about that.

She led him to another of those tenebrous tombs that was somehow more fetid than the one they'd just come from. At one of the shelves she gestured, and at Radek's nod, left him alone.

Radek inhaled. Dust and dampness scraped over his throat; he breathed in a century of empire history and yanked a tablet from its place.

He read the history of Gedrok and Dziove and seemed to see it all in his mind, hallucinating every action whether it felt true or not. He read because he was afraid of making their same mistakes, of being forever preserved in these annals as a harbinger of war and ruin. He read because he longed to know that this was his fate, and that in being destiny, he could not fuck it up. And he read in the hope of understanding the nuance of the role he had inherited. Ichor, gedroks, the astrok-mer, Suoduny—each facet of the arcane connected in a way Radek couldn't understand. He had accepted on a base level that the nature of existence was confusing. That investigating it might make him somewhat insane. That faith had become an inevitable part of his existence.

It had happened. In the end, it would be something Radek had to accept.

The emperor found him after an hour.

"Are you hiding from your husband?" came the voice.

"No, from the emperor," Radek mumbled back.

An exhausted laugh echoed. Izra sounded far away. Radek heard the scrape of metal, and then torch light bobbed into view. Lit by the warm glow, the shadows showed the harshness of Izra's jaw and cheekbones, the deep-set circles under his eyes. Radek felt his heart dislodge a fraction, felt it slip from the pericardium and wobble precariously over the drop to his stomach. Radek wanted to kiss him, but didn't.

"What are you doing down here, love?" Izra asked.

"Hoping the secrets of not fucking up an entire empire are hidden in amongst these dust mites."

"Hm," Izra mused. "And what have you found?"

Radek smiled softly. "Only more to fear."

"Then you, my husband, will be a good consort. Look at me. I have nothing but faith in you. And we are not alone." Izra leaned forward and kissed Radek's forehead. "Besides. We cannot hide down here much longer."

As if hearing their emperor, a choral striking of bells began to ring outside the castle; their bright peals were softened by the stone, but Radek knew a summons when he heard one. He turned back to the stone tablet, carved with memories of two long dead men, and slid it back into its place. He dug Emperor Dziove and Gedrok Ach Meedin out of his mind and relinquished them to the astrok-mer. His focus was on his husband. On this moment. On the future they would carve together. Radek became dimly aware that he was nervous, which felt so unlike him he almost laughed. But what was about to happen deserved his nerves, his giddiness. That little boy from Shoi Prya thrashed with excitement, and the adult in him felt, despite the nerves, that none of this was unexpected. He felt good.

"Let me take a look at you," Radek murmured to Izra.

The emperor was dressed well—of course, because Radek dressed him. He wore a knee-length tunic, covered by a shiny silver cuirass beaten with Suoduny's image, just faint enough the god was a spectral vision glinting gold. Black velvet cascaded from beneath the cuirass, the bottom half of the front-slit tunic patterned with layered black velvet resembling overlapping scales. Two armlets bunched the sleeves at the bicep and defined Izra's strong arms, which wasn't done so much because it was in fashion, but rather because Radek wanted to see those arms straining in the fabric. Over the hose were ceremonial greaves, poleyns haunting and shaped into the watchful stare of Suoduny. A sturdy silver circlet ran around Izra's forehead, and his thick black hair fell over it, framing his face. Around Izra's neck, he still wore King Zavrius's seal, as much a symbol of protection as one of unity.

It was a deliberate and beautiful stand: I am emperor, and this is my god. I am emperor and my god wills it. Izra Dziove had not conquered fate—fate had made him so. And as such, who would ever question his rule?

And in that moment, seeing him, the whole of him, as both emperor and his husband, the beautiful severity of Izra struck Radek. What a funny thing to look at someone and see, somehow, how every moment had led you to them. Every mishap, every triumph, had sent Oren Radek stumbling into Izra Dziove's embrace. He was every choice Radek had ever made.

"Remarkable," Radek whispered. Izra raised one big, calloused hand to rest against Radek's cheek. Radek had dressed to mirror him; long tunic in the blue and silver of the Rezwyn empire, in their style; gold thread flittered through Radek's layers as Suoduny's mark on him. Izra tilted his chin upward ever so slightly, so their eyes were locked. He skimmed a thumb over Radek's lips and smiled warmly. "And you: astounding."

There was a gentle moment of nothingness. Izra pulled him into an embrace, a truly intimate hold away from all the eyes of the castle. It was excruciating, in a base way. Sometimes even the strongest embrace didn't feel like enough of a touch.

"Bells," Izra mumbled, when the bells pealed out again as if annoyed their ringing hadn't yet mustered the emperor and his consort. "Ready?"

Radek put out his arm in answer and Izra took it. They ascended from the cuvari's crypt-like workroom to the upper levels of the castle, winding their way through empty corridors toward the grand doors of the feast hall. From within, a buzz of conversation seeped through the door. The energy was high. The energy was light. A celebration began within—for them.

Uncanny familiarity hit Radek so strongly he used his other hand to clamp down on Izra's forearm. He almost laughed from the way the feeling twisted in his stomach.

By the bones, his was a whorled and cyclic existence: months ago, he was led to these same doors by this same man. No one looked his way, then. No one knew his name. He had forgiven them what they did not know, thinking one day they would know him as the emperor's favorite merchant lord. Which was still technically true, but nothing like Radek's first dream. Not once had he thought he would return to this—like this.

Izra raised his hand and flicked the seal free with ease. The doors opened with a groan and the chatter and revelry quietened. The same old man who had announced Izra that first night turned to the pair of them now and swept himself low into a bow. Then he raised his horn high and declared them: the horn boomed throughout the hall, but it was little more than show by that point. Every eye in the room stayed on them. Every eye raked down Emperor Dziove and his husband, Oren Radek.

The crowd consisted of every empire noble who had pledged themselves to Izra, the governors who had bent the knee, and even the governor of Ostijan, who had declared their independence.

The herald proclaimed their titles, and Radek heard the words echoing in the hall, deep and resonant. "The True Commander, Blessed by Suoduny, He Who Weaves Our Fates, the emperor of all Rezwyn, Izra Dziove, and His Majesty, the Emperor Consort, Lord Oren Radek of Usleth."

There was an emotion, then, Radek didn't have a name for. It wasn't quite pride and it wasn't quite fear. It ran up his spine and curled around his heart, and he could feel the weight of it in his bones. The only thing that eased it, that edged the feeling back from the precipice of something disconcerting, was when Izra unhooked his arm from Radek's and clasped their hands together. Then, the warmth settled Radek and his chest swelled. He raised his chin and broke into a grin that he could feel splitting his face apart. Hand-in-hand, Izra and Radek walked the length of the hall to the twin thrones that lay waiting; the two of them together, holding each other as one so there was a blurring of the edges between them. And the cheer that sounded was practically music, an overture for Emperor Dziove's rule.

Familiar faces dotted the crowd: Hapina, cleaner than Radek had ever seen her, clapping wildly. Radek suspected she was celebrating more than Izra's succession—he had promised to favor her for the Usleth-empire trade routes, after all. Mirakel stood with a new ambassador from Usleth, having carted gifts and congratulations from King Zavrius reading: Well done, Radek. I hear he's very handsome.

And Luan was man of the hour, having been honored with the title of ambassador and paid handsomely from Radek's own purse. From Radek's own experience, quashing usurpers was an excellent way of stepping up in life.

Radek turned to bask in the celebration, his smile never leaving his face. But Izra wasn't looking at the crowd. He had turned to look at his husband—Radek could see him in his periphery—and when Radek turned, Izra stole a kiss. Barely longer than an inhale.

"All this has happened before," Izra murmured as he pulled away. "I have found you before. I have loved you before." Radek squeezed Izra's hand and let himself feel grounded. Izra continued, "How pure must it be, then, to survive something as final as death? That bond. The pull to you. You are my tether, Oren. Without you, I am lost."

And before he could say anything, Izra leaned down to him again. In a changing empire, in a faraway land he had never before dreamed of, Oren Radek kissed Izra Dziove and knew he would never leave him.

Glossary of Terms and Names

Astrok-mer: *The Rezwyn name for a spiritual plane known as the astral sea.*

Awha Stad: *A port city in Usleth and Oren Radek's birth place.*

Banonok: *A coastal empire city to the east near Barveck Bay, once considered for Radek's warehouses.*

Borviet: *The Rezwyn god of war, expansion, and conquering. Its symbol is a human-boar hybrid.*

Cizalec: *The Rezwyn word for foreigner. Occasionally used as a slur.*

Cres Stros: *A province in Usleth named after its principal city, the former Uslethian capital.*

Cuvari: *A Rezwyn academic caste dedicated to the preservation of memory and developing a living, authoritative collection of information on the empire.*

Doskor: *The capital of the Rezwyn Empire.*

Elkar: *A coastal empire city to the east, and one of the two cities that hosts Oren Radek's warehouses. Elkar used to be Uslethian territory before it was conceded in war.*

Emperor Dziove: *Historical ruler of the Rezwyn Empire. Gedrok Ach Meedin's contemporary.*

Gedrok: *Name given to the long-dead creatures found in Usleth, the source of Usleth's arcane.*

Gedrok Ach Meedin: *One of the first recorded kings in Uslethian history, also credited with discovering the remains of gedroks.*

Gulek Des: *Name given to an Uslethian strategy card game favored by Oren Radek.*

Hapina: *An Uslethian-born ship's captain whose love of the empire had her fighting in the war against her birth country. A contact of Oren Radek in the empire.*

Hulik: *An ex-soldier of the Rezwyn Army turned mercenary based in Ostijan and known to Izra Dziove.*

Izra Dziove: *Strix, Commander of the Uxbuh, and visionary advisor to the emperor.*

Kew: *Second-in-command of the Uxbuh and Izra's close friend.*

Kiriz: *City in the central north-east of the empire, known for its depravity.*

Lord of Veprak: *A young lord once promised to Izra Dziove in a betrothal orchestrated by the True Commander, before Suoduny showed Izra he had a fated man.*

Luan Zek: *An ex-Squadron Leader of the Rezwyn Army turned consultant. His leg was irreparably damaged in the war. Born and raised in Veprak, now based in Ostijan. Known to Izra Dziove.*

Mirakel: *Officer of the Uslethian treasury sent to accompany Radek and fund his trip.*

Muripej: *Rezwyn god of the sea.*

Neala Beumeut: *Second-born daughter to the emperor and the empire's High Priestess.*

Neve Beumeut: *First-born daughter to the emperor and the empire's General.*

Nio Beumeut: *The Rezwyn Emperor, also known as the True Commander.*

Ognmoksh: *Rezwyn goddess of the hunt.*

Oren Radek: *A merchant lord of Usleth sent to the Rezwyn Empire to investigate the sudden end of diplomatic ties between their nations.*

Ostijan: *A coastal empire city to the east near Barveck Bay, and one of the two cities that hosts Oren Radek's warehouses. Ostijan used to be Uslethian territory before it was conceded in war.*

Paqe: *Diplomat of Usleth sent with Oren Radek and Mirakel to negotiate with the empire.*

Port Sulvoy: *Port in the central south of the empire, closest to Doskor.*

Prauv Ocean: *The ocean surrounding the lower continent.*

Rezwyn Empire: *A conquering empire and the traditional enemy of Usleth, ruled by Emperor Nio Beumeut.*

Selvik: *The High Priest of Suoduny's nomadic temple.*

Semor: *Priest of Borviet.*

Shoi Prya: *Province in Usleth where Oren Radek was raised. Current seat of the Kingdom of Usleth.*

Strix: *Rezwyn word for those blessed with the arcane.*

Suoduny: *Rezwyn god of fate and destiny.*

Usleth: *The peninsula bordering the Rezwyn Empire to the east, ruled by King Zavrius Dued Vuuthrik.*

Uxbuh: *Soldiers of the Rezwyn Empire with a calling to the trade, commanded by Izra Dziove.*

Westgar: *Province of Usleth bordering the Rezwyn Empire.*

Wicjezst: *A tiny and fairly isolated port town to the north-east of the empire.*

Zavrius Dued Vuuthrik: *the King of Usleth, and last member of the Dued Vuuthrik dynasty.*

Zeljia: *Rezwyn god of sex and medicine.*

Zimsmrt: *Rezwyn goddess of death and winter.*

About the Author

Seth Haddon is a queer Australian writer of fantasy. He is a video game designer and producer, has a degree in Ancient History, and previously worked with cats. He lives in Sydney with his partner and their two furry children. Some of his previous adventures include exploring Pompeii with a famous archaeologist and being chased through a train station by a nun.

Since time immemorial the warriors of the Paladin Order have harnessed arcane powers to protect their rulers. For Balen, who has given up his chance at love and fought his way to the top of the Paladin Order, there can be no greater honor than to serve his king. But when assassins annihilate the royal family, Balen suddenly finds himself sworn to serve the very man he abandoned.

Now with their nation threatened by enemies both within and outside the kingdom, Balen must fight hidden traitors and unnatural assassins, while also contending with the biting wit and dangerous charm of young King Zavrius. To save themselves and their nation they will have to put aside their past and reforge that trust they lost so long ago.

Printed in the USA
CPSIA information can be obtained
at www.ICGtesting.com
CBHW041355180823
1004CB00001B/1